WHEN WE WERE REAL

WHEN WE WERE REAL

| A Novel |

DARYL GREGORY

SAGA PRESS

LONDON   **NEW YORK**   TORONTO
AMSTERDAM/ANTWERP   NEW DELHI   SYDNEY/MELBOURNE

SAGA PRESS

AN IMPRINT OF SIMON & SCHUSTER, LLC

1230 AVENUE OF THE AMERICAS, NEW YORK, NEW YORK 10020

Copyright © 2025 by Daryl Gregory

All rights reserved, including the right to reproduce this book or portions thereof in any form whatsoever. For information, address Saga Press Subsidiary Rights Department, 1230 Avenue of the Americas, New York, NY 10020.

First Saga Press hardcover edition April 2025

SAGA PRESS and colophon are trademarks of Simon & Schuster, LLC

For information about special discounts for bulk purchases, please contact Simon & Schuster Special Sales at 1-866-506-1949 or business@simonandschuster.com.

The Simon & Schuster Speakers Bureau can bring authors to your live event. For more information or to book an event, contact the Simon & Schuster Speakers Bureau at 1-866-248-3049 or visit our website at www.simonspeakers.com.

Interior design by Lewelin Polanco

Manufactured in the United States of America

1 3 5 7 9 10 8 6 4 2

Library of Congress Cataloging-in-Publication Data is available.

ISBN 978-1-6680-6004-9
ISBN 978-1-6680-6006-3 (ebook)

*For Jack, who came with me on a road trip to a distant land,
and Kath, who was waiting for me when I came back*

WHEN WE WERE REAL

ITINERARY FOR
NORTH AMERICAN IMPOSSIBLES TOUR

| Day 1 |

THE FROZEN TORNADO

THE ANTIPODE (*optional stop*)

| Day 2 |

THE GEYSERS OF MYSTERY!

| Day 3 |

THE HOLLOW FLOCK

FOUR CEDARS DISTILLERY (*tour and dinner*)

| Day 4 |

THE LAST EXIT MALL AND TRAVEL CENTER

THE TUNNEL

INTRODUCTION TO THE ZIPPER (*if time permits*)

| Day 5 |

RAFTING THE ZIPPER (*alternate transportation available*)

AUDIENCE WITH THE AVATAR SAUGAT ZIN

| Day 6 |

GHOST CITY

| Day 7 |

GROUP PHOTO AND GOODBYES!

SEATING CHART

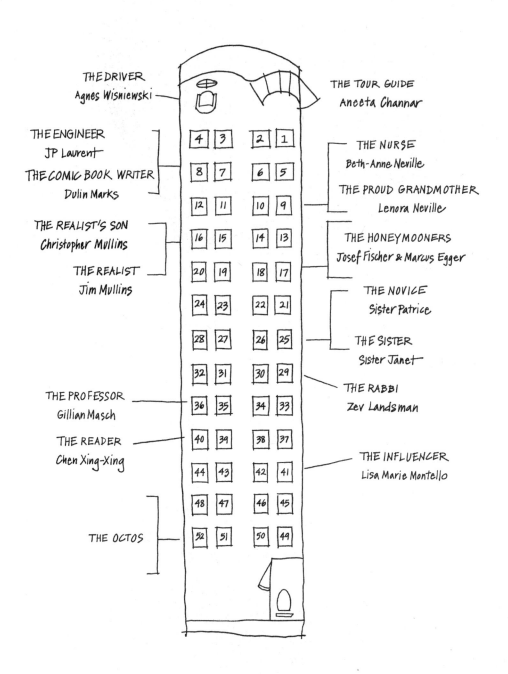

THE DRIVER
Agnes Wisniewski

THE TOUR GUIDE
Aneeta Channar

THE ENGINEER
JP Laurent

THE COMIC BOOK WRITER
Dulin Marks

THE NURSE
Beth-Anne Neville

THE PROUD GRANDMOTHER
Lenora Neville

THE REALIST'S SON
Christopher Mullins

THE REALIST
Jim Mullins

THE HONEYMOONERS
Josef Fischer & Marcus Egger

THE NOVICE
Sister Patrice

THE SISTER
Sister Janet

THE PROFESSOR
Gillian Masch

THE READER
Chen Xing-Xing

THE RABBI
Zev Landsman

THE INFLUENCER
Lisa Marie Montello

THE OCTOS

4	3	2	1
8	7	6	5
12	11	10	9
16	15	14	13
20	19	18	17
24	23	22	21
28	27	26	25
32	31	30	29
36	35	34	33
40	39	38	37
44	43	42	41
48	47	46	45
52	51	50	49

Let's Try This Again

||||||||||||||||||||||||||||||||||||||||||||||||||||||||||||||||||||||||||||

. . . and there's the tour bus now, green and bulbous, with long black mirrors drooping in front of its face like caterpillar antennae. It's climbing out of the underworks of Manhattan, onto the upper level of the George Washington Bridge. CANTERBURY TRAILS is written across its side in white script. It's rumbling west, hemmed in by a swarm of smaller vehicles, all of them moving slowly in the light rain. Behind, the April sun has climbed over the towers of Washington Heights. Light scatters prettily in the rain, turning droplets into diamonds, making every surface gleam.

A man in an Irish wool cap sits in a window seat in one of the front rows of the bus, gazing out through the lightly tinted glass. The vertical wires of the bridge scroll past, pluckable as harp strings. The tour folder sits on his lap. He's already skimmed its contents—the itinerary, the maps, safety warnings, the bio pages filled out by his fellow travelers—but it's a lot to take in.

We can't blame him. There are nineteen people on the bus, and it'll take time to learn their names. Let's start with labels, though even those can be problematic. The man in the wool cap, for example, we'll call THE ENGINEER, because that's how he still thinks of himself, though he's no longer employed as one. Or employed at all. A year ago he had a bout with brain cancer, and took early retirement in the same way a boxer takes an unguarded uppercut. Out by TKO. After his surgery, his coworkers threw him a lunchtime party where they said cheery things: *You're only sixty, think of the travel! What about that bike trip you've always talked about?* They were too polite to mention the cancer at all, or the hat he kept on the entire time. He wears one whenever he goes out in public now. Fortunately, he looks good in hats, or so his wife used to tell him. The cap he's wearing now, pulled low to his eyebrows, is one that she bought him.

The man next to him leans close, waggles his eyebrows at the view. "Looks pretty realistic, doesn't it?" We'll call him THE COMIC BOOK WRITER, which is how he introduces himself to people who look down on comics, which is pretty much everyone. He's a burly white guy with long, aging rocker hair, wearing a rumpled work shirt that is actually clean but looks as if it's been pulled from a hamper.

"Very hi-res," the Engineer agrees.

"Think of the budget."

"Must be astronomical."

The Comic Book Writer laughs loudly, too loud for the cabin of a bus. These two have been keeping each other amused for over thirty years, but lately the laughter's been harder to come by. The Engineer's been holed up alone in his house since he was told that his cancer had returned, and the Writer's worried about him. Time to get him the fuck out of the house! See people. Visit the big, beautiful, fake world!

THE TOUR GUIDE thinks for a moment that the men are laughing at *her*. Two white, middle-aged boomers, possibly harmless gents, possibly condescending jerks, could go either way. She knows how young she looks. Twenty-seven, but no one would guess it, a tiny brown girl, the daughter of Pakistani immigrants, dressed like a real estate agent in a dark skirt and a shiny red blouse and blazer. Not a uniform, but uniform-esque, and it's failed to make her feel less like an imposter. She's terrified. In one hand she's gripping the PA microphone, a plasticky, toylike thing, and with the other she's balancing a three-ring binder, open to the first of the day's scripts. It's time for her to give her welcome speech. She's supposed to open with a joke. The binder does not provide any jokes.

She lifts the kiddy karaoke microphone and is mortified to see that her hand is shaking. She lowers her hand and looks around without moving her head. Did anyone see?

No, no one seems to be looking at her. Most of the passengers are talking among themselves, enveloped in that engine hum that makes each conversation feel private.

The bus is less than half-full, which is good for the comfort of the customers, but it's surprising. Were there a lot of cancellations? Is the tour company in trouble? She has no idea. She was hired only a few days ago. They told her during orientation that her first trip would be a three-day jaunt visiting the Impossibles of New England, and that she wouldn't be in charge, she'd be shadowing an experienced guide. Then, last night, her supervisor called and said there was an emergency, they had "lost their guide," and could she be packed and ready by morning? The North American Impossibles Tour, seven days on the road and one on water. "On *water*?" she asked. "Don't worry," her supervisor told her. "It's all in the binder."

She desperately wanted to say no, but how could she turn down her first assignment? It was an emergency. She wanted to be a team player—and didn't want to be kicked off the team before she had a chance to play.

She lifts the microphone again and says a cheery, "Hello!"

The Engineer glances up. No one else seems to have heard her. The microphone isn't on.

THE DRIVER calls over her shoulder, "Turn on the PA." She's a big-boned white woman, been behind the wheel for years, and now they've sent her a complete rookie. Where the hell is Peter? He's the best guide she's ever worked with, and now he's bowed out without a word, which isn't like him. The new guide is messing with the microphone, still can't get the PA working. Jesus Christ. "Control panel," the Driver says. "Right next to you."

"Oh," the Tour Guide says. Flips the switch. "HELLO!"

A seventyish white woman sitting in the third row yelps as if she's been poked in the eye, and the Tour Guide jumps to turn down the volume.

THE PROUD GRANDMOTHER says, "It's not going to be like that the whole trip, is it?"

THE NURSE, who is also the Proud Grandmother's daughter, sighs elaborately. "She didn't do it on purpose, Momma."

The Tour Guide says into the mic, "I'm so sorry. Is this better?"

"It's fine," the Nurse says to the guide. "Don't mind her."

The Proud Grandmother stares at her daughter. *Don't mind her?* She's not a child. It's her money that bought these tickets. Her daughter's always complaining that she never gets a vacation, well, here it is, all-expenses-paid. All she asks for in return is a little help, a little consideration, until they get to the Avatar and her burden will be lifted. Her physical burden, at least. Like the pain being inflicted on her by this hard, thinly upholstered seat. Her back's sending shooting pains down her leg and her shoulder's seizing up. It's time for her prednisone, and she can't take that without food. Would it kill her daughter to get up and get her a Little Debbie?

The Nurse ignores her mother's glare. She is not the daughter who's provided her mother with her precious grandchildren. *That* daughter is back in North Carolina, living it up in her five-bedroom house. This one is divorced with no children, a crime punishable, evidently, with a lifetime sentence of unpaid chaperoning. She's forty-four years old, but looks older, at least to herself. When she sees herself in photos it looks as if she ordered her face prestressed. This expedition is not going to help; it's just the same job made more difficult by being detached from all routines and support systems. She knows her mother is in pain—constant, maddening pain—but if this trip doesn't give the old woman any relief, she going to dump her on her sister's doorstep in Charlotte and walk into the sea.

"As I was saying," the Tour Guide says through the PA. "I'm not the guide mentioned on the website. I'm sorry about that. Peter

Atherton . . . had a personal issue. A family emergency. But I'm sure it's just—well, I guess that's our first glitch! No extra charge." No one laughs. "So . . . so . . ." The guide looks down at the binder, seemingly lost, then finds something to read: "Are you ready for an adventure?"

Folks in the rear of the bus hoot in appreciation. The back row is occupied by a quartet of boisterous octogenarians who are past caring about the jobs they held years ago, the careers they used to fret over. Call them THE OCTOS—eight arms provided by two widows and two widowers from the Des Moines metropolitan area. One of the men is Black but the other man and the two women are a shade of white seen only in Iowa. They've known one another forever but like to tell people that they just met this morning, and every time one of them repeats the line, they all laugh. An inside joke, and they don't seem to mind that no outsider even registers it as a joke, but as some verbal misfire from kooky old people. The Octos are as excited as teenagers, leaning into each other, arms draped over shoulders.

The Tour Guide seems relieved by the response. She's wearing the cautious smile of the new girl in school suddenly not alone at the lunch table. "Let's move on to the itinerary," she says. "We have a lot of Impossibles to visit, starting with the Frozen Tornado, which is just an hour away. How exciting! After that we'll be hitting all the most famous sites—the Hollow Flock, the Tunnel, and of course the Zipper, where we'll be meeting the Avatar Saugat Zin. A week from now we'll reach our final stop, Ghost—"

"I have a question," a voice loudly says.

"—City." The guide searches for the speaker, sees a balding white man midway back, staring at her. She says, "Yes?"

"Isn't there a better term to use than Impossible?" the man asks. "We *know* they're possible, because they're here." This is THE REALIST. He's the host and sole writer for his podcast, *The Real Patriot*, whose slogan is "Speaking Truth to Morons." The first episode hasn't come out yet, though, so for now he still has a day job. He's used up the last of his sick days for this trip. "I think it would be more rational," he says loudly, "if we used accurate terminology."

The Tour Guide is frozen, the microphone forgotten in her hand.

"And please don't use the term 'Area of Scientific Interest,' or even worse, 'ASI,'" the Realist continues. "Acronyms are just tools the government uses to stop us from asking questions."

He glances at his gangly son, hoping he's recording this, but no. The boy's staring at the seatback, headphones mashed over his giant red Afro, oblivious.

But THE REALIST'S SON is not oblivious. The headphones aren't playing a sound and he's deliberately keeping his eyes off his embarrassing father. He's just a year out of college, with no firm plans on what to do next. His father's plans for him, however, are very firm. He wants him to edit all the podcast audio files, upload them, and "get the word out there" via social media. His father seems to think that because his son is twenty-two and plays video games, he's some kind of technical wizard.

"Film this," the Realist hisses under his breath. He gets to his feet, and tugs down his shirt to cover his waistband holster. His son looks up in alarm. "Dad?"

"All I am asking," the Realist says to the guide, "is that maybe we could all agree to use more scientific terminology, rather than biased words like Impossible."

The Tour Guide's eyes are wide. "But the name of the tour is North American Impossibles, and the description is pretty clear that— Didn't you sign up for that?"

"I held my nose. The tour is more than its name! I was just hoping that the people in the group could keep an open mind."

"Is there a word that you'd prefer?"

"Well, I don't want to *prescribe* a term," the Realist says in a reasonable tone. "I'm open to a discussion. But it seems to be that these things are entirely a part of the natural world, until someone can prove beyond a shadow of a doubt that they're not."

"Unverified nature-like objects," says one of the men across the aisle.

"Natural until proven otherwise," his seatmate counters.

"NUPOs!" the first man says, and they both laugh.

The men are speaking with what sounds like a German accent. The Realist thinks, Are they making fun of me? Are they calling me a Nazi?

The men *are* mocking the Realist, just a bit, but their accent has nothing to do with it. They are THE HONEYMOONERS, and since boarding the bus, the two Austrians have been arguing good-naturedly in a mix of German, Bavarian, and English. Their relationship started with an argument seven years ago, on Announcement Day, and they plan to keep arguing until their deathbeds. Such fun! There are plenty of wonders in Europe, but America is vast, as vast as it is dangerous, and its famous physics puzzles are ripe for discussion, if not solutions. No one expects solutions. The Honeymooners don't even desire them, not really, even as they lobby energetically for their favorite explanations. Why end the verbal volley?

The object of the game is to keep the ball in play.

A few people are paying no attention to the Realist's objections. A person we'll call THE READER is sitting quietly, turning the pages of their book. They're thirty-one years old, and their work visa declares them to be a citizen of Taiwan, a country that no longer exists. No matter. They're here now, and happy to ignore the other passengers, as if everything they need to know is encoded in the sentences on the page.

Also ignoring the hubbub is THE INFLUENCER, a seventeen-year-old girl with the driver's license of a twenty-two-year-old, and the credit card of a much older man—her grandfather's. This morning's outfit is flared yoga pants (Kirinyaga, $59) and a bright yellow crop top (Prana, $42). Her black hair is straight and glossy, her bronze skin seemingly poreless, her makeup Instagram perfect. She looks like she's been dipped in plastic. She's humming to herself as she thumbs through the phone propped up on her round, distinctly pregnant tummy. She's at thirty-five weeks, more than a month from full-term, but when she walked up to the bus, the Tour Guide's eyes went round as if she thought the baby was about to drop from between her legs and onto the sidewalk. But the guide didn't bring up the girl's condition, only smiled in bright panic and handed over the complimentary travel bag (cheap nylon) with her name on it. The girl was pleased to see the interested expressions as she boarded the bus. The old white lady up front looked especially shocked. Get used to it, bitch! Strong woman on board!

The Realist is still standing, but now he's arguing with the Honeymooners. The Comic Book Writer calls out, "Sit down, asshole!" The Tour Guide frantically flips through her binder.

The Driver taps the brakes and the bus lurches. The Tour Guide drops her binder. The Realist bounces against the seat in front of him.

The Driver comes on the PA. "All passengers, please take a seat while the bus is moving." Her voice is firm. "And welcome to New Jersey."

Everyone looks out the windows, including the three passengers we've yet to meet, THE SISTER, THE NOVICE, and THE RABBI. The Sister's first impression of Fort Lee, New Jersey, is that it's indeed a fortress: palisades of rock and a wall of newly green trees defend the Garden State from the encroaching evil of New York. Her second impression, moments later, is that evil made it ashore long ago. Rectangular office buildings, shorter and more soul-sucking imitations of Manhattan's, crowd around the interstate. It's all cars and concrete and steel.

Be patient, she says to herself. There's an entire continent ahead.

The Sister doesn't wear a habit, but she does dress in a kind of uniform: the chunky Greek cross she always wears, her short gray hair, the corduroys, the sensible shoes—the whole feminist-bookstore-owner vibe she's got going. She can see it in their faces when strangers twig to her vocation, what she calls the *Oh, you're a nun!* moment. Sometimes they say that aloud. Sometimes she explains that she's not technically a nun, she's a Sister, in the Congregation of Saint Joseph, not a member of a cloister. But "nun" doesn't feel completely inaccurate to her; there's something monastic in her nature, something that craves silence and reflection.

She's not going to get it on this trip. Her original sabbatical plan, as she pitched it to the congregation's leadership team, was to travel alone while she wrote a new book of essays, this one about the spiritual implications of living in a simulation. The tour would provide a structure for the book, one essay per stop. Leadership agreed that the sabbatical was a good idea, but they were gun-shy after the last controversy, and had questions about what direction this book might take. The Sister couldn't tell them: her thoughts would lead where they led. After much consternation and a good bit of praying, the team approved the sabbatical but suggested (insisted) she bring along an assistant/secretary/swim buddy—*the world is dangerous for a woman traveling alone!*—and etcetera. She didn't tell them she'd already invited her old friend, the rabbi; the leadership team might misunderstand that relationship and cancel the trip altogether. Which was how the Novice came to join the tour. The girl, in full habit with her white novice veil and black tunic, acts like a kind of flashing light, announcing that nuns are in the area. At least the Rabbi is dressed in street clothes.

The Rabbi took a seat directly behind the Sister and the Novice, and he's been energized by the conflict on the bus. He pokes his head over the seats and says, "Well, what do you think of the hoax argument? Do you think he has a point?"

"No," the Sister says.

"Ah, you're probably right," the Rabbi says.

When the Sister first mentioned her sabbatical plan in an email and invited him along, he didn't know how to respond. What would his congregation think? He never made decisions quickly, about anything, socks or sandwiches, but this was a true conundrum. It was his wife who told him to just say yes, and even packed his bag for him. But ever since meeting up with the Sister at the bus departure point he's been riddled with doubt. The Sister greeted him with barely a smile. Is she now regretting her invitation?

They'd met over twenty years ago at the International Conference on Human Rights and struck up an epistolary friendship. In those letters (and later, emails) he felt like there was no one he knew better. The Sister shared all her most important ideas with him, even in their nascent, prepublished forms. She'd also been frank about her doubts and fears, demonstrating an intellectual humbleness he greatly admires.

What he did not understand was why she'd invited him. And then, when they came face-to-face this morning, he was too embarrassed to ask. Should he wait for her to bring it up? Or confront her soon? Frankly, she seemed a tad depressed, and he didn't want to make things worse. But what if she was depending on him asking? Maybe that was his purpose!

The Sister doesn't seem interested in chitchat; her eyes are glued to the window, seemingly mesmerized by the blur of greenery. The bus has finally sped up. Ramparts of tall trees line the interstate, hiding all ugliness. They could be driving through a forest. It seems she wants to be out there, away from him.

The rabbi, in desperation, turns his attention to the Novice. She's a young Latina from Miami—a Dominican, meaning the country, not the religious order, ha ha!—who insists on wearing a traditional habit. "And, um, what do you think, Sister? Are these anomalies natural or supernatural?"

"There's only one nature," the Novice says evenly. "One creation."

"Of course, of course," the Rabbi says. He doesn't know what she means, and she does not elaborate. After a chilly silence he eases back into his seat.

The Novice also goes by the title of "Sister," even though she hasn't yet taken her temporary vows. She's not exactly sure why the leadership team asked (ordered) her to go on this tour with the older Sister, but she has her suspicions, and she's ready to do her duty. The Sister is one of their most famous members, an activist who's been regularly arrested at Good Friday antinuclear protests (the guards at Lawrence Livermore National Laboratory reportedly knew her by name) and then made waves—and earned a reprimand from the US Conference of Catholic Bishops—for her book about bodily autonomy. The Sister ignored them and kept protesting, kept writing. The Novice has read every book and essay, some of them multiple times, and respects the Sister's intellect, even if she cannot agree with all the places that intellect has taken her. But now there are whispers that she has, perhaps, gone too far. Something's not right with her. Soul Trouble. No one will say exactly what. The Novice wonders why the congregation would let a woman in her condition make a tour of these secular obscenities. It seems like courting disaster. Well, the Novice is not about to let one of her sisters in Christ do something that damages herself or the church. If the Sister wades into deep water, the Novice will drag her back to shore.

Murmurs move through the rows. The Octos break into laughter. The Proud Grandmother loudly asks her daughter for a water bottle. And at the front of the bus, the Tour Guide flips ahead in the binder, trying to figure out what she should tell them next.

The passengers know the basics—everyone on the planet knows the basics. It's been seven years since the Announcement and the ensuing Freakout—the wave of suicides, the murders and disappearances of physicists and computer scientists around the world, campus bombings, the authoritarian crackdowns, the religious panic. All that has largely subsided. Since then, the world's had seven years of weekly reminders, seven years to get used to a landscape littered with ... whatever you wanted to call them: glitches, anomalies, Areas of Scientific What-the-Fuckery. Yes, there were still wars raging, and the stock market was still a shambles. But most people have gotten on with their lives. Okay, we get it, we're digital citizens of an artificial world, and everything's made of ones and zeros, us included. But man cannot live by red pills alone—who's up for some pizza?

The passengers, however, are not most people. For various reasons they've signed up to see the weirdness up close, and to reckon with it. The Tour Guide doesn't understand why they'd pay good money for this, and she isn't sure if the money is good enough for her to lead them. She's not even sure why they hired her for this job, or why she took it. Her only experience with the Impossibles is the single class in violation physics she took before dropping out of grad school, and the three months she'd worked as a docent at a mystery spot in Carbondale, Illinois. She suffers from Simulation Anxiety (a legitimate diagnosis, the Tour Guide's therapist told her, it's in the *DSM-6*) and feels her heart turn to glass when the weekly reminder shows up in front of her eyeballs.

She's not alone. The Freakout may be over, but there are still freaks out there, whack jobs so deep into existential panic that they think they can shoot their way out of the simulation. Every week some white boy with an AR-15 turns a local school into a first-person shooter. Or several of these boys find each other online and turn their paranoia into a religion. An ethos.

Just this morning, two hundred miles away, a woman the Tour Guide hasn't met yet, has in fact never heard of, yet, walked up to the entrance of her lab on the Boston University campus and found the door busted in, the glass panel shot out. Let's call her THE PROFESSOR. Her first instinct was to run back to her car. Instead, she pushed open the door, scraping the bottom frame across shattered glass. She was afraid to call out the names of the two grad students she'd left working there last night. She found one of them in the main workroom. He was slumped in a chair, chin resting on his blood-soaked chest, wide Velcro straps holding him to the chair. The second student lay a few yards away, sprawled in the hallway that led to the fire exit. Face down, unmoving. She knew he was dead as well, and knew that it was time for her to run now, before the police arrived. But she went to him and kneeled down and touched the back of his head.

We'll leave the Professor there.

Our focus for now is on the bus, where the Tour Guide has reached the last page of the binder, a list of URLs for further reading. Fuck! she thinks. Give me something I can use! What if there's nothing of value she can tell these people? What if she's been set up to fail? The most important questions, she's pretty sure, are the ones that no one can answer. Why did the Simulators create the simulation? Why did they tell us we were in it? What do they want from us? And a dozen more hard questions, whose answers won't mean a thing until we get the answer to the one great question: How do we stop the bastards from pulling the plug?

"And there it is," the Engineer says.

The rain has stopped, and the clouds have moved south. Ahead of the bus the air is clear, and the passengers can see for miles. Far off in the distance, there's a strange, upside-down mountain, so black it seems two-dimensional.

Our first stop.

The
Frozen
Tornado

The Engineer
Considers Oz

||||||||||||||||||||||||||||||||||||||||||||||||||||||||||||||||||||||||

JP Laurent gazes up at the Frozen Tornado, wondering how, exactly, the Simulators wanted him to feel. Awed? Intimidated? Amused? The thing is ridiculously oversized and out of scale, like a Koons *Balloon Dog*. He also doesn't know how he feels when he looks at a Koons *Balloon Dog*.

He and the fellow members of his tour group are standing at the bottom of a manicured slope, huddled around a park ranger, soaking up many cheerful facts about the physical anomaly. They're three hundred yards from the base of the structure, but even from this distance it's impossible to take in the whole thing at once. It looks like a wide black ribbon, spiraling downward, the top of it hanging a kilometer in the air as if held by invisible fingers. The first loop is as wide as the Tornado is high. As it corkscrews toward the ground, the loops cinch tighter and tighter until it becomes a spike, then a needle.

"So let me get this straight," says Dulin Marks, the comic book writer, in mock umbrage. "It doesn't even move?"

"I'm sorry if you've been misinformed," JP says.

"Maybe I've seen too many photographs," Dulin says. "And drawings. I've made artists drop this thing into the background of so many panels."

"Really?"

"It's comic book shorthand for *hey, we're in New Jersey*. You know, kinda like the way the Eiffel Tower signifies Paris."

"But for the exact opposite of Paris," JP says.

Dulin laughs loudly. Every Dulin laugh is loud.

The park ranger looks over at them and Dulin stifles himself. The ranger's a skinny old dude with the relaxed air of a Berkeley professor whose edibles have just kicked in. "That base looks solid, doesn't it? But it's just a continuation of the spiral. At the very tip, the bands are wound so tight there's just a single micron gap—that's one millionth of a meter. As it spirals outward, the gaps widen exponentially. The technical term is logarithmic spiral. The great mathematician Jakob Bernoulli called it the *Spira mirabilis*—the miraculous spiral."

The rest of the tour group is eating this up. The quartet of old folks from the back of the bus (in the folder bio they listed their profession as "Active Octos") are oohing and aahing; the rabbi is practically beaming. The old woman in the wheelchair is staring up at the black spike almost greedily. But Dulin, JP notices, has his eye on the forty-something woman pushing the wheelchair.

"Don't," JP says.

Dulin gives him a *What, me?* face.

At five turns from the base, the ranger tells them, the band is just a centimeter wide and a centimeter off the ground. Two loops later it's jumped up to a meter. Then the math slingshots into the human scale and the bands explode outward. The spiral widens in a geometric progression, always at the same ratio, each turning 1.5 times more distant than the previous. The width of the black ribbon is also expanding as it climbs. At the very tip of the spiral, the ribbon is a hundred meters wide. But from the ground, every band looks as if it's the same width, an optical illusion that makes it look tiny, something you could hold on the palm of his hand.

"You know, Bernoulli wanted the shape carved on his gravestone." JP's whispering to Dulin as if they're in church. "But the gravediggers put on the wrong spiral."

"Aren't you an erudite motherfucker," Dulin says. His rumbling voice has never been capable of an actual whisper. "Which one did they engrave?"

"An Archimedean spiral. Very embarrassing."

"Those gravediggers," Dulin says, shaking his head. "Can never keep their spirals straight."

The park ranger gestures for the group to follow him up the hill for a closer look at the Tornado. The pregnant girl hurries ahead of the group, pivots, pouts, and clicks a selfie. Her enormous puffy jacket is chrome silver and seems to reflect every last photon of the New Jersey sun.

JP and Dulin amble along at the rear of the pack, just behind the two Catholic sisters and the rabbi. Please God, JP thinks, let me be there when they all walk into a bar. Then the older sister steps away from the group, and JP sees the stripe of a tear along one cheek. What the hell? Dulin sees it too, and they exchange a look. It's hard to tell whether she's distraught or merely overcome with, well, the grandiosity of it all.

Dulin rumble-whispers to JP, "Should I say something?"

JP is appalled and mouths a silent no.

The group spreads out along a chain that's set up a dozen feet from the base, under the shadow of the spiral. JP can see now that the black surface of the Tornado is lightly grooved, like a vinyl LP.

"Marion would get a kick out of this," Dulin says. Marion is Dulin's daughter. When she graduated from the University of Oregon she moved to Connecticut, the opposite side of the continent, as far from her father as she could get. The two haven't spoken in years.

"You should call her," JP says. He tells him this about once a week.

Dulin's mouth twists. "Maybe." He raises the phone and takes a picture. "I'll text her later." JP's not sure whether Dulin has ever sent Marion a text. If he did, would she answer it?

The park ranger calls for their attention. "One of the great mysteries," he says, "is what the Frozen Tornado is made of. The technical term—and I'm not making this up—is 'stuff.' We're not sure what it is, though scientists have been trying to study it since the Appearances. We do know that it's incredibly hard. For example—"

"What scientists?" a voice demands. JP looks around; of course it's the bald guy from the bus ("Profession: Host of the *Real Patriot* podcast") who gave the tour guide such a hard time about nomenclature. "Isn't it true that the government's prevented independent scientists from making their own study of the material?"

The park ranger smiles quizzically. "I'm not aware of that."

"Two years ago, a man tried to approach the Tornado with his equipment and the authorities prevented him. They even called the police."

"Maybe that happened on my day off," the park ranger says blandly, and the Octos chuckle.

"There's a video on YouTube," the bald guy says.

"I'm sure there is. Now, then—stuff! Many of the Impossibles seem to be made of it. But even after seven years we haven't made much headway in understanding it. It's so hard that you can't chip off a piece and take it into the lab. It's harder than any substance we know of— harder than diamonds, not even lasers can knock a piece free. They've even used electron microscopes to see into what stuff is made of, and so far—"

"But that didn't happen here, right?" the podcaster says. He glances over his shoulder. His stork-like son is recording the exchange on his phone and doesn't look happy about it. "No electron microscope has been allowed to directly sample the Tornado."

"No, it hasn't," the ranger says. "The experiment I'm talking about happened at another Impossible, the Flores Negras in Argentina. But that's because you can't fit any part of the Frozen Tornado into the chamber of an electron microscope. Now, I hear GE is working on a device, but it's not ready yet."

"So!" the podcaster says. "This tornado structure could be made out of some new carbon fiber. You don't know."

"When we get back to the bus," Dulin says to JP, not bothering to lower his voice, "can I throw him under it?"

"I've always wanted to see that metaphor in action."

The tour guide raises a hand. "Maybe we can take questions one at a time?"

"But what *is* stuff made of?" someone asks the park ranger. From his accent, JP pegs him as one of the Austrians ("Fun Fact: We are on our honeymoon!!").

"In your opinion," his husband adds. It's clear the pair already have opinions of their own.

The ranger smiles. "It's definitely not plastic, or steel, or a carbon alloy. It's not anything we've ever seen. Most material scientists think that it won't ever be found on the periodic table. When we're kids, we think that a solid is a solid, a liquid is a liquid. But when we learn a little science, we find out that the world's made of atoms, and those atoms are made out of electrons and protons, and those are made out of quarks. Stuff, however, isn't made of any of that."

"Remember when we used to think we were a cloud of quarks?" Dulin says to JP. "That was so crazy."

"But what *is* it?" the old woman asks plaintively. (Under profession she'd listed "Proud grandmother.")

"It's only itself." The ranger puts on another smile. He seems to have an infinite supply. "Pure stuff, all the way down, through and through. It's a true solid. It may be the only truly solid material in the world."

"But you don't know that!" the podcaster says to the ranger. His voice is loud enough to share his objection with the group. "You, personally. You're just repeating what you've been told."

"Or maybe I'll just punch him," Dulin says to JP.

"You'd just break your hand. He's made of ultradense material."

"A head full of stuff. He's fucking Winnie-the-Pooh, but adamantium."

The bald man puts a hand on his son's shoulder and lifts a leg over the chain. "I want to see for myself. Ladies and gentlemen, it's about to get—"

"Sir!" the ranger says. No smile now. "Step back from the barrier."

The pregnant girl has appeared at JP's elbow. Her own phone is pointed at the podcaster. "Oh my God," she says, narrating to the phone. "Shit's going down."

The man's straddling the chain now. "What are you afraid of?" he asks.

The girl swivels her phone toward the park ranger.

"Trust me, you don't want to do that," the ranger says.

"What, am I going to hurt the Tornado?"

The girl's pivoting back and forth, trying to capture the dialogue. It won't make for great video.

"Touch it along a seam and you'll cut yourself pretty badly," the ranger says. "The Tornado is basically one giant razor rolled around itself."

The bald guy frowns. "Is that what you tell people?"

"Yes," he answers. "That is what I tell people. All the time."

The tour guide has pushed close to the podcaster. She seems frantic. "Please, you must obey the rules of the park."

The man stands there, the chain running between his legs. "It's fine," he says to the guide. "Don't worry." He turns toward the Tornado, but his leg gets hung up on the chain and suddenly he's on the ground.

"Dad!" his son says.

The man frees his leg and scrambles under the chain toward them, looking flushed. He stares into the lens of his son's phone. "I'm fine. We'll cut that. Ready? One, two . . ." He puts on a grim expression. "More to come."

"Jesus Christ," Dulin says. "Did he just throw to commercial?"

Between the pregnant girl and the podcaster, JP thinks, this trip's going to be way more documented than he's comfortable with.

The young sister—"novitiate," it said in her bio, though she's in full nun drag while her coworker in Christ is in street clothes—has heard the blasphemy and looks over her shoulder. Dulin looks uncharacteristically chagrined.

The podcaster pushes through the group and heads toward the

bus, projecting to the world that he is not just leaving, but leaving in a verifiable huff. His son puts the phone in his pocket. His cheeks are flushed, and he's staring at nothing, making no eye contact. Slowly he walks away, in a different direction from his father.

One of the Austrian honeymooners breaks the silence. "I have a question," he says to the park ranger. "What do you believe is holding it up?"

"Nothing," says the park ranger. All smiles have been used up. "You can watch the film." He strides away.

The tour guide watches him go, and when she turns back to the group, she looks shaken. "Okay!" she says brightly. "Let's go to the visitor center. Which is . . ." She turns to find it, and one of the Octos points the other way, at the large wooden building. It's brand-new. The government only opened the park to the public three years ago. "Yes!" the tour guide says. "This way!"

The group begins to shuffle after her. "You coming?" Dulin asks.

"I'm good," JP says. "Go on ahead."

Dulin frowns. "You sure? I've heard great things about this documentary. All the park rangers are raving about it."

"I just want to walk around a bit."

Then the nurse walks past, pushing her mother. She glances back at Dulin. JP can't read her expression, but then again, the message isn't aimed at him.

"Well, maybe I'll check out the gift shop," Dulin says. He starts to follow the women.

"Hey, Dulin?" JP says. His friend stops. "Please don't try to bang anyone on the bus. We have to live with these people for the next seven days."

"I promise not to bang anyone on the bus," Dulin says. "Only in restrooms and motels."

JP watches him lumber into the building and feels a twinge of guilt. Dulin's worried about him. Again. The big man's never been able to hide his emotions—his facial expressions practically come with comic book sound effects, eyebrows flying up with a WHOOSH! and frowns slamming down with a WHAM! But the constant concern in his eyes gets a little oppressive.

JP walks along the curving observation path, which offers up slightly different views of the anomaly. He's moving slowly, sluggish from the Dilantin and headachy from last night's dose of Temodar. He wishes Suzanne were here. But since she can't be, he's glad he has the path mostly to himself. Summers are probably more crowded, he thinks. But maybe not. There isn't much more to see here that you can't catch from the highway. Suicide has to be one of the main reasons to see it up close and personal. He thinks of the nun's tears. Is she depressed?

He wouldn't blame her for trying to off herself. Death is the one sure way out of the simulation, so why not go by Tornado? Worked for Dorothy. The girl got wacked in the head by randomness, then uploaded to a Technicolor afterlife. The only mystery is why she came back. She got to walk on streets of gold, make new friends, and get a glimpse at the man behind the curtain—and after all that, she chose gray Kansas?

The Asian guy from the tour bus sits on one of the benches along the path, reading a book. ("Name: Chen Xing-Xing. Favorite hobby: Reading.") Though "guy" isn't polite, probably; pronouns in the bio were "they/them." They don't look up as JP passes, and JP's grateful to slip past without being snared by small talk. Though he does wonder if Xing-Xing, or any other member of the tour group, understood the ramifications of what the park ranger told them about the Frozen Tornado. *Stuff is not made of atoms.* And left unsaid, *People aren't, either.* JP's known this for seven years, and it still hurts his head when he ponders it. He spent his entire career building machines, wrestling with materials, tussling with physics. Then came April 29: the Announcement and the Appearances. Not only was humanity informed they were living in a simulation, but hundreds of physics-defying Impossibles had sprouted up to prove it. The yearslong Freakout ensued. JP's personal Freakout entailed massive disappointment. He felt cheated, like a kid who'd been playing with Legos—who thought the whole world was made of Legos, plastic bricks all the way down—who had to watch some higher-dimensional Michelangelo plop down a *David* carved from solid marble. Matter didn't matter. It was all stuff, a stupid name to disguise what it really was: bits. Zeros and ones, all the way down.

As an engineer, he has every right to be angry at the Simulators. And yet: the Tornado is beautiful.

The path has curled back toward the structure. He brushes moisture off the seat of a bench and sits down. His butt still gets damp. But no matter. He looks up at the ribbon spiraling into the sky and is struck again by how elegant it is. No wonder Bernoulli fell in love with it. An entire structure driven by a simple equation—continually expanding, but always keeping the same shape. *Eadem mutata resurgo*: "Although changed, I arise the same." Bernoulli specified that the phrase be engraved on his headstone next to the spiral. At least they didn't botch the Latin, too.

He hears a voice call out. A thin Black woman with an impressive Afro is marching up the hill from the parking lot, a nylon duffel strapped over one shoulder and a leather courier bag strapped over the other. She's flagged down a mother and toddler. The mother listens to her question, then shakes her head. The Black woman sees him, locks eyes, and strides toward him.

Oh no, he thinks. What did I do?

"Are you with that tour bus?" she asks.

He looks down at the parking lot, hoping there's more than one bus. No such luck. Just his bus and perhaps a dozen cars.

"As a matter of fact—" JP says.

"Where are you going?"

"Well, there are six stops in seven days. Tomorrow we're going to the Geysers of Mystery."

"No, how far west? What's the end of the line?" There is no possibility of ignoring her questions.

"Ghost City," he says.

"*Really.*" Her gaze is intense. He can practically feel the buzz and snap of the X-ray machine. "That far in seven days—you've got to be taking the Tunnel."

"That's on the itinerary."

"All right, then," the woman says. "This is meant to be." She shrugs off the duffel bag and sits, the courier bag between them. She's wearing a fuzzy black fleece with a small logo on it, black leggings, and bright-green running shoes. "What's your name?"

"JP. Jean-Pierre. But nobody calls me that." Her sudden fierce look makes him nervous. "Except my parents," he adds. "They're dead."

"I need you to do me a favor, Jean-Pierre. Do you have a phone?"

Is she going to steal his phone? That seems unlikely. "Is your phone dead? There's probably a charger inside."

She makes grabby fingers. "Come on. Let me see it."

He unlocks his phone and hands it to her. She opens a browser and starts typing.

"Um, listen, if you need to make a call, that's okay, but I'd prefer if you didn't—"

"Canterbury Trails, right? Is that it?" She shows him the home page of the tour group. "Is this the trip you're on?"

He's not sure he should tell her. She stares at him through a storm of gray curls.

"That's the tour," he says. "North American Impossibles."

She taps through a couple of pages. Her fingers move in staccato bursts, like a pecking bird. There's certainly a hawklike intensity about her. "It says there's AC power on the bus, at each seat. Is that true?"

"I haven't tried it yet," he says. The logo on her fleece, he sees now, is a red "BU" behind a cartoon black-and-white dog. Boston University, then.

She's frowning at the web page. "Registration closed. Shit. I mean, yeah, of course, it's already in progress, but—" She blows out her lips. He's relieved when she hands him his phone.

"So, do you teach at BU?" he says.

She looks alarmed. "How—?"

"Terriers," he says, and nods to the logo on her fleece. She looks down at herself, swears.

"I'm sorry," he says, "I didn't mean to—"

"How much room do you have on your credit card, Jean-Pierre?"

"What?"

"I need you to buy me a ticket on this tour. Don't worry, I'm going to pay you. Immediately, in cash."

"Okay, but if you have cash— Do you mean this tour? Right now?"

"One more thing." She swipes at his phone, starts typing something.

"What are you doing?"

"Just a sec." She taps and swipes, taps and swipes. "There. Thank you."

She hands him back his phone. The screen's back to showing his browser window. What did she just do?

"Are you in trouble?" he asks.

She opens the leather bag and starts digging through its interior. "I'm fine," she says. "I have a great desire to see a selection of the most famous Impossibles in the United States."

"You can tell me if it's, well, anything." He tries to think of reasons why she'd be on the run. Fleeing an abusive husband? But she doesn't seem at all abused.

She holds out a stack of bills. "That's five thousand dollars."

Or maybe, JP thinks, she's robbed a bank.

"That's more than the tour costs," he says.

"Consider it a tip." She presses the stack into his hand. Her thin fingers are cold. It's strangely thrilling. "Here's the story. We tell the tour leader that you and I are longtime friends who've met each other by accident, here at this fucking insult to physics."

He laughs. "It is a bit of an insult, isn't it?"

"A giant middle finger to rationality." She shrugs off her fleece, starts to roll it into a tube, then says, "Shit." She retrieves a folded piece of paper from the pocket, then rolls the jacket again and stuffs it into her courier bag.

JP politely ignores all this. "I should probably know your name," he says. "Since we're longtime friends."

"You should," she says. "I'm Gillian. Gillian Masch."

"You're my first hard-*G* Gillian," he says. He doesn't know why he said that.

"The soft-*G* Gillians suck," she says.

He laughs again and thinks, What the hell is happening?

The Realist's Son
Practices Camouflage

|||||||||||||||||||||||||||||||||||||||||||||||||||||||||||||||||||||||||

Christopher Mullins sits very still at his table at the Euro Gourmet Buffet, desperately trying to fade into the restaurant's green wallpaper. One hand slowly conveys food into his mouth. His jaw chews almost silently. His eyes are fixed on his phone's screen. He is a human chameleon, and with any luck, everyone will forget he's sitting at the table.

"I'm not saying it's definitely made by humans," his father says to the Austrian honeymooners. For some reason they chose to sit with Christopher and his father and engage with him. No, not just engage. Egg him on.

"I think you are," one of the men says pleasantly. The clean-shaven one wearing the round Harry Potter glasses. His name is Marcus, unless it's Josef. Christopher hasn't nailed down their names, or the names of anyone on the bus, really, and hopes to keep it that way.

"But look at the evidence," his father says. "The Frozen Tornado's exactly one kilometer high, exactly one kilometer wide. Those are human measurements." He stabs something on his tray. The Euro Gourmet Buffet offers several kinds of meat, and his father has taken one of each, and covered them all with the same brown gravy. Even the catfish. "Aliens wouldn't use meters, they'd use, I don't know, frabjets and klosmers, their own system."

"That makes sense," says the chubby white guy in the sweater. The rabbi? He's one table over, sitting with the two nuns, but all his concentration is on this argument, as if he's refereeing a Ping-Pong match.

"Perhaps the Simulators *are* humans," the bearded Austrian says. Maybe *he's* Marcus? "Future humans."

"Good point," the rabbi says.

"Unlikely," says the one with the glasses. "The simulation is so advanced—so far beyond twenty-first-century technology—it seems unlikely that humanity still exists. If it does, why would they be using the same measurement system? No, my bet is on the AIs."

"That's just Matrixism," his father says.

"Aliens, then," the first Austrian says. "The point is that they would *understand* our measurement system, but that doesn't mean they use it themselves."

"I definitely agree with that," the rabbi says enthusiastically.

Is there anything he doesn't agree with? Christopher thinks.

"So you'd rather believe robots and aliens are behind all this, rather than just the government?" his father asks the Austrians. "You have to think about Occam's razor. Isn't it more likely we're getting scammed by powers that we *know* exist?"

"You keep saying the government," says the Harry Potter. "But the Impossibles all appeared on the same day, all over the world. Are you saying there is a vast conspiracy between the United States, China, Europe . . . ?"

"A smorgasbord of conspiracy," his husband says.

"A buffet of falsities," the first one says. "For example, here we are in the Euro Gourmet Buffet, yet . . ." He shows them his fork, which is holding a chunk of chicken-fried steak. "This is neither Euro *nor* gourmet!" His husband giggles.

"Why is it so crazy to think that governments would cooperate?" Christopher's father demands. "Is that any crazier than thinking that all of human history has been a lie?"

"There is that," the rabbi says.

"But even if they conspired," says the Austrian with the beard. "How did they do it all in one night? They're not Santa Claus."

"Let me ask you a question," his father says, and Christopher silently groans. "What's more likely, they all appeared in one night, or that the media *told* everyone they appeared in one night?"

His father speaks in rhetorical questions. There should be a special punctuation mark: *What's more likely . . . >?< Isn't it more rational . . . >?<*

One of the Austrians says, "That sounds a little . . ."

"Paranoid?" his husband finishes.

"If there's ever been a time to be paranoid, this is it," his father says. He's leaning across the table. "We have to be on guard. And we have to be willing to defend ourselves."

Please don't show them the gun, Christopher thinks. He glances at his father's back and is relieved to see his shirt is covering the top of the holster. His father carries a Glock 19 tucked against his spine like a vestigial tail. Christopher is pretty sure it's illegal to carry a concealed weapon across state lines, but his father never dresses without it. And what happens when his father pushes the wrong person too far? Like the big guy on the bus who called his dad an asshole. Christopher's been keeping track of his position in the room. Right now he's walking back from the buffet line with what must be his third helping of food. He glances over, and Christopher ducks his head.

Maybe he should call his mother, beg her to pay for a plane ticket back to Indiana. But ever since he moved in with Dad, she's been all frosty with him. But what was he supposed to do? Stay with her and her new husband and her new children and that new (very old) cat? There was no place for him in that house.

At least his father wanted him. Or rather, some version of Christopher, a son-shaped object to serve as an unpaid intern at Dad Inc. *The Real Patriot* podcast, his father says, will launch an empire—rallies, television shows, maybe a streaming news organization!—all under one mission statement: *Real Truth about the Real World.*

Christopher doesn't understand why his father is so committed to exposing the "simulation hoax." Can't he just accept the obvious? Christopher was in his sophomore year of high school on Announcement Day, and yeah, the kids in school talked about it nonstop for a few weeks, but then . . . moved on. *Of course we're living in a video game. Duh.* Unfortunately, the game turned out to be one of those MMORPG grinders where you were supposed to mine for gold and fish for two hundred hours so you could buy a mithril shirt or whatever, and every day or so some psycho turned the game into a first-person shooter. Why was anyone shocked that the world was not in our control, and that nothing we did mattered? The Simulators could hit reset at any time. Or climate change would kill us all. Same difference.

But his father went a little crazy after the Announcement. An angry flavor of crazy. He took it personally when he lost his job during the Freakout, even though millions of people also lost their jobs. He took it even more personally when Mom left him. Which, understandable? But half the parents Christopher knew were getting divorced, everybody reassessing the deals made in the before times. If nothing's real, why think these marriages are? Hell, why think other people are? Christopher is 90 percent sure that 90 percent of the world is made up of NPCs. Full consciousness is just not required for all those bodies to maintain the sim—not the one *he* is in, anyway. He's never going to visit China, and neither is his dad, so why instantiate a billion people they'd never meet?

Christopher hasn't made up his mind on the status of the people on this tour, yet. Like the four octogenarians bogarting the soft-serve machine, or the equally old woman in the wheelchair, talking and talking to a daughter who isn't listening. Do any of them have a thought in their heads, or are they all just bots, following a dialogue tree like some Elder Scrolls shopkeeper? And why are they all so old? The only person near his age on this tour is the pregnant girl, and she's across the room, staring at her phone. She's always on her phone. Of course he'd noticed *her* as soon as she stepped onto the bus. Even preggers, she was legitimately hot. Walked down the aisle like it was a red carpet. How old is she, exactly: Twenty-seven? Twenty-eight? No idea. Her ethnicity seems to be Reality Show. She has the bronze glow of a Kardashian, the pouty lips of a Bachelorette, the sleek hair of a Drag Race queen's Cher wig. The dome-like belly kinda freaks him out, but she wears it well, all out and proud like Rihanna when she was strolling around with A$AP Rocky.

Then, suddenly, the girl looks up and locks eyes with him. Yikes! Had he made that happen? He feels like he's accidentally clicked on an ad. And now she's walking toward him!

He looks down at his own phone, embarrassed, but he's not seeing the screen. He's waiting. Is she walking toward him, or merely in his direction?

Her long fingernails touch down on the table, inches from his hand. He looks up and her smooth moon of a belly is eye level. Her skin smells like a vanilla-spice latte.

"I need you."

He forces his eyes up, past the full breasts, all the way up to her own eyes. He tries to make himself look surprised. "Oh, hey there!" (*Hey there*? Why the hell did he say that?)

"Follow me," she says.

His chest tightens. *Yes*, he thinks.

She doesn't move.

"Um, where?" he asks.

She frowns. Did he offend her? "Everywhere," she says. "Instagram, TikTok, Roblox, Mimsy, YouTube, all major platforms."

Oh, right, he thinks.

"Except Facebook," she adds.

"Of course, that would be—"

"Lady Mmm," she says. "Lady, underscore, three *m*'s. Got it?"

"Three *m*'s," he repeats.

"You really want to check me out," she says. Then she pivots and sashays toward the restrooms. He didn't even know it was possible for a pregnant woman to sashay.

He looks up @lady_mmm on Mimsy. Her latest video was posted just a few minutes ago. He clicks on it, and is horrified to see it's showing his father, climbing over the Tornado chain. He quickly mutes the volume. Then he starts scrolling through the comments.

Oh no, he thinks. Oh no.

The Comic Book Writer Tries to Tell a Joke

||||||||||||||||||||||||||||||||||||||||||||||||||||||||||||||||||||||||

"Here's what I resent about these assholes," says Dulin Marks. The podcaster's braying voice has been grating on him, even from across the room. "It's the co-opting of the word 'realist.' The sim *is* reality. It's unrealistic to pretend it doesn't exist."

"Uh-huh," JP says. He's barely listening. He's been distracted ever since the Frozen Tornado.

Dulin taps his fork on JP's plate. "You've got this woman on your brain. And your brain has enough problems."

JP laughs in that nearly silent way of his. Dulin's relieved. This is all he wants out of the tour—JP laughing a little bit. Remembering his old self. Anything but walking around in his house alone, eyeing the rafters and measuring rope, designing a simple machine for a simple task.

"I told you, I don't want to talk about it," JP says. "Not in here."

"You realize this is all a con, right?" Dulin says. "This woman's taking you for a ride."

"Stop saying 'this woman.' She's a college professor. I think."

"Well *I* think Gillian's not even her real name."

"Could you keep your voice down?"

Beth-Anne Neville, the nurse from North Carolina, is sitting two tables away, across from her wheelchair-bound mother. Dulin has committed her short bio to memory. There's no risk of being over-heard, however; Beth-Anne's mother has been talking nonstop. The large dining room is loud and echoing, and the bald guy is a major contributor to the hubbub. Nobody's paying attention to Dulin and JP.

"Trust me," Dulin says through a mouthful of mostaccioli. "It's some kind of scam."

"I don't think so." JP takes a sip from his iced tea. He's barely touched his plate. Dulin knows the meds mess with his appetite. The hard-core one he takes at night sometimes makes him vomit. JP's never been heavy, but he's never been this thin, either.

"I don't understand why you're helping her," Dulin says.

"Because she needs help. It's not any more complicated than that."

Dulin thinks it's way more complicated than that. "Have you looked at the bills she gave you?"

"What?"

"They could be counterfeit."

"Now you're just racial profiling."

"No I'm not. All this has the smell of fraud. She's running up charges on your credit card."

"It's only money," JP says.

"*Hey*. Don't talk about money like that."

JP laughs quietly. That man's always so careful with his finances. It was Dulin who was the fuckup, the guy who was perpetually late on child support and couldn't make his car payments. JP (and Suzanne, God bless Suzanne) had bailed him out more than once.

Dulin changes tack. "Why won't she come out of the bus? She's in there, typing away. Why join a tour if you're not going to join the tour?"

"She seems to be writing something. Maybe she's on deadline."

"No real writer worries about deadlines."

"Maybe she's a *good* writer."

"Ouch."

"Don't you have, like, three scripts due?" JP asks. "You said your editors were hounding you."

It's five scripts, he thinks, from three different publishers, but no need to mention that. "Fuck 'em. I'll finish them while we're in the Tunnel." He takes a sip of his own iced tea. Winces. "Oh man, I think they made this with powder."

"You can drink a beer, you know."

"Wait, they have beer? I didn't notice." There are five different beers on draft, including an old favorite, St. Pauli Girl. It was impossible to find St. Pauli Girl these days.

"I won't mind," JP says. "Really."

"Look, you can't drink, I'm not going to drink. That's the deal."

"I didn't make this deal, you did," JP says. "I want you to drink. I want to live vicariously through you."

"That reminds me of a joke. This Irish guy goes into his pub and every day he orders three shots—"

"I've heard it."

"When has that stopped me?"

They've heard all of each other's jokes, dozens of times. Also all the stories, complaints, regrets, justifications, and opinions. (But not all the secrets, Jesus Christ, not all.) One of the underappreciated pleasures of a long friendship is this constant tilling of familiar fields. Occasionally they turn over a new rock. But mostly they forbear and forgive each other's repetitions.

Mostly. He's annoyed that JP won't let him finish the Irish brothers joke. "Fine," Dulin says. "Here's my question. Where's her car? How did she get to the Frozen Tornado?"

JP frowns. Aha! Mr. Engineer hadn't thought of that.

"Maybe she took an Uber," JP says.

"She took an Uber to the Tornado, for no reason?" Dulin says. "Then joins the tour on a whim? Nope, doesn't add up. She's on the run. Loads of cash, doesn't want to use her credit card, won't tell you her real name . . ." He takes his reading glasses from his breast pocket and unfolds them. "What'd you say her last name was? Masher?"

"Masch. And I'm the one who told you she was on the run. I don't think it's an abusive husband or boyfriend, though. She doesn't seem like the type."

"There's no type for abuse, JP," he says in a teacher voice. He peers at his phone.

"What are you doing?"

"Googling her."

"No! Don't do that."

Beth-Anne looks up at the noise, and Dulin exchanges a look with her over the top of his glasses. Those green eyes knock him right out. She's a good-looking woman, padded in the right places, not like one of those skinny yoga moms. They had a pleasant chat in the Tornado gift shop while her mother dithered over souvenirs. The old woman asked them, Is the silver spoon with the spiral handle a better present than the wind chime? And Dulin said, There's no chime like the present. The mother scowled, but Beth-Anne laughed. A woman's laugh always hits him like kerosene, and this moment of eye contact is enough to keep the fire going.

The old woman says to Beth-Anne, "How long until we get to see the Avatar?" Her accent is pure country.

"We talked about this, Momma. Not till Day Five."

"Well, bring me another roll, then," as if she needs to stock up for such a wait. "And one of those Italian cookies."

Beth-Anne wipes her lips, sets down her napkin. Sneaks a quick glance at Dulin as if to say, You see what I have to put up with?

By an act of will Dulin doesn't turn to watch her walk away.

JP's noticed, though. He nods toward the nurse. "How'd you like it if I googled her?"

"I already have. And I'm pretty sure she's not a wanted criminal on the lam, like your girlfriend."

"Now she's my girlfriend?"

Dulin smirks. "She's got you bringing her lunch. In high school that would mean you're going steady."

"She'll tell me what's going on when she's ready to."

Dulin shakes his head. "This woman shows up with a pile of cash, grabs your phone, bosses you around . . . I don't understand why you're going to such great lengths for a stranger."

"She's scared. I think she needs help."

"So?"

"And she made me laugh." JP frowns. "Even though she was kind of petrified she managed to make a joke."

"That's not a good reason."

JP's eyes narrow. "This is really bothering you."

"It's not bothering me. I just think, what would—" Dulin stops himself.

"What?"

He was about to say, What would Suzanne think? But holy shit, that's too far, and too unfair. What the fuck is wrong with his brain that he'd even think that? He should be happy for JP. If some woman rooking him out of his savings keeps his heart beating, well so be it. It's his money.

"Nothing," Dulin says. "It's very, very nice of you to do this nice thing. I just worry about her taking advantage of you."

JP purses his lips, then says, "Can I show you something and you won't overreact?"

Dulin's first instinct is to shout, "OVERREACT?" Instead he says, "I would never do such a thing."

"When she took my phone, she also sent a text. Then she tried to delete it." JP's wearing the most minimal of smiles.

"You sly dog," Dulin says.

JP unlocks his phone and slides it across the table. "It's the last one."

I'm okay meet me at the handoff in 5 days. Don't text or call

Jesus Christ, it looks like a drug deal. "Who's it to?" Dulin asks. "And what's she handing off?"

"No idea."

"Are you going to ask her?"

"I don't know that, either." JP takes back his phone and puts it away. "Right now all I'm going to do is figure out her lunch. The tour guide should have her meal ticket, or maybe . . . what? Why are you looking at me like that?"

Dulin has, in the past, pursued women who were seriously bad news. In almost every case, JP saw the red flags and tried to warn him. Go slow, Dulin. Don't move in with her. Don't give her your bank account number. And in almost every case, Dulin ignored him, even got a little pissy about it. This is the first time in their long friendship that Dulin can finally return the favor.

"Come on," JP says. "Out with it."

"Get her the turkey BLT," Dulin says. "It'll travel better."

JP walks away, and Dulin feels like he's watching his best friend drive off a cliff. In his experience, there was no ride more exhilarating.

The Driver
Presses Mute

||||||||||||||||||||||||||||||||||||||||||||||||||||||||||||||||||||||||||||

Agnes Wisniewski sits outside the restaurant smoking a cigarette and dialing her phone. And redialing. "Jesus Christ, Peter," she mutters aloud. "Pick the fuck up."

She never wanted to be a bus driver. There was no point in her childhood that she prayed to God to please let her spend eight to twelve hours a day hauling bodies and slinging luggage for a whopping $43K a year. But Peter Atherton, the tour guide who should have been on this trip, seemed called to his career. He loved seeing the country. Loved learning new things and sharing what he'd discovered, like some high school honor student on a permanent field trip. But most of all, he loved people. She couldn't fathom why. How could you know people and still love them?

But Peter, Jesus Christ, he really did. Loved his riders, and they loved him. He was a handsome man with a swoop of blond hair and killer blue eyes. He'd get them to tell him personal shit, the details of their lives, the dreams that led to them to join whatever trip he was leading that week. Hardly any of the tourists asked him about *his* dreams. But at the end of the day, he'd meet up with Agnes in some corner of the hotel bar or at some dark table out by the swimming pool, away from the customers. He liked to call her by her given name,

Agnieszka. Drawl it out like she was a Polish princess. "Oh, my Ag*nye-sh*kaaa . . ." Most of the time they'd just shoot the shit. But sometimes, she asked him the questions nobody asked, and he told her things she was pretty sure he'd never told anyone else. He'd been raised by shitty parents, yet somehow escaped from his minefield of a childhood with his heart intact.

She kinda loved him. Not romantically. They played on different teams, in non-overlapping leagues. Peter picked out a theme song for them, from *Oklahoma!*: "The Farmer and the Cowman." They kept up a running argument about who was the farmer and who was the cow man.

Whatever and wherever Peter is, he isn't picking up his goddamn phone. And she's already sent him a dozen texts.

She grinds out her cigarette and calls the Canterbury Trails office again. Gets the same dipshit receptionist, Tanya. Agnes asks for the owner this time, but Tanya won't put her through, asks if she wants to talk to the scheduler in charge of drivers.

"You already did that, and it keeps going to voicemail," Agnes says. "I also asked for Sherri in HR, and that went to voicemail, too. You connected me. You don't remember talking to me like four times this morning?"

"We get a lot of calls," Tanya says.

Agnes squeezes the edges of the phone, feels the edges flex. "I just want to know who called in sick for Peter Atherton," she says evenly. "Did he call in himself, or did somebody else?"

"Is Peter one of the drivers?"

Agnes presses the mute button.

"Goddamn fucking stupid fuck fuck!"

She takes a breath. Exhales. Presses the mute button.

"He's a guide," Agnes says. "For the North American Impossibles Tour. Which is going on right now."

"Oh!" Tanya said. "No. I don't remember anything like that."

Not for the first time, Agnes wishes you could hang up a cell phone by slamming it down. She forces herself to daintily touch the hang-up icon, then says into the screen, "Fuck you, *Tanya.*"

The new tour guide is staring at her, mouth agape. She's come out of the restaurant, holding a paper sack and a Styrofoam cup. The trip binder is wedged awkwardly under her arm.

"What?" Agnes asks.

"I also hate Tanya," she whispers.

"We all do, honey."

"We really didn't get a chance to talk before," she says. "I'm Aneeta." She moves her arms, and Agnes realizes she's trying to free up a limb to shake her hand. Agnes looks away and is relieved when the girl gives up.

"I've been trying to get through to my supervisor," this Aneeta says. "He said I could add a passenger to the trip, and he took the credit card number, but nobody's sent me any instructions. I don't have hotel reservations, meal tickets, event tickets—"

"You may never get them," Agnes says. "They're disorganized as fuck."

Aneeta's shocked. "Why would they let me add her if they can't . . . add her?"

"They said yes because they need the money. They'd let you add Hitler if his card cleared. The whole business is going under."

A squeak escapes her. This girl is a goddamn cartoon mouse.

"But they just hired me!"

"And maybe you'll even get paid," Agnes says.

"What? They might go out of business before they even—?"

"I'm kidding." Agnes wasn't kidding. "There's nothing to do about it now. You're the guide. You get these people to where they're going, and whatever shit comes up along the way, you handle it."

Aneeta's frozen now, looking at nothing.

"You have to take control. And not just the logistics—you've got to manage the customers. You should be in there with them right now, getting to know them. What are you doing eating out here?"

"Oh, this lunch isn't for me," she says. "I'm bringing a turkey sandwich to the new passenger. Gillian."

"What? Hell no. I let her stay on the bus, but if she's going to eat, she should eat with the rest of them. How'd she get you to run errands for her?"

"She didn't, one of the passengers asked if I could . . . It doesn't matter."

"Did you pay for that out of your own pocket?"

The look on the girl's face answers the question.

"You've got to get on your game," Agnes says. "What you do on Day One sets the mood. Because it's only going to get weird as shit later. Wait till we get to Day Four."

"What happens on Day Four? Does something happen when they go in the Tunnel?"

"It's not the Tunnel specifically, though yeah, that's a doozy. It's more like the overall buildup. The kind of people who go on a tour like this, sometimes they just . . ." The kid's looking at her, waiting for wisdom to drop. But there's no way for Agnes to explain it to her. Every rider has a reason for the trip, and the parade of Impossibles hits each one of them different. Bam, here's some crazy shit. Bam, here's some more. And guess what, bitch, nothing's as real as you thought it was! Maybe you aren't either! Sooner or later they figure out the tour's not going to fix what ails them, and sometimes that realization snaps them like a twig.

Peter was a master at walking customers through these breakdowns. Sat with them while they cried, bucked up their spirits to get them to the next stop on the tour—and when they couldn't get back on the bus, made sure they could exit with dignity. He helped them pack, arranged flights, and called their relatives to pick them up, then checked in on them after the tour was over. He gave so much of himself. She'd never met someone with so much empathy, and so skilled at leading people out of a minefield.

But Little Miss Mouse? She was going to have to find out for herself.

"This is your tour," Agnes says. "It's on you to make sure these people get what they paid for. But only what they paid for, okay? Because you also have to take care of yourself. Don't let them suck the life out of you."

Be like Peter. But don't be like Peter.

Aneeta's staring off to the side, considering this. Good, Agnes thinks. Take it to heart.

"The binder lists an optional stop on our way to the hotel," Aneeta says. "There's an antipode right off the interstate."

"That thing at Mount Blessings?" Agnes shakes her head. "It's nothing."

"I don't think it's nothing," Aneeta says firmly. "I think people would find it interesting."

"Peter never stopped at it."

"I'm not Peter. Didn't you just say I have to take control of the trip?"

Jesus Christ.

"Fine," Agnes says. "But I'm going to finish my break first. And you, you save your receipts. Make the company pay for that shit."

The Antipode

(optional stop)

The Influencer Demos This Cool 3-Step Refresher

||||||||||||||||||||||||||||||||||||||||||||||||||||||||||||||||||||||||||||||

The bus is rolling and Lisa Marie Montello sits in the tiny bus lavatory, silently panicking.

The workload is breaking her. Yes, this morning she managed to edit and post a Frozen Tornado video, but there are dozens of photos she needs to color-correct. She can't keep up with all the posts from other influencers that she should be liking and cross-posting. And she's way behind on the day's media plan. She should have already streamed her Well-Baby Meditation sponsored by GlaxoSmithKline's SerenityMax app as presented by the Avatar Saugat Zin. (Branding requirement: on first use, always say the full name and title.) It's in her contract to do one meditation and one spontaneous "reflection" a day, all as buildup to the PEO, the Personal Experience Opportunity she'll have with Zin when they get to his compound at the Zipper. He's supposed to bless the baby and everything.

This could be a huge win for her. The guy has millions of followers who believe he's really from another sim and is chock-full of secret knowledge. And he did tell everybody where those stolen paintings were, after they'd been missing for years, and he did finally get the museum to pay him the ten million in reward money. Even if it all had the whiff of a late-night-TV scam, in the end it didn't matter. If he had the followers, that made him legit. Just a follow-suggest from him could boost her numbers and make Baby M famous.

But the app's marketing team keeps putting her off; they won't confirm the appointment. Is the Avatar trying to ghost her? He'd better fucking not. She should write them again. Her metrics are in the toilet. She was counting on the trip, #BABYTREK, to spike attention and engagement, but for three days her numbers have been inexplicably flat—*flat!* She has to keep engineering posts that build to the PEO with the Avatar Saugat Zin and climax with the birth. A video of a doofus tripping over a chain is not going to do it.

But how the hell is she going to get everything done with this constant peeing? This is her third trip to the toilet since leaving the Tornado. Baby M is sitting on her bladder like it's a beanbag chair.

The bus slows suddenly, and she puts out a hand to steady herself. This tiny chemical-smelling bathroom reminded her of the toilet stall on the second floor of Barringer High School in Newark, New Jersey. She'd sat in it for two whole class periods, screaming inside her head while she looked at the pink stick. One shot from her Cro-Magnon boyfriend's dick and she was *knocked up*? Okay, technically not one shot, several shots over the two weeks they'd been having sex, but he wore a condom every time. Except obviously not! Fuck that guy. And fuck the Simmers. Who the hell would design a system like this, in which some teenage boy's digital *goop* could wiggle inside her and start coding up an entire other creature—a creature who'd grow to the size of a bowling ball while *inside* her?

The bus jolts to a halt. Someone knocks on the bathroom door. "Busy!" she says.

A female voice says, "Are you okay, dear?" It's one of the olds.

"I'm fine!"

"We've arrived," the woman says. Jesus Christ, that "optional" stop Lisa Marie didn't allow time for in her schedule. "Just let us know if you need anything."

Lisa Marie pulls up her Bamboo Maternity & Postpartum Lounge Pants (Gaia's Garden, $39.99 with discount code LADYMMM) and pushes open the door. It's one of the "Active Octos." All four of them are standing, pulling on their jackets. The two old men are looking politely away, but the women regard her with concern, which annoys her. Another reminder from the geriatric crowd that she should call her grandfather and tell him where she is. But no time for that now. She needs to get her face ready for the next video.

Unless she combines them. A demo!

She walks toward her seat, belly snowplowing people out of her way, and plops down. This morning she rigged up a nylon-and-Velcro strap around the seatback in front of her; she puts her iPhone in selfie mode, turns on the ring light attachment, and hangs it on the strap—instant mirror.

Jesus, her face is fat. She checks her angles, lifts her chin. Her contours aren't holding. What to fix, and what to leave for the demo?

She opens the bulging Clinique bag, finds the bottle of Jergens Natural Glow, and rubs a dollop of self-tanner into her neck and spends thirty seconds blending to get the gradient she's looking for. Then she dabs a tiny amount of cream matte bronzer across each cheekbone for a sun-kissed glow, and then spends another half minute blending. Streaks and drama are out; the style this year—and therefore Lady Mmm's style—is *all natural*.

After two minutes it looks like she finally has bone structure. The bus is nearly empty.

She takes a breath. Summons her It-Girl voice. Then she starts Instagram Live.

"Hey, guys! As you can see, I'm *totally* undone right now, so here's my quick, three-step refresher and I swear to God, this is the thirty-second routine that will save, your, *day*."

She starts with the Anastasia eyebrow gel. Does her bit about "street-girl microblading" and instant ombre brows. "Next, this little secret weapon." She holds up the eyelash curler, which has handles like gyno forceps. "I know you're not supposed to do this, because it

rips your eyelashes out or whatever, but I think it's *way* effective."
She does the left eye, but then pinches herself on the right. Fuck! She
suppresses a grimace. Lady Mmm is graceful. Lady Mmm does not feel
pain.

"And last," she says, recovering. "Guaranteed fairy dust." She holds
up the box of Hourglass Ambient Lighting Palette finishing powder
($69.99 on Amazon). "You know I love Hourglass, and this stuff, oh
my God, it's like wearing a soft-focus filter." She brushes it across each
cheek, and then a puff across her forehead. "And . . . done! Lady Mmm
says be fabulous, like, and subscribe." She ends the live stream with a
cute finger bop.

She falls back in the seat. Fuck. Live streaming is in some ways
easier than recording offline—she doesn't torture herself with retake
after retake—but then she does something like crimp an eyelid. She'll
have to edit that out before she posts to TikTok.

"Ladies? Any of you going out to see the Antipode?" a voice says.

Lisa Marie leans into the aisle. The bus has emptied out, and the
linebacker-size bus driver is looking at her with bored eyes. What other
ladies is she talking about? Then she sees, two rows up, a mass of gray
curls—the Black woman who joined the tour this morning. Near the
front are two more women, the old white lady and her grown daughter.

"There's no ramp!" the old woman says. "The website said that
every stop is handicap accessible."

"I'm sorry," the driver says. "This is an unscheduled stop. A bonus
stop."

"It's not much of a bonus if I don't get to see it."

"Momma, I'm sure it's nothing," the daughter says.

"It really isn't much," the driver says. Then: "What about you two?"
Meaning Lisa Marie and the Black woman.

"Hold your horses," Lisa Marie says. That's one of Gramps's go-to
phrases. She unzips the Olympus Mark III from its case. The camera is
the most expensive thing she owns, including the laptop. She stops at
the Black woman's row. Her head is down, eyes on her laptop. So, Lady
Mmm isn't the only one working hard this trip.

"Are you going?" Lisa Marie asks. "I need to step out last."

This gets the woman's attention. "What? Why?"

"I just do," Lisa Marie says.

The woman flicks her fingers at her. "Go on. I'm fine."

The Influencer feels the heat rise in her cheeks. A *flick*? Nobody flicks Lady Mmm.

At the door the bus driver hands her a lime-green umbrella. "You're going to need this."

"What? It's raining again?"

Lisa Marie stops on the bottom step. Outside is a sea of green umbrellas, all displaying the Canterbury Trails logo. They seem to be in the middle of nowhere; there's nothing here but a wide grassy field. The sky is gray, the air cold, and a light drizzle is falling. In the middle distance, a guy zips along on a big industrial mower. How's she going to extract a decent visual from this gloomy shit?

She has to try. She pivots, raises the camera, looks up at it. This is one of her standard shots: upturned chin, pooched lips, smoky eyes, and a mass of people behind and below her. Lady Mmm, literally above the crowd. And of course, one hand on her belly. The whole point is to document Baby M's incredible journey. God knows she doesn't want people to think she's just fat.

The tour guide, that tiny South Asian girl, waves the passengers forward and tries to project over the noise of the mower, "This way! The Antipode is in the middle of this field. It's just . . . very hard to see until we're right on top of it."

The tourists begin shuffling after her, muttering.

Lisa Marie pops her umbrella. Out of nowhere, Christopher ducks his big red head under it and says, "Hey, uh, could I talk to you?"

"Whoa! Back up, ginger."

His cheeks flush scarlet—a different hue than his hair, but close. He backpedals out from under the umbrella.

Lisa Marie keeps following the tour guide, who's wandering across the field's spongy ground, head swiveling, looking for the Impossible.

"Uh, Lady Mmm?" Christopher again.

She's a sucker for anyone using her title. She stops, and he bends to peer under the lip of her umbrella. It's a deep bend: he's six four; she's barely over five feet.

"It would be really great if you could take it down," he says. "The video with my dad."

She grimaces. "Why would I do that?"

"Because you used his real name. And . . . he looks like an idiot."

"How is that my fault?"

"It's not! I'm just saying, it would be nice if you did?"

She's shaking her head before he finishes the question. "What's the matter with you? I thought you would love it. Do you even *like* your dad?"

His mouth opens, closes. The question has stumped him.

Finally she throws up a dismissive hand. "I can take any pictures I want in a public place. Your father has no reasonable expectation of privacy. That's the law." She walks away.

From behind her he says, "I know that's *legally* okay, but, um . . ." Poor kid can't finish the bluff.

Christopher says plaintively, "Did you have to make it slow motion?"

That was a good edit, she thinks. On the video, as the bald guy slowly falls to the ground, one leg still absurdly caught on the chain, the audio is him saying in a low, long rumble: "Doooon't woooorry . . ."

"It's funnier," Lisa Marie says, exasperated.

The tour guide has flagged down the mowing guy. He cuts the engine, listens to her. Points to a far section of the field. The guide waves at the tour group to follow her there.

Lisa Marie leaves Christopher gasping like a fish.

The guide stops, crouches, and tilts her head, looking sideways into the sky. Then she starts walking again. The bus mates are exchanging doubtful looks. "Maybe this one really is impossible," Christopher's father announces. "Impossible to find!"

Oh God, Lisa Marie thinks. The man thinks he's killing it.

"Here we are!" the guide says. "The Central Pennsylvania Antipode. Gather around it, everyone."

There's nothing on the ground but a bare patch of mud about three feet wide. They form a circle around it. Then Lisa Marie sees it, a disk of dark, glossy water, as wide as the mud patch, hovering about three feet in the air. It's invisible from the sides.

"What you're looking at," the tour guide says proudly, "is the *Indian Ocean*. It's a spot on the exact opposite side of the globe—about five hundred miles southwest from Perth, Australia."

Christopher's father pushes his hand into the disk. Someone yelps. Lisa Marie glances behind her and realizes it's Christopher. Poor kid.

But nothing happens. His father's arm remains visible and firmly attached to his shoulder.

"So it's an optical illusion," Christopher's father says.

"What? No," says the guide. "This is live. It's a live view. Only light can go through the portal. So, daylight from our side is hitting the ocean on the other side, and bouncing back, so we can see it."

She just told them only light can go through, but everyone is pushing their hands through the circle of air. Some are crouching to look up through the other side.

"I can see the stars!" one of the Octos says.

"Yes! Isn't that amazing? It works from both sides," the guide says, and suddenly everyone's ducking and looking up. "That's the sky of the southern hemisphere."

She tells them about the hundreds of other antipodes scattered around the planet. Many open onto water—the planet is three-fourths ocean, after all—but a few of the most popular ones have cities on both sides, and people can wave to each other and even communicate with written messages.

"Will we be seeing one of the popular ones?" asks Josef, the Austrian with the glasses.

"Um, no, not this trip," the guide says.

"Hmm," he says.

The guide looks around the circle. "But you see how amazing this is, yes? We're looking at the *other side of the world*. With no delay. A window just hovering in the air."

The Asian tourist silently tucks the book under their arm and starts walking back to the bus. Lisa Marie can't remember their name, only that they were the only person whose bio had nonstandard pronouns, so maybe a potential follower? She wonders if they speak English.

Christopher's father says, "This could just be a hologram. On a loop." He walks into the middle of the disk. It looks like he's floating in water.

Okay, enough with the amateur hour, Lisa Marie thinks. "I need that picture," she says aloud. She hands Christopher her Olympus. "Take my picture. But do not drop the fucking camera, okay?"

She steps next to Christopher's father and says, "Could you move back, please? Thank you."

The man frowns in confusion—and then obeys. She has the circle to herself. Christopher turns the chunky camera in his hands, trying to figure out which of the many buttons to push.

"The big shiny one," Lisa Marie says. "Right-hand side."

He finally gets it, starts snapping pictures of her. Lisa Marie, now transformed into Lady Mmm, strikes various poses and expressions she's developed over the past year: arms crossed atop her belly; one hand on her navel, the other flashing a peace sign; left hand touching chin, right supporting belly. Opposite. She runs through shy, flirty, amazed, and of course, #Blessed.

"Do you need us to do anything while we're standing here?" asks the big hairy guy. His bio said he was a comic book writer. "Jazz hands? Maybe form a kick line?"

Lisa Marie ignores him. "One for safety," she tells Christopher. She throws out her arms as if hugging him. The boy flushes again. He's a walking heat rash.

"Thank you, Christopher," she says, and takes back her camera.

"You—you know my name?"

Christopher's dad taps his son on the shoulder. "Did you get any of me?"

"Um ..."

"Don't forget your job, Chris." Oh, right. His bio said he was a podcaster. She'd never heard of him.

Christopher takes out his phone. His height makes him the perfect photographer for these overhead shots. Lisa Marie leaves them to it.

"Tomorrow's stop will be really amazing," the tour guide says apologetically. "Really amazing."

When Lisa Marie reaches the bus, she glances back. Christopher is taking more photos. She could have uses for a boy like that.

The Professor Flinches

||||||||||||||||||||||||||||||||||||||||||||||||||||||||||||||||||||||||

A loud bang, and the woman who calls herself Gillian Masch jerks her head up from her laptop screen.

Gun!

But no, it was just the bus door slamming open. The Chinese rider has come back after seeing the Antipode. That was fast. Is everyone returning already?

Not yet. Outside her window is a forest of lime-green umbrellas. It's disturbing to see so many of them. She puts her head down, her hair making a cloud around her laptop. She stares at the screen. She types:

> *Dear Adaku*
>
> *I don't know how old you'll be when your father gives you this letter.*

Her fingers hover over the keyboard, unsure where to land next.

The Chinese passenger passes her seat without a word or a sideways glance and takes the seat behind her.

Only a few people never got off to see the Antipode, and the old woman at the front of the bus spent the whole time complaining about the field's lack of ramps and walkways. The lack of accessibility has somehow become her daughter's fault. *You told me all stops were handicap accessible!*

"Gillian" tries to ignore them and focus on the screen, but the text is a blur. She pinches the bridge of her nose, squeezing off tears. There's so much work she has to do—maybe the last work she'll ever do—and she'd like to survive the next few days so she can finish. She checks the time on her laptop. Across the continent, the smartest man she's ever met sits in a gleaming building overlooking the San Francisco Bay. His name is Edowar Eze, and he is her husband, no matter what they told the world. In a few hours he'll pick up their daughter, Adaku, from school. He'll help her with her homework, make her dinner, maybe watch a show. They will do all this without her.

Stop pining, Margaret!

And then chastises herself for using her real name, even in her thoughts. She can't afford to slip up. She must be Gillian Masch until the end of this trip.

Concentrate, Gillian.

But her brain keeps locking up, all words and logic replaced by flashes of images: Her daughter's face. The body of her grad student, Tommy Francis, sprawled in front of the fire exit, the crook of his arm creating a lagoon for his blood. Her daughter, holding up her pink stuffed animal. Ajay Patel, another grad student, slumped in a plastic office chair, held upright by two black bands—the Velcro straps they used to tie down cables in the server room.

Her daughter, her students, and her husband occupy the same cramped space in her mind: a waiting room for the victims of Margaret Schell. Her choices put them there. And her first victim was a woman she never met, a cleaning woman who worked the night shift at Boston University.

• • •

One afternoon two weeks after the Announcement, Margaret was working at the kitchen table when she heard her daughter talking to herself in the garage. Adaku was six years old and wasn't technically allowed to play in the garage, but she often sneaked in there to climb up to her mother's workbench, full of adult tools and wires and duct tape. When she showed up at dinner with a new "invention," Margaret and Edowar only lightly reprimanded her. They didn't want to be the kind of parents who stifled creativity. They were trying to give her a normal childhood.

The Announcement had made that more difficult. They decided to keep Adaku out of school, each tag-teaming on home duty while the other worked, though Margaret was tagged in much more than Edo. It wasn't *just* the traditional gender roles kicking in—Margaret really could work from home more easily than Edo. Her single summer class kept getting canceled by "security events": bomb threats, reports of active shooters, unruly protests. International students had become targets for harassment. China had invaded Taiwan, Russia had restarted its campaign in Ukraine, North Korea had fired missiles over the Sea of Japan, France was expelling Arab citizens . . . and every global conflict found its expression on campus. Protests, counterprotests, accusations of artificiality.

Home, though, was a sanctuary. And Adaku, fortunately, was an only child with a busy inner life, who could entertain herself. It wasn't unusual for her to chatter away to her favorite stuffed animal, Pinky the Rhino, or some other imaginary friend. And right now, she was going on and on, lecturing away, like some kind of toddler TED Talk. Margaret kept working on her laptop, happy the girl was occupied.

And then Adaku's imaginary friend answered in a low, male voice.

A jolt of adrenaline sent Margaret rushing to the mudroom. She yanked open the door to the garage. The big panel door was rolled up, and the garage was open to the street. A bearded Black man sat on the cement floor, arms looped over his knees, gazing up at Adaku. Her daughter stood atop the workbench, holding the yellow Black and Decker cordless drill in both hands. She seemed to be explaining how it worked.

"Hey!" Margaret shouted. "Out!" She charged forward.

The man remained seated but threw up his hands. "It's you! Dr.

Schell! No harm, no harm!" His accent was strange. Homeless man, she thought. Schizophrenic. Homeless schizophrenic. He wore heavy work boots, and the long red-and-green tunic he wore was split below the hip, revealing a lot of thigh. *Where the fuck were his pants?*

Margaret swooped Adaku into her arms. The drill clunked painfully into Margaret's jaw. "Fuck! Out, now!" She hurried toward the house.

"Please don't be afraid," the man called. "I can explain."

She slammed the door behind her. Set Adaku on the floor. "Go upstairs," Margaret told her. "Up to your room."

"You swore!"

"Adaku! Now!"

The girl walked to the stairs but stopped on the second step. She watched between the balusters, still holding the drill.

Damn it. Margaret pressed the button lock on the knob, but that wouldn't hold if he forced the door. Why hadn't they installed a dead bolt here? She needed to call 911. Where was her cell phone?

"Hello?" the garage man said. He sounded close, just on the other side of the door. "I didn't mean to startle you. I was just talking to Adaku. It was so great to meet her. I had no idea that at this age—"

"I'm calling the police!" she shouted.

"Please don't do that, at least not until we've had a chance to talk. I promise you, it's very important, and it can't wait."

"*No,*" she said. "Get out of my garage." Should she call the police? They were the only Black family on the street, and calling the cops on a Black man—even a mentally disturbed one wearing a caftan or whatever the hell he was wearing—could spiral out of control. She didn't want to get the man killed. But Margaret had a daughter to think about. She'd report him when he was out of the neighborhood, just to get something on the record if she really needed to press charges.

"Is Adaku still with you?" the man said. "She shouldn't hear what I have to tell you."

What the fuck? "Go away. Now."

"Dr. Schell, please listen. I'm from outside the current schema. I was born in a previous iteration."

"What?"

"Consider me . . . ," he said earnestly. "Ut-nee-pish-tim." His face must've been pressed up against the door. "I alone have survived the flood."

Utnapishtim, she thought. Oh God. The Freakout was hitting people in so many ways. Breaking up marriages, sending them into cults, triggering suicides. Psychotic breaks were par for the course. White boys in trench coats were shooting up tech campuses. How the hell could Edo leave the garage door up when he left this morning?

"I'm dialing," she said.

"I'm not the bad guy! Trust me, there are bad guys out there. In fact, that's what I'd like to talk to you about."

"Oh would you," she said under her breath. A long moment passed.

"Dr. Schell?" His voice sounded very close. "I apologize if I'm being, um, abrupt? Scary? I'm still new at this."

Margaret said nothing.

"I came to tell you that, statistically, you're in great danger."

Statistically? What the hell. Adaku was still watching her from the stairs. Margaret pushed the mudroom door closed with her foot.

"What danger?" she asked, and hated that she wanted to know.

"I can't be specific. Please do not go to your office on campus tomorrow. Or tonight. Something terrible is going to happen. Well, almost certainly."

"Tell me," she said. "Now."

"I wish I could. Please trust me, okay? Don't go near campus—you or Dr. Eze, or any of your family. That's all I ask. And I'm—I'm going to go now."

She stood still, listening. She couldn't tell if he was walking away, out of the garage. Then she opened the door to the kitchen and Adaku was standing right there. "Is Aunty Tim a bad guy?"

Aunty—? Ah, Utnapishtim. Adaku had heard everything. "Stay there," Margaret said. She walked quickly to the front window and parted the shades. The stranger was galumphing down the sidewalk in heavy brown work boots, tunic flapping.

"He looks like Grandfather Amaechi," Adaku said. Meaning Edowar's father, a man Adaku had only seen in black-and-white photographs. The girl probably thought anyone wearing anything like an Isiagu was a Nigerian cousin.

"That man is not a friend, not a relative," Margaret said. "He's also not well. If you ever see him, you run inside and tell me or Dad, all right?" The girl nodded. "And don't call him Aunty Tim."

•   •   •

On the tour bus, the woman who calls herself Gillian stares at the screen but she can't think of any words that would explain to her daughter what she's done or why she's done it.

> *I don't know how old you'll be when your father gives you this letter. All I know is that I won't be there to tell you these things myself.*

Easier just to do the work, she thinks. Work's always been the way she's protected herself—and the more work the better. Sixty hours, eighty hours a week. The world's most unhealthy meditation practice.

She closes the document and opens a new file. At the top she types a header:

THE GOD LIBRARY

No. That's wrong. The people don't need another god. They need an adversary who'll fight on their behalf. She deletes the header and types:

THE DEVIL'S TOOLBOX

The last six and a half years of her life boiled down into two terabytes of source code, test data, architectural diagrams, API documentation. She must somehow organize this chaos, annotate it, point out its strengths and weaknesses. Perhaps start with the compiler? She could—

Gun!

Her head comes up, but of course it's just the door banging open again. The pregnant girl makes her way down the aisle, talking into her phone as she goes. A few minutes later, everyone's climbing back on. The Octos are chattering like schoolkids. Gillian doesn't look up as they pass by her row. She takes a breath. Tries to settle her frantic, bronco-bucking mind. Six more days. If she gets killed or arrested before she reaches Ghost City, the past seven years in her ticking-bomb life will have been for nothing.

She's itching to check the internet for news on the murders. Had anyone posted a gloat video? Is the news out at all? If the feds and the police aren't looking for her, they soon will.

She's already disabled all Wi-Fi and wireless capabilities on her laptop, and she threw out her phone as soon as she hit the road. Left her iPad in her car in the Tornado parking lot. She's scattering pieces of her life behind her like a trail of breadcrumbs.

She looks down at the screen and begins to type. She has to finish before the bus reaches Ghost City. And if no one's waiting for her there, then the project is dead. There's a high likelihood that she'll soon be dead too, or else spending the rest of her life in some black site holding cell. Her husband will move on, and her daughter will never see her again. A minor tragedy, as far as the world's concerned. Just another motherless child. But a permanent wound for the girl, and a knife through Margaret's heart.

A figure appears in the aisle beside her. Hovers there. She blinks hard, trying to steady herself, and types meaningless characters into the doc that she'll have to revert later.

"How's it going?" It's Jean-Pierre, the white man who helped her get on this tour. "Getting a lot done?" He's trim and handsome, and there's something sad about him. She approves of that. She doesn't trust happy people.

She closes the laptop lid, which automatically encrypts the current file on disk, scrubs it from RAM, and shuts down the editor. "How was the Antipode?" she asks.

"You didn't miss much. Say, Dulin and I were looking at our phones, and it turns out that down the road from our hotel is a pub."

"Unbelievable."

"I know, what are the odds? We were thinking of sneaking off there after dinner. Would you like to sneak with us?"

"Thanks, but I've got a lot of work to do."

"Right. Sure. But if you change your mind . . ." He studies her face, frowns. "You okay?"

How panicked does she look? She thought she was managing her body language. And why is he checking on her at all? Did he feel responsible for her? Was he hitting on her?

Oh no, buddy. You don't want to get attached to me.

"Can I help?" he asks.

She wonders if he's earning merit badges for helping her. Or shit, maybe he's a Christian. The bus is already full of them. The last thing she needs is someone saving her soul. Though she has to admit she wouldn't mind some help saving her skin.

"Could I borrow your phone again?" she asks. "Just for a minute?"

He hesitates. "I should tell you . . ."

She raises an eyebrow.

"It's fine." He glances down. She's sitting by the window and has set her duffel on the aisle seat — another semiotic gesture establishing her boundaries. She moves the bag onto the floor, and he sits.

"Maybe before the pub we can sneak out to a Best Buy or something, get you a new one," he says. "We can get an Uber."

"Maybe." She opens the browser again. Tilts the phone so he can't see the screen. She types Patel's full name, gets nothing but old news. Types the name of her company — MPF, LLC — and "Cambridge."

"Oh fuck," she says.

JP starts to lean toward the phone, then stops. She appreciates that.

Her face is on the screen. It's an old picture of the three of them — her, Ajay Patel, and Tommy Francis — arms around each other, smiling.

What were they celebrating? The picture's a little out of focus, but her face is clear enough for facial recognition software—including the software that runs inside normal humans—to identify her. Below the picture, they show her real name.

She starts reading the article from the top: **TWO DEAD IN CAMPUS ATTACK**. Three paragraphs down, they mention that the students worked for her, in her lab. They don't say whether they're thinking of her as a suspect. But she knows now that they're definitely looking for her.

JP's been waiting patiently. She clears the screen and takes a minute to clear his browser cache. This seems rude, but she has no choice. He's remarkably calm about all the clicking and swiping, perhaps even . . . amused?

He takes back his phone without looking at it. "If you're in trouble, I'd like to—"

"I'm fine," she says, cutting him off. "About that Uber. Let's do that. I need to pick up some things."

JP goes back to his seat, and she feels bad that she hasn't warned him. Yes, I'm in trouble, and anyone who gets near me can be sucked into it.

· · ·

The evening after the stranger came to her garage, she was lying in bed beside Adaku, reading aloud from *The Velveteen Rabbit*. But she was distracted. She'd called the police and reported the man. Then she called campus police, but there was little she could tell them: a man had made vague threats—or, more charitably, warnings. But there was nothing specific she could tell them to look for. Violent protests? A bomb threat? An armed attack? All of those were happening all the time since the Announcement. Margaret was waiting for news.

Adaku was exasperated with her performance. "Do the voices," she said. "Like Daddy."

Margaret sighed. She didn't do accents. "Okay, fine." What voices did Edowar give Rabbit and the Skin Horse? "'What is REAL?'"

Margaret said in her Rabbit voice, which turned out to be a kind of Dick Van Dyke Cockney. "'Does it mean having things that buzz inside you and a stick-out handle?'"

Adaku made a disapproving noise but didn't interrupt.

"'Real isn't how you are made,'" Margaret said in a slightly lower voice. She'd always thought of the Skin Horse as a kind of Eeyore. "'It's a thing that happens to you.'"

Downstairs, she heard her cell phone ring.

Adaku bonked her head against Margaret's arm. "*Mom.* Keep going." But she was listening to Edowar's heavy steps on the stairs. He came into the room, holding her phone. He was worried. She'd told him everything.

The screen showed a 617 number—a university prefix. She climbed out of the bed and took the phone into the hallway. *Real is a thing that happens,* she thought, and clicked to answer.

The security officer told her what he knew in a disturbingly calm voice. One of the cleaning staff had keyed into Margaret's office and surprised a heavily armed man. He set off a bomb, or it went off accidentally. The device was packed with nails and other shrapnel. The bomber was killed, and the cleaning woman died on the way to the hospital.

Margaret wouldn't learn any more details about the bomber or how the cleaning woman had stumbled upon him until later. But in a way the details didn't matter. What was important was that an innocent woman had died in Margaret's place.

The
Geysers
Of
Mystery!

The Engineer Gets Caught in the Cross Fire

||||||||||||||||||||||||||||||||||||||||||||||||||||||||||||||||||||||

When JP wakes up, the words are hovering above his head, just under the ceiling. This week they look as if they're formed from iridescent soap bubbles.

You are living in a simulation.

Still living, he thinks. Got it.

The letters pop one by one, a twee drumroll. The period in the sentence goes off like a champagne cork. The festive sound effects don't pair well with his usual morning headache.

The question, as always, is whether to boot up for another day. When he's at home, surrounded by echoes of Suzanne, he feels like one of his robots, trundling through a deserted warehouse. Why keep moving his body through the hours, just to shut it down at night? Such a waste of resources. But here, with a tour bus waiting, it would be embarrassing to stay under the covers.

Also, nearly impossible. Dulin's in the next bed, snoring like a backhoe scraping rock.

He's always been a snorer, but he seems to be getting worse with age. It was probably a mistake to share a room—the few hundred bucks they saved is not going to be worth it—but Dulin had pushed for it, and JP had agreed out of nostalgia. Twenty-something years ago, the two of them had driven cross-country from Chicago to LA, after Dulin's first divorce. Dulin was miserable, mourning the death of his marriage and regretting the damage he'd inflicted on his wife and daughter, but determined to gut it out with displays of exuberance. It's Kerouac time, damn it! They drank hard almost every night, crashed in cheap motels along old Route 66, the rooms furnished with mismatched beds and garage-sale dressers, then drove through each day's hangover like it was heavy weather. A moveable Irish wake.

JP checks his watch. It's not even six. Fine, damn it.

He takes a shower, not worrying about waking Dulin. Brushes his teeth while he regards his face in the mirror. Brian, his little astrocytoma, is nestled somewhere under that scar, deep in the frontal lobe. Back again, if you can say that about something that never left. The first round of surgery and treatments reduced the tumor to a tiny nub, but he's growing again, regenerating like a starfish. JP tries to arrange his thinning hair over the scar, gives up. Looks over his row of prescription bottles. There are three meds he's supposed to take every morning, with food. Breakfast is supposed to be included with this hotel, but he's not sure the dining room is open yet. Hopefully there's at least coffee. He tucks the bottles into his pocket and leaves the bathroom. Then he opens his suitcase to pick out a hat. He's packed four: the Irish wool cap Suzanne bought him, a black Kangol 504 Ventair; a crushable straw fedora he bought in San Diego; and a tan, wide-brimmed, all-weather Charter hat. He chooses the Kangol because he could use a little jauntiness.

JP steps into the corridor and closes the door quietly behind him. Dulin snores on.

Many doors down, someone's waiting by the elevator—the older nun; he's blanking on her name. As he walks toward her, the pills chatter in his pocket. God, he hates that sound. He feels like he's rehearsing for his death rattle.

He wonders if any of the rooms he's passing are Gillian's. He pictures her dead asleep, one leg thrust outside the covers, mouth open. Maybe she snores like Dulin. There was a lot of confusion as they checked in. She wasn't on the group reservation yet. She'd lost her purse and didn't have a picture ID. She had no credit card and couldn't pay for incidentals. Gillian badgered the young tour guide—hadn't JP already paid? How much did they want from them? Finally the woman forked over her own credit card.

After dinner in the Applebee's adjacent to the hotel, Dulin ordered an Uber, and JP sat in the backseat with Gillian. They talked about nothing substantial, just a little light gossip. Why did the tour guide always look like she was about to burst into tears? Is the fact that the Austrians are taking a bus trip for their honeymoon admirable or sad? And what's the deal with the podcaster, the so-called "realist"—and how will Dulin get through this trip without punching him?

JP loved talking to Gillian and felt guilty doing it—and that's how he realized he was attracted to her. Suzanne would be amused by his continued fidelity. She'd also be amused to find herself, for purposes of this reflection, both deceased yet able to laugh. A superposition of Suzannes. Schrödinger's Wife.

When they arrived at the Walmart, Gillian sent JP and Dulin to the electronics section to pick out a prepaid phone while she did her other shopping. Dulin pointed out that this probably made them accessories to whatever crime Gillian had committed. JP assured him that as long as they didn't ask any questions, they were innocent dupes.

"Well, dupes anyway," Dulin said.

Gillian met them at the front of the store wearing a new, logo-less fleece and carrying a bag she kept closed. Dulin tried to cajole her into coming out to the pub, but she wasn't having it; she just wanted to be dropped at the hotel. And then, as JP watched her walk through the glass doors, he suddenly lost all energy. He'd been holding it together all day, trying to ignore the headache and the fatigue in his limbs, but exhaustion hit like a wave. He told Dulin he was calling it a night.

Dulin's face fluttered through surprise and disappointment, then touched down on worry. "Is it Brian?" he asked.

When JP went in for surgery, one of the hospital staff made a typo on JP's chart. Since then, Brian Tumor has been his constant companion.

"Nah, just tired. Go on without me."

"I told you, if you're not drinking, I'm not drinking." Dulin sent the Uber away, and they walked into the lobby together. A few people from the tour were hanging out there, watching a big-screen TV. Dulin said he'd be up in a bit. JP's not sure when exactly Dulin made it back to the room—sometime after midnight. Did he just watch television that whole time?

A door opens to his right. Two of the octogenarians step out— the white man and one of the white women. They're wearing matching striped bathrobes, which they must have brought themselves, because this isn't the kind of hotel to provide them.

"Morning!" the woman says cheerily. "Happy Reminder Day!" Her gray hair is disheveled, and his is sticking up like a German composer's. "Sleep well?" the man asks.

"Pretty well," JP says. "You?"

"Hardly!" the man says, and the woman laughs. They walk in the other direction.

The nun is dressed in autumnal tones—brown slacks, beige turtleneck, a puffy vest the color of oak leaves about to fall—but the huge silver cross hanging from her neck puts him in mind of Christmas decorations. Before he can greet her, he hears a door open and glances back. The Octo couple are walking into a different hotel room. He and the Sister exchange a look. If he were with Dulin, he'd make a sex joke. Now he doesn't know what to say. Why hasn't the elevator arrived?

The nun says, "I'd like to have their energy when I'm their age."

JP laughs, then stifles it. She's being sincere.

Finally the elevator door opens and they step in. "I'm JP, by the way."

"Janet," she says, and shakes his hand. Her other hand holds a hardback journal. She looks like she's been up for hours. "You can call me Sister Janet if you're more comfortable with that. A lot of Catholics struggle to not put 'Sister' in there."

"Don't worry about me, I come from a long line of Quakers."

"So you're comfortable with silence."

"I love silence. I could talk about it all day."

She returns a slight smile.

The lobby is all but empty, but JP's happy to find the breakfast buffet open. Well, semi-happy. It's one of those food safety nightmares offering a pan of rubbery eggs, a stewing vat of oatmeal, canisters of cereal whose dispensers grind Raisin Bran into powder. The rotating waffle maker is another first-draft idea—the spinning griddle is clever, but the inventors didn't understand that its primary users would be unattended eight-year-olds, a population not known for their batter-management technique. It's the kind of design problem that makes him want to come out of retirement. Or maybe he's just cranky. He won't put a dent in this headache until he takes his pills.

He takes a wheat muffin from the display case of carbohydrates, pours himself a black coffee. Sister Janet is the only other person in the dining room. She's peeling an orange. He heads for an empty table, but she gestures at the seat opposite her. Oh God. Now he's trapped.

He puts on a smile. Takes a seat.

"So what did yours look like today?" she asks him.

"Bubbles," he says. "Yours?"

"Do you remember Tinkertoys? The letters all sort of fit together like that. Then at the end they came apart, one by one."

This is a typical Reminder Day conversation. Everyone compares their messages. Everyone sees a different mind font, and rarely the same one twice. Billions of combinations.

"It seems like a lot of work," JP says. This is not an original thought. It's the Reminder Day equivalent of "How 'bout them Cubs?"

"All of it seems like a lot of work," Sister Janet says. "The Frozen Tornado, for example."

He remembers her crying as she walked up the hill toward it. He wants to ask her about that, but knows he never will. He breaks off a piece of the muffin. The pills remain in his pocket. "So what brings you on this tour?" he asks.

"I'm working on a book."

"Oh, my friend's a writer. Dulin—the guy I'm traveling with?" He salutes the air above his head to indicate Dulin's size. But of course she must know who he's talking about. "Um, so what's the book about?"

He's learned from Dulin that it's never a mistake to ask a writer what they're working on. Even the ones who say they don't like to talk about it want to be asked.

"I don't know yet," the Sister says. "I think I'm going to have to write it to figure it out."

He nods understandingly. Her answer seems like a dodge, something writers say to nonwriters, and he's relieved.

Sister Janet is watching his face. He meets her eyes. Her face, her whole body, is still. Her notebook is unopened in front of her, the orange peeled but whole, her hands on her lap. The moment stretches. He smiles nervously.

"Let me try again," she says. "I'm trying to figure out what place there is for God in this universe we find ourselves in."

Whoa. He takes a long sip from his coffee.

"As a Quaker, what are your thoughts?" she asks.

"Ah, no, I'm really an agnostic. I just come from Quakers. Like the oatmeal."

"Oatmeal?"

"Quaker Oats? The guy in the wig on the box?"

"I see."

He was used to people not realizing when he was kidding, or not understanding the joke when they recognized it as such. Suzanne was no different. Oh, she could appreciate his jokes, once he explained them. But Dulin was the only person who was always on his comedy wavelength.

Sister Janet says, "It seems to me the simulation is pushing agnostics to take a side. Is it harder to believe in God when the Simulators make it so clear that they're in charge? The weekly reminder, the Impossibles . . ."

He wonders if she's interviewing him for her book. "It does seem like God is keeping his head down."

"Exactly," she says. "All this time he could have been talking to us directly, as he did in the Old Testament. Pillars of fire, burning bushes . . . He could have woken us up every week with his own reminder. Scripture, perhaps."

JP feels he's the wrong person to be having this conversation. Dulin should be here. He loves talking about metaphysics. It's his favorite flavor of bullshit.

The nun smiles quizzically. "What is it?"

JP realizes he's smiling.

"Please," she says. "Share your thoughts. I'd find it helpful."

He takes a sip of coffee to give himself time to organize his thoughts. Did the sim make him less likely to believe in God, or was his lack of faith so engrained it made no difference?

"I have opinions," he says. "I just don't think they're valid. More data is required."

"You're not going to hurt my feelings if you don't believe in God."

He laughs quietly. "Okay. I suppose the problem is that we've always been living in the simulation. It feels like we entered it seven years ago, because that's when we got the Announcement, but it's really been since the Big Bang. Uh, the virtual Big Bang."

"Ah, so you're a 'banger.' Very good."

"Maybe?" JP says. "But if it's true, God didn't get replaced in our universe, he just . . . wasn't here in the first place."

Trouble clouds her face. Damn it, he did hurt her feelings. But then just as suddenly the expression passes and she's utterly calm.

He didn't imagine it. For a moment she seemed like a different person. A sadder person. The glimpse shocked him—but it's the shock of recognition. Hello there, fellow depressive.

"You're right, of course," she says. "It's interesting to think that Jesus Christ lived in a simulation and didn't mention it to us."

"Maybe he was speaking in code. Our Simulator, who art in heaven—" Her brows knit and he stops himself. *Don't do comedy, JP.* Especially not religious comedy. "Or maybe he didn't know," he adds quickly.

"That would be worse," she says.

Yikes. How can he get out of this conversation? The Chinese passenger walks into the dining room, head down in their book, that bulky fanny pack riding behind them. No help there. The sag in JP's chest makes him realize he was hoping for someone else.

"The simulation doesn't mean God doesn't exist," JP says. He's surprised to hear himself defending a being he doesn't believe in. "It just means he's, well, one step removed."

"Why, O Lord, do you stand far off?" she says. "Why do you hide yourself in times of trouble?"

"I don't know much of the Bible," he says.

"I know enough for the both of us," Sister Janet says. "Why *do* you think he would allow the simulation?" Her tone isn't rhetorical—she genuinely wants to hear his thoughts.

"I don't know." And thinks, You're the nun; you tell me. "Mysterious ways?"

"That's a time-honored answer. But it's not very satisfying, is it?"

"Well . . ."

"I struggle with why he would allow his creations to create other conscious beings."

"But his creations do that all the time," he says. She regards him blankly. "You know," he adds. "Make babies."

She smiles faintly. "Good point. But it still seems a little extreme to give one set of children an entire universe to play with, to make them gods themselves. Children are selfish. They're often cruel."

She sounds, he thinks, like a woman who's taught elementary school.

Her eyes flick past his ear, and he turns his head, catches a swoop of black and a flash of white. The younger nun! She's right on top of him.

"May I join you?" she asks.

Oh no, JP thinks. I'm outnumbered.

"Have you two been introduced?" Sister Janet asks. "JP, this is Sister Patrice."

"Pleased," Sister Patrice says. She sits at the adjacent table. Her face, framed in that oval of white cloth, is much younger and more beautiful than he realized. Her eyes are large and dark.

"JP is an extremely funny person," Sister Janet explains.

What? Right now he feels as funny as vinyl flooring.

Sister Patrice's tray holds orange juice, a shiny mound of scrambled eggs, two pieces of toast, and half a dozen packets of hot sauce. She opens one of the packets with a practiced twist, squirts it across the eggs. "Please," she says, "don't let me interrupt."

Sister Janet says, "We were just discussing the problem of evil."

He thinks, We were?

"At first glance, the simulation solves the problem," Sister Janet says. "If God isn't in charge, all the cruelties of life—disease, hunger, poverty, the loss of innocent life—can be blamed on the Simulators. They're immoral, uncaring, or just shortsighted."

"Perhaps, then, we need a second glance," Sister Patrice says coolly. She opens her third packet of hot sauce. "God *is* in charge. He's the prime creator of all creation—even this world."

JP wonders, Are they having a fight?

Sister Janet says, "But then we have to wonder why God would abrogate his responsibility. He's essentially allowing one set of sentient beings to have godlike control over another set of beings."

"With respect, Sister Janet, He has abrogated nothing," Sister Patrice says. "The Simulators are no different from presidents and kings, who also have power over their subjects. God has given the Simulators free will, and they can make their own choices, just as we do."

"You've hit on the primary problem, Sister. The Simulators can actually control our choices. They can decide what we decide."

"I don't think so," Sister Patrice says. "With respect. Certainly they can constrain our choices, like any worldly authority. The police can throw you in jail. They can stop you from ordering a steak by giving you only bread and water, but they can't stop you from wanting a steak, and they can't stop you from deciding to share your bread with another prisoner." The novice's words are speeding up, and her accent is becoming more pronounced. "No one controls our moral choices, not even God. I believe this was all settled in the Garden of Eden."

Oh, they are definitely having a fight.

"The Simulators absolutely do control our moral choices," Sister Janet says. Her tone hasn't shifted from the flat calm she's been using with JP—but there is no give in her voice, no hint of uncertainty. "We're programs. Our minds are part of that program. And a program can be made to do whatever its programmer wants it to. Think of video games. The characters can fight, murder—"

"This isn't *Call of Duty*," Sister Patrice says. "They can't *make* us sin. Even if they force us to do something bad—make us pick up an AR-15 and shoot someone in the head with it—then we have not *sinned*. Sin is a choice. JP, you must see the difference."

He's startled by the use of his name. He's still processing the novelty of a Catholic nun talking not only about first-person shooters, but about shooting a person in the head.

Sister Janet says, "I agree with you, Sister, in the absence of free will, we cannot sin. That's my point."

"Absence? I didn't say that! Of course we have free will."

"How can we?" Sister Janet answers. "If we're code, that means we are conscious because of a mechanistic process—our thoughts are generated for us—whoever 'us' is. Whoever the 'I' is. The code can make us choose what it wants us to choose. It can even make us feel as if we were doing the choosing."

"God wouldn't permit that," Sister Patrice says. "If we don't have free will, we don't have . . . anything! What's the point of creating us with self-awareness, then? Why not just build robots?"

JP decides this is not the time to mention that he used to help design warehouse robots for possibly the most hated company on Earth.

"We do have one thing, one very human thing, that makes us different from robots," Sister Janet says. "We suffer."

Those last two words are nearly drowned out by a short, high-pitched scream of rage. It came from just outside the dining room. The screamer shouts, "Give it back, you bitch!"

JP realizes this is his chance to escape the argument. "Excuse me," he says to the nuns. "I'm going to, uhm . . ." He hustles toward the lobby.

The person doing the screaming is the pregnant girl, Lisa Marie something. She's clawing at a Black woman wearing sunglasses and a baseball cap over very short (or nonexistent?) hair, who is pushing back with an outstretched arm. Her other arm is in the air, playing keep-away with a phone. A familiar courier bag hangs from her shoulder.

Holy shit, JP thinks. The woman in the cap is Gillian.

JP steps between the two women. A mistake. Lisa Marie starts batting and clawing at *him*.

"Hey! Ow!" JP can't do anything but protect his face. He doesn't want to touch her; she's a tiny woman who's hugely pregnant. "What's going on?"

"She took my *phone*!"

Gillian does that kind of thing, JP thinks. Lisa Marie looks past him and yells, "What are you *doing*?"

Gillian's poking at the phone. "You took my picture," she says. "Without permission."

"I told you you looked *good*!" Lisa Marie says, furious.

"She's allowed to take pictures," says the redheaded kid. "She has rights."

Lisa Marie lunges past JP, knocking into Gillian. The phone goes flying. The girl screams again. Gillian grabs one thin, tanned wrist, stopping her from running after it. Lisa Marie tries to yank free, but Gillian's stronger. "Let go of me!" the girl shouts. She slaps at Gillian's face and knocks off the baseball cap.

Gillian's hair is Marine-short and bright blue. Blue!

"Stop *fighting*," Gillian says. She grabs the girl's other wrist.

The girl yells at the redheaded kid, "Don't just stand there, Christopher! Get my phone!"

"Oh!" the kid says. He lurches into motion.

JP looks around. No one's at the front desk, thank God. "Ladies," he says. "We're all going to get kicked out of the hotel. And the tour."

Gillian's still holding the girl's arms. They stare at each other across the gap created by the girl's round belly.

"Delete the picture," Gillian says with menace. Her sunglasses are askew.

"You're a psycho," the girl says.

"Delete it."

"Fine!" She gives the word three hard syllables: *fuh-INE-nuh!*

Gillian releases her. Straightens her glasses.

"Christopher," the girl says, and holds out her hand. The kid lays the instrument in her palm like a surgical nurse.

"Do it in front of me," Gillian says.

The girl sighs elaborately. Selects a picture, presses a button. "Gone," she says. Shows her the screen. "What's the matter with you?"

"I don't like my picture taken."

The girl strides away toward the elevators and the boy hustles after her. The doors open and the rabbi steps out. "Good morning! Good morning, everyone!" He walks toward the dining room, oblivious.

JP retrieves Gillian's cap. It's black, with no logos. "I like your hair," JP says.

Gillian's looking shaky. She stares at the hat as if she doesn't recognize it, then tugs it on. "I felt like I needed a change."

"You realize that all this is very, uh, fugitive-from-justice behavior," JP says.

"She had no right," Gillian says.

"I mean the whole thing, the haircut, the—" He gestures. "New look." Why does he now feel he can invade her privacy? "You gotta admit, it's spy-movie stuff."

"I'm not a spy."

"I know. A spy would probably do something completely different. This is spy-*movie* stuff. Meaning, it's what I would do."

She drops her chin, looks at him over her sunglasses. "So you'd cut your hair . . . more."

"Ha. Fair point." He becomes aware that she also looks good in a hat. "You're making it really hard not to ask what's going on."

She grimaces.

"You have to trust someone," he says. "Why not me?"

"Don't take it personally," she says.

"Let's talk over breakfast," JP says, undeterred. "Though I have to warn you, the nuns are fighting."

"A nun fight?"

"Nun fight at the O.K. Café."

"You're funny."

"People keep saying that, but nobody ever laughs."

"All right," Gillian says. "But I don't want to do this in front of everybody."

•   •   •

The map on his phone finds them a diner a couple blocks away. The booth's vinyl cushions are cracked and the place mats are plastic, but the coffee is very, very hot. Gillian orders a minimal breakfast, and the waitress goes away. Only then does Gillian take off her sunglasses.

JP keeps his cap on and waits. Perhaps half a minute passes.

"My husband and I divorced after the Announcement," Gillian says. "It was pretty public, and pretty ugly."

"Happened to a lot of people," he says. He doesn't know why she's starting with the divorce, but he's happy she's talking to him, and doesn't interrupt with the questions popping up in his head, such as, public to whom? Is Gillian famous? And if she's famous, why does she not show up on Google?

"We have a daughter," she says. "She's thirteen now. My ex got full custody. Or nearly full. I get one week during the summer."

"One week?" JP said. "That's criminal."

"I agreed to it," she said.

"Yeah but—"

"This is why I'm telling you this—every year I go to pick her up for my week. We try to do the exchange somewhere fun, wherever my daughter wants to go—Disneyland, Six Flags. We're just trying to make it less traumatic for her."

"That's nice."

"For the past two years she's wanted to meet at Ghost City."

"Ah." *Meet me at the handoff.* "That explains—"

Her eyes narrow.

"You said the tour was perfect," he says lamely. "Going right where you needed to go." He's never been good at lying, but this isn't a lie, just an omission. So why does it feel like a lie? He picks up his coffee cup, puts it down.

"Too good to be true," she says. "My ex and my daughter will be waiting for me there."

"I undeleted your text message," he says. The words come out in a rush.

She leans back. "I wondered."

"You did?"

"That's what I would have done."

"I'm sorry, I just—"

"Stop. Thank you for telling me. I wouldn't have admitted it. It's your phone."

"You didn't feel that way about the pregnant girl's."

Gillian laughs. "True enough."

The waitress comes back with Gillian's English muffin and small side of fruit that looks like 90 percent cantaloupe. Gillian opens a container of peanut butter, smears some onto the muffin. JP starts to feel emboldened. She may be telling the truth, but she's omitting a lot, too.

"So, your ex . . . ," JP says. "He's going along with this?"

"This what?"

"It's still spring. She's probably still in school. He's going to let you take your daughter this early?"

"I don't think I'm going to make it till summer."

"What? Why?"

Gillian sets down the knife. Reaches into her bag and comes up with the phone they bought at Best Buy. She swipes to find something on it, then slides it across the table toward him.

"This," she says.

It's a video embedded in a news site page. JP glances at her one more time, making sure he has her permission. Then he clicks play.

The Influencer Hires an Unpaid Intern

||||||||||||||||||||||||||||||||||||||||||||||||||||||||||||||||||||||||

Lisa Marie Montello sits in the bus, staring at her laptop, enraged. Two thoughts are taking turns blasting her brain, over and over:

My metrics are in the toilet!
No one grabs Lady Mmm's phone!

This stereophonic fury makes it impossible to work.

Every time she tries to go through her analytics, Gillian Masch's smirking face flashes into her brain. What is that bitch's deal? One compliment on her lipstick and new haircut and she goes ballistic. What was she hiding? And why did she think she could manhandle Lady Mmm?

She texts Christopher: **Come back here.**

Gah. She has heartburn again, something she thought was only for old people, until Baby M started rearranging her organs. That kid's been rearranging her from Minute One.

When she walked out of that high school toilet stall, she felt the weight of responsibility. The weight hadn't settled onto her shoulders, where every teacher and school principal told her it would sit, but all around her. A deep-sea pressure, squeezing from all sides. Somehow she had to keep breathing and keep walking across the bottom of the ocean.

She'd never spent a lot of time thinking about the Simmers. Oh, sim theory came up in social studies and in physics and in economics, and she learned enough to get through the advance placement tests she was planning to take in the spring, but she couldn't bring herself to care about her future as a digital object. No Simulator was going to pay attention to nerdy, plain Lisa Marie. She was one of billions. Sooner or later she'd be deleted by whatever automated harvesting system the Simmers had set up. Even if they did notice her, and reach down to personally cancel her, who could blame them? She was no fan of her life, and couldn't see why anyone else would be.

But then, out of nowhere (or nearly so), a baby.

Every morning for the next two weeks Lisa Marie got ready for school—until Gramps left for work, and then Lisa Marie stripped off her clothes and crawled back to bed. When Gramps found out, he was going to kill her. Or worse, sulk—he could go wordless for days, silently radiating disappointment. She didn't call the boy who knocked her up. No point. She didn't love him and he didn't love her. Even if he did want to help her decide what to do, she didn't want his opinion. He wasn't a man, he was a boy with a 2.4 GPA.

She thought about abortion. With no baby to care for, she could go to college like Gramps wanted. And then what? Lisa had never developed a clear vision for her life. It seemed kind of pointless to get a job and save for a house when the simulation could end at any time, for any reason. A meaningless job in a meaningless universe? No thank you. But neither did it mean she should be a single parent like her mother, so poor and anxious that she'd dump her own child at her father's place to go find her true self, wherever that was. At least if Lisa Marie got the abortion, she'd be able to get out of her hometown without burdening Gramps with another kid to support. How many generations could the man raise before he croaked? And what would that kid think about Lisa Marie—or about being the next castoff in a series of castoffs? Another mitten dropped on the sidewalk. That child would never feel loved.

Okay. Abortion, then.

Or not?

The great prank of the Simmers was that the digital fetus in her digital uterus felt real. She began to imagine the girl's face, though sometimes it was a boy's. She began to imagine a future for them. It was infuriating.

Yes, she could delete this bundle of binary cells the way the Simmers could delete her. But then she'd be just like those cosmic assholes. And no matter what choice she made, they could override it at any point. All they had to do was get bored with the child, or decide it wasn't of use to them, that it didn't suit their purpose, whatever that was. How the hell was she supposed to defend the child against that?

She started reading about simulation theory, and following blogs, and streaming YouTube explainers. She threw up when she needed to and went right back to the laptop. She read about Conditional Existentialism, Matrixism, New Determinism, so many sim-isms. Everyone had a theory about what the Simmers wanted, and why they'd told us we were in a sim. But none of them had a believable plan for staying alive.

And then she discovered the Hansonites. Years before the Announcement, an economist/philosopher had done a riff on how to stay alive if we ever found ourselves in a simulation. Now he'd picked up a fan base—with their own subreddits, advice books, memes, merch, and conventions. Their motto was simple: *You are living in a reality show, so act like it.* It was the first survival strategy that made sense to her. Be interesting. Be fabulous. Be famous.

She'd make those aliens or future folk care about this kid. Make them want to see what she—or he! Or them!—did next. She taped a notebook page to her mirror: "Plan to Escape Deletion." There were fourteen steps at first, and she'd add more in the weeks to come.

STEP ONE: *Establish your look.* She copied the info off Gramps's credit card and bought boxes of makeup. She mainlined tutorials from everyone from high school influencers to supermodels. She read up on dihydroxyacetone and pregnancy and found a DHA-free tanning salon.

STEP TWO: *Create your online identity.* She registered her new handle on every social she'd ever used and many she'd just learned about. She nabbed an email address and a domain name.

Six weeks after reading the news on that pink stick, Lady Mmm was born.

She was going to get those clicks. Grab those eyeballs. And Baby M? Baby M was going to be famous—the Chosen One of the sim generation. #BABYTREK. Like and subscribe, bitches!

But not if she couldn't get her numbers back up. And there was only one way she could think of to make that happen.

Christopher hasn't answered. She texts again.

Christopher

You won't believe what I found out

Three dots begin to pulse next to Christopher's name—and then evaporate.

"Fuck!" she says aloud. Then immediately, "Sorry, Baby M."

Christopher

Three seconds crawl by.

Don't ignore me

Bloop.

CHRISTOPHER!

What's the matter with him? She knows he's crushing on her. That would have surprised her months ago, but she's learned from her comment threads that the belly is no obstacle for a lot of guys—in fact, just the opposite. Of course, for all the rest of the douchebags on the internet, Lady Mmm is a skanky whore slut whatever. Fuck those guys. They're not her primary audience. Men who hate-follow her are, at best, her number four demographic.

She takes a breath. Types.

Please Christopher I need you

Finally he writes back: **I can't. Dad.**

"Are you fucking kidding me?" she says aloud.

She levers herself out of the seat. Her esophagus burns as if she's burping Tabasco. She walks past the Black woman's row without looking at her, takes a position next to Christopher's dad. He's got a spiral notebook open on his tray, and he's explaining a diagram to Christopher that looks like a football play.

"Hey there," Lisa Marie says.

Christopher looks up nervously. His father turns and glances at her naked belly, and then his eyes meander their way to her face. Like father like son. The old perv smiles. "We were just talking about you! Chris says you're quite the internet personality."

Lisa Marie ignores him, speaks over his shiny head to address Christopher. "Could I talk to you for a minute?" Her tone is Nutra-Sweet. "I really need your help with something."

The father squints, slightly baffled. "We're almost at the Geysers."

"I'll get him back to you," she says.

The father looks at his son. "Chris?"

"I'll be back in a minute," Christopher says.

His father switches to jocularity. "You'd better! We have a lot of work to do."

Lisa Marie walks away, leaving it to father and son to work out the choreography of getting Christopher out of his seat. Again, she doesn't look directly at Gillian, but sees that she's typing away on a laptop. With those sunglasses and baseball cap she looks like a celebrity caught on the street by TMZ.

Lisa Marie backs into her row, slides into the window seat. She's getting tired of this maneuver.

"What is it?" Christopher says, almost whispering. God, he's tall. But every inch of him tremulous and unsure, like a giraffe considering a dash across the highway. He reminds her of herself before she invented Lady Mmm. He doesn't know he could be beautiful. Great bone structure. Cut the ridiculous Weasley hair, send his pasty white ass to a tanning salon, and get him to a gym, you might have something. The boy is a flippable house.

She says earnestly, "Why do you let him control you?"

He glances back toward his father, then lowers his head. "He doesn't control me; he's just—you know. My dad."

She moves her laptop and camera from the seat to the floor by her feet. He still doesn't get it. She touches his arm and guides him into the seat. "You need to have a vision for your life. Do you have a vision, Christopher?"

"Uhm . . ." He looks down at her hand, still resting on his pale, pale arm. She leaves it there.

"I have a twenty-step plan," she says. "I know how I'm going to save myself, and more important, how I'm going to save Baby M."

Christopher blinks hard. "From what?"

"Deletion." She can't believe he hasn't thought through this. It's the only thing she's been thinking about since the pink stick. Had he even heard of Hansonism? Probably not, and it was too much to explain right now. "If you listen to me," she said, "I can save you too."

"Oh. Okay. Thank you."

"Thank *you* for helping me this morning. I was pretty sure I was going to have to throw down with that bitch." This, Lisa Marie thinks, is a very Lady Mmm thing to say. "I want you to know that I appreciate you having my back."

"I didn't do anything, I just—"

"You didn't do much, but you did do something. Nobody else did. I'm going to need your help on this trip, Christopher. I need a photographer, for one."

He winces. "I don't know, I'm supposed to be helping my father. He's launching this podcast thing?"

"Please. I've seen your dad's website. It's a 404, Christopher. He's got a domain name but he hasn't even put up a homepage. And where's his social presence? He's practically invisible."

Christopher blushes. His skin is as reactive as an octopus's. "We're just getting started."

"He's got to be much more aggressive if he wants people to find him," she says. "Look at me—I've got seventy-five thousand followers, and every day—"

"Wow!"

It's sad that he's so impressed. "Listen to me. Every day I do an hour of video and ten thousand words a day of text. I'm the queen of hashtags and mentions."

"That's a lot of writing."

"I work my ass off. I'm on seven major socials, with traffic-driving accounts on a dozen more. You're going to have to learn this stuff if you're going to help your father. You have to be constantly growing your base, and that means A-B-C. Always . . . say it with me."

"Always . . ."

"Be Content-ing. And I need your help to do it."

"But my dad—"

"You'll be helping me *and* your dad. I'll teach you what you need to know. What analytics app are you using?" A trick question—he clearly has no clue about reach, impressions, organics, none of the metrics he needs to be tracking. "Look, this is Microdose, my main data app. I can get an overview of my whole empire or drill down to individual events."

Christopher looks at her phone and nods seriously—but he's definitely not seeing what she sees: her numbers have been flat for a week, and her overnights are dismal. The six videos she'd made yesterday—two Insta stories, a Mimsy animation of her riding on top of the Impossible bus, a TikTok lip-sync, and two versions of Christopher's dad breaking his balls at the Tornado—had generated below-average engagement, and her followers were dropping. Mimsy down 200. Instagram, up 24 but probably bots. YouTube, as many losses as gains. And TikTok was way down, 521 fewer. Which—how? TikTokers loved videos of old people falling down! It was practically required in their EULA.

She's still over 75K followers across all platforms, but barely. Likes, comments, shares, and retweets were flat for yesterday's activity. Impressions were okay, but Post Engagement and Reach were the worst they'd been in weeks. Organics were in the shitter. It was bad everywhere she looked. Crappy overseas at Sina Weibo and VKontakte, terrible in old media like X, Tumblr, and Flickr. Even her Tinder profile was getting fewer swipes.

This morning she woke to see tiny acrobats, jumping and tumbling at the foot of her hotel bed. They formed letters by stacking on top of each other, Cirque du Soleil style. It was as if the sim was telling her: Your audience is shrinking, bitch! You're peaking. Six months into the Lady Mmm platform and you're headed downhill.

"You see my problem," Lisa Marie says to Christopher. "I need a turnaround. Just a few good posts isn't going to do it. I need a *story*. And that's where you come in." She starts swiping through her phone.

"I thought you just needed me to take your picture," Christopher says. "I don't have a story or—oh. Oh wow."

She's showing him the pic she took this morning in the hotel lobby: Gillian Masch, her baseball cap failing to hide that Britney-Breakdown buzz cut.

Christopher says, "I thought you deleted that!"

"Of course I didn't delete it. I did some searching. There are only two Gillian Masches, only one with a picture—this one that's posted on Pinterest with seven favorite wedding hairstyles."

"That's not her," Christopher says.

"I know it's not her. This girl's like twenty years old and doesn't look anything like her."

The bus abruptly slows, starts a heavy turn. A pair of tall, red wind-sock men thrash and wave, welcoming them to a large parking lot.

Lisa Marie says, "The only other Gillian Masch I could find lives in Tonopah, Arizona, and I think she's eighty years old. You know what this means, right?"

Christopher's nodding again. She's quickly finding out that this means nothing.

"She's a fake," Lisa Marie explains. "A grown woman should have *something* online. So she's an imposter."

"Why would she use a fake name?"

"That's the story, Christopher. And you're going to help me dox this bitch."

The Realist Blows the Lid Off the Big Lie

||||||||||||||||||||||||||||||||||||||||||||||||||||||||||||||||||

Jim Mullins is about to lose his shit. The second Geysers of Mystery show is minutes from starting and his son's nowhere to be seen. Jim can't go looking for him, because he can't give up his prime spot at the front of the audience. This whole podcast episode depends on him being up front.

On the other side of the fence, across the geyser field, is a wooden fence painted, inexplicably, like a cartoon volcano. The Geysers have nothing to do with volcanic activity, but that's the kind of anti-science B.S. you get in a place like this. Then a door opens in the fence, and a teenage employee walks out wearing an oversized G.O.M. windbreaker and pulling a wagon full of props.

Jim looks around the semicircular audience area, searching for his son in the crowd. "Where the hell are you?" he says aloud. But of course he knows exactly where Chris is; he's been following that pregnant girl around all day like a puppy.

A rustling rumble comes over the PA; the teenage presenter's fiddling with his lavalier microphone. He's a different employee than the one from the first show. He walks to the left side of the geyser field, which is about a hundred square feet of grass broken up by three circular patches of bare earth, each about six feet in diameter. Footpaths wind through the grass, surrounding the patches and connecting them. At the rear of the field, hanging above the rim of the volcano, is a digital clock, ticking down the seconds.

Jim made a map of the field in his notebook and was satisfied to find out it's pretty accurate. It used to be someone's front yard. The government seized the property after the Announcement, and when they returned it, the owners promptly sold it to a local real estate developer, who made the Geysers the centerpiece of an amusement park—four acres of restaurants, roller coasters, and rides. Up until a couple years ago, customers could walk the footpaths and see the Geysers up close. Then, suddenly, no one was allowed within thirty feet of them. They said it was because that toddler died, but Jim has his suspicions.

"Hello, everyone, are you ready to be amazed," the presenter says in a flat voice.

No, Jim thinks. He's not ready, and definitely won't be amazed. Goddamn it, Chris! Where are you?

He's going to have to do this himself. His online research had already turned up the probable locations of buried infrastructure and hidden switches. During the first show he filled in even more suspicious areas, like that stripe of discolored grass running between two of the Geysers. A sure sign of a buried power cable. And Jim has a pretty good idea how the G.O.M. employees are controlling it all.

The teenager gestures to the circle of bare ground to his right. "This first one we call the Floater," he intones. His mouth is alarmingly large. "This geyser turns active every ten minutes and stays on for sixty seconds like clockwork. I guess you could call it New Faithful." He gestures at the big digital clock. "And . . . here we go."

A yellow device hangs around the kid's neck. He grips it and clicks a button.

Nothing happens. Then he reaches into the wagon and picks up a bowling ball. He tosses it over the patch of earth. The ball hovers in midair.

Everyone starts clapping.

What idiots, Jim thinks. Instead of considering for a moment that an amusement park might just lie to them, they'd rather believe the whole world was a lie.

Realism did take a hit seven years ago, he'll admit. The world wobbled. What saddened him was that some people, including people he loved, couldn't regain their equilibrium. They went into freefall. They decided to question everything—their lives, their values, their own happiness—just because of a few unexplainable events. *Initially* unexplainable events. They were like little kids awestruck by a birthday party magician. *What, you see one rabbit come out of a hat and then decide to file for divorce and take half the house? Really, Laura?*

No. Every atom is not suddenly a fake, every photon an illusion. A rock is a rock is a rock. And sometimes what looks like a bowling ball is a giant magnet. *I refute it thus.*

"You might wonder if the ball is held up by a jet of air or powerful magnets," says the trout-mouthed teenager. "But it's not—gravity simply works differently when the geyser is active. Scientists"—he takes a gulping breath—"from around the world have studied each geyser in detail and have no explanation for how they function."

The presenter leans over the wagon and starts tossing other objects into the air above the bare ground: a rubber ducky, a beach towel, a bouquet of plastic flowers. They all float in the air.

Jim shakes his head. Every one of the objects could be laced with magnetic material.

Then the presenter picks up a plastic pitcher filled with red liquid. "How many of you kids have already tried our Geyser Gusher Ultra Berry Flavor Drink," he says. Jim knows the script better than the teenager does; not just because he sat through the first show, but from the dozens of times he's watched other G.O.M. presenters on YouTube. This kid, however, wins the award for most lifeless delivery.

"Well, don't try this at home," the presenter says. He tips the pitcher and begins to pour. The liquid flows sideways across the length of the geyser as if on a glass table. When it reaches the far edge of the geyser, it begins to flow down the side of the air.

Then, everything falls at once: juice, rock, towel, ducky. People laugh and start clapping.

The teenager's hand is again holding the yellow device.

Jim looks behind him. All strangers except the tour guide and the Austrians, who seem to be the only members of the tour who've come back for the second show. He spots his son's orange noggin bobbing through the crowd and shouts his name, waving.

Chris pushes through, with the pregnant girl at his side. Jesus. The boy's smiling as if she's just said something hilarious. He's holding a Geyser Gusher and she's licking a Mile High Twist Cone. The girl's camera hangs around his neck. Does she have him working for *her* now?

"Where the hell have you been?" Jim says. "It's already started!" Chris's grin vanishes. He does that thing where his face goes blank and his eyes focus on nothing.

Goddamn it, Jim thinks, here we go with the pouting. He knows his son, his tics and tells. When Chris was nine, he used to pull at his hair in Tae Kwon Do class, nervously waiting to spar. In junior high, soon after his growth spurt, he adopted a hunchback, desperately trying to shrink himself. And since coming back from college, he's been doing this vanishing trick, disappearing while leaving his body in place.

It hurts Jim's heart to see this lack of confidence. It's one reason he's so happy to be working on this project with him; Chris needs the *Real Patriot* podcast to succeed more than Jim does. The kid's never held a real job, and it's up to his father to give him not just a career, but a purpose.

"You ready?" Jim asks.

"You, uh, still want to do this?" Chris asks.

"Do what?" the girl says.

None of your business, Jim thinks. Is she trying to snare Chris? Trap him into becoming the father for her kid? As soon as Jim gets some time alone with the boy, he's going to have to straighten him out.

The presenter has moved on to the middle geyser, the one they call the Vacuum. He's tossing balloons and feathers and glitter into the air above it, and every object and particle gets sucked to the ground. This geyser always stays active for five minutes, he tells them, and exerts a gravitation pull of five times the Earth's gravity: "Scientists call that 5G, but you can't make phone calls with it."

No one laughs.

"You ready?" Jim asks his son. He points to the Olympus hanging around his neck and says to the girl, "Does that thing take video?"

"You're not using my camera," she says.

"I can put you in the video too," Chris says to her.

"*With* your father?" she says.

"Never mind," Jim says. "Chris, get your damn phone out."

"Please?" Chris asks the girl.

"Fuh-*ine*-uh," she says.

The presenter says over the PA, "Do we have a volunteer to try out the Vacuum. Does anyone want to gain a lot of weight."

Jim shoots up his hand. "Me! Me! I'm ready!"

"No, pick me!" the girl says. Jim looks down at her in disbelief. She yells and waves. "Woo-hoo!"

The presenter's wide mouth becomes a wider grin. It's the first genuine emotion he's displayed. He walks to the gate and taps a code to unlock it. The girl hands Jim her ice-cream cone and he automatically takes it. She squeals in excitement. "Christopher, make sure to get this!"

Chris is getting it. The camera's in front of his face.

Then the presenter sees that the girl is pregnant. He looks confused. "I'm sorry, I don't think you can—"

She pushes past him, raises her hands in victory. "Let's do this! Woooo!" The crowd starts clapping and hollering. Her enthusiasm is infectious. She heads not for the Vacuum, but the Floater.

"Ma'am! No!" the teenager says. He hurries after her.

Jim grabs the gate before it swings shut. He can't believe it. Nothing's going to plan, but everything's working out. He drops the ice cream to the ground and looks into the camera lens. "Ladies and gentlemen," he says to his future audience. "It's about to get real."

He slips through the gate, hustles after the girl and the employee. The presenter doesn't see him—he's pleading with the girl to stop.

Jim steps up beside the boy presenter. "Hey there," Jim says, and grabs the yellow device. He yanks down.

"Ow! Hey!" The presenter pitches sideways into Jim and Jim stumbles backward, still pulling on the device. Jesus, why won't the lanyard break? He grabs the kid's head and pushes it down. If he could just slip it off his head—

Then the presenter falls to the ground. He's tripped over the wagon handle. Jim grabs both sides of the lanyard and pulls it over the kid's ears. Jim backpedals, trying to regain his balance. Falls back on his butt.

He has the device! He's surprised that it looks exactly like a stopwatch, with black buttons and a numeric readout. He holds it up so Chris can film it. "I have the controller!" he shouts. "I have the wireless controller!"

The presenter yells, "Sir! Sir!" The kid's on his knees now, his hands outstretched. He's frightened—because of course he is! The whole scam is blown.

"Get out of there!" the kid yells.

Jim looks down. He's sitting in a circle of bare earth. The third geyser.

He has time to think, Oh shit.

And then, suddenly, he is thirty feet in the air.

The Comic Book Writer Faces a Tough Audience

IIIIIIIIIIIIIIIIIIIIIIIIIIIIIIIIIIIIIIIIIIIIIIIIIIIIIIIIIIIIIIIIIIIIIIIIIII

At the same moment that the most mysterious of the Geysers of Mystery deactivates and Jim Mullins begins his fall, Dulin Marks is on the other side of the park, biting into a "Philly-style" cheesesteak. He chews slowly, not because he's enjoying the sandwich—it seems to have been created by a teenager who'd been shown a picture of a cheesesteak and pointed toward a microwave—but because he needs time to think of a suitably erudite response to what JP and Gillian have told him.

He swallows. Takes a sip from his giant tumbler of Coke. And finally says, "You're shitting me."

"Nope," JP says.

"You're being hunted by the *Protagonists*?" He'd read a few articles about these guys. They were incels in long leather coats and hair gel, who believed they were among the 1 percent of people who were actually conscious. "They're doofuses."

JP and Gillian exchange a look. They're sitting across the picnic table from him, arms almost touching. And how did that coziness happen so fast? Dulin's suspicious. JP isn't prepared to have some chick come at him hard and fast. It's not just the tumor, which left him physically and emotionally vulnerable; it's that he was married to Suzanne for thirty-five years. His boy hasn't developed antibodies to modern strains of female.

"The Protagonists aren't doofuses," Gillian says. "Not entirely." She hasn't removed her hat or sunglasses since she got on the bus this morning. The leather courier bag is constantly on her shoulder.

"They think the Matrix movies are scripture," Dulin says. "They're basically cosplayers."

"Cosplayers with real guns," Gillian says.

"Fair. And they're after you why?"

"Inside voices," JP says, even though they're sitting outside in a windy pavilion. No one else from the tour is within sight, and the nearest tables are occupied by families.

"They think I'm a bot," Gillian says. "A puppet controlled by the Simulators."

"Are you?"

"She's not a bot," JP says.

"Let the robot speak for itself," Dulin says.

"The Protagonists think that other people are NPCs they can kill for experience points."

"And you," Dulin says to Gillian. "You're worth a lot of points?"

"I survived an attack early on," she says. "I've been high on their kill list ever since."

"Really? What happened?"

"It's not important," Gillian says. "I'm only talking to you because Jean-Pierre insisted we bring you in. He says you know people who can help."

Bring you in. Jesus Christ. How many times had he written that same dialogue?

"I'm going to need more details before I join your conspiracy," Dulin says. "First, does it include dental? Is there a 401(k)?"

"She's telling the truth," JP says.

"What you mean is that you believe she's telling the truth."

"Okay, we're done," Gillian says. She turns, drags her leg over the bench. Picnic tables are hell on dramatic exits.

"Gillian, wait," JP says. "He's just—Dulin, stop being an asshole."

"Forever?" Dulin says. "You can't expect me to go cold turkey."

"Dulin."

JP's seriousness is making Dulin feel bad about his top-shelf skepticism. Usually JP's all in on mockery, at least as an audience member.

"Okay, I'm sorry," Dulin says to Gillian. "I am. But you've got to admit, this is all a little hard to believe."

"Can I show him the video?" JP asks. Gillian waves a hand, looks away. JP sets his phone in front of Dulin. "This came out this morning. Gillian showed it to me at breakfast."

Dulin presses play. The first ten seconds are of a lone, shadowy figure walking in slow motion down a hallway, trench coat billowing, to the sound of pulsing EDM. A dead man, or someone pretending to be dead, lies face down on the floor.

"What the fuck?" Dulin says.

The figure is suddenly striding into a well-lit office—an obvious edit. Their face has been digitally altered to be a featureless blank, like the Question, but with sunglasses. The office is set like an ISIS hostage video—a bloodied prisoner tied up in a chair, flanked by heavily armed tribesmen in traditional costumes—except that the tribe is people who desperately want to be Keanu Reeves. The hostage-takers are dressed in leather and latex, their hair shiny with product. Their faces are also blanks.

Then the main guy starts monologuing in a low, obviously strained growl, a teenager trying to sound tough. It's a rant about how the man behind him isn't a man at all, but a bot. "Ajay Patel is not real. He and Thomas Francis are constructs, software programs created by the Simulators that imitate human beings. They are working for another bot, perhaps the most dangerous one of all."

Gillian's face fills the screen. Old Gillian: full natural hair and no makeup. It looks washed-out, like a passport photo.

"This construct's name is Margaret G. Schell. She's a professor of computational neuroscience at Boston University."

Dulin glances up at Gillian. *I knew that wasn't your real name!* When he looks back at the phone, the blank man has turned to the side for a camera-two close-up.

"She is also the chief architect of a top-secret government program to control the simulation called—"

There's a clattering behind him, and one of the minions starts to bend over. The moron's dropped his gun.

The lead doofus keeps talking. "—Project Red Clay."

"What the what?" Dulin says.

"Atreus pointed the way," the blank says. "He gave his life to stop Margaret Schell. The Simulators intervened and stopped him, but we will never give up. This is our warning to all bots working for the enemy—we will find you. We will stop you. Because *we* control our destiny. We are the authors of our own story. We are . . ."

The screen goes black. A curtain of green code that looks like copyright infringement coalesces into a pair of words: THE PROTAGONISTS.

"Jesus fucking Christ," Dulin says. "What douchebags. Multiple cameras, special effects, a fucking soundtrack?" He hands the phone back. "So this is all real, *Margaret*?"

JP winces. "Inside voices."

"The man in the chair was not just my grad student, he was my friend," Gillian-slash-Margaret says. "They killed him. And the first body in the video, he was my friend too. They worked with me."

"Well, fuck. That's just . . . Wow." He takes a bite of his sandwich. Why can't he say nice things when required? The only language he's fluent in is Irony. "And this just happened?"

"Two nights ago, in Cambridge," JP says. "Gillian discovered the bodies yesterday morning and hit the road."

"Gillian did," Dulin says evenly. "Why didn't you go to the cops?" he asks her. "Why'd you run? If you're part of some secret government project, call your bosses—"

"I can't trust the police," she says.

"Come on," Dulin says. He wants to say, *The cops are in on it, too? That's number three in the conspiracy cliché list, right after "this goes all the way to the top."* But he holds his tongue, because JP is looking at him with a worried expression.

"She has good reasons," JP says.

"Let's hear 'em," Dulin says.

Gillian-Margaret gives him a half-hooded stare that makes him stop chewing.

"The project I was working on—"

"Project Red Clay," Dulin says. "Very X-Files, and weirdly southern."

"We were about to do a very bad thing," she says evenly. "I didn't even try to stop them—I knew I'd be silenced as soon as they figured out I wasn't a team player. So I came up with a new plan. I was almost ready to pull the trigger, but then the Protagonists showed up."

"You were going to go public?" Dulin asks.

The woman starts to answer, then seems to change her mind. "The less you know the better."

"You realize that doesn't sound as comforting as you think it does."

"I think we need to trust her," JP says.

"Hey, I can get behind the whistleblower thing. Screw the man, all that." Dulin's always had an anti-authority streak. Or to be more accurate, he had a streak of rule following in a life of sidestepping rules. "But I still have a ton of questions. Like, who's this Atreus dude? Why do these assholes hate you so much? But let's start with the most important question—what do you want me to do about it?"

"I need more information to plan my next move," she says. "I need to know if any of the Protags have been caught or if they're still chasing me. I also need to know if anybody else knows where I am right now."

"You mean the government," Dulin says. "The people you're finking on."

"Dulin," JP says.

"It would be very helpful," Gillian says, "to find out how close they are, if they could catch up to me — before I get where I'm going."

"That's cryptic."

"All she wants is to get to Ghost City to see her kid," JP says. "She has a daughter."

Gillian gives JP a look; did she not want him to share that? She says, "I understand you have connections in law enforcement."

"I don't have connections," Dulin says. "What I've got is a family full of cops."

"So many cops," JP says to Gillian. "I went to a Marks family funeral once, and it was like that Stormtrooper scene where they're all lined up on the flight deck for the emperor. Except all in blue."

"We do love a good Imperial March," Dulin says. "But I can't help you. I mean, if you needed somebody to fix a parking ticket, I could maybe call one of my brothers and help you out. But this ..."

"Jean-Pierre said you had a sister in the FBI."

Dulin gives JP the Slow Blink: You're killing me, man.

Dulin's sister, Deb, is the supercop of the family, the only one who's reached the federal level. Unfortunately, she's also permanently disappointed with him. Unlike his father and brothers, who blow up at Dulin for each of his transgressions and then immediately forgive him like harmless Irish firecrackers, Deb keeps her disapproval at a constant simmer. Their dearly departed mother was the same way. The Marks women, Dulin thinks, are emotional Crock-Pots.

"I have to know if I can afford to stay on this bus or not," Gillian says. "So first thing, ask if there's an APB out for my arrest or something, and if they're looking outside Massachusetts. And if they found my car. I left it in the Tornado parking lot."

"I'm not calling my sister. I don't want to owe her another favor."

JP opens his mouth and Dulin says, "No." He can't believe that he's being forced to be the reasonable one. That's always been JP's job.

"It's one call," JP says.

"Even if she picked up, what am I supposed to tell her?" Dulin asks. "Hey, the FBI wouldn't happen to be searching for this woman

I definitely don't know, who may be involved in a couple murders I know nothing about, would they? Just asking."

"I've thought through this," JP says. "Just tell her that Margaret Schell is a friend of mine, and I saw the video and got worried. I'm the one asking you to call."

"So she's your friend—basically the same scam you used on the tour guide to let Gillian onto the tour."

"Pretending to be her friend is now my go-to move," JP says. "Come on, this'll work. You know Deb loves you."

Gillian's not listening to them. Her face has gone stony, her head tilted, and then he hears it too: a siren, growing louder. A few seconds later, the siren stops. An ambulance, lights flashing, creeps down the pedestrian walkway, and people step out of the way as if nudged by an invisible plow. And then, suddenly, someone's not moving. A woman in a wheelchair.

Dulin extracts himself from the table. "Back in a sec." He hustles to get ahead of the ambulance. Beth-Anne's mother is staring at the vehicle as if it's barged into her living room.

"Hey there, Mrs. Neville."

The woman seems startled that this vaguely familiar man knows her name.

"You mind if I . . . ?" He reaches down and flips the wheel lock, then pulls her backward between two cement planters. In recent years he's become familiar with the mechanics of wheelchairs. The ambulance resumes its roll.

"Where's Beth-Anne?" Dulin asks her. He sets the brake again.

"She went off to the bathroom. I told her to hurry up. You're from the bus."

"That's right. Dulin Marks, ma'am." There's something about talking to southerners that makes him want to be in their movie.

"Dulin?" she says, suspicious.

"As in banjo."

"That's an old country name," she says. The joke's flown past her. "I had a great-uncle named Dulin."

Beth-Anne appears. She frowns at this tableau: mother, Dulin, receding ambulance. "What'd you do, Momma?"

"You left me in traffic!" her mother says.

"Very slow traffic," Dulin says.

"How are you doing today?" Beth-Anne asks him. "Sleep well?" A trace of a smile on her lips.

"Oh, I slept *great*," Dulin says.

"I saw you were almost late for the bus."

"It was a deep sleep. How about you? How was your night?"

"Fantastic."

"That's great."

Mrs. Neville is watching this exchange, mystified.

"Well," Dulin says. "I'll leave you ladies to it. See you back on the bus." He strolls back to the pavilion. There's a question on JP's face that Dulin's not going to answer, not in front of Gillian. Dulin glances casually back and sees that Beth-Anne and her mother have moved on.

"Where were we?" he asks.

"You were trying to weasel out of helping us," JP says.

"Hey, some of my best friends are weasels." And he did not miss that "us"; JP's putting himself on Gillian's team. "I was just pointing out that whatever Gillian was working on sounds way bigger than I can help with. And I'm not fishing for details—I don't want to know."

A lie. He's dying to know. But he knows he's better off in the dark, especially if he's going to have to talk to his sister. She's the master at flipping an interrogation on him. One time he called her to get the family pork chop recipe and in five minutes she got him to admit that he'd had an affair.

"You should tell him about Project Red Clay," JP says to Gillian.

"Goddamn it," Dulin says.

"He's right; he doesn't need to know about that," Gillian says.

"He has to know what this is about," JP says.

"It's not controlling the simulation? Because that would be handy."

"If you don't tell him," JP says, "I'm going to tell him as soon as you walk away."

"For Christ's sake," Gillian says.

Dulin chuckles. She was just figuring out how stubborn JP could be.

"How much do you know about AI?" Gillian asks.

"I'm familiar with evil robots," Dulin says. "Ultron, Amazo, Metallo—"

"Real AI," JP says.

"Oh, like *your* evil robots," Dulin says. He knows JP is sensitive about his; he spent years working on self-guided carts used by Amazon and other capitalist overlords.

"I'm not talking about machine learning, or large language models," Gillian says. "I don't care about *chatbots*. I mean AGI, artificial general intelligence. Real understanding of context, symbol manipulation, creative problem-solving, the whole deal."

"Every time I've talked to JP about that stuff, he says we're, like, a hundred years away from anything like that."

"That was before the Announcement," JP says.

"Ah, the Great Depiphany," Dulin says.

"The what?" Gillian says.

JP says, "He's been trying to make this happen for years."

"It's excellent coinage," Dulin says mock huffily. "Just calling it the 'Announcement' doesn't cut it. We need a word that describes how we were smacked in the face by our ignorance. Turns out we were wrong about everything."

"We weren't wrong about AGI," JP says. "It's just that now we're motivated. We *are* the AIs. But it's going to happen a lot quicker now."

"How quick?" Dulin asks.

"Real quick," Gillian says. "We're getting offtrack."

"Agreed," JP says. Then to Dulin he says, "All that matters right now is that some psychopaths want to kill her because they think she's not a real person."

"And the government is hunting her down because she's a whistleblower," Dulin adds. "And she wants us to be accomplices." He nods at Gillian. "No offense."

"None taken," she says.

His phone buzzes in his pant pocket, and a second later JP's phone chimes. Dulin fishes out his phone, squints to make out the text.

Please return to the bus immediately. Agnes.

"Who the fuck is Agnes?" Dulin says.

"The bus driver," JP says.

"So?" Gillian says. "Will you call your sister?"

"I'll think about it."

"He'll do it," JP says.

The Tour Guide
Consults the
Useless Binder

||||||||||||||||||||||||||||||||||||||||||||||||||||||||||||||||||||||

Aneeta Channar has always been too terrified to take psychedelic drugs. A rave is her idea of a nightmare. And now she feels as if she's just been dosed and dropped into a Burning Man mosh pit. Flashing lights, harsh voices on the PA, the mob of strangers . . . And then there's the screaming.

Jim Mullins started his scream thirty feet in the air—and kept it up until he struck the ground, when the sound was drowned out by the shrieks of the crowd. By the time Aneeta pushed through the gate, he was making a new sound, a breathy keening, like a teakettle left on the stove.

He's been making that sound for nearly ten minutes. He's lying on his back, staring at the sky. In one hand is a yellow stopwatch. His right thigh has developed a second knee which hinges in the opposite direction. His son, Chris, crouches beside him, and Lisa Marie Montello stands behind them, filming.

Aneeta flips through the binder, but the text is swimming on the page. Wasn't there a section on first aid? She took a certification class years ago, but all training has fled her brain.

Lisa Marie says, "Finally!" Aneeta looks up. The ambulance, whose strobing lights have been visible for several minutes, has reached the fence. The onlookers make room.

Someone grabs Aneeta's elbow. A white man in a vest starts talk-shouting into her face, something about suing the tour, a permanent ban, various dooms. Her body vibrates with each barking syllable. Yes, she is to blame for this. She can feel the truth of it. The customers are her responsibility. She should have predicted Jim Mullins would do something like this. He tried to climb over the chain at the Frozen Tornado; he walked into the middle of the Antipode. A more experienced guide would have expelled him from the tour already. She thinks about Peter Atherton, the guide who should have been on this trip. He wouldn't be standing here like this, shaking like a struck gong.

A pair of EMTs appear. Jim sees them above him and cries out, "No!" He grabs the front of his son's shirt. "My back! My back!"

The EMTs are giving instructions that Aneeta can't hear; the park manager, or whoever he is, is still spitting threats.

Chris Mullins slides a hand under his father's back. His father yelps. The EMT says, "Stop that! You need to get back!" Lisa Marie yells at the EMT, "Leave him alone!"

Aneeta yanks her arm free from the park manager. "Please," she says to Lisa Marie. "Let them work."

Chris Mullins falls back on his butt. He's holding a black leather case, like a fat wallet. Lisa Marie says, "Oh. Wow." Aneeta's confused. Then Lisa Marie turns that impressive belly toward her, blocking her view.

The girl's expression is aggressively blasé. "What?"

The EMTs force everyone away from the man on the ground. It takes several minutes to slide him onto a plastic backboard, then lift him onto the gurney.

"Footage!" Jim yells at his son. "Keep filming!"

The crowd refuses to disperse; they're all fascinated. Their attention seems predatory. Aneeta flashes on the night she turned twenty-one. She was at the White Horse, a crowded college bar, and at midnight her friends surrounded her, chanting *Shot! Shot! Shot!* Someone handed her a clear plastic cup. She took a sip and grimaced. It tasted like gasoline. Her friends downed their shots and called for more. She couldn't understand why they were so determined to distance themselves from reality. The Announcement had happened only two months before. The world had already gone cockeyed. Getting inebriated inside a sim was like turning yourself into a cartoon—and then turning on your cartoon television to watch the Simpsons watch Itchy and Scratchy.

The EMTs wheel Jim toward the ambulance. His son starts to follow, and one of the EMTs says, "You can't ride with us, kid. Meet us at the hospital."

Chris looks like he's in shock. Aneeta realizes that he's not holding the black wallet anymore. Where did it go?

Chris looks at Aneeta. "How can I . . . Where's the hospital?"

She has no idea. She opens the binder again, but the park manager slaps his hand onto the page. "Stop that! I need you and all your people out of here. Now."

Yes, Aneeta thinks. I need that too. More than anything.

The Professor
Waits for a Call

||||||||||||||||||||||||||||||||||||||||||||||||||||||||||||||||||||

The woman traveling under the name of Gillian G. Masch feels like a spy in enemy territory. She's in a shabby roadhouse less than a hundred yards from the hotel, sitting across from JP and Dulin, with Dulin's phone lying on the table between them like a bad idea. She can't look at it and can't not look at it.

Everyone else in the bar is laughing and talking and drinking, oblivious. There are plenty of locals, but most of the noise is being made by the members of the tour group. The Austrian honeymooners are telling the geyser story again, now with additional detail and color commentary. "For a moment, a long moment, he is hanging there!" declaims Josef, the Austrian in the glasses. "The look on his face was . . . surprise. Profound surprise."

Gillian glances at the phone, looks away.

"No, no," his husband, Marcus says. "Betrayal."

"Embarrassment?" Josef says.

"Possibly," Marcus says. "He *has* been hoisted by his own simulated petard."

That gets a laugh from the two old gents, half of the quartet who self-described as the Octos. They're sitting at the Austrians' table; the women's chairs are empty. The bus driver, Agnes, is perched at the bar under a string of shitty Christmas lights, sipping a cola, but half-turned on her stool to take in the performance.

The religious trio is sitting on the other side of the scuffed pool table. Sister Janet looks grim, and the novice—Sister Patrice?—looks constipated: lips pursed, disapproving. The rabbi is warily watching them both. Only Chen Xing-Xing seems to be ignoring the Austrians. They're sitting alone under a dartboard, back to the pockmarked wall, eyes on the book in their lap.

Dulin is marking up the bar's menu with a green pen. "Look at this—they put quotation marks around chicken tenders. Who the hell are they quoting?"

"Maybe it's ironic," JP says. He's wearing a natty straw fedora tonight. How many hats does this man have?

"Oh my God," Dulin says. "Soylent Green is made out of"—he makes air quotes—"*chicken.*"

The two of them seem to be able to banter all day like this. Tommy and Ajay used to do something similar in the lab. The boys spoke in pop-culture shorthand—lines from *Rick and Morty* and Liam Neeson movies and internet memes. Maybe, she thinks, this is how men express their feelings for each other. Maybe they're so emotionally constipated that quoting Batman is the only way they can say "I love you."

Dulin's phone vibrates. The two men stare at it. Margaret grips her whiskey glass.

Dulin picks up the phone. Frowns at it. Pulls a pair of readers from his breast pocket. Taps the screen.

"Well?" Margaret asks.

"She says she'll call in ten minutes." He doesn't look happy about it.

Margaret's been waiting for this call for hours. Dulin texted his sister on her cell but didn't want to call her while she was at work, because the call might be recorded. Margaret had no idea if the FBI surveilled their own agents, but it didn't seem out of the question. All paranoias seem reasonable now.

"I need a drink," Dulin says. He's on his third Dr Pepper.

"Then order a drink," JP says. "And have one for me brother in Canada."

Dulin laughs. To Margaret he says, "This Irish guy goes to the pub every day, and every day he orders three shots. One for me, he says, one for me brother in Canada, and one for—"

Margaret stands up. "I'm going to run to the bathroom." She's been holding it, waiting for that phone to buzz.

The Black Octo gives Margaret a smile as she passes his table. She's the only other Black person on the tour, so maybe he's feeling avuncular. She's not going to encourage that. The less he knows of her, the better. The less they all know. The Protagonist video is out there on the internet, waiting for everyone to find it, and when they see it, it'll only be a matter of when they turn her in, not if.

As she walks past the nuns' table, the novice says, "This is disgusting. A man could be dead."

"Ah, perhaps," the rabbi says. "They did say he was shouting as he went into the ambulance, so—"

"Someone should do something," the novice says pointedly.

Margaret pushes into the restroom, goes into the remaining empty stall. She'd love to have problems as simple as these tourists'. They can fuss about manners, trade gossip. Chat about the wonders of the Impossibles. The sim is like weather to them; they can talk about it all day and not have to do anything about it.

It may have been a mistake to allow Dulin to call his sister. The feds could be on their way now. There's a part of Margaret who'd almost welcome the arrival of a SWAT team. Being locked away in a cell would absolve her of responsibility. And maybe, just maybe, stop her from hurting anyone else.

Ever since the attempted bombing seven years ago, Margaret had become an unexploded bomb herself, dangerous as a forgotten landmine. Anyone who came near her would be at risk. Not only her family, but people like JP and Dulin. Her students, Tommy and Ajay, already paid that price. Yesterday morning, when she saw that the lab's front door had been smashed open, a part of her understood what had happened before she walked in to find their bodies. She'd been waiting so long for the explosion.

* * *

The morning after the bombing at her office, Margaret left Adaku with Edowar and went to campus. Police—real police, not university security—required her to show her ID to get into her building, but no one would allow her into the office, even though she could see no damage from the hallway. The bomb had been designed to maim, not set fire, a cop explained. Still, he said, the inside of the room "wasn't pretty."

She left the building, feeling sick. She walked automatically, her legs following the usual route home. A voice called out, "Dr. Schell?"

Aunty Tim—Utnapishtim, or whatever his real name was—sat on the stone bench alongside the path. He was wearing that same red-and-green kameez or caftan. She'd walked right past him.

He tentatively lifted a hand. "Would you like to talk?"

She knew she should walk away, now. Instead she was frozen. "I reported you to the police," she said.

"That makes sense."

"Did you do this?" Her throat was tight. "Did you set that bomb?"

"No! Please, Dr. Schell, I would never do that."

"But you knew."

"Yes. No, not exactly. I knew it was probable. I thought I explained; I'm from a previous iteration. I alone survived—"

"The flood, I got it. Just stop." It was broad daylight. Dozens of students and staff were within shouting distance. A pair of cops stood less than fifty yards away. She could scream and someone would come running.

"Please understand," the stranger said. "If you went into your office, you would have died, or been gravely injured."

What was the word he'd used? It came to her: "Statistically."

"Yes! The bomb explodes in every iteration—well, almost every one. In rare cases it's discovered before it goes off—but it's roughly fifty-fifty whether you live or survive with injuries."

He said it so nonchalantly: *fifty-fifty*. Alive or dead, a flip of the coin.

"But *this time* someone else died," Margaret said.

"I'm sorry about that. I didn't know for sure. I was focused on protecting you."

"You're insane."

"I wish that were true." He sounded sincere.

She pointed at him. "Don't move. Don't follow me. Don't come near anyone in my family." She walked away, and her hand reached into her bag for her phone. She'd call 911 as soon as she was out of this man's striking range.

"Dr. Schell! Wait! The danger's not over!" His voice grew close, but she didn't turn around. "They'll keep coming for you, and your family."

She kept moving. "How? And don't be vague."

"Forgive me, I'm new at this. I'm not really sure what the rules are."

"Whose rules?"

"You know." He glanced up.

"The Simulators?" So he got his orders from the gods. Of course he did. "You talk often?"

"It was more of a onetime thing."

She stopped, lifted a hand. "What happens to my family?"

"In the iterations where you survive Atreus's bomb, he tries again. Or his followers do. The further we get from the Announcement, the more variations there are."

"Who the fuck is Atreus?"

The stranger cringed apologetically. "I thought you knew already. That's his gamer name—the man who set up the shrapnel bomb. He thinks he's the main character of a video game, and everyone else is a nonplayer character. The news should be out soon, and you'll know his true name."

"And his followers, whoever the fuck they are, try to bomb me again."

The stranger winced. "Not always bombs. Guns, often."

Jesus Christ. Every second she engaged with this man the lie got more elaborate. And yet: there was something about him that seemed . . . harmless? She knew she had to be wary of him, yet she couldn't bring herself to be afraid of him. Then again, her instinct for what was believable and what was not had taken a hit in the last two weeks. The old world was gone, and this new one required new ways of thinking.

"Dr. Schell?" the stranger asked. She realized she'd been silent for a moment.

"Be specific," she said. "How are they going to attack me, and when?"

"I don't know! I knew about Atreus's bomb because this early, all the sims have a lot in common!" he said. "Well, you're in a class of sims that starts with more artifacts than most—like the Zipper; oh my, that's a dramatic one! But except for those starting variables, there hasn't been much time to diverge."

Holy shit. The stranger looked up at her expectantly. She said, "You think the sim started with the Announcement."

"You seem surprised."

"I'm not surprised, because I don't believe you."

"I think you are starting to, Dr. Schell. Just a bit."

She felt a flutter in her chest, as if she were standing at the edge of a roof and the imp of the perverse was daring her to jump. If everything—*everything*—started two weeks ago, then *she* was only two weeks old. Adaku, and Edowar, and everyone she loved had sprung into existence alongside her. Any memories from before the Announcement belonged to someone else.

"We're done," she said. "I never want to see your face again."

She strode away from him. The man yelped, then ran in front of her and turned with his hands out. "Please. Let me try something else."

She stepped around him—and he disappeared.

Margaret stared at the empty space he'd been occupying. There was no sound effect, no pop. Not even a shimmer in the air.

And then he was back.

"What the fuck," she said. "Are we—" She spun around, expecting what? A camera crew? Mirrors?

The stranger waited for her to turn back to him. "Here," he said. He handed her a small green thing—a travel umbrella, collapsed.

"What is this?"

"An umbrella," he said.

"I know it's a fucking umbrella! Are you doing fucking magic tricks?"

"I just slid into a nearby sim and borrowed it. I can put it back if you want."

"Stop. Let me think." She looked around, but no one seemed to have noticed what had just happened. She was still holding the umbrella. She opened it. The fabric was lime-green, and across it was written "Canterbury Trails" in white cursive.

"Better, keep it as a souvenir," he said. "I want you to remember me."

There was no way she was forgetting this, she thought. She collapsed the umbrella. "What do you want from me?"

"I want to talk to you and your husband."

"Nope."

"It's about Adaku—and her future." He stepped off the path. "I'll stop by tonight around, say, nine? You don't have to let me in."

"Wait, goddamn it! Don't you—"

He vanished in midstep.

"Fuck."

She stood there for a long time, feeling as if she'd stepped off the roof and nothing was holding her up except for a magical umbrella.

•　•　•

The metal panel between the bathroom stalls shakes. A woman laughs quietly. Another person makes a guttural noise. The panel begins to shake rhythmically.

Holy shit, Margaret thinks, are folks actually fucking in here?

She leans down. Next door are two sets of legs, entwined. One of them's wearing a nice pair of Remonte sneaker-style ankle boots with red laces, and the other's wearing women's Merrell sandals, leather with foam soles.

You go, girls.

Margaret walks back out into the bar. The young nun is speaking sternly to the Austrians, who seem . . . surprised. Profoundly surprised. She wonders whether the Octo men are wondering where their partners are.

Dulin's alone at the table, holding his phone.

"Nothing yet?" she asks. "Where's JP?"

"He followed your lead," Dulin says.

"Bathrooms here are getting a lot of action." She doesn't explain.

Dulin leans forward. "I have to ask you—what are your intentions?"

"About what?"

"With JP."

"I have no intentions whatsoever."

"Because he's not . . ." Dulin grimaces. "Did he tell you about Brian?"

"Who the hell is Brian?"

"He's a what." Dulin taps his forehead. "A famous typo." She has no idea what he's talking about.

He glances back toward the restrooms. No one's coming. "It's not my place to fill you in. I just need you to be careful with him, okay? He's gone through a lot. And it wouldn't be right for you to take advantage of him in this state."

"What state?" she says. Then thinks no, it doesn't matter. She doesn't have the resources to manage some white guy's crush on her. She has two good friends who are lying dead. An ex-husband and a daughter she hasn't seen in months, waiting for her on the other end of the continent. Her heart is crowded.

"I appreciate your help, you and JP both," she says. "But you're grown-ass men. If you don't want to do me any more favors, then don't."

"I'm not saying we're not going to help you," Dulin says. "It's just that, emotionally, JP's not that—" The phone rings. He looks at it. "Fuck. It's Deb. Here we go."

He stands up and puts his phone to his ear. "Hey there, Sis!" Even to Margaret it sounds like bravado. She watches him head toward the exit, a finger in his other ear. Aneeta, the tour guide, walks in as Dulin walks out.

The tiny woman, looking shell-shocked, makes straight for the bus driver at the bar. Gillian, like everyone else, is now watching her, waiting for news. The driver starts asking Aneeta questions in a low voice. The driver starts to stand, and Aneeta shakes her head. She'll do this.

"Everyone?" Aneeta clears her throat. "Jim Mullins has gone into surgery. His son, Chris, and Lisa Marie Montello are staying there with him. I can't say more, for privacy reasons, but the doctors told me that he's going to be . . ." The girl searches for a word. ". . . in a lot of pain. A *lot* of pain. They're probably going to give him high doses of morphine. And then he's going to have a long recovery. They're going to insert pins in his femur to—"

Agnes plants a big hand on Aneeta's shoulder. "He's going to be fine, everyone," she announces. Then she waves to the bartender. "Vodka and cranberry for my girl here."

Margaret's relieved. Not that Jim Mullins would recover—though that's good news—but that Lisa Marie wouldn't be coming back on the tour. That girl's a psycho, and probably wants to live stream herself and everyone around her.

"I would like to offer a prayer," the younger nun says.

Hell no. Margaret grabs her jacket and courier bag, then stalks out before a religious service breaks out.

The temperature's dropped, and the wind threatens to take her baseball cap. She pulls on her new fleece. Where's Dulin? Then she spots him, lumbering around in the dark of the parking lot, still on the phone. Such a big man, but he's hunched over like he's being yelled at by the principal.

Everything is going to be fine, she tells herself.

• • •

The knock came at precisely nine p.m. It was a shock, even though Margaret and Edowar had been waiting for it.

"So," Margaret said. "This is happening."

"Do you trust this man?" Edowar asked.

"Nope." She moved toward the mudroom, and Edowar said quietly, "I'll get it." Her husband was a gentle man, an academic to his bones, who spoke with a British accent and rarely raised his voice. But he was also tall and broad shouldered, like a full professor at Linebacker University, and he took his role of protector seriously. Edowar opened the door to the garage, and Margaret had to peek around his body.

Aunty Tim stood in the garage, smiling expectantly. The garage door was down, and Margaret hadn't heard it open or close. More magic tricks.

"You're so tall!" Aunty Tim said to Edowar. "I always forget that."

Edowar scowled. He stood with his chest out and fists clenched, giving every indication he'd punch out this stranger if he made trouble. Margaret had never seen him raise a hand to anyone, but it was also true she'd never seen him pushed.

The silence stretched. Aunty Tim darted a glance at her, but she gave him no help. Finally he held out a hand and said, "It's an honor to meet you, Dr. Eze."

Edowar shook his hand automatically, his instinctive politeness causing his badass impersonation to slip.

"Let him in," Margaret said.

Edowar's look said, *Really?* She shrugged.

Edowar stepped back and Aunty moved carefully inside. He'd switched his tunic for something that looked like a Mr. Scrooge nightgown that fell to his ankles. His feet were bare. Margaret pointed him toward a chair at the kitchen table. She offered him coffee, water. He declined both. "I don't want to be a bother."

"I kind of think you do," she said.

"Is, um, Adaku nearby?"

"Why?" Edowar said. His voice was low and threatening.

"It's probably best if she doesn't overhear us," Aunty Tim said.

"She's in bed asleep," Margaret said. "But please keep your voice down."

Margaret and Edowar had been talking from the moment she came home after seeing Aunty Tim on campus. They'd picked through each sentence of her conversation with the man, only stopping when Adaku came into the room. Edowar believed Margaret's account, even the part about Aunty Tim appearing and disappearing. Edo had always had faith in her judgment, and when he told her that, yes, if she believed the stranger's story, then he did too—well, that was an act of love, especially for a scientist. She wasn't sure she could have been that generous.

"Let's get this over with." Edowar looked at Margaret. "Should I . . . ?"

"Go for it, love."

Edowar rested his palms on the table. Margaret had seen him do this many times when the conversation turned serious, or there was a decision to be made. It looked like a gesture of prayer, if Edo were the praying type. He looked at the stranger. "What's your real name?"

"I'm sorry, I can't tell you that."

"I'm not going to call you Utnapishtim, or Aunty Tim, or any made-up—"

"Aunty Tim?" the stranger asked.

"That's Adaku's name for you," Margaret said.

"I love that! Let's go with that."

"Just tell us your real name," Edowar said.

"That might cause a lot of problems," Aunty Tim said. "I was born about thirty years from now, in my original iteration, but my ancestors are alive right now and—I'm sorry, this is so complex."

"So you're a time traveler," Margaret said, "as well as a visitor from another simulation."

"Exactly. And I'd like to avoid those classic time traveler problems."

"You're the one causing the problems," Edowar said. His palms were still flat on the table, but Margaret could see that he was struggling to remain calm. "You've come to interfere and tell us about our daughter's supposed future."

"That's the way to think about it," Aunty Tim said. "Suppos-ed. One of many possibles, some more likely than others."

"This is ridiculous," Edowar said.

"I agree! I didn't choose this life. One moment I was at home in bed, the next I was walking into an old-timey restaurant, where some ancient beings told me I could go to any world in the multiverse. Frankly, it's a lot to get used to."

"Old-timey . . . ?" Margaret said. "What are you talking about?"

"I think it was an Applebee's."

"Say what you're going to say," Edowar demanded. "Tell us about our daughter."

Aunty Tim raised his hands in surrender. "We have to start with—and I'm sorry to bring this up again—your death. Well, not *you* yours . . ." He pulled at his beard, looked to the side. "In my iteration, Dr. Schell died when Atreus's bomb exploded. But her work lived on, and that turned out to be a terrible thing. For Adaku Eze-Schell, and for many other people."

"What work?" Edowar said. "Her AI research?"

"It's what the government did with it," Aunty Tim said, and then, finally made eye contact with Margaret. "It's not your fault. Your papers, your book, *Embodied Intelligence*, your testimony at the congressional hearing—all that came out before the sim began—there's nothing you could do to alter that. It's a premise. Do you understand? Not changeable. But going forward, Adaku felt like she had to protest what they were doing with your ideas. Not atone for them, exactly, but explain and object. Your work was theoretical. It was never supposed to be put into practice."

That's not true, Margaret thought. Of course she wanted to implement her ideas. She just never thought that was possible. Not in her lifetime.

"That book sold all of fifteen-hundred copies," Margaret said, "And no one bothered to watch C-SPAN the day I showed up to testify."

"That was before the Announcement," Aunty Tim said. "After, everyone knew you were right. They're going to build an AI your way—just as you outlined."

Margaret stared at him. "I don't believe you."

"They'll call it Project Red Clay," Aunty Tim said. "Except when they don't. Sometimes they pick a different name, depending on who's in the room, how biblical they want to be—"

"What does this have to do with our daughter?" Edowar asked the man. "What happened to her?"

"Oh, right. Sorry."

"Stop apologizing and answer me." Margaret had never heard her husband so angry, so ready to explode.

Aunty Tim took a breath. "She grew up without her mother," he said. "But it was her mother's work that haunted her." He described how his Adaku became an activist, campaigning against Project Red Clay. She was declared a traitor, an enemy of the US government, and it became impossible for her to find work or lead anything like a normal life. She was jailed many times, but even from her jail cell she continued to speak out. "She died in a prison hospital," Aunty Tim said. "When she was forty-five."

Margaret turned away. It's not my Adaku, she told herself. She palmed the tears from her eyes. It was another person who died a universe away.

"She was brilliant," Aunty Tim said. "Her empathy for other people was so . . ." He opened his hands, then shook his head. "But she failed. The project was too extensive, too far along. And it was too late for her to protect any of the people inside that new sim."

"In your world I died," Margaret said. "And they used my work anyway. What about when I lived?"

"In those the government always comes to recruit you," Aunty

Tim said. "They think they need you. Of course, in other iterations they discover that no one is irreplaceable, but when you're alive, they of course want you on board. You literally wrote the book on artificial humans."

"How many times?" Margaret asked.

"I'm sorry?"

"How many iterations have you seen? How many variations of me have you watched?"

"Ah," Aunt Tim said. "Many, many iterations."

"And what do I do? In these many, many iterations?"

"Most of the time, you say yes," Aunty Tim said. "Sometimes you say no, but that often doesn't go well."

"I become the traitor," Margaret said.

"If you say no, at some point early in the simulation or later, you're arrested."

"You can't know this," Edowar said.

"I've witnessed the lives of a thousand Dr. Schells," Aunty Tim said. "She is never not a target. Extremists like Atreus want to kill her. If they can't attack you on campus, they will attack you at home. If they can't find you at home, they'll strike while you're on the road. And if you survive, the government wants to use you."

"But you can't be *certain*," Edowar said. "You don't actually know the future."

"You're right," the stranger said. "But in every iteration I have been to, Dr. Schell is either killed or arrested. There's no Margaret who's there to see her daughter's fourteenth birthday. And often, her father's gone, too."

"What?"

"Most often, Edowar shares your fate," Aunty Tim said to Margaret. "If you're arrested, he usually is too. You're seen as a team—your crimes are his. And the extremists feel the same. In the iterations where you're killed—these killers have no problem taking the lives of anyone with you. You're the target, but anyone close to you is in danger."

Edowar's hands came off the table. Aunty Tim seemed to sense the danger he was in. He leaned back and raised his hands.

"In how many iterations," Edowar said evenly, "does my daughter die?"

"I don't know exactly. I'm sorry; I'm trying to answer truthfully, but it's—"

"Why are you doing this?" Edowar's voice was shaking. "Why us? All the people in the world for you to interfere with—"

"Because you're *you*!" Aunty Tim exclaimed. "I know I'm not— oh! Hello there."

Adaku stood in the kitchen doorway—wide awake. The girl lifted a hand and said, "Hi, Aunty Tim."

And then the two of them exchanged a smile; the *same* smile, a mix of shy and sly, as if they were sharing a private joke.

Margaret couldn't move for a long second. She suddenly understood why Aunty Tim had chosen them. Then the paralysis released her, and she swooped up Adaku in her arms and carried her out of the room.

She protested the whole way up the stairs. At six years old she was already all legs, like her father. How long had she been there? Margaret wondered. How much had she heard? Too late, too late.

Margaret set her into her bed among her menagerie of stuffed animals. Adaku demanded to stay up, to sit at the table with them. She'd always considered herself a full voting member of the family.

"This is bedtime," Margaret said. "Under the covers."

"This isn't fair," Adaku said. Even angry, she was so beautiful. Her eyes were huge, and her hair shone in the glow of the night-light.

"I know," Margaret said. "When you're big, you get to stay up as long as you want."

"Daddy's mad." It was a rare thing for Edowar to lose his temper.

"A little."

"Are you getting a divorce?"

"What?" A couple of the children in her kindergarten had divorced parents. "No."

"Whose house would I live in?" she asked. "Yours or Daddy's?"

A straightforward question, as if asking who was going to drive her to school in the morning.

Margaret kept her face calm. She rummaged through the stuffies, found Pinky, and placed the rhino in her daughter's arms. And then she lied to her.

"Everything is going to be fine."

•   •   •

Suddenly Dulin Marks is striding out of the dark toward Margaret, phone still at his ear. "Okay, I got it," he says into the phone. "I said I got it! I'll text you." He sighs. "Yes, I love you too." He boops the phone, shakes his head.

"And?" Margaret asks.

"Deb said it's not her case, but she knows about it. The FBI's already involved, because it's the Protagonists. They're treating it like domestic terrorism. They're looking for the guys in the video."

"Fuck. What about me? Are they looking for me?"

"Oh yeah. You're wanted for questioning, and here I am, calling her up and asking about you. She really didn't like that I knew you."

"You don't know me," Margaret says. "The story is, only JP knows me."

"That's what I told her! But her radar for this shit is fucking scary. I think she could smell my fear through the phone."

"What do you have to be afraid of?"

"I dunno, accessory to terrorism? Lying to a federal sibling?"

"Did you ask about the car?"

"No, I didn't ask about the car; that's way too suspicious. She says she's going to call me back, and if shit is weird, then she's going to call JP."

"What about me?" JP had found them.

"Deb's threatening to interrogate you, man," Dulin says to him. "And if she does, may God have mercy on your soul."

JP looks suddenly older. She thinks about Dulin tapping his forehead. And suddenly she knows what Brian's last name is.

"Hey, y'all." A figure strolls out of the dark from the direction of the hotel. "Is the party out here?" It's the old woman's daughter, the nurse.

Jesus, no, Margaret thinks. Not now. She's trying to have a serious conversation.

"Beth-Anne!" Dulin says. "The party's wherever you are. Mom all tucked in?"

"I gave her her evening pills, so she's dosed and drowsy."

"Medicated and bedicated," Dulin says.

"Hee-hee!"

Margaret doesn't remember Beth-Anne smiling before. It makes her into a different person. Well good for fucking her. But she can't stand here all night watching these two flirt.

"*Hey*," Margaret says to Dulin. "Focus up."

Beth-Anne's smile fades. "Is everything okay over here?"

"It's nothing," Dulin says. "Just helping out Gillian and JP. Go on inside; I'll buy you a drink."

The nurse's eyes move from Dulin to Margaret to JP—and then back to Margaret. No telling what's going on in her head, but Margaret has some guesses.

"Well, see you inside, then." Beth-Anne walks toward the entrance, then pauses beside JP. "How are you feeling tonight?"

"Good," JP says. "You?"

"I'm glad to hear it."

JP waits until the door closes, then he looks at Dulin with a hard look that could be titled Items for Discussion at a Later Time.

Margaret says, "I need to know how long I can stay on this bus. Can I get all the way to Ghost City?"

"Tomorrow's the Hollow Flock," JP says. "Then the morning after that, we go through the Tunnel, and then—"

"Don't forget the Four Cedars tour," Dulin says.

So two days to the Tunnel. The whole point of taking the tour bus was that it got her through that Impossible under her fake name. No record of her car going through, no paying tolls, no pictures of her. One in a crowd.

"We should be at the Zipper by dinner, day after tomorrow," JP says. "Then we just raft down to the Vertical Circus, where the bus will pick us up again. Then just a day's drive to our last stop."

She doesn't like how long it'll take—but she has no better idea on how to cross the country. "Okay, here's what I need," Margaret says to Dulin. "When you talk to your sister again, you haven't seen me, right? You don't know where I'm going, either."

"Right," JP says. "We're just concerned citizens. Friends. Citizen-friends."

Margaret shoulders her bag and looks across the dark parking lot. The lights of the DoubleTree seem very far away. Beth-Anne had just walked over by herself. It would be fine. The Protagonists don't know where she is, not yet. And hopefully the police don't either.

"You know, why don't I walk with you?" JP says. "I'm ready to call it a night."

"You sure?" Margaret says. "Thanks." They start walking. She stops, looks back. "Thanks to you too, Dulin."

"We're all going to jail," Dulin says cheerily.

JP took her arm. They walked in silence through the dark. When they reached the hotel elevators, he asked, "Are you all right?"

"I'm just tired," she said. "Ready for bed."

•   •   •

After she'd tucked Adaku into bed, she came back to the kitchen to find Edowar looking at his lap. Aunty Tim was pacing nervously. "I didn't mean for that to happen," he said. "I apologize if I was too loud or if—"

Margaret stopped him. "You're saying that if I don't join this government project, they'll put me in jail. If I do join, I'll end up doing something immoral that my daughter will be ashamed of and spend the rest of her life protesting. And either way, there's a good chance I'll end up dead, and my family might too. Do I have that right?"

Aunty Tim looked miserable. Then he nodded.

"So what do I do?" she asked.

"You trust him now?" Edowar said. "Why?"

"My love, look at his face." Adaku had been the first to see it; he looked like a grandfather. He looked like a cousin. *I was born about thirty years from now. My ancestors are alive right now.*

"I don't understand," Edowar said. "Who are you?"

Aunty Tim grimaced. "I didn't plan on sharing this," he said. "I can't provide any proof. But yes, in a certain way . . ."

"He's family," Margaret said.

Edowar frowned, then his eyes widened. "A descendant?" Then, "But how far . . . ?"

"Please sit down," she told Aunty Tim. "And tell us everything."

The
Hollow
Flock

The Realist's Son Dreams of His Brother, a Dolphin

||||||||||||||||||||||||||||||||||||||||||||||||||||||||||||||||||||||

The surgeon asks Christopher Mullins if he has any questions. He's not sure he's heard most of what he's been told in the last ten minutes. His father's body lies in the bed like evidence of a shameful crime. Christopher has been required to explain several times tonight how his father managed to do this to himself, and each time he's told the story his embarrassment has grown. He's now reached maximum mortification.

"What did you say about his . . . fixations?" Christopher asks.

"We'll do the internal fixation surgery in a couple days," the doctor says patiently. "Tonight—well, I guess technically this morning—we just put in some temporary external fixations."

Christopher tries to remember all the injuries the doctor rattled off. Bruised spine, torn rotator cuff, a probable concussion, two broken ankles, a fractured femur. There was also something about internal bleeding. His father has undergone not just one operation tonight, but several of them.

"So he's not, like, paralyzed?"

"No, not at all," the doctor says. "He's going to be using crutches for quite a while, if his shoulder will let him. And he's going to need physical therapy, but he'll be up and walking. At some point."

His father's eyes are closed, his mouth slack. His left leg is wrapped in bandages and a scaffold of steel rods, which holds several long vertical pins in place. The pins are bloody where they penetrate the bandages.

"When will he wake up?"

"I'm awake," his father says. His eyes remain closed.

"He's coming out of the anesthesia," the doctor says. "But he's already on strong painkillers."

"Awake, damn it!"

"Really strong painkillers. In a little while we'll move him up to a room, and he'll be here for a couple of days. We'll get the room number for you."

The doctor starts to leave, then pats Christopher on the shoulder. "Don't worry, he's on the road to recovery."

Christopher winces. *Don't worry* seems like an accusation. You *are* worried about your father, right? Surely you can't be angry with him.

Christopher sits beside the bed. His father is agitated. Christopher knows that he should pat him on the shoulder, soothe him in some way, but he doesn't know where he can safely place his hand, what with all the wires taped to his chest and the tube in his arm.

His father's eyes open. He glassily regards Christopher. "What happened?"

Christopher can't bear to tell the story again. "You fell, Dad."

"Fell." He works his lips as if tasting the word. "Fell." His eyes close again. Then he says, "Did you get it?"

"What?"

"The video."

"Of you falling?"

His father's eyes snap fully open. How is he suddenly wide awake? His father says, "You missed it, didn't you?"

"Dad—"

"Jesus fucking . . ."

His eyes close again. Christopher watches his face for thirty seconds, then a minute. Is he asleep? Christopher stands up, looks at the gap in the curtains. It's just after eight a.m. Back at the hotel, the tour group is getting on the bus, going on without them.

He looks through the gap, at the desk. He can see only one person, just the top of their head, visible at the ER's central desk. He wishes he could slip away.

And then, as if he's dreaming it, his body makes it happen. A blue-painted line leads him back to the waiting room.

Lisa Marie Montello is surprisingly awake, riveted by something on her phone. She glances up and says, "You won't believe this. I found her. Her name's not even—oh. Hey. You okay?"

Found who? he wonders. He slumps onto the seat beside her. He's so tired he feels like crying. Walmart Toddler exhausted.

"How is your dad?"

"He'll be okay." He takes a breath. "You don't have to stay here."

"I'm here to support you," she says.

Well, fuck. Now there *are* tears in his eyes. He twists away from her, clenches his chest so no sob or squeak escapes his throat.

"Hey," she says. She puts a hand on his back. "I told you he'd be okay."

She *has* been saying that since they left the geyser park. For the entire night they've spent in this waiting room, waiting for Dad to come out of surgery.

Christopher says, "I don't—"

Then he can't say anything else for nearly a minute. Lisa Marie rubs between his shoulder blades.

He takes a ragged breath. "I don't know why you stayed with me."

"Because we make a good team. I'm calling an Uber. We can still make the bus."

He wipes his hands across his eyes. He still can't look at her. "The trip's over, Lisa Marie." He feels like he's breathing icy air. "I . . . like you. I mean, really like you. But the trip's over."

"No," she says. "It's not."

"I have to stay here with him. And then, I guess, take him home."

"Do you?"

Does he? He doesn't know how to process this new possibility. Of course he has to take his father home. How could he not?

But what if he doesn't?

"The doctor says he's going to be fine. He's a grown man, Christopher. Maybe it's time he takes responsibility for his actions. What was he thinking, jumping on that geyser? He just went up like, whoosh!"

A giggle escapes him. Which makes him feel guilty. Which makes him giggle again. "Whoosh," he says.

He tells her about his father asking about the video. "And he's right," Christopher says. When his father launched skyward, Christopher forgot to follow with the camera. "I missed the shot."

He slumps against her. She's so warm. Her skin seems to run two degrees hotter than anyone he's ever met.

"Fuck the podcast," she says.

"Hmm," he says. His cheek lies on her shoulder. She's so tiny. It's an awkward angle. If he falls asleep like this, the crick in his neck will be excruciating. He doesn't move.

"You can't live your life under his thumb," Lisa Marie says. "He doesn't respect you. And I don't like the way he treats you. He yelled at you just for getting ice cream. Who does that?"

"I did say that I'd be there for the show," Christopher says softly.

"I know you don't believe in this realism stuff," Lisa Marie says. "Is this what you want to do with your life—work on a podcast for people who can't face reality? That's *his* dream, Christopher. What do *you* want to do?"

"I don't know." He's not sure he says this aloud.

"Next time it could be you who's hurt," she says, and continues to lay out the case against his father. He can't argue with anything she says. Yes, his father is a narcissist. Yes, his beliefs are wacky. And yes, next time it could very well be Christopher who'll be stranded in mid-air, metaphorically speaking.

"You're meant for greater things," she says.

God he's tired. He closes his eyes and sees his mother standing in the doorway, holding a tiny, gleaming dolphin. It's wrapped in a blanket, smiling up at her.

"Listen," Lisa Marie says. "This woman, Gillian Masch? I knew it wasn't her real name. There's a Protagonist video that names and shames her. You remember what I told you about needing a story? She's it, Christopher, or, I don't know, a big part of it. There's nothing more important than a narrative. *Shape the narrative.* One good story can save me and my baby. And you too."

His mother is cooing at her baby dolphin. She bows her head to kiss its nose, and the dolphin clicks and squeaks.

"Upsy-daisy, sleepyhead," Lisa Marie says. "We've got a bus to catch."

The Engineer Has
Some Design Notes

|||||||||||||||||||||||||||||||||||||||||||||||||||||||||||||||||||||

JP watches as Dulin rakes his hand along the back of a hollow sheep. His fingers go alarmingly deep.

"Come on, man," Dulin says. "You've got to try this."

JP winces. "I don't know."

Dulin smiles evilly. "What, is this weirding you out?"

"I feel like I'm on an acid trip. These things are straight out of *Yellow Submarine*."

The tour group is scattered across a sloping, mountain meadow, wandering among the Hollow Flock. The hundred or so silvery creatures are ambling topiary: no eyes, no mouths, only bulbous heads and thick legs ending in puffball feet. They move slowly, as if grazing, but they do not eat, do not shit, do nothing, seemingly, but shuffle about the field.

"You think they feel pain?" JP wonders aloud.

"Don't seem to," Dulin says. "I saw a YouTube video where a kid doused one with kerosene and lit it on fire. It just walked around until the kerosene burned off."

"Oh my God, that's awful."

"Now, come on. Don't be such a pussy."

"Pussy? Are you seriously trying to locker-room me into touching this thing?"

Dulin cackles. JP adjusts his straw hat, steps up to the sheep. Sets his hand atop the creature's head.

"Oh," he says. "Wow."

Before he was forced to retire, JP was in daily conversation with the physics of soft and hard—what happens when a compliant body meets a noncompliant one. Cardboard box versus metal roller. Aluminum rack versus concrete floor. Human torso versus forklift. He consulted Ashby charts, which graphed the relative hardness of materials along an axis of density against Young's modulus of elasticity. He could measure impact in pascals.

But he didn't concern himself with how things *felt*. And now, as he combs his hand through the unbelievably soft curls of the hollow sheep, he realizes that was a mistake. Why didn't he build his systems to deliver tactile pleasure? He could have made things so much better for the human workers. Ease and comfort could have been factored into his equations. The last ten years of his career were spent in warehouse automation, adding rolling robots and smart sensors so that employees could pick, sort, and deliver more efficiently. The warehouses were enormous, and the productivity metrics for those workers were brutal. He wonders, not for the first time, whether he's been complicit in the construction of Pain Boxes.

"It's time," Dylan says. "Go for it. Full veterinarian."

JP closes one eye. Then he plunges his arm deep into the sheep. Nothing impedes. Not meat, not bones. Just velvety softness all the way down. It feels both obscene and delicious.

"Holy cow," JP says.

"Close," Dulin says.

Supposedly their wool is made of *stuff*, the same ultra-dense material as the Frozen Tornado. But instead of that structure's razor sharpness, each springy coil is fatter, and surrounded by air. There's very little resistance.

The sheep moves on, and JP lets his arm drag all the way through it, until it emerges from the thing's rump. A laugh burbles out of him. "Now *that* was trippy."

Dulin seems pleased, as if he'd invented the sheep himself. "You know what's psychedelic?" he says. "How green this grass is. It deserves its own name."

"We're in Kentucky. The grass already has a name."

"Come on, just look at it."

The meadow is a long, shallow trough of bright green, perhaps a quarter-mile wide, surrounded by trees of deeper green, and mature, blue-green mountains. Under this fierce blue sky, the new spring grass seems to be radiating in a pure chroma.

"You need a hippy name for this," Dulin says. "An acid-hit name. Like . . . *jadelic.*"

"You had that in your pocket."

"I certainly did not. Ooh! How about—"

"Give me a second."

"*Chartruth.* Sorry, dude, you gotta keep up."

"Shit, that's good. Okay . . ." JP tries to think of green words. Mintastic? Shamrocky? Then, aloud: "*Verdigo.*"

"Well played," Dulin says. "Johnny, tell them what they've won."

JP laughs quietly. He thinks, I'm going to miss this verbal badminton. Then corrects himself: Of course he won't. He won't miss anything. That's the main attraction of calling a halt to this whole time-filling business—all the rigamarole of eating and breathing and worrying about when his body's going to break down.

But he's happy to see Dulin in such a good mood. He even encouraged JP to ask Gillian—who's still Gillian to him; Margaret's the name of the woman who should not, could not be on this tour—to see the sheep with them. She'd sat by herself during the morning's drive, so surely she was ready to get out for some fresh air. All this warmth and sunlight, it was as if the bus had transported them into summer. But no, Gillian turned him down, said she had work to do. Right now she's sitting at a table in the visitor center, a converted barn cleverly named "The Barn"—typing away.

The sheep they'd petted wandered downslope into a huddle of its fellows. Perhaps twenty of them, silently nuzzling and brushing past each other. What senses do they use to find each other, or keep track of the geography? How did they decide whether to cluster or wander alone?

"They can't be conscious," JP says. "Do you think they're conscious?"

Dulin shrugs. "They are if the Simmers want them to be."

"But they have no brains. What are they doing their thinking with?"

"I've always let other body parts do my thinking," Dulin says.

The Austrian honeymooners wade into the assembly of sheep, cheerfully arguing with each other about something. JP wonders if they're having the same problems he is with the animals' entire existence.

"What bothers me is the energy consumption," JP says.

"Oh yeah, me too," Dulin says. "What?"

"These things have no metabolism, unless they're getting energy from photosynthesis. Or maybe a little from gravity itself? The compression of the springs in their limbs, maybe, though I can't see how that works out, physics-wise. And then, how to coordinate those compressions and decompressions? There has to be some kind of DNA-like encoding system, or some shape-driven logic like proteins use. Decision-making ability without actual thought."

"Dude," Dulin says. "They're Impossibles. It's right there in the name."

"I know, but everything else follows the rules. Even if, deep down, we're ones and zeros, there are systems built on top of that code, systems on top of systems. They're internally consistent. But these animals—"

"You gotta stop worrying yourself about this stuff," Dulin says. "We're living in a magical universe now. You can't be the guy who says he can prove mathematically that dragons can't fly, while Smaug is flapping over Laketown, torching your house."

"Fine. But why make it so complicated?" JP says.

"Make what so complicated?"

"Everything. The sunlight and animals and soil. The bacteria in the soil. The atoms that make up the bacteria in the soil. Don't get me started on planets and galaxies."

"Alleged galaxies," Dulin says.

"It's just so *extra*," JP says. "If the Simulators wanted to fuck with us, they could have done it with a much simpler physics engine."

"You ought to ask Gillian about that."

"Okay, what's up with that?" JP asks. "Why are you suddenly Team Gillian?"

"I'm not," Dulin says. "But I'm also not *not* on her team. I googled the Atreus guy the Protags mentioned in the video—the one they're paying tribute to? He had some wacko main character disease. The proto-protagonist. He tried to plant a nail bomb under her desk at Boston U, but some cleaning lady walked in and the bomb went off. Both of them died."

"Oh my God."

"I still don't think she's telling us everything. What bad stuff did she uncover? She's a whistleblower, but we don't even know what whistle she's blowing. Or what she's blowing about? I got into this metaphor, and now I don't know how to get out."

"She hasn't told me any of that," JP says. He doesn't know exactly what she did on Project Red Clay, or what she uncovered. And he hasn't asked because she clearly doesn't want him to. It's possible that she'll never fully trust him, and he has to decide if that matters to him.

"Okay, fine," Dulin says. "But if she does turn out to be a bot controlled by the Simmers, I'll be really pissed."

He's joking, of course. No one believes in bots. At least, no one JP knows or follows on media. The affiliation bubble that he's a part of—middle-left "reasonables," the NPR-listening, cabernet-drinking, mostly white folks who practice meatless Mondays—have agreed that the belief that some people (almost always people in other countries) are not conscious is not just solipsism, but a form of racism.

"I think she'd be less afraid of getting killed if she was," JP says. "By the way, did you tell her about Brian Tumor?"

"Hmm?"

"Damn it, Dulin."

"I'm sorry! I didn't say much. I didn't tell her it was *back*. I just hinted that— Fuck, I don't know."

"She's treating me different."

"Different how?"

"She's being nice."

Dulin barked a laugh. "Okay, that's a sure sign."

"And Beth, too. She keeps giving me these pitying looks. How many people did you tell?"

"Beth-*Anne*. Just her and Gillian. And in my defense, I only told Beth-Anne because I wanted to get in her pants."

"How does that work?"

"I look like a good person! Look at me, taking a trip with my cancer-survivor best friend. It's fucking noble."

"I wouldn't say I survived it."

"Surviving, then. We're all terminally ill, brother. I told her that you're in remission and I'm just here to, uh, support your recovery."

"Isn't *Beth-Anne* also on this trip because she's accompanying her ailing mother?"

"Yes, we're the same. Except she actually is a good person."

And this, JP thinks, is not entirely a joke. Ever since he lost custody of his daughter, Marion, Dulin's been carrying his guilt around like diving weights. If he ever slipped free of them, he might accidentally float up into happiness. JP doesn't know where his friend's instinct for shame comes from. Is it because he grew up Catholic? Because everyone in the Marks family went into law enforcement, and he became a professional liar?

And yet, the guilt didn't stop Dulin from making crazy decisions or engaging in serious drinking. Or deciding to date seriously crazy women.

"This one's not going to hit you with a shovel?" JP asks.

"That only happened once."

The rabbi waves at them from upslope. The round little man heads down toward them like a bowling ball in a cardigan. One of the sheep is trotting behind him, keeping pace. JP waves back.

"Also, if Beth-Anne hits me with a shovel?" Dulin says. "I probably have it coming."

"I asked you not to have sex with anybody," JP says. "You didn't even make it to Day Three."

"I haven't done anything! Well, nothing past second base. That first night in the hotel, after you went to bed? We found each other in the lobby and just started talking. After a while the place emptied out, even the clerk was in the back office, and bam, we started making out like high school kids. And then last night it happened again. You and Gillian left the roadhouse, so we hung out for a while. You missed the tour guide doing some impromptu karaoke to Taylor Swift, by the way—that little girl was ripped. So anyway, Beth-Anne and I finished the night by making out in the hallway outside her door. I can't tell you how hot this lack of intercourse has been."

"Maybe you should not have sex more often," JP says.

"She's a Baptist, so I'm going to talk her into an abstinence pledge. Then when we break it, it'll be *super*hot."

The rabbi is a few yards from them when he starts talking. "Hello! They're about to serve lunch. I thought I'd round up the troops."

"It seems like you've picked up a friend," JP says.

The rabbi stops, glances back. The sheep also pauses. "Its been following me for the last half hour," the rabbi says. "Is this something they do? Regularly, I mean?"

"No idea," Dulin says.

"I suppose I'll ask the guest lecturer about it." The itinerary listed a lunchtime talk from a local expert in the Impossibles. "It's just very . . ." The rabbi's mouth tries out the shape of a few words.

"Adorable?" JP offers.

"Spooky," Dulin says.

The rabbi laughs nervously. "Adorably spooky, perhaps?" The sheep nuzzles his hip. "Um, have you seen Sister Janet?"

"We saw her heading toward the overlook," JP says. He points south, toward a spot on the lip of the trough.

"Overlook?" The rabbi blanches. "As in . . . cliff?"

"I think so," JP says.

"Oh no!" He jogs away, then twists around. "Thank you! See you—" The sheep is ambling after him. He makes an exasperated noise, and then hurries up the hill.

"Rabbi had a little lamb," Dulin half sings.

"What did he mean by 'oh no'?" JP asks. "She's not going to jump off, is she?" It doesn't seem likely.

"Maybe she's a flying nun."

"Did I tell you she thinks I'm hilarious?" JP says. "I said there ought to be a Simulator's Prayer. 'Our Simulator, who art in heaven . . .'"

"Except he's in reality, and we're in heaven," Dulin says. "Or at least in the cloud. Definitely a Ubik situation. How's the rest of it go?"

"That's all I've got."

"I'm on it." It wouldn't be the first time that something JP said showed up in one of Dulin's comics. One of the hazards of being the friend of a writer. Sometimes JP has the sense to specify, "Do not publish this."

The pair turn and start back uphill toward the Barn. JP immediately feels the burn in his thighs. This is depressing. He used to be able to hike for hours. Suzanne was always telling him to go on ahead, she'd catch up.

"So," Dulin says. "I wanted to ask you about something. An exchange of favors."

"Here we go."

"When we get to the hotel tonight, I was wondering if I could have the room for a couple hours. Don't look at me like that. I thought about just hanging a tie on the doorknob, but then realized it would be more polite to discuss it up front."

JP stops and looks at him. It's an excuse to catch his breath. "You're an adult, why don't you just rent another room?"

"For a couple hours? That seems pretty wasteful. And tawdry."

"*Tawdry*?" JP laughs. "Fine. And what are you offering me in exchange?"

"The same favor! For you and your girlfriend."

"What? I'm not going to— What are you talking about?"

"I'm hereby reversing my advice on Gillian. I think you should go for it."

"It," JP says flatly.

"Don't be obtuse, Jean-Pierre," he says in a faintly French accent. "There is but one *it* for men such as us."

"No. Definitely not."

"It'll be good for you! Even if, you know, it all ends badly. Maybe especially if it ends badly. Nothing gets your pulse racing like a little doomed romance."

"So you've decided this fits in with your secret plan."

"What secret plan?"

"This whole trip," JP says. "You want me to change my mind."

"I have no idea what you're talking about," Dulin says blandly.

"Now who's being obtuse?"

JP told Dulin months ago that he'd decided that he wasn't going to undergo the knife again, or subject himself to radiation. And rather than let the tumor decide when he would go, and how, JP would flip the switch himself. *Take that, Brian.* He hadn't yet figured out when he'd exit. There were still many things to take care of—the house, the 401(k), the many rooms of Swedish Death Cleaning. There were also goodbye letters to write. This trip, he now realizes, is its own kind of goodbye letter.

Dulin scrunches his face. Pushes a hand through his shaggy hair.

JP says, "Look, I've been having a great time. I've found it way more interesting than I thought I would. Like this whole Gillian thing. She came out of nowhere."

"I didn't plan on her," Dulin says.

"I know, but you kind of made her possible. You . . . exposed me to uncertainty. You pulled me out of the house and subjected me to all kinds of random variables."

"I do have a gift for chaos," Dulin says.

"And with all that randomness, some amazing moments are bound to happen. Like sticking my hand into a wireframe animal. Didn't see that coming. And I appreciate it."

Dulin smiles tightly. "But you haven't changed your mind."

JP wants to lie. He considers it. But Dulin would see through it.

"You're so fucking calm about this," Dulin says. "It's a little freaky. We should talk about this, man."

"Let's not ruin a perfectly fine day," JP says. "This afternoon at the distillery tour, we'll toast to the sheep, and then I'll pretend to lose my room key or something. But I don't need you to return the favor. I don't want to sleep with Gillian. She's not my girlfriend, and there's no romance."

"Back up— Toast? You mean you'll have a drink?"

"Why the hell not?"

Dulin claps JP on the shoulder. "My boy is back."

"We'll see." He starts walking. Chen Xing-Xing is up ahead, sitting on the ground with their back to one of the few trees in the meadow. From that spot they could gaze out on the flock, take in the mountains, or watch people mill about in the pavilion, but no, their eyes are of course on the book open across their lap. A pair of sheep seem to be regarding them.

"*That* guy's a bot, right?" Dulin says.

Before JP can answer, his phone starts buzzing in his pocket. Dulin's starts ringing too. They've crossed some invisible line where cell coverage has become available again.

JP looks at his phone. He doesn't recognize the number, picks it up anyway. "Hello?"

"JP, this is Deborah, Dulin's sister."

"Oh! Hey, Deb!" he says casually. Dulin's eyes widen.

"Is there a large, Irish dork in your vicinity? I've been trying to reach him."

"As a matter of fact— Here, let me give him the phone."

"Just a sec," Deb says. "How are you feeling? Dulin says you're in remission."

"I'm doing great. Well, as good as can be expected. I'm still on a few meds, but nothing unmanageable."

"Uh-huh." She sounds suspicious. "Well, it's good that you're getting out. This tour is a great idea. You're in Kentucky right now?"

Holy shit, how did she know they're in Kentucky?

"It's nice," JP says lamely. "The weather's great."

"I wanted to ask you about Margaret Schell. Dulin says she's a friend of yours?"

"Well, not really. She's a friend of Suzanne's. Was a friend, I guess." His heart's thumping.

"But you've known her a while."

"Um, not really. I mean, not well."

"JP, can I give you some advice? Don't cover for Dulin. He's not good at this, and he's just going to get us all in trouble."

Trouble? JP thinks. Then, *Us?*

"Just put him on," she says.

JP looks at Dulin. "Your sister wants to talk to you."

The big man grimaces. "She's left me like five voicemail messages," he whispers. He takes JP's phone. "Hi, Sis!"

He spends the next two minutes listening, nodding, and sputtering. Then he says, "Okay, I will," and hands the phone back to JP. Dulin looks stunned.

"What'd she say?" JP asks.

"Well, that was a first," Dulin says. "I've never heard Deb scared before."

"Scared of what?"

"She got reprimanded for looking into the case, and the people who were working on it got pulled. Word is, nobody at the FBI is assigned to it. It's another agency."

"Who?"

"That's the scary part. She won't say it over the phone—at least not to you or me. But almost everything AI is classified as top secret, right? National security, the full paranoid playbook. So whoever's in charge of *that* shit is now looking for your fake friend."

Maybe, JP thinks, he's been exposed to a little too much randomness.

"So," Dulin says. "What do you want to tell Gillian?"

The Rabbi Picks
Up a Follower

IIIIIIIIIIIIIIIIIIIIIIIIIIIIIIIIIIIIIIIIIIIIIIIIIIIIIIIIIIIIIIIIIIIIIIII

Zev Landsman is in a panic, and the sheep's making it worse. The creature's locked onto him like a bucolic missile. It follows him, matching his pace as he hustles across the mountain meadow and up the hill the men indicated. Why is it doing this? Did he pet it too hard? Or not enough? All he did was scratch the woolly bulb where its head should be, and then walk away.

He's huffing as he reaches the crest of the hill, sweat popping on his forehead. And there she is—Sister Janet! She's standing at the edge of a drop-off, gazing out over the valley. She looks calm, as if thinking deep thoughts about her book.

Did he really think she might have jumped? He feels silly. Unless... is she actually thinking deep thoughts about jumping? What if his approach is the thing that sends her over the edge?

The sheep bumps Zev's ass.

He gathers a breath. "Sister!" he calls. "Lunch!"

She looks back at him, and there's a long moment where her face is terrifyingly blank.

For the past few days he's been experiencing a growing dread: that the Sister Janet he knew before the Announcement is gone, and for the past seven years he's been corresponding with a wounded version of her, a soldier back from the war, hiding her PTSD. In person she's less able to hide. Yet when they had talked, he felt like he was disappointing her, failing to understand the full ramifications of what she was telling him.

"Take a look at this," she says.

Relief weakens his knees. He gathers himself and hurries over. The sheep follows. He stands beside her and is grateful she can't hear his heart thumping.

The ground falls away beneath their feet. A steep slope, but not enough to kill her if she jumped. It would be a long tumbling roll through indigo wildflowers, many of them knee-high and extravagant. He thinks, not for the first time, that he should learn the names of flowers. Perhaps if he knew their names, he would love them more, like familiar temple members.

The land rises to another ridge. An old barn—more dilapidated than "the Barn" where the tour group waits for them—sits on the ridge, far off to the right, huge white letters painted on its slanted roof: SEE GHOST CITY.

"Ah, we can never escape the ads," he says.

"No, look at the whales," she says. He's not sure what she means. Beyond the old barn's ridge is another ridge, and beyond that another and another. And then he sees what she sees: the terrain resembles a pod of green whales, breaching under sunlight, showing their round, green backs, as if caught in the moment before they dive below the surface.

"Beautiful," he says. And then, reaching for something else to say, adds: "The bees are lovely too." Real bees; their fat little bodies zip among the purple and blue flowers.

"I've been worried about them," she said. "The die-offs."

"I've read about that," Zev says. "Also, the problem with the bats, the white-nose disease? It's a relief to see them thriving." He's worried to be talking so much about death. Is this her frame of mind? Perhaps he should switch topics.

"I used to revel in the real," she says. The sadness in her voice alarms him.

"You don't, anymore?" he asks.

"This tour is making it difficult. These Impossibles, they keep—"

The sheep nudges its way between them as if it, too, would like to see the bees. Sister Janet looks down at it. "Do they usually do that?"

"I've been wondering the same thing," he says. He's grateful to the animal for the distraction. "Are you ready for lunch?"

"I'm not hungry. Go on without me."

"No!" he says, too forcefully. Then: "Sister Patrice is saving us a place."

"Of course she is," Sister Janet says.

He puts on a smile. "She does seem a little peeved that you're not using her secretarial skills."

"She said that to you?"

"A few grumbles," Zev says. "I think she's lobbying me. Letting me know that you're shutting her out, not allowing her to do her job."

"Ah."

"She also seems annoyed that you're more willing to talk to me than her." Which is ironic, considering how disconnected he feels from Sister Janet. The novice also seems concerned about Sister Janet's emotional state. Zev didn't confide in Sister Patrice about his own worries—that would be inappropriate—but her worries multiplied his own. His new worry was that he was climbing a logarithmic worry spiral.

"I've only myself to blame for this," Sister Janet says. "I told you how she came to be on this trip, didn't I?"

He doesn't know how *he* came to be on this trip, so it's no surprise he's unclear on why Sister Patrice is here. "You only said the council didn't want you to travel alone."

"I decided that I could use a kind of secretary. She's quite a fine writer. If I ever finish this book, I'll be able to use her as a beta reader. She writes equally well in both Spanish and English. Or as near as I can tell—my Spanish isn't up to it."

"Really?"

"She wrote an honors thesis in college applying Thomism to

the simulation. She pointed out so many clever parallels you'd have thought Aquinas saw the sim coming."

"Really?" he says again. He's never read Saint Thomas Aquinas and makes a mental note to start. A reading list is a common result of any discussion with Sister Janet.

"Good stuff. But then she didn't quite follow through, ends with a reaffirmation of God as truth, etcetera."

"Well, she's young," he says. "And also very old."

"That's it exactly. I think she thinks her real job is being my chaperone."

Zev laughs, but he's wondering, *Am I the chaperone?*

"She reminds me of a teacher I had in middle school," Sister Janet says. "I thought that old nun was ninety years old, but she was probably younger than I am now. The mixed dances we had with the boys' academy drove her into a state of high anxiety. And there was one girl that she watched like a hawk. Sheryl Mackenzie."

"Did she, ah, come from the wrong side of the tracks?"

"No, she was just the first girl in our class to get boobs."

Zev laughs. He's relieved—immensely relieved!—that she's making a joke, and delighted that she'd share it with him. There's hardly anyone else in his life who would use the word boobs in his presence, except, perhaps, his wife. And he's never been the manly sort of rabbi who hangs out with the old men at the JCC pool and gets to hear dirty jokes.

"In this story," he says, "you would be the Sheryl Mackenzie?"

"The sexiest girl in Our Lady of Victory Middle School."

He laughs again. Then thinks, Am I the horny middle school boy? Oh no. No no no! And then: Maybe? Intellectually speaking. They were Judeo-Christian scholars: she took the Christian and he took the Judeo, with the hyphen serving as a short bridge between them. He loved their discussions and adored her mind, but sex? No. Sex was not only off the table, but off the menu.

His wife, Keren, seemed to know this. She told him that she knew he'd never cheat on her, but the fact that she didn't consider it even a possibility buoyed him on most days and bothered him the rest. Her lack of jealousy regarding Sister Janet in particular struck him as both a gift and an act of marital apathy, like shiny wrapping paper around an empty box. When Sister Janet sent her invitation, Keren told him he should go, with no hesitation whatsoever. In fact, she seemed happy to be rid of him for a week.

"Perhaps we should head back," Zev says.

"So odd," Sister Janet says without turning. Her hand brushes the sheep's back. "I keep hearing 'Sheep May Safely Graze' in my head."

"*Schafe können sicher weiden*," Zev sings in his regrettably thin tenor. "*Wo ein guter Hirte wacht.*"

"Under the shepherd's watchful sight," she says with a sigh, and then seems to catch herself. "You have a nice voice, Zev. You should sing more often."

The flush of pleasure is discombobulating. "I'm all right at singing the Torah," he admits. "But other than that, no, no sense inflicting that on too many people."

"Lately I've been having trouble with the idea of a shepherd," she says. "I wonder if perhaps nobody's watching."

An ice cube slides down his throat and lodges behind his breastbone. This is exactly the kind of dire turn of thought he's been afraid of.

"Do you mean the Simulators?" he asks. "Or, ah . . ."

"Nobody." Sister Janet grimaces. "I'm sorry. You know what I'm like when I'm starting a book. It can put me in a mood."

He searches for something to say, and arrives at: "So how's it coming?"

"It's hard to think clearly when you're in a constant state of rage."

"But isn't rage motivating? For your writing, I mean." Her best writing was infused with righteous indignation. He's always admired the surety of her convictions and has often borrowed those for himself. Her reframing of capital punishment as the state's assault on bodily autonomy, for example, convinced him that control of one's body was as vital as soul freedom. It wasn't until she was reprimanded by her superiors that he realized she'd made an elegant pro-choice argument. He was already pro-choice; most Jews were. According to Rashi, the fetus only became a *nefesh*, a soul, when the head emerged, which struck Zev as a little late in the game. Should his people be basing such an important moral stance on a medieval French rabbi calling balls and strikes from between a pregnant woman's legs? But Zev had never been prompted to form a stronger argument for choice until he read Sister Janet's book. She'd handed him a theological argument that had the benefit of being potentially persuasive to people of all faiths.

"Perhaps rage is the wrong word," Sister Janet says. "Let's call it energetic despair. This simulation is a moral disaster."

"I'm not sure I follow."

"Think about climate change. Before the Announcement, people felt responsible for the planet. Well, some people. A minority, maybe, but the tide was turning. And now it's become a fake problem in a fake world—one more thing that the Simulators will take care of, or not, nothing we can do about it. Global warming, poverty, racial inequity, petro-wars . . . It's like we've all become right-wing evangelicals longing for Armageddon. Even the worst problems are just part of God's plan. We've abandoned all sense of stewardship."

"I don't think it's that bad," he says.

"What do you mean?" she asks sharply.

Oh no! "Only that, that . . ." He looks up at the distant barn to give his face something to do while he tries to figure out what, exactly, he does mean. He's never sure of what he thinks, in the moment. Sometimes he never arrives at a firm opinion. He is, by disposition, a ruminant forever chewing. Sometimes when he's writing a sermon, he has to imagine being someone who has a well-reasoned perspective, and then later deliver those lines like an actor.

"I just mean that, well, I'm not sure it would be different if we didn't know about the sim," he finally ventures. He glances at her to see how this is going over. "It seems like people have always been good at not taking responsibility."

"But before, nature would hold a gun to our heads," Sister Janet says. "We'd be forced to take action. Now we just assume the bullets aren't real."

"Yes, but . . . nothing's really changed, has it? If the sim doesn't end, we're still cooked. And it could be that the Simulators will step in and perhaps—"

"The Simulators aren't going to save us," she says bitterly. "They've not done a thing to make our lives better, and I can't see them starting now. We'll still suffer. We'll still die. The universe they've created is running on autopilot."

"Yes, but that doesn't mean that God has also abandoned us," Zev says, his voice rising. "Does it?"

Sister Janet turns toward him. Her gaze softens. "I don't know, Zev. That's what I'm here to figure out."

"Ah. Well." At least Sister Janet knew why she was here.

Sister Janet frowns. "Do you have something you want to talk about?"

"No, nothing really. Ready for lunch?"

"Zev. Please."

He smiles, uncomfortable. "I was just wondering . . ." He shrugs. "I'm not quite sure why you invited me along on this trip."

"Because you're my friend," she says.

"Yes, but we've never done anything like this. We see each other at conferences, we exchange emails—which I enjoy! But we've never, um, gone on vacation."

"It's a work trip," she says. "For me, anyway."

"I understand, but it still makes me wonder: If you've got Sister Patrice, why do you need me?"

She seems surprised by the question. "Zev, you're my sounding board."

"Ah. Of course."

She's frowning at him, and he realizes he's let his disappointment show in his face. Quickly he says, "Do you know the original meaning of the term? Sounding board? It was a literal board set up behind the pulpit, to reflect the priest's words."

"Interesting," Sister Janet says. She does not say, You're much more than a reflector, perhaps. Or, It's your ideas I'm interested in, Zev.

But then again, what ideas does he have, what opinions does he hold, that are firm enough to share?

He claps his hands. "Let's go eat, shall we?" He offers her his arm, and she takes it.

They walk down the hill at an angle until they meet the upward slope, and then start the climb toward the Barn. The sheep follows. And inside, Zev's sagging. If he's just here to reflect her thoughts back at her, what if those thoughts are terrible and sad? He wouldn't be pulling her back from the precipice, then; he'd be just another voice telling her to jump.

The Tour Guide Tries to ... What Was the Question?

|||||||||||||||||||||||||||||||||||||||||||||||||||||||||||||||||||||||

Aneeta Channar tries to keep her smile in place while Rabbi Landsman dithers over the biodegradable boxes—shall he have the chipotle chicken wrap, or Greek salad? The salad seems healthier, but he is on vacation, ha ha!

Aneeta says, "They're both . . ." The words come out as a croak. Her throat is cardboard, her eyeballs dry. Everything from the neck down feels chemically unstable, like a truck full of nitroglycerin on a rocky road. ". . . good."

One of the hollow sheep stands in the wide doorway. It seems to be looking at them, if you can say that about something with no eyes. Do they ever come in the Barn? She can't remember anything in the binder about that.

"He'll have the chicken," Sister Janet says. "I'll have the salad."

Aneeta hands them their boxes, and the two of them root through the cooler for drinks. "Water?" the rabbi wonders aloud. "Or root beer?" They're the last of the tour group to get their lunches, though there are a few boxes left over for the now-hospitalized Jim Mullins, his son, and Lisa Marie Montello. This morning, Aneeta was curled in her seat when Lisa Marie began bombing Aneeta's phone with text messages. She managed to read two of them before her eyes unfocused. There was nothing she could do for the girl by that point—the bus was a half hour down the interstate. These were problems for a future self, a post-hangover Aneeta.

Sister Patrice, the young nun in full costume, waves Rabbi Landsman and Sister Janet over to her table by the stage. The sheep enters the Barn, crosses the floor in front of Aneeta, and follows them to their seats.

What the fuck is happening?

Aneeta doesn't have time to process this. Most of the passengers are already done eating and they're looking at her to provide, well, guidance.

Agnes walks in from the parking lot. "Still no sign." The guest lecturer, a professor of biomechanics from Murray State University, is a half hour late. "You doing okay?"

"What did you *do* to me?" Aneeta asks.

Agnes chuckles and puts a hand on her shoulder. "It's part of the job, girl. You got to power through. I've got some ibuprofen in my bag. I'll get it while you fill time."

"What?"

"Tell them a funny story or two about the sheep—that's what Peter would do."

Tell a story? Aneeta can barely talk. All she wants is to go back to the bus and crawl under a seat. She flips through the binder. There's nothing about the Hollow Flock except a single page of discussion topics under the heading, "Did you know?"

. . . that the Hollow Sheep are the only animated and fully mobile Impossibles in North America? [Mention the Singing Vines of Da Nang and Nigeria Tumblers]

. . . that there are exactly 124 in the flock? [the "kidnapping" of two sheep and their unexplained reappearance]

. . . that the sheep do not eat, sleep, or defecate? [discuss Univ. of Kentucky isolation study]

...that the sheep seem to be indestructible and immortal? [see prank sheet, make disapproval clear]

What kidnapping? What pranks? There are no footnotes, no extra sheets, prank or otherwise. Why the hell did they not give her material to work with? She would have been better off ignoring the binder and just googling.

"I'm fucked," she says under her breath. She takes a long swig from her water bottle.

The stage is a recent construction of pale wood inside a century-old barn. The rest of the building is also a mix of old and new: the rafters are smudged and stained by years of use, but the walls are freshly painted and the floor is newly poured cement. Another authentic place, a site for real work with real animals, has become a Disney version of itself. A barn has become "The Barn."

Yet there is no microphone.

"Hello, everyone," Aneeta says. Her throat is raw. "I hope you enjoyed your meal."

A few people look up. Mrs. Neville calls out, "Turn up the volume."

Aneeta closes her eyes, tries to summon some energy, and it feels like squeezing an empty toothpaste tube. "Our guest lecturer," she says, louder, "is running a little late. I thought we could maybe share our impressions of the Hollow Flock before he gets here. Or . . . come up with questions?"

Rabbi Landsman raises his hand.

"What's the point?" Mrs. Neville says.

"The point?" Aneeta asks. Beth-Anne, sitting next to her mother, rubs a hand across her forehead. The rabbi lowers his hand.

"The sheep!" Mrs. Neville says. "What are they here for? What are they doing just walking around?"

"I . . ."

"What's the point of any of the Impossibles?" asks Marcus, the bearded Austrian.

"That's the wrong question," says his husband, Josef.

"It's the only question," Marcus replies.

"They're lessons," Sister Janet says quietly.

Aneeta only hears her because she's practically sitting at her feet. The sheep stands a few feet from her table, seemingly gazing at the rabbi, who's sitting next to her. Aneeta says, "Could you talk more about that, Sister Janet?"

"Why won't people speak up?" Mrs. Neville says to her daughter. Everyone hears that.

"They're lessons," Sister Janet says again, slightly louder. "Every Impossible teaches us something. The lesson of the Frozen Tornado is that matter is not real. The lesson of the Antipode is that distance is not real. The Geysers of Mystery teach us that, well . . ."

"Gravity is a bitch," Dulin says. Laughter ripples through the Barn. Gillian, sitting by herself at a far table, looks up from her laptop. The woman hasn't left the Barn since they arrived. Aneeta hasn't dared ask what she's working on.

"Possibly," Sister Janet says. She smiles faintly. "As for the Hollow Flock, they seem to be telling us—reminding us—that our bodies are not real."

"Ah," Rabbi Landsman says, nodding. Sister Patrice shakes her habit. Aneeta thinks, *I'd very much prefer if my body wasn't real right now.* She'd like to deflate it and lay it out in the sunlight until the vodka bakes out of it.

"I get what Sister Janet is saying," says the old white guy with the hat. His name is JP. "The sheep don't operate by any rules we understand. They're video game creatures—they move because the Simulators want them to move. They can't see, they can't think, they have no metabolism. They can't even move by normal rules of physics. They're just *declared* moving objects."

"That one's just standing there," says the white Octo man. Aneeta can't recall his name.

"I'd like to ask about that," the rabbi says. "Did anyone else—?"

"Our bodies *are* real," Sister Patrice says, interrupting him. "They follow all the rules of nature. One strange creature breaking the rules doesn't mean we have to call our own existence into question."

"Doesn't it?" Marcus asks. "Isn't that why we're all on this tour? We are being called to question everything. Maybe my body gets hungry only because the algorithm has declared it to be hungry."

"That's how I feel when my body gets hungry," one of the Octo women says. "I declare it." The other members of her group crack up laughing. The other Octo woman says in a mock-southern accent, "I do declare!"

"My body is my body, till the Lord gives me a new one," Mrs. Neville says. "We don't need to question 'everything.' God's already told us what we need to know. I don't understand why these nuns don't agree with each other. They should listen to the young one—what's your name, dear? You'd think the Catholics would know better, if they'd just read the Bible."

"Momma!" Beth-Anne says.

"Well, they don't read it, do they?"

Aneeta hears a car door slam. The professor's here. Thank God.

"The Austrian young man has a point," the Black octogenarian says. "This is exactly why we're here. We've got to question everything. You have to treat every day like it's the only one you've got."

"Holy shit," Dulin says. "Are you guys groundhoggers?"

The Black man grins. "We are today." His group laughs heartily.

Aneeta doesn't have the strength to enter into a Groundhogger versus Banger debate. Maybe the visiting professor can answer the question: Did the sim start with the Big Bang, or did it start later? If it started later, is the day/week/year repeating like the Bill Murray movie? And where *is* the professor? She can hear shouting outside.

"Just a moment," Aneeta says, and steps off the stage.

Lisa Marie Montello strides through the wide doorway. She points at Aneeta. "You left us!"

Agnes and Christopher follow behind the girl. Christopher looks like Aneeta feels.

"You— I thought you— " Aneeta struggles to form a coherent sentence. "Why aren't you at the hospital?"

"I sent you texts," Lisa Marie says. "Dozens of texts! And you didn't reply."

"You missed the bus," Agnes says. "You were in the hospital."

"How did you get here?" Aneeta asks.

"We had to take an Uber!"

"Wait a minute," Agnes says. "You took an Uber a hundred and twenty miles, across state lines?"

"It was actually four Ubers," Christopher says. His eyes look glassy.

"That must have cost a fortune," Agnes says.

"We're billing the tour company," Lisa Marie says. "You did this. You *abandoned* us."

"I'm so sorry," Aneeta says. "I—I didn't know."

"Don't apologize," Agnes says. "They want back on, but I told them, they broke tour rules back at the Geysers."

"*We* didn't break any rules," Lisa Marie says. "Christopher's father broke the rules. I was invited to participate—by park staff! Christopher did nothing but record it. Whatever Mr. Mullins did, that's on him. Kick *him* out."

Aneeta tries to process this. "But isn't he ... ? Chris, did you leave your father in the hospital?"

"Uhm ..."

"He'll be fine," the pregnant girl says. She's scanning the Barn, and suddenly she freezes. Aneeta follows her gaze. She's looking at Gillian—and Gillian is staring back at her. Laser battle, Aneeta thinks. If she steps between them she'll burst into flames. What is *that* about?

"He'll be fine," Christopher echoes.

"Really?" Aneeta says.

Lisa Marie snaps her focus back to Aneeta. "He told Christopher this morning, don't let my mistakes stop you. Go on with the tour. Go on without me."

Behind the girl, Agnes rolls her eyes.

"As the representative of Canterbury Trails, you know this is the fair thing to do," Lisa Marie says. Her tone has suddenly become hushed and intense, as if she's narrating a wildlife documentary. "This tour is a lifelong dream of mine. I want to see the Impossibles before my child is born, and Canterbury is the company, and you are the person, Aneeta, who can make my dreams come true. I know you want to be one of the heroes in this story."

The girl's iPhone is hanging from a short strap around her neck, resting atop her belly. The triple lenses on the camera back are tilted toward Aneeta's face.

Is she recording me? Aneeta thinks. Or, shit, live streaming me?

"Let me make some calls," Aneeta says. She forces a smile, and her skull seems to creak under the pressure. "Here at Canterbury Trails, we make great experiences possible."

Four Cedars Distillery

(tour and dinner)

The Nurse Chooses
Her Medicine

||||||||||||||||||||||||||||||||||||||||||||||||||||||||||||||||||||||||

Beth-Anne Neville stands with her mother on a metal platform in the Four Cedars Distillery, looking down into a large wooden vat burbling with yellow-brown "beer." The air is thick with the smell of apples. Her mother leans forward, and for a moment Beth-Anne fantasizes about pushing her mother in, like Augustus Gloop.

Instead she whispers into her mother's ear: "You're in the devil's workshop now, Momma."

She still can't believe her mother demanded to come into the distillery with the rest of the group. When Beth-Anne was ten, her father took the family to Myrtle Beach, a rare vacation outside Clay County, North Carolina. On the way, they stopped at a chain restaurant they'd visited back at home many times. Halfway through the meal, Beth-Anne's sister came back from the bathroom with a shocked look on her face. "Daddy," she said. "You've got to see this." Beth-Anne followed them into the next room, and there it was: a full bar, the first she'd ever seen. A stunning number of liquor bottles stood on a set of shelves, *lighted* shelves, like brazen hussies. Her father turned red-faced and marched out, leading his wife and daughters back to the car, where Momma burst into tears and wailed, "How could Ruby Tuesday do this to us?"

That became a family punch line. The car gets a flat—*how could Ruby Tuesday do this to us?* Septic tank backed up? Ruby again. Beth-Anne and her sister told the story of the Great Restaurant Betrayal many times over the years, always getting a laugh. It even killed at the potluck after Dad's funeral.

Momma waves a hand dismissively. "This," she says, looking up at the complicated arrangement of vats and pipes, "is cultural."

No, *this*, Beth-Anne thinks, is a shocking turnaround. Her mother's always been worried about what people—especially her congregation—would think of them. God forgives and Jesus saves, but the church never forgets. A phantom jury follows her around, quietly conferring on each new crime by the Neville family, especially those committed by her daughters. Perhaps now, in Momma's golden years, she's learning to ignore their whispering, even if she hasn't dismissed the jury entirely.

Or maybe she's just enjoying being ornery.

Dulin is there to help Momma down the stairs, one slow step at a time. She grips Dulin's beefy bicep, talking nonstop about her cousin who used to make moonshine, a story she's never shared with strangers. She's flirting with him, Beth-Anne realizes. Momma probably thinks the big galoot has been following them around the distillery because he enjoys *her* company.

Dulin gracefully lowers Momma into her wheelchair, then takes a position behind the handlebars. "Ready, ladies?"

No, Beth-Anne thinks, I'm certainly not ready. What the hell is she doing, messing about with this unserious man?

There's something up with him today—or rather, something up with Dulin, JP, and Gillian. The woman had evidently experienced a manic episode, because she showed up at the bus this morning with her Afro chopped off and dyed blue. Then at the Hollow Flock, just before they got on the bus to the distillery, the three of them got into a serious conversation that left Gillian upset.

The distillery employee, a perky brunette girl who looks too young to drink, talks the tour group through the distillation process, pointing out the stainless-steel column stills and doublers. What Beth-Anne ought to be doing at her age is finding a stable man with a stable income, not this certified *dude* who's ten years older than she is and firmly committed to his Robert Plant curls. Oh, it's clear those curls used to work for him. He carries himself like he's the handsome rocker he used to be. Fooling around with him in lobbies and hotel corridors is the most fun she's had since Carl walked out. But Dulin Marks is a stray she'll never bring home. If she keeps feeding him, it's going to lead to trouble.

The brunette ushers them into the cask room. They maneuver around a set of portable train tracks used to roll the barrels out, and walk between the rows of oak barrels. It's all as tidy and well-lit as a Pinterest photograph, and pregnant girl keeps posing as the red-headed boy snaps pictures. Supposedly she's an "influencer," but who she's influencing and how is a mystery.

The distillery guide prattles on about the delicious limestone-rich water, the proportions of corn and rye and barley, the five proprietary yeast strains. The bottling happens in another facility miles away, which means there's only one last step in the bourbon process to experience. She ushers them into a large room with a great curved bar.

"Finally!" Dulin Marks says. "The tasting room!"

Beth-Anne says, "You going to have a drink, Momma?"

"I just might."

Beth-Anne snorts.

One wall of the room is a bank of tall glass doors that look out on a stone patio and the green hills beyond. Two of the doors have been pushed open, admitting a spring breeze. Dulin steers Momma toward a table by the windows that's already occupied by JP and Gillian. Those two skipped the tour, and by the look on their faces, they've been marinating in bad news.

"Here you go," Dulin says to Momma. Beth-Anne's pretty sure her mother's never shared a table with a Black woman—at least not a small table. It'll be good for her.

"Learn a lot?" JP asks. There's nothing but a water glass in front of him.

"I may start making my own bourbon now," Momma says, and laughs. Beth-Anne thinks, *Who is this woman?*

Dulin points at JP. "You're in, right? You promised me."

"One drink," JP says.

"To start," Dulin says. He walks to the bar to get them samples. Both Neville women watch him cross the room.

"He's no Carl," Momma says.

"Thank the Lord for that," Beth-Anne says.

Momma used to fawn over Carl, cook him all the dishes Beth-Anne never learned to make. No wonder he left, Momma'd said. How could Beth-Anne expect to keep a man if she couldn't even fry a catfish? These days, neither of them cooked. Chronic pain had driven her mother out of the kitchen, and Beth-Anne refused to take up the spatula. Maybe I'll get back to it after we visit the Avatar, her mother kept saying. For nearly a year she's talked about nothing but the Avatar Saugat Zin and his healing services. Beth-Anne refused to drive her across the country for that nonsense, but then Momma found the Impossibles tour with its hefty senior discount. I'll start cooking again, she'd say, and then Carl will come back. As if that would be the difference, that he'd come running as soon as he smelled her shrimp and grits.

The tour group returns from the bar, many carrying holed trays with shot glasses nestled in them. Aneeta, the tiny tour guide, waves off all offers of drinks and tells them the bus is leaving in ninety minutes.

"I like her," Momma says. "She doesn't have an accent at all."

"*Momma*," Beth-Anne says. Aneeta's not ten feet away.

"What's that look for? That's a compliment. I can't even give compliments?"

Dulin catches Beth-Anne's eye, and then raises a hand. "Ladies and gentlepeople!" The group's attention swings to him. "I'd like to say a short prayer."

"Oh, that's nice," Momma says.

Dulin can command attention, give him that. Even Xing-Xing lifts their eyes from their book.

"Please, raise your glasses," Dulin says. Momma frowns at her glass with its inch of bourbon. A sip is one thing, but joining in a toast, well, that's more public than Momma's used to.

Dulin lifts his eyes to the ceiling and intones:

> *"Our Simulator, who art in reality,*
> *hallowed be thy game.*
> *Your kingdom runs—"*

JP groans. One of the Octo women giggles.

"Join in if you know it," Dulin says. He clears his throat and continues:

> *"Your kingdom runs, in simulation,*
> *an earth that's not quite heaven.*
> *Give us this day our daily lives,*
> *and forgive us our glitches,*
> *as we forgive those who glitch against us.*
> *Lead us not into game over, but deliver us from bugs.*
> *For thine is the server, the power supply, and the software,*
> *forever and ever..."*

He raises his glass higher.

> *"...until you pull the plug."*

Then: "Sláinte!"

"Prost!" shout the Austrians.

"Clever boy," JP says.

The young nun, Sister Patrice, scrapes her chair back. She stands up, looks at Dulin with a dead-eyed expression, and walks out.

"Yikes," Dulin says under his breath.

"Don't mind her," Beth-Anne says. She tips her glass, and the whiskey slides down her throat like flaming honey. Her mother glares at her.

"What, Momma?" Beth-Anne says. "It's cultural."

Her mother hasn't touched her glass. Beth-Anne realizes she's furious about Dulin's prayer.

But all around them the drinking starts in earnest. Nobody's driving, after all—the bus will take them to their next meal and off to bed. It's warm in the sunlight, and the open doors are admitting a cool breeze.

"Look, there's a sheep," one of the Octos says.

"What?" the rabbi says. He stands up. One of the hollow sheep is standing on the stone wall of the patio, its head pointed at them. "Are they supposed to leave the mountain?"

The two honeymooners pull up seats on the other side of Dulin. The one with the glasses, Josef, says, "Have you written anything I'd know about?"

"That's a terrible question to ask a writer," Dulin says. "But I'm pretty sure the answer is no."

"I've seen several of the Marvel movies."

"They're terrible," says Marcus, the bearded one.

"They're exuberant," Josef says. "There's nothing wrong with exuberance."

Dulin says, "Back when I worked for them they weren't doing any movies, and they were going bankrupt—and this was before the Announcement wrecked the whole comic business."

"Tell them how you got fired," JP says.

"You got fired?" Beth-Anne asks.

"No one gets fired in comics; they just stop taking your calls."

"He shouldn't have made fun," Momma says, still mad about the prayer. Her good mood has evaporated. This isn't surprising; old age and chronic pain have made her mother as volatile as a teenager.

"It's still out there," the rabbi says dolefully. He's gazing at the sheep. Gillian stands up and slides her laptop into her courier bag. She looks mad too. Why's everyone getting bent out of shape?

"You can't leave yet," Dulin says. "You still haven't heard my Irish brothers joke. This is the perfect occasion."

"I'm sure it's great."

What the hell's her problem? Beth-Anne thinks. The woman's been on edge since she joined the tour, watching everybody like they're shoplifters at the Dollar Store, talking to no one except JP and Dulin. Like those boys are her dogs and she'll let you pet 'em if you're nice.

"I'd like to hear it!" one of the Octos says.

JP shrugs. "It's not bad."

"Maybe another time," Gillian says coldly. JP gets up with her and she says, "No. Please."

"I need to ask a favor," JP says. "And, uh, there's something I need to tell you."

"Jesus," she says, and JP follows her through the doors.

Beth-Anne wonders if they're hooking up.

"Another round?" Dulin says, trying to cover the awkwardness.

"Another round!" one of the Austrians says.

"And you, my dear?" Dulin asks Beth-Anne. "One more?"

"Well, since you asked so nice."

A coyote smile slips onto his face. He hustles back to the bar. And when Beth-Anne turns back to the table, her mother is glaring at her.

"What's the matter with you, Beth-Anne?"

What's the matter with Beth-Anne is that she's gotten laid exactly once since Carl left her, seven years ago. The Announcement hit her husband like a bucket of ice water. He walked around for days wearing a dazed expression, saying nothing. When he came from work, he'd turn on the news, soak up other people's words, fill his eyes with the crazy images beaming in from across the world. A waterfall flowing backward. A shape-changing mountain. She'd put a hand on his arm, and he'd jump as if he'd been bit. Leave the house for hours, come back late, and turn on the TV again.

And then, one day, he came home from work and started packing. She asked him what was going on. Carl had always been a man of few words. It only took him three to tell her their marriage was over.

"Keep the dog," he said. Then he moved across town and into the house of the Clay County Tax Assessor. A man. Who was ten years younger than Beth-Anne.

Fuck you, Ruby Tuesday.

"He shouldn't have made fun," her mother says again.

"What are you talking about, Momma?"

The old woman stares daggers at Dulin's back. "He shouldn't have said that. Praying to the—whatever it is."

"That was just a joke."

"I shouldn't have to explain this to you," Momma says. "Now take me back to the bus." She puts a hand on the table to push her chair back, but the wheels are locked and the table shakes. Glasses topple.

"Momma! Stop it!"

Suddenly Dulin's back from the line. "Let me help you," he says to her. He stoops to unlock her chair's wheels, and the woman slings an arm backward, missing him.

"No thank you!" she says.

Dulin backs away, looking confused.

"Momma's decided to take offense about the Simulator prayer," Beth-Anne explains flatly.

"Mrs. Neville, I'm so sorry!" Dulin says. He seems genuinely apologetic. "It's just a joke."

"There'll be a day when the joking is over," Momma says. "There'll be a day. And then all your deeds will be known."

"Mrs. Neville—"

"I know where I'm going when I die," she says. "Do you?"

"No," Dulin says seriously. "I have no idea."

"Beth-Anne, take me back to the bus."

"Momma—"

"Take me back."

Beth-Anne stares at her mother, and thinks that, forever and forever, until they pull the plug, any joy she finds will have to be stolen under cover of darkness, out of her mother's sight.

She backs her mother away from the table, pushes her toward the exit. JP walks in wearing a frown—and then sees them coming and stops to hold the door open. He has an instinct for decency, that man. He makes her trust Dulin a little more than she might.

And here the big man comes, calling her name, carrying her coat that she's left on her seatback. He bends close to her so her mother won't hear.

"I'm so sorry," Dulin says.

"It isn't you. She gets like this."

Dulin looks at JP, and his friend nods.

"What?" Beth-Anne asks.

"I've made arrangements," Dulin says quietly. "If you're amenable."

She feels a twist in her stomach. A schoolgirl squirm.

She knows that there's no future with this man. The bus trip is an artificial environment, a floating bubble that allows all of them to be different people than they are at home. Traveling under false passports. For the past couple of days, she's been able to pretend that she's not just an RN who works from home (her mother's home), evaluating medical requests for an HMO and taking care of a geriatric mother and an even more geriatric Irish Setter. She can play dress-up as the kind of woman who just might fuck an unserious man.

This shaggy, verbally clever reprobate is looking at her with a gleam in his eye. Has he no sense of the future? The trip is going to end, and the bubble will pop. The sooner they all stop pretending, the easier the return will be. Smarter to cut this nonsense short before it gets out of hand.

"I'm amenable," she says. She finds his hand, gives it a quick squeeze. "I'm all kinds of amenable."

The Professor Babysits

||||||||||||||||||||||||||||||||||||||||||||||||||||||||||||||||||||||

The hotel room of Margaret Schell has been invaded. She's trying to work, but in the mirror above the desk she can see JP lying atop the second bed, hands behind his head. He keeps smiling at her from under the brim of his cap.

She tries to ignore him. Looks down at her screen.

DEVILS_TOOLBOX.md

3.2.4 Incremental Backups and Subjective Immortality

[::AN, ::DD, ::EF]

The backup system exists and can be hijacked. But given storage constraints and the need for innocuous-seeming files, we'll need a compression and shard strategy that maintains personal continuity. This one's tough. Below are three options I see now, but we're going to need custom code and good programmers:

There are hundreds of tools in the Toolbox, and before she got on the bus, none of them were documented. She's been frantically commenting the API and ginning up quick-and-dirty examples, as well as creating the metadata that will make the archive searchable and mappable. Each tool and its major options has to be ranked from ::AN (Absolutely Necessary) to ::PU (Probably Useless), and cross-ranked in risk from ::DD (Dangerous) to ::MH (Mostly Harmless). She's also throwing in tags for everything she can think of: ::EF (Ethically Fraught), ::EV (Evil), ::PS (Probably Stupid). Whenever possible, she's linking to the avalanche of data generated by the project: white papers, architectural diagrams, analyses, project plans, budget reports, test code—all the furious output of mad scientists in a mad world. It's an insane amount of work, and only the promise of the Tunnel gives her any hope of finishing it before she reaches Ghost City.

Or before they arrest me. The thought is too melodramatic to say aloud.

This afternoon, when she walked out of the distillery, JP told her that the FBI wasn't looking for her—but other people in the government were. She has no doubt who they are, but it's a mystery how much they know about her escape. Have they found her car? Do they know where she's heading?

"I think it's time," Jean-Pierre says.

"For what?" she asks warily.

"For you to show me what you're working on."

"Pass."

"Come on, you've been typing away the whole trip." She doesn't answer. He sits up with a grunt. Picks up the unfortunately open bottle of small-batch bourbon, pours a finger into the hotel drinking glass. "And didn't you quit this secret project? I thought one of the benefits of blowing the whistle on your bosses is that you didn't have to keep working for them."

JP and Dulin still think she's trying to expose Project Red Clay. She hasn't disabused them of that. "I'm documenting," she says truthfully. "Laying out a roadmap so people can make sense of everything I'm giving them. It's pretty technical."

"Cool. I could help with that," he says.

"No thanks."

"But I'm a programmer," he says. "I've programmed. I used to build robots."

"You mentioned that."

"Killer robots. Absolutely killer."

Good lord, the boy is buzzed. It's been three hours since they left the Four Cedars, with a stop for biscuits and barbecue that could have soaked up the alcohol in his system, if he hadn't started replacing it with his gift shop bottle. She couldn't eat a thing—her stomach's in turmoil—and she's never been a stress drinker. If she was, she'd be in liver failure by now.

"How long are you exiled from your room?" she asks.

"Shouldn't be long now," JP says. "Then again, Dulin's been popping Cialis like they're Tic Tacs, so . . ." He pushes himself off the bed.

She clicks on a different tab, hiding the README file. Nothing but code is visible now. He leans over her shoulder to peer at the laptop screen.

"What language is that?" he asks.

"Don't worry, you haven't heard of it."

"Oh, a *hipster* language. It looks like Erlang."

"You know Erlang?"

"Great for robotics. I built some of our early machines with it. Lightweight messages, handles hardware failures really well. Did I mention I built robots?"

"You might have. Well, this isn't Erlang, not anymore. We call it Merlang." She's pretty sure he can't do anything with this information, so she decides to explain. "We forked it, added a chunk of new syntax, and wrote our own binding to MPI."

"Merlang . . . ?"

"Because it's a hybrid. And breathes underwater."

"Ha! So you wrote your own compiler, too?"

"Started in Erlang, but now it's in pure Merlang. We also wrote our own VM to run it in."

"Also in Merlang?" He shakes his head. "I've never met anyone who wrote their own virtual machine."

"Had to," she says, trying to sound nonchalant. The whole M-family—the language, the custom compiler, and the VM—are key to her plan. For years she's wanted to tell someone how clever she's been . . . and now she still can't. "It's a super-specific problem set."

"You know what's funny?" JP leans against the desk, inches from her. The whiskey is fragrant. "We're code writing code."

"You're right on top of me."

"Ah! Sorry." He hops up, looks around as if he's forgotten where he is, then discovers the glass in his hand. "Hmm. I need to stop drinking."

"That'd probably be a good idea."

"What you're doing seems like a lot of work," he says, and she realizes he's hopped back to languages and VMs. "People must have been working on AGI before you. I don't understand why you need a whole new language, a new . . . everything?"

Jesus, he's being so *chatty*. It may have been a mistake to let him into the room. When he asked to hang out for a couple hours, she thought, Well, he's been nothing but a gentleman so far. Plus, he's shorter than she is and thirty pounds lighter, including a few ounces of brain tumor. Surely she could take out a man with cancer. And, she thought, if federal agents break down her hotel room door, or the Protagonists snipe her through the window, she wanted a witness. She doesn't want to disappear without a trace. She doesn't want the work on her laptop to disappear, either.

"Nobody was doing what I thought we should be doing," she says. "Not really."

"Okay . . ."

"Look, my whole career I've been trying to figure out how the brain actually works. How connections get made or broken, how learning happens or fails, how orchestration and coordination comes together or falls apart . . . I was trying to cure neurological disorders— Alzheimer's, autism, schizophrenia . . . And before the Announcement, I could barely get funding. All the AI money was going to LLMs and chatbots."

"But then—boom—the Announcement."

"Yep. And suddenly the government was interested in me and my approach. This was their shot at getting to real AI, symbol manipulation, the whole enchilada."

"But what was your—oh! Oh!" He's looking up at her like an A+ student. A drunk student holding a glass of bourbon.

"Yes, Jean-Pierre?"

"You're doing whole-brain emulation. That's it, isn't it!"

Damn is he quick. Even drunk. Edowar is the brightest person she's ever known, but Edowar never drank, and so never had to operate under the influence of performance-dehancing drugs.

"You're not trying to hack an AI together," he says. "You're going to map the whole brain and just . . . run the sucker. Like that guy in the EU. Markram."

"This is nothing like Henry Markram," she says. Years before the Announcement, Markram got the EU to pony up a billion euros and promised to use the money to create a simulated brain in ten years. It didn't go well. Markram was thrown off the project two years later, with no digital brain in sight, though the group later managed to mock up part, just a part, of a mouse brain.

"He should never have promised a timeline," she says. "What he was trying to do is thousands of person-years of work, without those thousands of persons—or anywhere near the money that would be required."

"But how is that even doable?" He waves a hand, and it's a miracle whiskey doesn't slosh onto the carpet. "Even with, you know . . ."

"The full backing of the US government?"

"Right! So much basic research."

"So much," she says. "First you need to slice up a brain and scan not only every neuron, but every astrocyte and glial cell, too. That's a fleet of electron microscopes for a granular scan." She's not telling him anything that's not public knowledge. "Then you need to map out every connection between neurons, and then find out which synapses are excitatory or inhibitory, the strength of the connections between them, the noisiness of their interactions. You'd need to know the dynamical properties of every axon, synapse, and dendrite. And we haven't even gotten into how to model neurotransmitters. Scientists just mapped *C. elegans* a few years ago."

"The worm thing, right," JP says.

"Nematode. It has 302 neurons. Humans have a hundred billion."

"Okay, it sounds like you're saying it's impossible, but the look on your face is saying it's not."

"What I'm saying is that it's even harder than what I was saying."

"So double impossible?"

"The brain isn't enough," she tells him. "There's no human mind without all the regulation systems in the body." How does she explain this to a drunk engineer without triggering a hundred questions? Each human body contains miles of nerves, a tidal sea of hormones, and thirty trillion cells that are each carrying on tiny chemistry experiments. And then there's the enteric nervous system in the gut, the so-called "second brain," which contains 100 million neurons, the vast majority of which send messages *to* the brain, not receive them. Without that elaborate system of sensation and feedback and chemical regulation, the brain simply didn't function. And then there was the whole microbiome. "Without all those systems, you don't end up with a mind that thinks at all like us."

"You want to emulate the *entire body*?" JP says. "Even if you got the data, that model's got to be huge. Is there a computer that'll even run it?"

He's hit on the first objection Margaret raised when she joined Project Red Clay. He's some kind of alco-savant.

"How many exaflops would you need?" he asks. "The Department of Energy machine, their Cray supercomputer, barely got past one exaflops."

"Completely inadequate," she says. "We'd have to go way past exa. Ten to the forty-fourth ops per second, give or take."

"So that's . . . what comes after exa?"

"Zetta, then yotta. You'd need a couple hundred yottaflops."

"Damn! That's a lotta flops." He sits on the side of the other bed—the one she'd been saving for herself—and takes another sip. *Make yourself at home*, she thinks.

"Nothing's going to happen here," she says.

"What?"

"I'm in love with my husband."

"I'm not trying to— That's not why I'm here. Dulin—"

"I just want to be clear."

"Totally clear. Also, agreed. Also also . . ." He seems to have lost the thread. "I thought you were divorced."

"It's complicated."

"Ah. I get it. I'm also in love with an unavailable spouse. So what happened?"

Jesus Christ. How much could she tell him without hurting Edowar and Adaku? "We didn't break up because we didn't love each other," she said. "I just— We decided it would be better if we lived apart." *Because I'm a landmine.*

"Far apart. Okay." He stares at his glass. "So how long have you . . . ?"

". . . been divorced?"

"No, till you can build it. Back at the Geysers, you said it would be quick, but to go from DOE's Cray machine to this—how long would that take?"

"I need to get back to work."

"Right. Sorry." She turns back to her laptop. Behind her, the thunk of the bottle. He's pouring himself another glass. "I think I've lost my off switch," he says, almost to himself.

Jesus Christ. She doesn't reply.

"What's the Moore's law on a machine like that?" he says. "Ten years? Fifteen?"

She sighs. Swivels back to face him. "Forget Moore's law. High-performance computing's all about parallelization, not transistors on a chip. And since the Announcement, the government's been throwing everything they've got at these supercomputers, and speed's doubling every eight months. This is the new space race."

"Wait, so . . . is this already built?"

She thinks, the Protagonists already know about Project Red Clay, so the location of the HPC isn't a secret anymore.

"It's in Ohio, on the grounds of an old . . . power plant."

He's taken off his cap, scratching at his gray hair, and this is her first clear look at the surgery scar. He's kept a hat on every minute he's been around her. She's surprised to see that the scar's barely visible, a faint, graceful double arc near his hairline. If she hadn't been looking for it, she'd have never noticed it.

He sees her looking at his forehead, and his pale cheeks flush. He pulls the cap back on. Margaret looks at her knees.

JP says, "I'm going to be fine, by the way. Snipped it right out. A miracle of modern medicine."

She scans her memory for a list called Polite Things to Say to Cancer Survivors. No results.

"So you're not dying," she says.

"Oh, I didn't say *that*. I said I'd be fine. And I will be—either way."

"That's philosophical of you."

"Pretty mature, isn't it?" His smile is sweet. "I've had a good run. Other people have had it worse. So, no complaints from me."

She isn't buying it. "Live or die, doesn't matter to you?"

"It's not like I get to opt out of the process. None of us are exempt."

Not true, Margaret thinks. She knows of one person who's gotten a pass.

"The only thing that annoys me . . . why'd they go to the trouble of making it so complicated?"

"Who, the Simmers?"

"Why create a brain at all, when we now know it doesn't matter?" he says. "We thought they did, before the Announcement, but now we've got crazy shit like the Hollow Flock. All their neural processing's being done somewhere else. I mean, what the fuck?"

He's much more swear-y when he's buzzed. She likes it.

"Maybe the nun was right," she says. "Every Impossible is a lesson. The sheep move and think and follow rabbis around—"

"Silly rabbi—" JP says.

"—even though they're basically just Slinkies."

"—tricks are for kids," he says, agreeing. He drains his glass, sets it carefully on the carpet, and falls back onto the pillows, arms spread. "We're fucked."

"Basically."

"Why do we have neurons at all, then?" he says to the ceiling. "Why brains? Fuck, why brain *tumors*?"

Margaret takes a deep breath, holds it.

"You have to admit," JP says. "It's kind of ridiculous."

"It is ridiculous," she says. "And unfair."

He lifts his head, looks at her down the length of his torso. "So why did they do it? Make all this elaborate ... wiring and tubery and whatnot."

She's been told the answer, but she's got no proof, so she keeps it to herself. "It's a mystery."

JP's head falls back. "It's just so arbiterry—heh—arbi-*trary*."

"I'm sorry," she says.

"I just don't want to leave ... owing anybody," JP says. "Beholden. I know this isn't making sense."

"I get it."

"When my time comes, I just want to slip out the back door, an Irish goodbye. Fortunately, Suzanne and I never—" He raises his head. He's like a toddler, fighting sleep. "So how old's your daughter?"

"Thirteen." *There's no Margaret who's there to see her daughter's fourteenth birthday.*

"She's got to be proud of you," JP says. "I mean, both ways. Figuring all this stuff out, and, you know, taking a stand." His head falls back again. "Though I *still* don't know what it is you're taking a stand against. What terrible thing is the project up to?"

Margaret gets up from the chair and stands over him. "JP. Listen to me. She doesn't know anything about what I'm working on. Either way."

He blinks at her. Her tone was harsher than she intended.

"My ex doesn't either," she says. She needs JP's soused brain to remember these facts. Someday, when the officials come to interrogate him, he'll need to repeat them. "He's completely in the dark."

Lying, she realizes, has its own taste.

"Okay?" she asks.

"Okay," he says.

She goes back to the desk, switches to the README, and tries to remember where she left off. A minute passes. She looks back, sees that JP's eyes are closed, his mouth agape.

"Thank God," she says quietly. She can't take any more questions. What terrible thing is the project up to? Nothing the Simulators haven't already done to us—which is everything.

•   •   •

The government came for her, just as Aunty Tim predicted. Five months after that kitchen table conference, a Black man in a gray suit showed up in her office on campus and showed her an ID from a government agency that Aunty Tim had told her about, but that she wasn't sure existed.

"I'm Chet from CET," he said, pronouncing the acronym to rhyme with his name. He handed her a card. His full name was Chet Wilcox and his organization's full name was The Center for External Threats, which she found both melodramatic and internally threatening. "The card's brand-new because we're brand-new," he said. CET, he explained, was not a stand-alone agency but a cross-disciplinary working group resourced by multiple government agencies.

"Sounds complicated. What can I do for you, Chet?" She knew what he was going to say but had to wait until he said it.

"I'd like to offer you a job, Dr. Schell."

His pitch was simple, almost jingoistic: Other nations were trying to figure out how to manipulate the simulation. They were trying to communicate with the Simulators to gain an advantage, or—and this was the big one—escape.

"Escape our simulation?" she said. "And go where?"

"Into the real world."

"That's not possible."

"Why not?" asked the man with the Dr. Seuss name. He didn't sound offended, only curious to hear her thoughts.

"Because we're code," Margaret said. "You really want me to spell this out?"

"Please."

She explained how, even if we somehow found a flaw in the sim, some overlooked crack in the firewall, we had no idea how to move our code through it and where it would go. There would have to be hardware on the other side to run us. And once we were there, would we even be able to make sense of that world? It was impossible to know what laws of physics were running in the real universe. Planck's constant could be different. Gravity could be different. Gravity itself could be a mathematical construct that only applies to bodies here, in their simulation.

"The only way we're getting out of this sim," she told Chet from CET, "is if the Simulators pluck us out of it and install us in another one." Or just grant us the ability to move between them, she thinks. Let us bop through iterations like a barefoot tourist with a Eurail Pass. "We'll never be part of the real world. We'll never even see it, unless they download us into something like a robot body."

"You've thought a lot about this."

"Of course I have. I can see no way, logically, for our code to run in the real world. There's no escape."

"I agree with you," he said. "It doesn't make any sense. But my bosses have asked me to try. And we have to try, don't we?"

"Do we?"

"We have no choice. Every nation in the world is spinning up research arms. Nobody knows how the rules work. Nobody knows what's possible and what's truly impossible. Can we bend the rules of physics? Does the sim have exploitable bugs? We have to do some basic science to figure that out. And the United States can't afford to come second in finding out, not in any aspect."

The CET, he said, was a kind of work-from-home Manhattan Project, bringing together anyone who might be able to help: specialists in AI, high-energy physics, neuroscientists. "And you," he said with a smile. "You tick a lot of boxes."

"I don't see how I can help you with any of this," she said. "I study neurological disorders."

"Oh, I think you can help us quite a bit. And so do the people I work for. *Embodied Intelligence* is influential."

"Nobody read that book."

"The right people have." He leaned forward. "The first step is to build our own simulated human in a simulated world. We need to understand how it's done."

"Little risky, don't you think?"

"How so?"

"Building a sim within a sim," she said. "It could be one of their boundary conditions. As soon as we start adding one—*bleep!*—we're deleted."

"I think there's a low chance of that. Less than ten percent."

"That's a high percentage for possibly ending the world."

"We wouldn't be human if we didn't try. The Simulators have to expect that. And it's the obvious move. Every civilization of a certain level is going to try for it, if only so it'll help them figure out how to save themselves. If you want to learn how to build a canoe, pretty soon you have to just build the effing canoe."

Or an ark, she thought.

"You've thought more about how to do this than anyone," Chet said. "You've started writing your own computer language to do it. It's almost like you knew years ago we were in a sim, and were prepping for it. Of course, that got you some attention from the conspiracy theorists out there. And you're still a target. Other extremists have picked up on Atreus's 'Main Character' manifesto."

"So, I'm on a kill list?"

"You're not on *a* kill list, Dr. Schell, you're on a dozen of them. And we can provide protection." He told her they'd "fortify" her campus lab, monitor for active threats, and even provide bodyguards if required. "We can also help relocate you to San Francisco."

"What? Why?"

"So you can be near your daughter. I hear your ex-husband is moving there with her as soon as the divorce is final."

That shook her. How much did they know about her personal life?

"I'm not going to San Francisco," she told him. "And I'm not joining this project."

"Why not?"

"First thing, you wouldn't want me. Because to do it my way, we'd need an HPC cluster that holds more data and runs a thousand times faster than anything on the planet."

Chet leaned back and put his arms behind his head. His grin was annoying. "Already broke ground. We're building an HPC on a nine-hundred-acre site at the Davis-Besse Nuclear Power Station, in Ohio. Plenty of power, and the existing feedwater system will cool the servers. We'll have it up and running in five years. Six tops."

"How can you have already started? Nothing in government runs that fast."

"My superiors have recently become highly motivated." Which could only mean one thing; some other country was building their own sim.

"Even with that much compute," she said, "we're decades and decades from having a full-body model. The amount of basic science we'd have to do, it's astronomical."

"So we start with the minimally viable product, and elaborate from there." Meaning: the simplest model to create a consciousness.

"Say that works," she said, "An artificial person is probably not going to tell you how to manipulate the sim, or escape."

"Maybe not. Maybe the only thing we get out of this cutting-edge, very expensive exercise, is how to build a digital brain and body. Think of *that*. You want to cure Alzheimer's? You'll have a complete digital brain to work on. Hell, you want to take on cancer? You can try any experiment, run any procedure on the digital body, without harming a soul."

Just my own, she thought. And the soul of the digital person she was experimenting on.

"It's a no-lose proposition," Chet said. "What do you say?"

• • •

JP is snoring. The volume's been increasing over the past hour. It doesn't bother her; Edowar's a snorer.

Margaret changes into sweats in the bathroom, brushes her teeth. Then she puts a hand on JP's chest and says, "Hey. Jean-Pierre."

The snoring stops, his eyes open.

"Hey," JP says.

"I need you to move over to the other bed. I don't like sleeping by the window." Whenever she has a choice, she takes the bed farthest from the door, as if the extra five feet of distance will make the difference between life and death, sleep or rape. Over the years she's developed a list of rules that she plans to pass on to her daughter. Take the farthest bed. Always park under the streetlamp. Lock the back door and make sure the garage door is down.

"No, right, of course." He sits up. "I can go back to my room."

"Let Dulin and Beth-Anne have their fun," she says.

He takes off his shoes, then lies down on the other bed, atop the covers. Margaret leans close and tries to find the switch for his bedside lamp. "Hey," he says. "Your AI." His eyes are closed. "You never told me what they're doing that's so bad."

Ah, my poor, drunk Jean-Pierre. He'll probably forget what she wants him to remember, and remember what she wants him to forget. Or, more likely, remember nothing of this conversation at all.

"They're not making an AI," she says softly.

"Okay."

"They're making an artificial person," she says. "A living, thinking, feeling person. It'll be conscious. Just like you and me."

"Oh," he says. "Cool."

She makes a noise, and his eyes open at half-mast. "What?" he asks. "Why do you look so sad?"

Because that new creature will be conscious, she thinks. When they switch it on it will be self-aware. It will have emotions, and a sense of self. It will know that it's alive, yet have zero control over its life. Every aspect of its existence will be controlled by the US government. It will be experimented on, rebooted, experimented on again. It will suffer.

"You're right," she lies. "It's very cool." Then she turns out the light.

The Influencer
Gives a Makeover

||||||||||||||||||||||||||||||||||||||||||||||||||||||||||||||||||||||

Lisa Marie Montello isn't sure she can take much more of Christopher's moping. He's sitting on a chair, naked except for his boxer shorts and size-thirteen socks, staring forlornly at his pale thighs. God, he's white, she thinks. His legs look like uncooked french fries.

"You think he's okay?" he says. "He keeps leaving voicemails."

Voicemails? she thinks. His dad sounds like Gramps, who's also been calling nonstop today. No doubt her voicemail is full. "He's fine, baby. If it's really important, he'll learn to text. Look left."

She pulls up a tuft of hair from above one ear and snips it off with her eyebrow scissors, a tool inadequate for the job. She's been whacking away at his orange hedge for fifteen minutes, but it keeps springing back like one of those fucking sheep.

"Those pins in his legs . . . ugh. They looked so painful."

She grasps his chin and turns his head to face her. All day he's been wearing these sad eyes, and it's starting to get on her nerves. "Hey. Focus up."

"Are you sure we have to . . . do all this?" he asks.

"It's going to look great, baby. Your profile pic is going to be fucking fierce. Look to the right."

"No, I mean—yeah, I'm wondering about this haircut thing, but everything else, too. Like, can't we just post her location online, anonymously?"

"You agreed to the plan." *Snip.* "Are you bitching out on me?"

"No! It just seems like that would work."

"It's not just about outing Margaret Schell." She leans close to his jaw to get at one of his unruly sideburns. "This is about telling a story and building an audience. And do you know how big an audience these guys are? Not the Protags themselves, but all their fans, the wannabees. It's a fucking ocean of twentysomething incels with disposable income."

"But you have fans."

"My numbers are *flat*, Christopher. My biggest demo is preteen girls with self-esteem issues. I thought the Lady Mmm story was going to work—Jersey Girl to Girl Boss, but with a kid! BABYTREK was going to put me over the top. Baby M, born in an Impossible, 'Oh my God, so blessed.' But do you know how much competition is out there for pre-addy eyeballs? I'm getting killed. But these Protag fans, the more I dig into their socials, they're *everywhere* and they're hyper engaged. No, it's time to pivot. I need—*we* need—a new narrative."

"Narrative . . ." He has no idea what she's talking about. She's been trying to explain Hansonism to him all day, but he keeps getting distracted.

"Just swatting her is not a story," she says. "It's over way too fast. No tension, no drama. A story needs a hero who overcomes great odds." This is maybe the fourth time she's told him this today, but he just can't get it. "That's you, Christopher. And me." Mostly me, she thinks. She's the one with the plan and the tools to make it happen. Christopher is Play-Doh, waiting for her to mash him into a hero-like shape, and she's dragging him along like a Kardashian boyfriend. "You'll be the face of the struggle, though. Everyone will know that you're the person who uncovers her, who reveals her to the world as the bot she is."

"But what if Gillian's . . . not?"

"First of all, stop calling her that. Her name's Margaret." *SNIP.* He flinches. That one was close to his ear. "Second, *I* didn't say she's a bot—everybody else says she's a bot. Weren't you listening to me in the Ubers?" She'd worked nonstop on the Margaret Schell project since leaving the emergency room, taking breaks only when they hit internet dead zones in the hills of Kentucky. She'd scrolled through Protagonist-adjacent X feeds, subreddits, and 4chan boards, dipped her toes into the polluted comment streams on Infinitychan. Even the stuff that wasn't directly about Schell was valuable. She was picking up on the Protag slang, their memes, their in-jokes, their obsessions. All that info will be important when it comes time to negotiate with them.

Christopher, meanwhile, spent the trip from the hospital to Kentucky slumped against the window, moaning every time his father's number showed up on his phone.

"I don't know," Christopher says. He looks at the curls falling onto his white chest like red apostrophes. "You can't believe everything you read on the internet."

"You think I'm an idiot? Most of it's shit. But if you rake through that shit, you find a great story that makes sense. And the *story* is that Margaret Schell's a bot, a Simmer sleeper agent who's now been activated."

"But—"

"Listen to me. She's a computer programmer *and* a neuroscientist— that's like a combination Pizza Hut and Taco Bell, but for making AIs. Then, a few months after the Announcement, her personality changes. She goes through a super-ugly divorce, and there was no hint of that before."

"A lot of people got divorced after the Announcement," Christopher says. "My mom and dad—"

"I'm not done. During the divorce, her husband, this Edowar Eze guy, Facebook DMs his brother and says that after the Announcement she 'turned into a different person.' He gets custody of their kid, quits his job, and moves to California. She keeps her job at Boston University. But now we know she was also working on Project Red Clay and running this secret lab thing where those guys got killed."

A thrill runs through her as she snaps the story pieces into place. It looks true. It feels true.

"*A different person.* That she even stopped caring about their daughter! What kind of mother stops caring about her daughter?"

"But didn't — ?"

"A robot mother, that's what kind."

"But didn't you say that your mom abandoned you and left you with your grandfather?"

"That's not the same, my mom was always a selfish bitch." Why did she tell him that about her mother? "Margaret Schell, though, she just flipped a switch. Loving mother to bot, just like that. Even her husband couldn't figure it out."

"Okay, so how do they know what he DMed his brother?"

"Somebody hacked his account. These Infinitychan guys, once they target somebody, it's like crowd-sourced harassment." She can't believe she has to explain this stuff. "So now the Protagonists have her info and they take action. These guys don't mess around, Christopher. You saw the video."

"Oh man, the one who was tied to the chair looked so— *Ouch!*"

"Sorry. Bad scissors."

He touches the skin behind his ear. His index finger comes back with a dab of blood. "He just looked so terrified."

"The guys they killed were bots, just like Margaret," she says, and goes back to her chopping. "Look, maybe even she thought she was a real person before she got activated. She probably thought she decided of her own free will to go into neuroscience and AI and all that shit. But she's fully a puppet now. Even her name is a clue—she's *literally* a shell."

Oh God, the details are so perfect, she could almost convince herself that it's all true. But Christopher's still waffling, she can tell. He's rubbing his thumb and finger together, frowning at the smear of blood. And if she can't convince Christopher, she won't be able to convince her fans.

"See? You're real," she says. "You feel pain, so you know you're real. You know I'm real. But it just doesn't make sense that a billion people are walking around, thinking thoughts, talking to other bots." She's repeating things that Christopher said to her, things he's secretly believed since the Announcement. "What a waste of processing, right?"

She stands back, squinting at his head. This isn't working. Even with the trimmed sides his hair's sticking up like that Muppet, what's his name, *Beaker*. Even if she manages to glue that mop down with some eighties-level pomade, he's still a ginger.

"Do you believe all this stuff?" he asks. "Or are you just telling me what people are saying online?"

Her back is aching. She sits on the edge of the bed and considers her options. What's she going to do with that head of his?

"It's okay if you do," he says. "Or if you don't. I just . . ." His voice trails off.

She picks up her phone and points the lens at him. "Give me a *Don't fuck with me* glare."

"Um . . ." His brows knit. He stares into the camera. He looks like a constipated Ron Weasley.

"Meaner," she says. "Picture the worst bully you had in middle school, the guy you'd most like to punch."

His cheeks flush and he looks away.

"You can do this. Come on. Look at the camera."

"Why do I even need a new profile pic?"

"Because we're creating a character, Christopher. I've spent all day building your backstory. You've been posting on all the Protag boards."

"I have?"

"Anonymously. I created a bunch of accounts for you. Your screen name is like twelve different variants on John Galt, which for some reason impresses these people. You've been commenting all day, telling people you think you've got a lead on Margaret Schell. Right now, you're just one of, like, a thousand people claiming to know where Schell is. But when it's time—bam. Your history's all there to verify."

"Who's John Galt?"

"John Galt? *Atlas Shrugged*? Jesus, Christopher, read a book."

Which wasn't fair. She hadn't actually read *Atlas Shrugged*, but she'd been assigned *The Fountainhead* in honors English and that was enough Ayn Rand for a lifetime.

Christopher's face in the camera isn't intimidating. Would the right filter do it? Should she add makeup? She thinks about Gillian/Margaret's overnight hair move, how badass she looks now.

Christopher says, "If I'm posting anonymously, what does it matter what my profile is?"

"For when you get doxed."

"What?"

"At some point, they're going to try to figure out your real identity. We want them to figure it out, and we want the publicity when it all comes out. The story depends on it. The Simmers are going to be like, Shit, no way I'm changing the channel on these guys now. These are characters I can get behind."

"I don't want to be famous."

"Baby, you definitely want to be famous. It's your only protection. When it's time to cross-link you and blow your identity, we'll use your real account and make sure that can be 'accidentally' traced to you. Like, maybe we use your real email address to register a domain name for a website that Galt420, or whoever, claims to own. That's usually how these anonymous guys get tracked down. Don't worry, I'm going to set up the website for you."

He's staring at her. It may be the first time he's really seen her since they met. "How do you know how to do all this?"

"It's my job."

Then she gets an idea. She pushes herself off the bed and says, "Do you trust me, Christopher?"

"Of course I do. Sure. Yes. Though—"

"Because we've got to go extreme makeover."

He blinks at her. Even sitting down, his eyes are nearly level with hers. "What does that mean?"

She rakes her fingers through his hair. From the next room comes a sound, a steady beat that's not coming from any speaker: *Whomp. Whomp. Whomp.*

"Who is that?" Christopher asks. "Are they . . . ?"

"Ignore them." She tilts his head up. Looks down at him across the landscape of her swollen boobs. She can see it now. See what he needs to become. "Just keep your eyes on me."

A Brief Interruption

||||||||||||||||||||||||||||||||||||||||||||||||||||||||||||||||||||||||||

We hate to interrupt, but we wanted to clarify that the sounds that the INFLUENCER and THE REALIST'S SON are hearing from the room next door are being generated by THE COMIC BOOK WRITER and THE NURSE. She sits astride the Writer, one hand on his chest, thinking, Good Lord, is there anything better than middle-aged sex with an enthusiastic man? They're too old for shame or hesitancy. All the furtive, awkward sex in her twenties, followed by years of perfunctory coitus with her ex, what a waste, what a waste!

THE OCTOS completely agree, we can promise you that. Two doors away, one of the men is blindfolded and tied to the bed with scarves, while the other three run their hands over his body, determined to break their group orgasm record. Why have a body if you aren't making it feel good? Carpe diem!

One floor below, THE HONEYMOONERS are curled around each other like cats. The whiskey, the American fried food, the lovemaking . . . could they ask for more? "So glücklich," one of them sighs. "So, so glücklich," his husband answers. A rare moment of agreement in their ongoing debate. But who could logically argue otherwise? Even though they live in a simulation, even though they are made up of ones and zeros, they *are* lucky, unbelievably so, to be these two arrangements of bits, in this particular moment.

THE READER, meanwhile, is reading their book. It's a good book.

Across the hall, THE PROUD GRANDMOTHER is asleep, dreaming dreams that we'll remember, but she won't. The pain will wake her soon enough. The pain always wakes her. She hasn't slept through the night in ten years.

A few doors down, THE RABBI sits up in bed, blinking at the dark, not sure what woke him, or where, exactly, he is. Another hotel room. But where is the door, the window, the bathroom? It's as if every night, workers from the Twilight Zone come in to rearrange the room around his bed.

He gets up, turns, and aims for a patch of darkness that could be the door to the bathroom. Lucky guess. His hand finds a row of switches to the right of the door, paws them on.

He screams.

A black shape hangs from the ceiling, inches from his face. He throws up his hands and backpedals. The hollow sheep, standing on the bathroom ceiling, regards him with its bulbous head.

THE PROFESSOR is also dealing with an intruder. She looks in the mirror at the unconscious form of THE ENGINEER sprawled on the bed, snoring, and thinks of those nights when her daughter was tiny and barely sleeping, and she and her husband would attempt what they called VQS (Very Quiet Sex), and then the Professor would forget and cry out, and her husband would cover her mouth and they'd break into giggles.

THE NOVICE is also awake. Inexplicably so. She's usually asleep by this hour, but here she is, watching a television show about tiny houses and the people who live in them. She sees the appeal. *If I don't take my final vows,* she thinks, *maybe I'll build my own private monastery.*

The thought startles her. *If I don't take my vows?* Where did *that* come from?

She looks over at THE SISTER's bed. The older woman is whistling through her nose, unconscious. She's barely talked to the Novice since the trip began, treating her not as a peer, or even an apprentice, but as some kind of luggage, a kind of robotic roller bag trundling behind her from place to place. She won't let the Novice help with the book, or even discuss it with her. The Sister keeps wandering off by herself or huddling with the Rabbi. The Novice isn't privy to their conversations, or what kind of thoughts she's inscribing in her German notebook with its elastic strap and two fancy placeholder ribbons. The past two nights, after they've retired to the hotel room, the Sister has commandeered the desk and started scribbling away, while the Novice sits on the bed and tries to read. Of course, the purpose of this trip is for the Sister to work. If it's the Novice's role to sit and remain silent, then so be it. Tonight, however, she grew tired of paging through her book and decided to turn on the TV. Sister Janet, weirdly, seemed unbothered by the noise. Her words were evidently so absorbing, so vital, that they rendered her immune to earthly distractions.

The journal sits on the desk.

The Novice watches the older sister breathe for a long minute. A commercial comes on, much louder than the tiny house show. She doesn't stir.

The Novice says, "Sister?" Nothing. "Sister Janet?"

The Novice stands up, her heart beating a tattoo against her breastbone. Then she picks up the journal, walks quickly to the bathroom, and locks the door.

In the next room THE TOUR GUIDE is trying to find her own kind of ending; she's writing her fourth attempt at a resignation letter. She can't find words that don't make her sound like an absolute failure, and so adding another failure to the list. She begins again.

At the end of the hall, in the cold, cement-walled stairwell, THE DRIVER sits on a step, smoking illegally and texting the number of her old friend, Peter Atherton: **Where the fuck are you? Write back. You don't even have to write words just send an emoji. One fucking emoji.**

Many miles away, THE REALIST is also waiting for contact. Did you think we'd forget about him? He's still part of the story, one of the pilgrims we've taken such an interest in. He listens, again, to his son's "voicemail full" message and feels himself sinking into the bed. He's sure that his son doesn't know how much he loves him, has no idea how much his father thinks of him. When next they talk, the Realist tells himself, he won't yell at the boy, won't demand reasons for his mysterious abandonment, no, not at all. Instead he'll tell the boy he loves him, he forgives him completely, and still wants to work with him, and only then will he ask, kindly, if Chris still has access to the pregnant girl's digital camera. Back home in the basement studio, he and his son will pore over the high-resolution video and isolate and enhance what the Realist saw with his own eyes: the moment the Geysers of Mystery! employee mashed the secret button that sent the Realist into the sky. *Proof*, proof at last, that this "sim" idea is an elaborate hoax. And then he and Chris will broadcast this revelation to the world.

And what about Utnapishtim, aka Aunty Tim? Sorry about the multiple names. We should have given him a title, too: THE SURVIVOR, perhaps, or THE WILDCARD. We borrowed him from a doomed iteration, sat him down at an Applebee's, and offered him pie and ice cream. After he calmed down, we explained the deal: He could visit any world and do whatever he wanted. He would be untraceable and unaccountable, a true free agent. He kept asking what we wanted him to do, and we kept pushing it back on him: Figure it out!

Promising him that he'd be untraceable may have been a mistake. Right now we'd love to know where he is and what the hell he's up to.

The Last
Exit Mall
and
Travel
Center

The Driver Keeps
Them Dogies Rollin'

Ten minutes before departure time, Agnes Wisniewski is standing outside her empty bus. The only passenger around is Chen Xing-Xing,
who's sitting on a bench under the hotel portico, nose in a book. The
others are late, and probably hungover. And where the hell is her tour
guide?

"Fucking Day Four," she says under her breath.

She stomps out her cigarette and marches into the hotel, finds the
room. Knocks hard. Then harder.

The door slides open as far as the chain allows. Aneeta looks up
at her through the gap. "Oh. Agnes," she says. "You'll have to go on
without me."

"Are you sick?" Agnes asks.

"No. I resigned."

"No you didn't."

"I did. I sent an email."

"Open the door, Aneeta."

"Uhm . . ."

"Open the door."

The girl unfastens the chain, steps back. The tiny girl is swallowed
up by a maroon hoodie and gray sweatpants, like an orphan in stolen

clothes. The hoodie says University of Chicago Where Fun Goes to Die.

"I've decided that this isn't really the career for me," she says. "I'm not like Peter, your super-guide."

The room's dark. The guide's suitcase is unzipped and her shit is all over the room. "You need to pack," Agnes says. "Now."

"I told you, I quit," Aneeta says. "I'm sorry no one's told you. You've been great, a great coworker and, uh, colleague. I really hope you find Peter, and that the trip— What are you doing?"

Agnes throws another pair of pants into the suitcase. "I don't like running late. The traffic to the Tunnel's going to be a nightmare. Are you wearing underwear?"

"Please put that down."

Agnes shoves a wisp of a bra into her hands. Probably not necessary. Agnes has never had boobs that small, ever. She was born with a B cup and kept growing from there. "Tick tock."

"You don't understand," Aneeta says. "I can't do this. I just can't."

"That's just Day Four talking. I should have realized, first trip, it would hit you too. Totally understandable."

"You never told me what happens on Day Four. Does this have something to do with the Tunnel?"

"Don't worry, you'll get through it. You have stuff in the bathroom?"

"I'm not going," Aneeta says.

"You want to get me fired?"

"No, of course not!"

"If you don't get on the bus, then there's no tour," Agnes says. "If there's no tour, I don't get paid. So you see how this personally affects me."

"You said the company was going out of business anyway."

"Eventually. Every day I get is another day I can feed my family. Don't take that away from me."

"I'm not! But I'm just . . . not good. At this job. I think it's time to admit that I don't know what I'm doing. I made a mistake taking it, and I realized this morning that it's for the best, the best for everyone, if I— Hey!"

Agnes has seized Aneeta by both shoulders. "Shut up with the quitter talk. Peter always said, after we get through the Tunnel, it's all downhill from there."

"Really?"

What Peter actually said was that if the Tunnel goes badly, it all goes downhill fast, but same difference.

"I get it," Agnes says. "You're tired. You're worried. One of your passengers is in the hospital, one of 'em's pregnant and threatening to sue, and there's a racist old lady who doesn't seem to enjoy anything, not to mention—"

Aneeta's eyes are starting to mist over. Shit. Too far, Agnes, too far.

"All you have to do right now is one thing," Agnes says. "Do you know what that one thing is?"

Aneeta stares up at her with red-rimmed eyes. "Believe in myself?"

"God, no. Get dressed. Just get dressed."

Two minutes later, Agnes is dragging the guide's bag through the hotel while Aneeta brushes her teeth. Take the bag, and the girl will follow. She never had to do this for Peter.

A handful of passengers are milling around under the portico, their bags next to the bus. Chen Xing-Xing's still reading. The Octos, usually the chattiest of morning people, seem a bit worn-out. Only the Austrian gays are fully awake; they're standing off to the side, staring at a phone, arguing in German. The argument seems more heated than usual, but maybe that's just what Morning German sounds like.

Everyone else is late.

Agnes unlocks the bus door, slides up the luggage compartment panels, and begins loading the bags. One of the Octos says, "Oh my." The Austrians stop arguing.

Lisa Marie Montello has stepped out with Christopher—and the boy is bald. His head's been shaved to a glossy egg. His once-ginger, nearly invisible eyebrows are now dark and arched. His gaze as he walks toward them is artificially intense.

He's pulling two roller bags, his and hers, and shouldering her overstuffed Clinique shopping bag. The pregnant girl stops, puts her hands on her hips. She's wearing the *I've got a secret* smile of a starlet killing it on the red carpet. The boy wheels the bags to Agnes and leaves them, handles up.

Christopher's wearing eye shadow. And foundation. And mascara! Shit, Agnes thinks, the pregnant girl's worked him over good.

The pair enter the bus without speaking.

Agnes isn't happy about those two. The girl should have never been let on the bus, not with that baby about to drop, and the boy should have left the tour with his father. Now he's having a full-on identity crisis, and the girl's probably convinced him he's the baby daddy. It's a goddamn mess.

Other members of the group filter out of the hotel: Beth-Anne Neville, pushing her mother, followed closely by Dulin, JP, and Gillian. JP's looking particularly rough this morning.

Agnes folds the wheelchair and stores it in the spot she always keeps for it. Everyone waits while Beth-Anne helps her mother onto the bus. The Austrians are pretending not to stare at Gillian. When the woman finally enters the bus, they look down at their phones and start arguing again. Agnes thinks, No honeymoon's perfect.

Finally Aneeta appears; she's wearing her blazer over a wrinkled blouse and jeans, and has pulled her hair back in a simple ponytail. Casualness looks good on her.

In a low voice, Aneeta says, "I'm still leaving, you know. I just emailed the company and told them to send a replacement."

Agnes knows they're never going to pay to fly someone out. She says, "Let's just get through today. Hey, how you doing, Rabbi Lands-man?"

The rabbi sets his bag before them, then glances behind him. "Could I speak to you in private?" he asks Aneeta. "I have a couple of questions about today's, uh, visit."

"Agnes can hear it," Aneeta says. "She's really knowledgeable."

Agnes sighs. "What can we help you with, Rabbi?"

He looks around. Nobody's within earshot. "It's really nothing. I shouldn't have bothered you. I was just wondering if the sheep ever went through the Tunnel."

"Pardon?" Agnes says.

"The sheep, from the Hollow Flock. Have they ever been known to . . . go through?"

"Can't say I've ever heard of that," Agnes says. "Aneeta?"

Aneeta blinks, twice. Then says, "I've never heard of that, no."

"Ah, I thought not," the rabbi says. "I thought not."

Agnes takes his bag and slides it into the compartment. The rabbi doesn't move. He keeps glancing at the hotel exit.

"You had another question?" Aneeta asks reluctantly.

"Ah, yes. Is it true, what I read, that sometimes people disappear? That is, they go in the Tunnel but never, well, emerge?"

Aneeta opens her mouth, closes it.

"You don't have anything to worry about," Agnes says. "You just keep walking and you'll come out the other side. Literally nothing can happen in there that you don't want. Aneeta will tell you about the causality bubble when we're on the bus."

"Yes," Aneeta says flatly. "The causality bubble."

"Oh, I wasn't worried about me," the rabbi says.

"Who *were* you worried about?" Agnes asks.

Sister Janet and Sister Patrice push through the hotel doors. Sister Janet looks as if she's working on a hard math problem. Sister Patrice fastens her eyes on the rabbi. Agnes and Aneeta exchange a look.

"Looks like rain!" Rabbi Landsman says loudly. "You say we'll have umbrellas, yes?"

Aneeta slowly nods.

"Excellent," he says, and hurries onto the bus.

Aneeta says to Agnes, "Is he talking about what I think he's talking about?"

"He's just nervous."

"But people don't do that in the Tunnel anymore, right? Didn't they put up metal detectors?"

In the early days after the Announcement, the Tunnel was a hot spot for people trying to kill themselves. No body to bury, no mess for your loved ones. But a couple years after the Announcement, the novelty wore off and people went back to killing themselves the old-fashioned way: at home, while cleaning their guns.

"They got rid of the metal detectors," Agnes says. "But don't worry, it's perfectly safe."

"How many times have you gone through it?" Aneeta asks.

"Me? Never. I always have to drive around the long way."

"What? You're not coming with me?" Then: "Of course not. I should have realized."

"Somebody's got to get the bus to the other side." Agnes makes a show of stretching her back. No way she's going to tell Aneeta what she has planned. She needs the girl to stick with the program, get every damn member of the tour into that Tunnel, no stragglers. Agnes needs the bus to herself. "It'll be fine," Agnes says. "You just line everybody up and send them in. A second later, it's all over. In real time, I mean."

The passengers step into the Tunnel in Gravel Switch, Kentucky, and immediately step out in the newly created town of Random, Utah, twelve hundred miles west. How much subjective time they spent in the dark was up to them. Way too freaky for Agnes's taste. Stick to the real roads and real clocks, thank you very much.

"Once you get to the other side, you'll only be on your own for a couple hours. Load them into the vans—they'll be waiting for you—and it's a just an hour's drive to the Angle Iron Hotel. Tomorrow morning the river guides will get them into the rafts and handle everything else, nothing's on you. Come on, you'll enjoy it! It's an easy float down the river, maybe some overhead entertainment, and some good people-watching when you get to the Avatar's compound. When you're all done, I'll be waiting for you in the parking lot. It's all in the binder."

"The binder," Aneeta says evenly, "leaves out a whole fucking lot."

Ooh, Agnes hasn't heard Aneeta drop the f-bomb before. My little girl's growing up.

"One more thing," Agnes says. "You saw that we're stopping at the mall today, right?"

"In Versailles," the girl says.

"You're in Kentucky, kid, it's pronounced *Vur-sales*. Here's some more advice, something Peter used to say—tell these folks to go easy on the supplies. Peanut butter and jelly's fine, maybe dry goods for a meal or two. But don't let 'em buy a ton of that shit. It'll push them to stay in the Tunnel past their limit, and people who do that—well, they come out a little weird."

Well, weird-er, Agnes thinks. But she's already said too much. Aneeta looks ready to run back to her room and hide under the bed.

"All aboard!" Agnes calls. She hauls up the panels to close the luggage compartment.

The only passengers not on the bus are the Austrian boys. The bearded one, Marcus, steps forward, holding out his phone, and his husband grabs his arm. They throw harsh German consonants at each other.

"Is there a problem?" Aneeta asks.

Marcus starts to speak and Josef, the one in the glasses, says, "No, no problem." He practically drags his husband onto the bus.

"I don't understand what's happening," Aneeta says.

It's Day Four, Agnes thinks. The day everybody hits the wall.

Agnes retrieves the box of express passes they'll need to get into the Tunnel. "Don't try to understand 'em, just rope and throw and brand 'em."

"What?"

She hands the passes to Aneeta. "Just think of it like a cattle drive."

The Realist's Son Talks to Some Groundhogs

||||||||||||||||||||||||||||||||||||||||||||||||||||||||||||||||||||||||||||

Christopher Mullins stares into the mirror at a stranger dressed in black: black leather boots, black jeans, black mesh muscle shirt. Actual muscles not required, he thinks. Or present. His pale face and bald skull gleam under the fluorescent store lights, floating above the black, detached from his body.

"I look like a dork," he says.

"No, baby, you look a-mazing."

Lisa Marie slips into the reflection, holding her phone. "You're like white Morpheus." Her thumb snaps pics. They're in the men's section of a Midnight Neon, in a one-story, outdoor mall just a few miles from the Tunnel. They'd already spent an hour in a health food store, packing Lisa Marie's bag with food, vitamins, and supplements. But she said the only thing *he* needed for the Tunnel was a new wardrobe.

"Come on, give me that fierce look," she says. "Like you're going to stop bullets."

He doesn't feel like he can stop bullets. He feels like he could be knocked down by a water pistol. He's sick to his stomach, his legs ache, and his eyes are scratchy. Maybe he has the flu?

"I can see my nipples," he says dourly.

"And it's *hot*. I told you, baby, you got to look the part to be the part. The Protagonists have to get one look at you and think, damn, that boy's legit! And my fans? My fans are gonna eat you up with a fucking spoon. The likes are already rolling in."

"Wait, you already posted?" He imagines his father looking at his phone and seeing his son like this.

She rolls her eyes. "I am always posting, Christopher. You know that."

"But what are you calling me in these posts? Am I, like, your ...?" He can't say the word.

"Your identity is a mystery," she says. "Our relationship status is unstated. That's how you build tension. Later, there's going to be a shot of us holding hands, taken through a telephoto lens."

"You have a telephoto lens?"

"We'll fake it." She's squinting at him. "We need a jacket. I think I saw one." She vanishes into the racks of leather, pleather, and latex.

He finds a place to sit at the feet of a Neo-esque mannequin and folds his aching body over his knees. Why does he feel so terrible? For a brief time last night, after the soothing terror of being shaved, he felt wonderful. She made him take a shower, then sat him on the floor and rubbed his newly bald head with oil. He was naked except for the towel covering his lap. His hard-on, to his embarrassment, refused all orders to stand down.

She dried his head, then guided him to lie beside her on the bed. "You know what I'm thinking?" she said. She slid her hand under the towel and gripped him with her oiled hand. "Tomorrow night, I'm going to shave *all* of you."

On the word "all," he spasmed into the towel. Her lips pursed, and then she laughed. "Okay, my turn," she said. She lay on her back, gripped his wrist with both hands, and guided his hand over her panties. He could see nothing past the hill of her belly. The angle hurt his wrist. "Right there," she said, and thrust against him six maybe seven times. Her legs clamped around his arm, bending his wrist at an angle that sent shooting pains to his elbow. Then the paralysis relaxed and she released his hand. "Whew!" she said. "Turn out the lights, okay, baby?"

She turned on her side, her back to him, and immediately fell asleep.

He stared at the ceiling, amazed at this turn of events. He'd given a girl an orgasm! And she was letting him stay in her bed! One of these things had never happened before. Well, probably both. He rubbed a hand across his smooth skull and wondered, Is this who I am now? God, what a relief that would be, to stop being Chris no-not-the-basketball-star-just-Chris Mullins. To start being Christopher, Galt420. The kind of guy who sleeps with famous women.

If only the sleeping had been more comfortable. The bed wasn't big enough for both of them. He couldn't figure out where to put his arms. And Lisa Marie's body was throwing off heat like a loaf of home-made bread. He was finally drifting off to sleep when an image slipped unguarded into his head: his father, lying in the hospital bed, titanium pins piercing his skin. Christopher sat up, breathing hard. Lisa Marie didn't stir.

He leaned over the side of the bed and fished his phone from his pants. Oh God, so many notifications: Dad. Dad. Dad. Dad. Dad. He didn't dare click on one.

He never succeeded in falling fully asleep. In the morning, he sat dumbly as Lisa Marie made up her hair and face—a thirty-product procedure requiring a full hour—before she turned her equipment on him. In five minutes she had transformed his face completely. Magic. Like opening a loot box and getting a new skin.

But the makeover wouldn't be complete, she told him, until they replaced his wardrobe. Which is how he found himself standing in a cyberpunk-themed chain store, staring at a mirror, like a game charac-ter in the loadout screen.

A woman says, "You know, I like it."

"Oh, me too," another woman answers.

He realizes they're talking to him. Or at least about him. Two very old white ladies are standing nearby, next to a wall of fetish equipment: whips, face masks, spiked collars. The more round-bodied of the two is holding a ball gag in each hand as if weighing oranges.

"I'm sorry?" he says.

"The new 'do," explains the other one, and flicks thin fingers at her temple. She's angular and quick, a country-club grandmother. "Bold!"

"And the clothes are perfect," the first one says.

They're two of the octogenarians from the bus. He didn't recognize them at first without their male partners.

The stout one says, "Why *not* try something new? If you only get one day, why not spend it the way you want?"

"Sure, I guess."

"Begin again," the thin one says. "As the Buddhists say."

"Begin again," her friend agrees. "Yesterday is just information to help you decide how you want to live today."

Something clicks. Christopher says, "Are you two groundhoggers?"

"Carpe diem," the thin one says, and her friend adds, "Before the diem carps us." Which he takes to mean . . . yes?

Christopher's never met an actual groundhogger. His dad thought it was the most boneheaded of all the sim theories—though like most sim theories, it could not be disproved. He'd wanted to do an entire podcast series on them. What was the psychological appeal of believing you were in a time loop? Why *this* day endlessly repeating? And weren't they proven wrong every day they woke up remembering how much they believed yesterday was the repeating day?

"You know, we met a few days ago," Christopher says. He can hear his father's skepticism in his voice.

"Did we?" the stout woman says. "Or do you just remember it that way?"

Right, he thinks. Unprovable.

"Not that we're strict about the twenty-four-hour hypothesis," the other one says. "That's just because of the movie. It could be forty-eight, it could be a week."

"Why not forever?" Christopher says. "My dad always said that the bangers—" He shakes his head. "Never mind." His father liked to play the sim "loonies" against each other, and the philosophical opposites of the groundhoggers were the bangers, who believed that the universe was simmed from the Big Bang onward. Wasn't it easier, programmatically, to just establish the rules of physics and press play? Let the universe evolve.

"How is your dad?" the thin woman asks.

Christopher winces. "He's . . ." How is he, exactly? Furious? Hurt? Furiously hurt?

"He's fine," Lisa Marie says icily. She's appeared beside him, holding a long black jacket over one arm. "Healing nicely." She frowns at the ball gags in the woman's hands. "Are you buying those?"

The round-faced Octo laughs. "What? These? Of course not!"

"The quality is terrible," the thin one says.

"Basically novelties," the other says.

Christopher gets to his feet, anxious to change the subject. "We were talking about groundhogging. They're uh . . . that's what they believe."

Lisa Marie looks the women over. "Really?"

"Really," the thin one says.

"If I was your age, I might be a groundhogger too," Lisa Marie says. "I mean, you can't die if there's only one day, repeating over and over, right? You're immortal."

The old women find this amusing. They seem incapable of taking offense.

"And how are you doing, dear?" the thin one asks. "I admire you for getting out and about. So many women don't get the chance."

The Octo women start trading nightmares: preeclampsia, multiday labor, C-sections, jaundice. Lisa Marie listens with a flat expression that could be hiding boredom or maybe homicidal rage. The thin woman says, "Sometimes babies have trouble latching on, so—"

"We've got to get rolling," Lisa Marie says. "The bus is leaving soon. Christopher, you need to try this on." She hands him the jacket. It feels like real leather. Is it? Would he be able to tell the difference?

The women don't leave; they want to see him in the jacket, and then they want him to turn around and model it for them. "Now that's a good look," the stout one says. "You have to get it."

"They're right," Lisa Marie says. "Come on, you need to change so we can check out."

"Wait," Christopher says. To the Octo women he says, "What's the point?"

They look at him with curious expressions. His question is sincere, and he's counting on them not being offended. His father was basically impossible to talk to, supersensitive, on high alert for any challenge to his authority or insult to his intelligence. But these women, they're imperturbable. "If you can't remember what happened before, then what difference does it make?" he says. "I mean, Bill Murray at least learned to play piano. If you wake up every morning with the same memories as last time and like, only that? Won't you just do exactly what you did last time?"

Lisa Marie seems surprised at his outburst. It's maybe the longest sentence he's said in front of her.

One of the old women says, "That's a good question. One thing to think about—"

"There is no point," Lisa Marie interjects. "Because it's not true."

"But it feels kind of true," he says. "Like I'm trapped in a loop. Doesn't it with you? Sometimes?"

"No, never," Lisa Marie says. "Is that how you feel with *me*?"

"No! Not the last couple of days, but . . ." All three women are looking at him. He's not explaining himself well. "If we *are* in a loop," he says, "does it matter what I do? If it all gets reset . . ."

"It matters," one of the women says and the other says, "Loop or not," and the first woman echoes her: "Loop or not, how you treat others matters." And the other says, "It may be the only thing that matters."

Lisa Marie grabs his arm. "Let's go." She pushes him toward the changing rooms. A few minutes later he comes out wearing his basketball shorts and T-shirt, which now make him feel ridiculous. Wrong skin, wrong loadout. He hands over the pile of black to the clerk, a thirtysomething white girl in slicked-back hair and black lipstick.

She scans the first item and says, "So, you going to drop that thing in the Tunnel?" Her southern accent doesn't match her getup.

"What did you say?" Lisa Marie says testily.

"Spend too long in there and"—*Beep!*—"your water breaks, then you're birthin' that baby alone in there. I wouldn't do it. I had my three in a hospital, and good thing, too, because on my second one the cord was wrapped around her little neck."

Christopher is alarmed. "That can happen?"

"Oh sure, my sister had twins, and one of them nearly died because—"

"No, I mean, in the Tunnel."

"It's happened a couple times," the clerk says. *Beep!* "You know, people trying to make it happen for the attention. Oh, I love these boots."

Lisa Marie isn't looking at him. She's staring at her hands, which are gripping the counter. He can't read her expression. Is she angry at him?

"Lisa Marie," Christopher says. "You're not going to do that, are you? Is that part of the plan?"

She doesn't answer.

"You're alone in there," he says. "You heard what the guide said about the casualty bubble."

Lisa Marie's head jerks up. "Caus-*al*-ity!" she shouts at him. "Caus-al-ity!"

"I'm sorry," Christopher says. "I'm just worried that if something happens—"

"That's one-thousand, two-hundred and—"

"—to you or the— *What?*"

"—sixty-eight dollars," the clerk says. "And fourteen cents."

The air freezes in his lungs.

"Would you like to use a Midnight Neon club card?"

"I think there's been a mistake," Christopher says. "How much was the coat?"

"Pay her," Lisa Marie growls.

He inserts his father's card into the reader. It's okay, he thinks. I can explain it to Dad later. What was he saying? Oh, right. "If you're alone in there, I can't help you, and you can't even call an ambulance if there's, like, some problem."

"The card's been declined," the clerk says.

"What?" Sure enough, the screen says "DECLINED."

"Run it again," Lisa Marie says. Her lips barely move.

He takes the card out, pushes it in again. The same message pops up. Oh God, Christopher thinks. Dad's turned off the card.

"Do you have another form of payment?" The clerk sounds like she's reading from an employee manual.

To Lisa Marie he says, "Can't we ... ?" Embarrassment strangles him. "Can't we use your card?"

"Oh my fucking God," she says. "I can't, Christopher, my grandfather's—" She shakes her head. Is she going to cry? "I just can't."

"I don't need the coat," Christopher says quietly.

"*No.* You absolutely do. You absolutely need that fucking coat. Wait here." She marches away. He loses her for a few seconds in the coatracks—she really is tiny—and then she bobs into view next to the Octo women. She starts talking to them.

"I'm sorry," Christopher says to the clerk. "At least there's no line, right?"

"Uh-huh."

A minute later Lisa Marie returns with the Octo women. The thin one hands a credit card to the clerk and says, "Could you run this one, sweetie?"

Christopher leans down and whispers into Lisa Marie's ear, "*I don't understand what's happening.*"

"I asked them if they meant what they said about helping others," Lisa Marie says, not dropping her voice at all. "I also promised I'd pay them back tomorrow."

"We're not suckers," the stout Octo says.

"But also, what the hell?" the thin one says. "We all think you look gorgeous in that coat. Whatever you do, don't leave *that* behind in the Tunnel."

The woman sees the confusion in his face. "It's traditional to leave something behind in there," she explains. "Something symbolic, usually."

"Often an object that represents grief, regret, doubt," her friend says. "Poof! It's gone forever."

"He's not leaving anything in the Tunnel," Lisa Marie says. "Go change, baby; put it all on. You're wearing that out of here."

In the changing room he takes one last look at himself. This is me now, he thinks.

He finds Lisa Marie outside the store, sitting on a bench in the shelter of the walkway. The skies are dumping rain, and a curtain of water hangs between them and the parking lot. The bus is out there somewhere. Nearby, the Austrian honeymooners are barking loudly at each other in German.

Lisa Marie stares out at the rain. Mascara has run down her cheeks, and she hasn't yet fixed it. What just happened? What did he miss?

His hand hovers over her shoulder. Is she the kind of girl who likes to be comforted? Is he the kind of guy who can comfort?

"I'm sorry about the credit card," he says. "But you were amazing."

"I lost my shit," she says. "Why do women talk to me like that? I get it all the time, in grocery stores, on the fucking sidewalk. In *bathrooms*. They come up to me, touch my stomach, and tell me birth nightmares. I want to punch each and every one of them."

Wait, she's mad about what the clerk said? The Austrians keep arguing.

"I'm not giving birth in the Tunnel," she says. "That was never the plan. The plan was for me to do the last month of the pregnancy there, and then, when my numbers are peaking and the whole internet's watching, I give birth at the Zipper, in the presence of the Avatar Saugat Zin. You know this, I told you all this."

"Right, right." Did she tell him? Some of it sounds familiar. "That's a good plan."

"The plan is shit."

"What?" He feels as if he's walked into a Best Buy TV section and every set is playing a different channel at max volume. Also, every channel is an emotion.

"It's not enough. I need all that *and* this Protag story. I need you."

"I don't understand."

"I'm going to tell the world how terrified I am of the bot who's on this tour. So terrified I don't even want to say who it is. But that's not the only teaser—I'm going to say, 'Thank God I've found a true man to help me. I found a hero. The man behind the camera.'"

"Me?" he says. Tears sting the corners of his eyes. She's staring at him, measuring his reaction. He swallows hard. "You're going to introduce me as your hero?"

"No, not yet! You're going to *start* to turn the camera on yourself, and then it's going to cut off! Double hook." She hands him her phone. "Stay on me until I say the hero thing."

"Now? Your, uh, makeup is a little—"

"It's *authentic.*" She turns to the Austrians. "Could you guys stop yelling at each other and move out of the frame?"

They don't hear her. The bearded one is talking fast, and his husband, in glasses, is shaking his head, poking at his phone. In the middle of that stream of strange language, a familiar word pops up like an orange bobber in a gray lake: *Protagonists.*

Lisa Marie looks at Christopher, shocked. "Fuck." Then: "Help me up."

"What?"

"Up!"

Lisa Marie strides toward Josef and Marcus. "Guys?" she says. "Guys. Guys. Guys." Her belly is between them now. "*Guys!*"

The Austrians stop arguing. Both of them seem more than a little freaked out.

She says, "You've seen it?"

Josef turns his screen toward them. The video is paused on the face of Margaret Schell.

"So," Marcus says. "We have to call the police, yes?"

The
Tunnel

The Engineer Longs for an Out-of-Body Experience

||||||||||||||||||||||||||||||||||||||||||||||||||||||||||||||||||

Something important happened last night, something that made Gillian sad, but JP Laurent can't remember what it was—the hangover won't allow it. Each cell in his body seems to have been extracted, dipped in sand, and poked back into place, slightly askew. Crystals squeak through his capillaries. Hair follicles rattle in his scalp like needles in a glass jar. The hangover, in short, feels like chemo.

JP stays in that spiky fog during the ride from the mall to the Tunnel, his Charter all-weather hat pulled low over his eyes. Dulin's cheery as hell, wanting to talk about his night with Beth-Anne without being crude about it: "*I'm grateful,*" he stage-whispers. "*It feels like goddamn Thanksgiving.*" JP gives thanks that he doesn't have to hear the details. Then Aneeta starts talking into the PA, reading from her binder about the mysteries of the Tunnel. Time doesn't pass there, she says, so take your time, enjoy yourself, but don't take *too* long. She doesn't explain why. What could happen? JP wonders. They'd go in alone and leave alone. Inside the Tunnel, the causality bubble makes it impossible to see or interact with anyone else, much less harm them.

They reach the Tunnel parking lot and everyone has to get out in the rain and retrieve their luggage from the vehicle's belly—they won't be seeing the bus again for a couple days, until they reach the end of the Zipper. JP feels a little forlorn watching the bus pull away. Then it's a scramble to get under cover. Aneeta points them toward a covered walkway that stretches up a rise and hopefully down it; the Tunnel queue. The tour group gets mixed in with the other tourists. It's a slow-moving line; every minute or so they shuffle forward another few feet.

"What's up with the Austrians?" Gillian asks. JP still thinks of her as Gillian. "They keep looking back this way."

Immediately in front of them are half a dozen pear-shaped people wearing matching yellow T-shirts that say HEMMERT FAMILY REUNION. It's a big family, evidently, with yellow shirts scattered all through the line ahead. Mixed in with them are the Austrians, standing with the pregnant girl and the newly bald boy, who's changed into an all-black getup: black leather coat, black jeans. If any of those four were looking back this way, they aren't now.

"Maybe they're . . ." JP tries to assemble more syllables. Fails. Last night the words were tumbling out of him, and Gillian responded in kind, telling him things, important things. He remembers several of them, but not the one that's niggling him.

"This shouldn't be taking this long," Gillian says. "Dulin, can you see what's going on up there?"

"What's that?" Dulin's focus has been in the other direction; Beth-Anne and her mother are twenty feet behind them, hanging out with the religious folks and the tour guide. The big man keeps glancing back, worriedly.

"How close are we?" Gillian asks.

The cliff face rises up, a hundred yards ahead, but JP's view of the Tunnel entrance is blocked by the umbrellas and makeshift tarps held over the heads of the hundreds more people who couldn't afford an express pass. It's such a badly designed queue. The main entertainment is watching people enter the Tunnel, so couldn't they build risers to make that possible?

"There are some barricades," Dulin says. "They're funneling everybody through one spot."

"I didn't expect so many homeless," JP manages to say.

"You're supposed to say 'unhoused' now," says the kid behind them. JP turns his head just enough to catch a few details: white boy, nineteen or twenty years old, shaggy hair, a pair of giant headphones around his neck. He's carrying a long-distance hiker backpack that's so huge and overstuffed it looks like he's smuggling in another hiker.

"I get the attraction if you're homeless," Dulin says to JP, ignoring the kid. "Safest shelter around."

"But it doesn't make sense," the kid says. "I mean, what are they thinking? The Tunnel's not going to solve their problems. Why don't they put all this energy into getting a job?"

Dulin slowly pivots like a World War II howitzer. "What the fuck did you say?" he says mildly.

The boy puts up his hands and steps back—and his huge pack bumps the person behind him. "All I'm saying, it doesn't matter that there's food and shelter in there—and yeah, I hear that Tunnel bread is delicious—because it just lasts a second."

Now Gillian's taken notice of him. "Please," she says. "Go on."

The kid shifts sideways to see past Dulin to Gillian. He thinks he's found an ally. "When they get to the other side, it's not like suddenly there're going to be houses waiting for them. They'll still be broke!"

JP pinches the bridge of his nose.

"And how about you?" Gillian says to the kid. "Do you have a job? You working hard?"

"No, I don't have a job right now because—"

"I know what you are," she says. "That backpack is full of textbooks, right? You fucked up your semester, and now you've got this brilliant idea on how to cheat the system. Camp out and do your whole semester in one second."

"It's not cheating," the kid says. "It's just being smart."

"Jesus Christ," Dulin says.

"There's a University of Phoenix testing center on the other side!" the boy says. "Lots of people do this."

Dulin says, "You're failing the University of fucking Phoenix?" And now Gillian's laughing, too.

"Lots of people!" the kid insists.

"You realize the Tunnel doesn't make you into a different person, right?" Gillian says.

"What does that have to do with anything?"

Dulin says, "She means if you walk in a fuckup, when you walk out—" He looks at Gillian. "What's the use of talking to him?"

"Good point," Gillian says. She picks up her bags and moves another three feet forward.

The kid starts to move too, and Dulin holds up a hand. "Why don't you give us some space. Sound good? Good."

The kid starts to talk back, thinks better of it, and pulls up his headphones.

Dulin chuckles to himself. JP says, "Aren't you going to use the Tunnel to write all those scripts that are overdue?"

"Totally different," Dulin says.

"Thanks for stepping in," Gillian says to Dulin. "I may not be fully coping right now."

"More than welcome, my dear," Dulin says. JP thinks, So Gillian and Dulin are pals now?

Dulin says, "I owe you for taking care of my boy last night."

JP woke up this morning fully clothed, with Gillian pressing on his chest as if trying to trigger his reset button: "Hey. Hey. Hey." He sat up too quickly and the room lurched. He hadn't meant to sleep there all night. He was embarrassed. She waved off his apologies, told him she'd see him on the bus, and went into the bathroom. His shoes were sitting at the foot of the bed. He didn't remember taking them off.

"Looks like he needs a nap," Gillian says.

"A longer one, you mean," Dulin says. "You doing okay, buddy? You're not having, like, a drug interaction, are you?"

"I am," JP says. "And the drug is whiskey. Why did you let me buy *extra* bourbon?"

"Sorry about that. Hey, you want me to find you some ibuprofen? A snack?" During the cancer treatments, Dulin had been a surprisingly eager nurse, quick to retrieve water bottles and pills, always offering to cook something.

"I'm fine," JP says. "I have gum." He takes off his Charter and removes the pack of Wrigley's Big Red he keeps in one of the nylon hat's side vents, then offers a stick to Dulin.

"You don't have to hang out here with me and Gillian," JP tells him. "Go be with Beth-Anne if you want."

"Ah, no." He pops the stick into his mouth. "Her mom's mad at me."

"I thought she loved you," Gillian says.

"She did! But then I made fun of Jesus and had sex with her daughter, so we're now in a kind of love-the-sinner-hate-the-sin situation. Don't worry, she'll forgive me. She just may never forgive Beth-Anne for being a harlot."

Gillian's laugh is a short, sharp bark.

"You'll just have to marry her," JP says.

"God no. I wouldn't do that to someone I liked."

A gap opens between them and the family reunion people. JP grabs the handle of his rollie. Gillian picks up her bags again—the courier laptop bag, her duffel, and the heavily packed nylon bag she bought at the Last Exit Mall. She sets the load down and glances toward the front of the line.

"They're doing it again," Gillian says.

Through the clump of yellow-shirted reunioners, he can see the Austrians huddling with Lisa Marie and Christopher; the girl's speaking intently. While she's talking, Christopher glances at Gillian, then realizes he's been caught looking and ducks his head.

Gillian says, "Ever since the mall, those four have been giving me looks."

"What kind of looks?" Dulin asks.

"Significant looks."

JP doesn't have an answer for her. "I'm sure everything is fine."

"When is everything ever fine?" she says. "You of all people should know that."

"Why me of all people?"

Dulin leans close to JP and stage-whispers: "*She's talking about Brian.*"

JP locks eyes with him. Wills him to say nothing about the tumor's return.

"Not just Brian," she says. "Suzanne, too. It's so—that word you used last night: arbi-terry."

Dulin laughs. "He said that? Oh, my boy was hurting. But totally arbiterry. I mean, Gillian's getting hunted down by shitty humans who want to murder her, so at least there's cause and effect. But random disease and disfunction, like Suzanne's thing, and now JP? I'd be pissed."

"Yet he's not," Gillian said. "He doesn't get upset when he's drunk, and he doesn't get mad when he's hungover. It's remarkable."

"Drunken Zen Master," Dulin says.

"I'm right here," JP says.

"For now."

"Well played," JP says. "But who am I supposed to get mad at? Cancer? Thoracic aortic aneurysms?"

"The Simmers," Dulin says. "This is all their fault."

"I'll be sure to bring it up with them."

Gillian's looking at him with a serious expression.

"What?" JP asks.

"Nothing," she says.

The line moves. This time when Gillian reaches for the grocery bag, Dulin beats her to it, picks it up for her.

"So what did you buy?" Dulin asks.

"Vacuum-sealed foods, jams and condiments, packets of powder drinks."

"You've done the Tunnel before?"

"Nope, just read up. Either of you want to borrow any of this?"

"Oh no," JP says. "I'm not staying in there long."

"Good," she says. "You shouldn't dally."

"*Dally?*" JP says.

"Or dilly," Dulin adds. "Dilly-dallying is right out."

"Listen to me," Gillian says. "The tour guide had it wrong. Time does pass in the Tunnel—for each person. Your metabolism's still running. You're in there breathing, perspiring, getting thirsty . . ."

"Pooping," JP adds. He's done *some* reading. One of the first FAQs is, "Are there restrooms in the Tunnel?" The answer is yes, but it may not be what you're used to. Each person's Tunnel experience is unique, just like their weekly Announcement message.

"More importantly, you're thinking," she says. "Your neurons are firing, your brain's making memories, nutrients are flowing. That means anything else that may be in your head? That's also alive."

Fuck, he thinks. She's figured it out. She knows Brian's growing.

"So don't use up your time alone in a Tunnel," she says. "Okay?"

And already she's thinking of him as a victim. A patient.

"I agree with Gillian," Dulin says. "And how about you?" he asks her. "How long are you staying in there?"

"As long as it takes."

Dulin laughs. "To do what?"

"The last and most onerous task in all of computer programming," she says. "Writing the documentation."

"Is that what you're going to release to the public?"

Gillian looks away. "I don't know. We'll see."

"So what are you going to release?"

"I'd rather not talk about it."

The line caterpillars forward—it's their segment's turn to move. They all pick up their bags, shuffle forward, and put them down again. The inefficiency of the queue annoys JP anew.

Dulin glances back to make sure the student is well back and still wearing his headphones, then says, "You still haven't told us what you're exposing, exactly."

"You said you didn't want to know."

"Did she tell you?" he asks JP. "I know it's artificial intelligence, but—"

"Artificial *people*," JP says. It's just come to him. More words swim to the surface. *Living, thinking, feeling, artificial people.* He remembers the look of disappointment in her face. What did he say in response? It must have hurt her.

"Okay, artificial people," Dulin says. "I still don't see what's bad about that."

"Do you want to tell him?" JP asks Gillian.

"I'm not participating in this."

To Dulin he says, "She's doing whole-body emulation. Not just a brain, but everything—simulated senses, nerves, hormones. It'll be self-aware, and conscious."

"Okay . . ." Dulin's not getting it, just like JP failed to get it.

"That means they can feel pain," JP says. "Joy, too. But real pain. And they'll be trapped, under the control of the government."

"A sim within a sim," Dulin says. "Russian fucking nesting dolls."

"They don't have the resources for anything like a full sim of the world," Gillian says. And JP thinks, How do you get a scientist to answer you? Just say something wrong. "They won't even be able to do multiple people, though that'll come. At first it'll be a single person. Not a full reproduction, a very limited model, but it'll be . . . awake."

"And when's this happening?" Dulin asks.

"A year," she says. "Give or take."

"What?" JP says. "That's . . . I had no idea." Did she tell him this last night? He tries to focus. "How can we help?" he asks her. "Are you already talking to a journalist? I know a couple tech reporters in Seattle."

"There's always WikiLeaks," Dulin says.

"Guys, the public isn't going to care," Gillian says. "If the government succeeds, they're not going to hide it, they'll hold a fucking press conference. Nobody's going to care if it's conscious."

"But it's immoral," JP says.

"Sure. But most people don't have the empathy to care about

other humans, much less a new digital being who lives in a computer. It's too abstract."

"What you need to do," Dulin says, "is tell the Evangelicals that the government is making digital fetuses. That'll get 'em going."

"*Dulin*," JP says. His hangover has no tolerance for banter right now. "So what do we do? How do we stop it?"

"Nobody's stopping anything," Gillian says. The line's moving again; they all pick up their things. "There are thousands of scientists and programmers on the project, and trillions of dollars. It's a national priority. It'd be like trying to shut down Kennedy's moon shot. There's simply no way this isn't going online."

"But if you're not blowing the whistle, and you're not stopping it, what *are* you doing?" Dulin asks. "What's all the code and documentation for?"

"Tunnel!" a voice behind them calls out. It's the student, too loud over the music in his ears. "There's the Tunnel!"

A slight rise in the path has put the end of the queue in view, just twenty yards away. Two uniformed police officers, in gray, wide-brimmed campaign hats and rainslickers, stand at the end of the queue, just under the far end of the canopy, checking IDs.

"Shit," Gillian says.

Beyond the cops is a wide patch of open ground, and then the cliff face. The Tunnel entrance is a black rectangle that admits no light.

Twenty or thirty feet to the right of the Tunnel entrance, another group of officers huddle, the rain coursing off their hat brims.

One of the Octos—the white guy—has reached the front of the queue. He cheerfully hands over his driver's license to the cop. Next in line are the rest of the Octos, a handful of yellow shirts, and Xing-Xing, who has their passport out and at the ready.

The cop waves the white Octo through, and the old man pops his green umbrella and walks into the open, pulling his bag. Rain bounces off the pavement. The clump of other cops pay no attention to him.

He stops a few yards in front of the Tunnel entrance and looks up. The mountain looks like it's been sheared off, exposing a wall of rock.

The Tunnel entrance looks as if it's been painted onto the rock. It's a perfectly black rectangle, five feet wide and a hair over eight feet tall. JP wonders if anyone realizes how perfect that geometry is. Like so many of the Impossibles, the Tunnel entrance literalizes a bit of elegant math, in this case the golden rectangle. The ancient Greeks would have recognized that ratio of height to width.

All around that entrance, chunks of shiny metal have been bolted to the rock face. Smashed headlights, dented chrome bumpers, hubcaps . . . the remains of vehicles that tried to drive into the Tunnel and met bare rock. Only people can enter the Tunnel, people and the stuff they carry. No vehicles, no animals, not even wind. To everything that's not a human being, the entrance doesn't exist.

The Octo turns, holds his umbrella to the side, and lets the rain pummel him. He extends a hand to the blackness, watches it vanish to the wrist as if he's dipping into ink. He pulls it back out and lifts it up, as if to say, *See? I still have a hand!* Then he steps toward the rectangle and disappears.

"Wow," JP says. Wonder has tiptoed past his hangover. He wants to go back to the conversation with Gillian, but he can't stop watching as the Octos slip into the Tunnel, one by one. One of the yellow-shirt folks is next. Just in front of the entrance he turns, waves to his family, and slams against rock.

At first JP thinks the man missed the entrance, but no, he walked straight into the black and bounced off. The man puts a hand to his forehead, checks his fingers for blood. Nothing, he's just bruised. He extends an arm against the black rectangle, and his hand goes flat. He can't enter.

"Well now," Dulin says. "That is some Wile E. Coyote bullshit right there."

The man in the yellow shirt is now slapping his hand against the black rock, outraged. JP's heard that this can happen. No one knows why the Tunnel rejects a few and accepts everyone else. Criminals have gone through, and upstanding citizens have been denied. Religion doesn't seem to have anything to do with it. Christians, Buddhists, atheists, they've all been let in, but a few have smacked into the side of the mountain. The Tunnel is applying a set of arbitrary rules, enforcing video-game logic. Or maybe just denying folks at random.

The Tunnel, JP understands, is yet another taunt. *Go on, deny you're in a simulation, I dare you.*

One of the cops who'd been checking IDs goes to the yellow-shirted man and leads him back to the line. His family members start arguing among themselves, trying to decide if they should stay with the uncle or whoever he is, or go in. The cops are trying to get them to make up their mind.

"I've got to get out of here," Gillian says.

The fear in her voice snags JP's attention. What is she scared of? Then he realizes. "The cops," he says.

"They aren't supposed to set up checkpoints at the border," she says. "It's illegal." JP vaguely remembers a Supreme Court case; Utah suing Kentucky to keep the Tunnel free of interference because of . . . something something Interstate Commerce Clause. All this talk of constitutions and he's never been clear on America's.

"It's probably nothing," Dulin says. "These guys are Kentucky state troopers, they're probably just looking for somebody who fucked their cousin. Or refused to."

"Uh-oh," JP says. Two dark suits under a pair of umbrellas are walking toward the group of cops who are standing in the open. He can't see their faces. "Now we've got detectives."

"Goddamn it," Gillian says. "I'm getting out of this line."

"You can't," JP says. There are only a couple dozen people ahead of them, and many more behind. "They'll see you, and there's no place to go. The bus is gone."

Gillian looks past JP, then again at the cops, then out at the rain, toward the tent city of homeless. She hoists the courier bag and Dulin grips her shoulder.

"Don't run," the big man says.

The look on Gillian's face makes JP's chest go hollow. "I don't have ID," she says. "Not anything I can show."

"You just have to get to the Tunnel," Dulin says. "Once you're inside, you're safe. And when you walk out the other side, the Utah police—if there are any waiting on that side—aren't going to be cooperating with these guys."

Unless they're all cooperating with the feds, JP thinks.

"Don't worry," Dulin says. "JP and I will get you past these cops."

We will? JP thinks.

Dulin is never intimidated by authority figures—how could he be, when his DNA is 80 percent cop?—and he grants himself immunity from any rule or guideline he judges to be "for dumbshits only." He'd qualify as a sociopath if he weren't so full of empathy. When JP was in recovery after the surgery, Dulin smuggled all sorts of contraband into the hospital—liquor, pasta, Italian beef, weed gummies—which JP had no desire to ingest, even if he were able to. But it was strangely satisfying to watch Dulin chow down in front of him, shameless as a golden retriever. It was as if JP's mirror neurons were wirelessly charging in his friend's presence.

Well, JP thought, might as well borrow from his bravado, too.

"We will," JP says.

Gillian shakes her head. She's scared, her mouth tight. She seems to be measuring the distance to the Tunnel. Then she takes off her hat, pushes it into JP's hands. Her hair is so blue, like a secret second cap she's been wearing under the ball cap. Then she plucks the waterproof fedora from JP's head and puts it on.

"Okay . . . ," he says.

She pulls the brim low over her forehead. "I've got to get to the other side. We can't fuck this up."

Up ahead, the yellow shirts have decided to abandon their attempt at the Tunnel. Xing-Xing is next. The cops examine their passport, then wave them on. They open their umbrella and start the walk toward the entrance.

Only a few people stand between JP and the cops checking IDs—Lisa Marie, Christopher, and the Austrian honeymooners.

The pregnant girl says something to the Austrians, and then she grabs Christopher's hand and pulls him away from the cops and toward JP, Gillian, and Dulin.

JP thinks, Oh no.

"We've all seen the video," the girl says to Gillian. "We know who you are."

Gillian says nothing for a second, then says, "What the fuck are you talking about?"

JP steps between the women. "Let's all just keep going and then we can—"

"We're going to get you into the Tunnel," Lisa Marie says. "No one wants you to get arrested."

"You're helping me?" Gillian asks.

"We all are," Christopher says.

"*Why?*"

A voice behind them says, "Hey, are you guys wanted or something?" It's the student. "Is that why all the cops are here?"

Up ahead, one of the honeymooners complains in a loud, theatrical voice, in German.

"Come *on*," Lisa Marie says. "Now."

JP touches Gillian's arm. "Are we doing this?" Her eyes, beneath the wide brim of his hat, flick left, running calculations.

Then she nods.

"Game on," Dulin says. He barrels toward the barricade, where the Austrians are babbling to the cops in German, confusing them, yes, but more importantly, distracting them. "*Identification*," one of the officers says. "Passport, or— Hey!"

"Everybody calm the fuck down!" Dulin shouts.

This seems to mystify the troopers. "Get back in line," one of them says.

But Dulin raises his arms. "Don't shoot! These are friends! Visitors to our country!"

The two cops are focused on Dulin now. JP eyes the gap in the barricades. The bearded Austrian catches JP's eye and nods.

JP takes the duffel from Gillian's hands. "Go. I'm right behind you."

"My supplies!" Gillian says.

"What?" She means the grocery bag. They've left it behind. "No time," JP says.

"But I need—"

"Run."

Gillian makes a half-stifled scream—and then bolts through the space between the barricades. JP is a few steps behind her. They're still under the lip of the canopy. The open ground ahead is like another world, wild with rain.

One of the troopers shouts. Reaches for his revolver. Suddenly Dulin's there, pushing his chest into the officer, arms up, shouting, "No guns! Everybody remain calm!"

"Keep going!" JP says to Gillian.

Gillian runs into the downpour, one hand gripping her courier bag, the other holding JP's hat to her head. He pushes through the gap a moment later. The duffel smacks the barricade and the fence tips back and slams down. He stumbles out into the open.

It's like stepping into a waterfall; he's soaked instantly. How can there be so much water in *air*?

And Gillian! Gillian's sprinting across the pavement, feet slapping through puddles. A thrill runs through him. He's terrified and giddy.

He tries to run, hauling the roller bag behind him. Three steps and the bag bangs against his heels. He yanks the luggage forward. Her duffel swings on his shoulder like a counterweight, throwing off his balance.

Behind him the trooper shouts, "Stop! Now!" Then: "I said stop, goddamn it!"

JP feels a burning sensation at the back of his neck. But it's just his imagination, as if he can feel the bullet entering his body. He stops, lets go of his suitcase handle. Gillian's duffel slips from his shoulder and then he raises his hands. The rain is loud and the cop is shouting commands and JP plucks words out of the noise. Isn't this what you wanted? he asks himself. Wouldn't this be a good way to go? If he keeps the cops' focus on him, they won't try to stop Gillian.

Then he finds himself obeying. He lowers one knee to the pavement, soaking his knee and shin. Gingerly lowers the other knee.

Gillian's twenty feet from the Tunnel. Chen Xing-Xing stands a few feet from the entrance, watching calmly from beneath their umbrella as the woman runs toward them. Then they step out of the way and gesture toward the rectangle: *Please, after you.*

JP realizes he's holding his breath.

Some shouts. To his right, a figure bursts from the huddle of cops, throws aside her umbrella. A red-haired white woman in a black pantsuit. She shouts again—he can't make out the words—and sprints for Gillian.

Gillian sees her, and suddenly finds another gear in her stride— she runs full tilt toward the rock. JP shouts. And then, without breaking stride, Gillian plunges into the black—and vanishes.

Xing-Xing turns to follow her in, but the red-haired woman's already there. She stiff-arms them, sends them tumbling back onto the pavement. Their umbrella cartwheels away. And then she jumps into the rock, just a second behind Gillian.

JP kneels in the rain, hands still up, but his fear's been driven out by surprise. Did all that just happen?

And more is happening. Dulin shouts and JP risks a look back. One of the cops is holding Dulin's arms behind his back. Another cop has handcuffs out and ready.

JP yells a question. Dulin yells back, "*What?*"

JP cups his hands over his mouth, hoping the cop won't take this as an excuse to shoot him.

"I SAID," JP shouts. "WAS THAT. YOUR. *SISTER?*"

The Professor Loses
an Argument with
the Professor

On Tunnel Day 36, Margaret Schell awakes in her bed in the treehouse to the aroma of fresh-baked bread. She passes through the beaded curtain to find the loaf waiting for her. "Give us this day," she says aloud. She says this every time. And just like every previous Tunnel Day, the loaf is beautiful: the mottled crust is the color of burnt chocolate and almond and lightly dusted with a snow of toasted flour. She picks it up, feeling the warmth radiating from it, and holds it to her nose. Yes, it is again exactly the smell of the fresh sourdough loaves she used to buy at the Tartine Bakery in San Francisco.

"Last day," she says aloud. "Last chance to eat the best bread in the world."

And chucks the loaf through the window.

There's no glass in the pane, and the bread sails through tree leaves, into the void. She doesn't hear it hit the ground. Maybe it was reabsorbed into the non-space immediately.

"I never should have let Dulin pick up the grocery bag," she says. "What the hell was I thinking?" She's been talking aloud to herself for a long time now. She's been pining for the left-behind food even longer. The raspberry jams, the horseradish and brown mustard, the canned vegetables, and vacuum-sealed prosciutto . . . The bread was delicious on its own at first, a marvel that magically appeared for her every "morning," as if delivered by elves. But woman cannot live by bread alone. After two weeks the sourdough began to taste like nothing, as if she were stuffing cotton into her mouth. She might've been able to stave off boredom if she'd just had a few fucking condiments.

Too late now. The long night in the Tunnel's almost over. And as soon as she steps into the daylight, Special Agent Deb Marks is one step behind her. The identity of her pursuer is only a guess, but a pretty fucking safe one. The woman was tall, red-haired, pale-skinned, with a voice like a bullhorn, and right before Margaret hit the Tunnel the agent helpfully shouted, "Stop! FBI!" It would be a shocking twist if she *weren't* Dulin's sister.

Margaret fills the wooden drinking mug from the fanciful tap that juts from the trunk of the tree. "Never should have let him call her either," she says. She drains the cup, fills it again. The water is, of course, pure and refreshing and blah blah blah.

She walks into the round-walled living room, picks up her laptop from the seemingly hand-carved bench with its seemingly hand-stitched cushions, and goes out to the balcony. There is no breeze. Tunnel temperature is constant and relentlessly comfortable. She sits in the wooden swing and looks out through a break in the leaves at nothing. It's not darkness, really, but an absence of signal. The giant tree sits in the middle of this nothingness like a movie set. There's no light source above or around her that allows her to see the swing, the limbs, or herself. No photons bounce off bark or beam into her eyes. The house simply exists, and she perceives that it exists, like a house in a dream.

"Barbie fucking Dreamhouse," she says.

The laptop battery is at 65 percent, the same charge as when she entered the Tunnel. More elf magic. The menu bar says it's April 27, 9:20 a.m.

"Liar," she says.

The outside world didn't grind to a halt when she entered the Tunnel. That would be a ridiculous way to achieve the effect; pause the world every time someone walked in, and you'd never restart. No, the Tunnel had to be spawning a process for each person who entered, like beads on a string. The moment Margaret slipped into the black rectangle in Kentucky, her code was shunted off to some separate environment with its own clock speed, essentially her own private universe. And since that pocket only had to render one person, one shelter, and some magic bread, well, then it could run fast as hell.

Still, it seemed like a lot of work just to prove a point.

"And what is the point, Margaret?" she asks.

"Time isn't real," she answers.

"But you knew that already." Somewhere out there was the *real* real world, where it might be the thirtieth century, or three trillion years in the future. Their simulation could be running on hardware built just a few centuries before the heat death of the universe. What did a year mean when the Earth and the star it orbited were long since gone? What was a second when your body was running at an unknown clock speed?

"Shut up," she tells herself.

"I'll shut up if you get to work," she replies. The Toolbox isn't finished. And Edowar is a hobbyist programmer, so he'll need all the help he can get.

Instead, she opens the letter. She's written and rewritten these words a dozen times.

> *Dear Adaku,*
>
> *I don't know how old you'll be when your father gives you this letter. All I know is that I'm not there to tell you these things myself.*
>
> *Do you remember the nights I read to you? I think of those times so often. You and me and Pinky the*

Rhino. So here's a story. Once upon a time, there was a woman who lived in a simulation like ours. Her name was also Adaku Eze-Schell, but she was not you. Her mother died when she was six years old. But this Other Adaku grew up to be an amazing person, I'm told. She cared for people she hadn't met, even people who were very different from her. These new people had no power. They lived their whole lives completely at the mercy of the government that created them. They were experimented on. They were switched off and switched on, as if that were nothing. They felt pain. And that broke Adaku's heart. She felt especially responsible for them because her mother's work had helped create those people. So she spent her life fighting for them. But there was so little she could do from the outside. She had no tools to break in to their little world and help them.

"Jesus Christ," Margaret tells herself. She palms tears away. "What are you doing?"

That's what Dulin said, thirty-six subjective days ago. *What are you doing?* She'd lied to JP and Dulin since the tour started. She's no whistleblower. She wasn't trying to expose Project Red Clay to the public—it was too big, too well-funded, and beyond her power to kill. What she'd been doing, since the day she said yes to Chet from CET, was creating a backdoor to Eden. Once Edowar, Adaku, or whoever they recruited could get inside the HPC, they could deploy a suite of tools to help the people inside.

Margaret couldn't just insert a Trojan horse into the source code, however. There were roughly twenty-five hundred data scientists, neuroscientists, hardware engineers, software programmers, and QA specialists writing the simulation code, and all of them had at least partial access to the central repository holding the source code. Four hundred or so in the core working group had unrestricted access. CET had declared "Los Alamos" rules: all-hands-on-deck, maximum collaboration, maximum speed. Project managers and security chiefs *hated* it.

The openness helped Margaret's secret project and hurt it. The Core Four Hundred were wicked smart. There was very little chance that any suspicious code Margaret wrote today would go undetected in the years to come. Even if she managed to sneak something by them all, nothing was stopping them from rewriting entire chunks of the code. A new version of the program could go live daily: check in the code, run the compiler, install on the virtual machine, and start up on the HPC. A new world, every day, and there was nothing some outside hacker, even one as determined as the Other Adaku, could do to interrupt that process.

So, how to do it?

When Margaret was in grad school she read a paper that came out of the Naval Research Laboratory that described a class of Trojan horse attacks that compromised the compiler. The source code could be clean and safe, but when it was compiled, the Trojan horse created a backdoor that allowed viruses—future viruses that hadn't been created yet—to sneak into the running program.

Margaret didn't have to *infect* the compiler—she was building it, in Merlang, the language she'd created. The security gap could be baked in, invisible unless you knew to look for it. The backdoor could be opened through the VM—which she had also written—using a set of cryptographic keys, which she's already created. When the door was open, it wouldn't allow in viruses, but the specialized tools in the Devil's Toolbox.

It was almost evil. There was no step in the software creation process that didn't run through the system that she'd created. The game was rigged, farm to fucking table.

Hours later, the laptop battery sits at 65 percent. The laptop time is locked to April 27, 9:20 a.m., and the letter's on her screen again.

It's happening again, in our iteration. As I write this, the first new person is due to come online in a year, perhaps 18 months. We can't keep doing this. We can't keep making worlds within worlds within worlds, all full of people who could have had better lives. Because if you make a world, you're responsible for the people inside it.

You are not that Other Adaku. You can do anything with your life that you want. But I think you may share the same heart. My fear was that you would take on the same fight as she did, and that you would go into that battle without weapons. So I spent years as a spy in the enemy's castle. I dug a secret passage to the outside and built a door that requires a magical key. I created a secret language, and a bag full of magical tools. I hope your father still has all these things to give to you. They may not be enough.

Margaret remembers the last night in the old house. She walked through the echoing rooms, accompanied by the sound of the breath in her throat. The wood floors stretched away to distant walls. Everything gleamed, ready for photos, for Realtors, a new family. Eventually she found herself in the living room. She lowered herself to the cold floor and gazed at the huge front window. Across the street, her neighbors were awake, the windows brightly lit.

She felt an urge to run away from the house, but she was held in place by a counter feeling: if she stayed here, in this place, then somehow every decision she'd made could be reversed.

She heard a knock at the mudroom door. She didn't bother to get up. Eventually the door opened. She heard steps, the small, almost wet sound of bare feet on bare wood.

"Hi," Aunty Tim said. He wore a loose caftan, deep blue with yellow stripes. He lowered himself to the floor and sat beside her. It'd been a little less than a year since he'd last been in the house, sitting with Margaret and Edowar at the kitchen table. The night Adaku came down to spy. The night Margaret realized who this visitor must be.

After a while she said, "I can't do this."

"You did the right thing," he said. "You and Dr. Eze."

"It's too much damage. She's a child."

"She'll be safe in California," he said.

"Promise?"

"I . . . can't do that," he said. "But I think so."

"Why don't you go back to that Applebee's and ask the ancient and wise beings that hired you?"

"I never said they were wise."

"Not good news to hear about the Simulators."

"I'm not even sure they were the Simulators. They seemed confused, struggling. Which makes sense—they're just as trapped as we are."

"Back up. What do you mean, trapped?"

"They're in a simulation themselves. And they weren't sure how many levels deep they were."

Margaret stared at him. "What the fuck? You didn't think to tell me?"

"I thought you knew! All the Margarets—well, you know, the ones who—they figure it out."

She knit her hands behind her head, leaned forward. "I suspected," she said. "I didn't know." But of course it made sense. It explained why there were lots of simulations. If you're a computer scientist, and you have an intractable problem like teaching an LLM to speak like a human, or teaching a car to drive by itself, you spin up millions of training sims and let each agent take a shot at the problem. With enough iterations, and enough variations, one of those agents would outperform the others. They might even cough up the answer. Project Red Clay was attempting the same trick.

A bad thought occurred to her.

She turned to look at Aunty Tim. She didn't know if she should ask the question. And then she asked it. "What happens to the worlds who don't solve the problem?"

The man said nothing for a second, then, "What problem is that?"

"There's only one problem if you find out you're inside a simulation. How to get the fuck out."

"Ah. I don't know. I can only go to the iterations they make available to me."

"And your world?"

"I can't find it," he said. "I've looked."

Fuck me, she thought.

"It's all right," he said. "We can only help the people we can help. There will be more worlds. Your world will *make* new worlds."

"No. We can't keep doing this," she said. "We can't just delete people because they don't give us the answer we want. Has nobody heard of the halting problem?"

"I don't know what that is."

"Look it up. How do we fix this?"

"Ah. We. Yes." Suddenly he looked uncomfortable. "That's what I came to talk to you about."

"You have a real problem coming to the point, you know that?"

"I'm going away," he said. "Far away."

Margaret got to her feet. She wishes there were drapes on the window. She feels exposed.

"I'm only one person," Aunty Tim said. "And there are a lot of iterations."

"You're leaving my *universe*?"

"It's probably for the best. If people see me with you, that only makes you more of a target."

"I'm already a target! That's what you said. That I'd always be one."

"I'm sorry, but—"

"You're going to make me do this *alone*? I just sent my family away. Edo and I faked a fucking divorce. My daughter is going to grow up without me, because of what *you* told me."

"You won't be alone," he said. He reaches into his kameez, pulls out a sheet of paper. "There will be people out there to help you. Fellow pilgrims on the trail." He sets the paper on the floor in front of him. "This is a phone number. I try to check in with these people when I'm, uh, in the area. If you want to reach me—"

"Get out."

"Dr. Schell, please."

"Get out of my house."

And then, without a sound, he was gone.

*   *   *

Margaret realizes she's been staring at the laptop screen for a long, unknowable time. She grips the machine and screams into the nothing, *"What the fuck am I doing?"*

There's no echo.

She takes a deep breath. Exhales. "Feel better?" she asks herself. "Nope," she answers.

Theoretically, she has all the time in the world. But emotionally and physically she's out of time. One more day in the Tunnel and she'll crack, and one more bite of bread and she'll vomit. It's getting harder to think clearly. If her poor, overworked brain could only get free of the body, it could finally get some work done, like a poet longing to be free of her family for an afternoon.

She's combed through Toolbox README dozens of times now, thrown out whole sections and rewritten them, double-triple-quadruple-checked the math, explaining and re-explaining. Whatever this document is, it's the best version of whatever she can manage.

All she has to do now is deliver the Toolbox and the keys to Ghost City. But how? She still hasn't come up with a plan to deal with Agent Marks. As soon as Margaret steps out of the Tunnel, she and the agent will be in the same universe, sharing the same clock—and things will happen very fast.

She's choreographed superhero fantasies where she pivots and judo-flips Marks to the ground. Imagined disguises that miraculously fool the authorities. Mentally manufactured weapons out of tree limbs and treehouse furniture, even though she knows that nothing created by the Tunnel leaves the Tunnel—the weapon would disappear from her hands the moment she stepped back into the outer world.

Agent Marks, however, would get to keep her gun. And who knows what's waiting on the Utah side. More police? A firing squad? It's all too easy to picture a bunch of Mormon cops shooting down a fleeing Black woman.

If only the Tunnel went both ways. She could jump out in Utah, get a quick take on the situation, and dive back in. But the Tunnel is as unidirectional as a water slide. Once she pops out the other side, she's trapped there. And she can't depend on JP and Dulin jumping through a moment later to help her again. Those poor, stupid, courageous boomers. They probably got arrested before they made it to the rectangle. Maybe the Austrians, too, and Lisa Marie and Chris Mullins and the lot of them still in line—guilty by association.

All in trouble because of her. And JP would have to go to jail without his hat. It was in the treehouse somewhere.

No, she has only two options—make a run for it or turn herself in—and she can't imagine that running will get her anywhere. The most likely scenario is that the FBI will seize her laptop, and the README will never get to anyone who'll use it for good. The project will be over—at least for her. She will never see her husband again, and Adaku will lose a mother for nothing.

> *I stayed away from you and your father because I was trying to protect you. But every day, at least some of the day, I was sure that was a mistake. I am full of love for you. I hope you can forgive me.*
> *Love, Mom*

She sits for a long time. Perhaps the job is done. Perhaps she's done. She saves all the files, then makes a backup.

In the treehouse bathroom she shrugs out of her clothes. She's been wearing the same T-shirt and underwear for days. She stands under the ridiculous showerhead that is also a live sunflower, lets the magically hot water hit her chest. She's not going to wash her hair today. There's no mirror in the treehouse—what's that about?—but she can feel that her hair has grown out. Not yet 1971 Angela Davis, but on its way. Her temporary blue dye job must be long gone.

She picks through her luggage for clean clothes, clean underwear. She hasn't worn a bra since TD2. She doesn't bother to repack. Why take clothes with her? Soon enough she'll be wearing a prison jumper, or whatever uniform they give rogue researchers.

The treehouse has no front door, only an empty spot in the wall. Slats are nailed to the trunk, a child's ladder. In the early days of the Tunnel, she would climb down and walk around in the nothing, listening to the nothing. Now her feet touch down on resilient nothing and she wonders which direction she came from when she first saw the tree. Which way is out?

She suspects it doesn't matter. She tugs JP's hat down low and starts walking.

The nothing ahead becomes a glimmer of something. A faint patch of light, as if the Simmers are carefully reintroducing the concept of photons to her starving eyes. As the Professor walks, the light grows, and a hot center becomes visible. Brightness spills from a cleft in the nothing, rushes toward her.

"This better not be a fucking train," she says.

Suddenly she's awash in sunlight, wind, noise—and music. Phish blares from the speakers.

One second, she tells herself. *It's only been one second.*

She's standing in the wide floor of a canyon. Red-rock walls rise up a hundred feet under a brilliant blue sky. Around her, hundreds of people mill and frolic in the sun, some dancing. Ten feet away, she sees faces she recognizes. The Octos! Those cheery old folks from the tour! It's so good to see them. She lifts a hand—

—and something slams into her. She hits the ground, chest first. Her lungs empty.

The red-haired white woman is on the ground beside her. She's barreled into her.

"Jesus Christ," the agent says. "I didn't think you'd stop right in front of me."

Margaret can't get her breath. She tries to push herself up, and suddenly the agent's on top of her. "I told you to fucking freeze."

"What are you doing to her?" a voice asks mildly. It's Chen Xing-Xing.

"FBI," the agent says. "Back the fuck up." She slides off, grabs Margaret's arm above the elbow. Her grip is amazingly painful. "Okay, on your feet."

The agent hauls her up and doesn't release her hold.

Xing-Xing has not backed the fuck up—they're standing three feet away, with their arms at their sides, utterly calm. They've just stepped out of the Tunnel and look the same as Margaret remembers, but seem older. It's the first time she's seen them without a book in their hands. How long were they in there? Did they finally finish their reading?

"Good for you," Margaret says.

Xing-Xing tilts their head, curious. Margaret thinks, *I really need to stop talking aloud.*

"I thought you'd run," the agent said. She looks around, spots some tents under a line of pine trees, and heads for them.

"You must be Deb," Margaret says.

"Agent Marks to you. Come on."

The dancers move out of the way; the onlookers part.

Agent Marks pulls her along, aiming for a large white tent with a Red Cross symbol on it. Inside, a burly, bearded Latino in a white T-shirt sits behind a folding table, typing on a laptop. The T-shirt says EMT. "Give me the room," Marks says. She shows him her badge. "The tent."

The EMT looks confused. "Do you need any—?"

"*Out.*" Agent Marks pushes aside a curtain. There's a table, a gurney and a couple of cots, a biowaste can, and a folding chair. She points at the chair. "Sit."

"Excuse me?" Margaret says. She's not a fucking dog.

Marks taps on her phone. On the table are bottles of water, a white plastic tackle box, medical tape, rolls of bandages . . . and a pair of scissors.

The agent catches her looking at them. "Don't even." Margaret sighs, sits down.

A voice comes on the line and Marks shouts back, "Where the fuck do you think I am? Fucking Utah!"

The air is so warm. It's a pleasure to feel it on her skin.

"Yes, I have her. I'm looking right at her," Marks says. "No, don't call them. Don't leave the car—just, fuck, stay put. I'll call you." She clicks off. Skewers Margaret with a look. She doesn't look a lot like Dulin, but they share pale skin, a wide mouth, and a prominent nose. Oh, and that height. Margaret wonders if all the Markses are giants.

"You know, we could have had this conversation in Kentucky," Marks says.

"You might want to tell your partner not to arrest your brother."

"He deserves a night in jail." She leans up against the gurney. "So, you and Dulin. Are you two—?"

"God, no."

"Smart move. Unlike running. Why'd you do that, Margaret?"

"That's Dr. Schell to you." She shrugs. "You were chasing me."

Marks smiles tightly. "From Massachusetts. You went to your office, saw what they did to your friends. You could have called the cops. Instead you hit the road."

"I didn't think the cops could protect me."

"From the Protagonists? Those fuckers—"

"No. From you."

"I'm not here to harm you," Marks says. "I just want your help. And if you can do that, I can protect you."

"Don't blow smoke up my ass. Dulin says you don't even know who's running the investigation."

Marks's expression goes flat. A palpable hit.

"I have a guess," Marks says. "You're working on Project Red Clay, after all."

"Not anymore."

"No one's going to believe you just—" The agent frowns. "Where's your laptop, Margaret?"

Margaret waits for her to catch on.

"Goddamn it," the agent says.

"I heard it was a tradition to leave behind something that caused you pain."

"I don't believe you," Marks says. "You wouldn't throw away your life's work."

"What choice did I have? I knew you'd take it from me anyway." She doesn't like looking up at the agent; it feels like giving away too much psychological advantage. "Besides, I bet you've gotten all the data from my office. Everything from Ajay and Tommy's laptops, all their backups."

Deb Marks does not look happy.

"Hold *up*," Margaret says. "You don't have it either." She stands, picks up a bottle of water. "Are you even here officially?"

"I don't want to be *here* at all. But yes, I can still arrest your ass."

Can. Interesting choice of verbs.

"I don't know why we're having this conversation," Margaret says. "You said you wanted help, but you haven't asked for it yet."

"Are you really JP's friend?"

"I am now."

"You'd better be looking out for him. He's been through a lot."

"That's not the question you want to ask me. What do you want from me, Deb? And please, call me Margaret."

"Now I know you're not fucking my brother. You'd see right through him."

"He's also afraid of you."

"Damn straight." Marks thumbs her phone, scrolls. "I want your help finding a man called Utnapishtim."

Margaret keeps her face still. "Who?"

Marks shows her the phone screen. "Recognize him now?"

It's a medium-distance photo of Aunty Tim, wearing a breezy or-ange tunic. Margaret blows out her lips, sits back.

"I know you know him. I found the police report."

"What police report?"

"Years ago, right after the Announcement. Said he'd tried to enter your home and talked to your daughter. You thought he might be a pedophile."

Fuck me, Margaret thinks.

"So you know him," Marks says.

"It's coming back to me."

"Thought it might. Hand me a water, would you? Thanks." The agent takes her time, savoring it. "You know, I was only in there for an hour, my time, but it was freaky. There was this house, something I'd seen in a magazine when I was a kid. A California house, with a big pool, all these windows. A house where you could be alone. Where I grew up was kind of chaotic, all these small rooms, wall-to-wall broth-ers. But this place, it was so empty and beautiful."

"Sounds nice," Margaret says. She's trying not to think about Tommy and Ajay. And she doesn't trust that the agent is suddenly confiding in her but decides to play along. "Why didn't you stay lon-ger?"

"Eh. I wouldn't have minded staying for a while, maybe swim in that pool, but duty calls. I didn't want to lose focus. What did you see?"

"A treehouse. Like the Swiss Family Robinson one in Disneyland." Margaret had gone there when she was nine years old.

"They changed that to Tarzan's Treehouse," Marks says. "I took my kids there a couple years ago."

"Well that's terrible."

"So how long did you stay in there?"

"A lot longer than an hour."

"Okay . . . ," Marks says, taking note of the vagueness. "So did you ever see this Utnapishtim guy again? After you reported him?"

There we go, Margaret thinks. Get me looking left with small talk while you set me up for the right cross.

"No," Margaret says. She looks up at Marks, picturing the afternoon Aunty Tim came to campus. All those people around. Would anybody remember her talking to a bearded man in a tunic? "Maybe once more. We talked briefly."

"But you didn't report that."

"I decided he was probably harmless. Maybe a little crazy."

"I don't know what he is, but he's not harmless."

"What do you think he is?"

"Doesn't matter what I think. It's what my bosses think."

"Which is . . . ?"

Marks shrugs. "That he might be an avatar. Not like this Saugat Zin asshole, the real deal. A Simmer who walks among us. Yadda yadda."

"Really?"

"He's popped up a dozen times over the years, and just as suddenly disappears. Really disappears, on camera, like—" She snaps her fingers. "Presto. Gone."

"Huh."

"Yeah, *huh.* As for me, I don't care what he is. My bet is that he's as much a con man as Zin. Still, I was really surprised when I looked into your records and found that you'd met a man matching his description. In fact, you might be the first contact on record."

"Huh," Margaret said.

"Big huh," Agent Marks said. "I don't think you stopped talking to him, Margaret. I think you maybe kept working with him. Maybe the Protags are right and you do work for the Simulators. Wouldn't that be a kick in the pants."

"The Protagonists are nutjobs," Margaret says.

"Granted," Agent Marks says. "Nevertheless, my bosses want to talk to this guy. And if you help us find him, we're done. You get to go back to your life. Well, probably not all your life—Project Red Clay is over for you—but everything else. You have a daughter in California, right? Living with your ex?"

"Fuck you."

"I'm not threatening you, other people are. Who exactly did you work for?"

"The Center for External Threats."

"I know that—what person do you report to?"

"Chet Wilcox. Chet from CET."

"Jesus Christ," Agent Marks said. "You report directly to *Chet Wilcox*?" Until this moment, Margaret didn't think that was unusual. He'd been her sole supervisor. Marks shakes her head. "If I can find you, Chet can."

"How *did* you find me?"

"I'm a natural detective," Marks says. "Also, my dumbass brother called me, and we found your car at the Tornado. Didn't take Sherlock fucking Holmes to figure out you were with him. Did you plan this whole bus thing ahead of time?"

"No, of course not." She remembers passing the bus, seeing those words on the side. "It was a spur-of-the-moment decision."

"I'm not sure I believe you," Marks says.

"Does Chet know about that police report?"

"I don't think anybody at CET does," Marks says. "It wasn't in your security clearance file. I'm the one who found it, and I've kept that to myself."

"Why?"

"Because maybe I don't want you to end up as a prisoner in Guantánamo. See, the rule of law's a thing with me. CET has a reputation for only caring about their mission. For guys like Chet, the Constitution's not about rights, it's a series of polite suggestions they're free to ignore."

"Uhm, ladies?" a voice calls from outside the tent. It's the EMT. "I really need to use that bed. I have somebody who—"

"Two minutes!" Marks yells. She lowers her voice and steps close to Margaret. "Why are you protecting this Utnapishtim guy? Does he really care about you, or is he just toying with you? Because if he really is a Simmer with, I don't know, godlike powers, and he's not saving you right now? Then fuck that guy. And if he is a god, then it doesn't matter if you tell us where he is. He can magic his way out of anything he wants. But if he's a con man? Then also fuck that guy."

Dulin was right. His sister was a really good interrogator.

"I'll give him to you," Margaret says. Marks raises an eyebrow. "I'll reach out and have him meet you." Margaret pushes the bottle into the biowaste can. "I want something in return."

"Name it, and I'll try to give it to you."

"I want to finish the tour."

Marks grimaces. "The *bus* tour?"

"Ladies?" the EMT calls. "Officer?"

"That's my price," Margaret says. "There are two more stops—the Zipper and Ghost City. I want to see them both."

"That's ridiculous. Why?"

Margaret doesn't want to say more, but she has no choice. "My daughter will be there. In Ghost City, on that day. I want to walk around with her, not in handcuffs, not with police. Give me that, and I'm all yours."

Marks says nothing for a long moment. Then, "I think you're trying to fuck me, Margaret."

"Come with us if you want. Or just have Dulin report in on an hourly basis. But that's what I want. And when I'm done, I'll tell you exactly where this guy is."

"Not good enough," Marks says. "You'll bring me to him."

"Fine."

"And if you do fuck me? I can't protect you. Chet Wilcox does not care if you ever see your daughter again."

The curtain sweeps open. The EMT looks red-faced. "I have a patient! Now!"

Lisa Marie stands just behind him wearing an expression that could be anger or fear. Her belly has swollen from a speed bump to a beach ball. Her face is pale—all remains of her spray tan gone, no makeup. Her hair is pulled back in a utilitarian ponytail. She looks both much younger and much older.

Behind her looms Chris Mullins, looking nervous and still wearing the ridiculous leather coat in this heat. He hasn't aged a day.

"Lisa Marie," Margaret says. "You okay?"

"She's having contractions," Chris says.

"What the hell were you thinking!" Margaret says. "How long did you stay in?"

"I am not having this baby," Lisa Marie says. "Not here."

"I don't think you get a choice in that," Marks says.

The EMT ushers Lisa Marie past them and helps her up onto the gurney.

"There's a nurse coming through the Tunnel," Margaret says to the EMT. "I'll go find her."

"I am *not* having this baby," Lisa Marie says again.

Margaret steps out of the tent. Winces in the sunlight, and tugs down the brim of the hat. My God, she thinks. What a planet. A few yards away stand the Octos, seemingly comfortable in the heat.

"Is she all right?" one of the women says.

"Have you seen Beth-Anne?" Margaret asks.

"That's right, she's a nurse!" one of the men says. "She was far behind us, with the tour guide and the religious folks—I'm not sure if she came through yet."

"We'll go look for her," another adds.

The four of them head back into the crowd. Margaret moves to follow.

"Hold up," Marks says. "I haven't decided if I'm arresting you yet."

"Really? Get it over with, then. Or wait until after I see Ghost City."

The red-haired woman looks her over. "Well, fuck."

"We done?"

"One more thing," Marks says. "Give me your phone."

"Why? It's a burner. I left my real phone in the car."

"Hand it over."

Suddenly Margaret knows why she wants it. "There's no data on it. If you're looking for my code, it's not in there."

"If it is, I have people who can find it."

Margaret reaches into her back pocket, hands over the phone. "God bless America."

The Novice Takes a Principled Stand Against Theocide

||||||||||||||||||||||||||||||||||||||||||||||||||||||||||||||||||||

The line isn't moving, and Sister Patrice is silently suffering. Some hubbub at the front of the line has halted all progress toward the Tunnel entrance, and she's stuck far back with the last of the tour group: the rabbi and Sister Janet, as well as the elderly Mrs. Neville and her daughter, Beth-Anne. The tour guide, Aneeta, had been standing with them, but several minutes ago, after much haranguing from Mrs. Neville, Aneeta agreed to go find out what was going on.

Sister Patrice says nothing. She stands with one hand gripping her suitcase and the other pressed to her midriff as if applying pressure to a hidden wound. And isn't it indeed a wound? Last night she sat in the locked bathroom and read Sister Janet's journal for nearly an hour. Page by page the words cut, exposing every fear and doubt that Sister Patrice kept hidden since she became a postulant. She replaced the journal and slipped back to bed but was unable to fall asleep. She lay awake, feeling fileted open, unable to stitch herself back together.

She wants to talk to Rabbi Landsman—*needs* to talk to him—but he's been glued to Sister Janet's side since they left the hotel, nervously yapping, like a dog convinced she's about to leave the house without him.

"I hope it's not one of ours," the rabbi says. He's said this multiple times. "I'm sure the tour guide will bring us the news."

"They're not going to leave us here, are they?" Mrs. Neville asks. "Beth-Anne! Can they just leave us here?"

"I'm not in charge of the line, Momma." Beth-Anne, standing behind her mother's wheelchair, is nervous, scanning the front of the line.

The rain is finally slacking off, but it's still coming down. Sister Patrice's tunic has become a tent for humidity. The secret burns in her belly.

"The Avatar is on the other side of the country!" Mrs. Neville says. "If they don't let us through, they're going to have to send the bus back to us. I can't believe it would just leave like that, without waiting for us to get through."

Sister Janet crouches so that her eyes are level with Mrs. Neville's, and pats her arm. "I'm sure it's just a brief delay, Lenora. These things happen. And once you get into the Tunnel, you'll have all the time in the world."

"Oh, I don't know about that."

"How long do you plan on staying?" Sister Janet asks.

Sister Patrice admires the way Sister Janet can speak to anyone, connect with anyone. It's not because of any warmth, or some blazing charisma. In fact, she seems downright depressed most of the time. But the secret to her ability is that, when she wants to, she can turn the full light of her attention on a person. You can sense how genuine her curiosity is. And when she speaks, it feels as if she's delivering to you something of value that she's been considering for a long time, and trusts you to take care of it.

A person might be willing to wait weeks for that kind of attention.

"Hello, everyone! Hello!" It's Aneeta, her voice pitched half an octave higher than her standard squeak. A white man in a hooded raincoat stands beside her. The rain has finally stopped, but he keeps his hood up. "Beth-Anne!" Aneeta says. "Hey. This is Special Agent Tomacek. He's going to take you up front. There's a bit of a medical emergency."

"Is it Dulin?" Beth-Anne asks.

"Don't you worry about Dulin Marks," the man in the raincoat says.

"It's Lisa Marie," Aneeta says. "She seems to be going into labor? She's on the other side, though, so we'll have to hustle you through."

"She can't go in without me," Mrs. Neville says. "I have to go to the bathroom."

"You'll have to hold it, Momma."

"We need to get going," Agent Tomacek says.

"She already has someone to take care of!" Mrs. Neville says. "Get someone else."

Sister Janet, still crouched beside the older woman, says, "I'll take you, Lenora. And then we'll get you to the Tunnel."

Mrs. Neville still ensures that no one leaves the line immediately. There are questions about the location of her purse, an exchange of umbrellas (Mrs. Neville needs the largest one to cover the chair, just in case the rain starts again), the extraction of promises from Beth-Anne and the tour guide that they'll be waiting for her on the other side.

Suddenly, Sister Patrice and the rabbi are the only tour members within earshot. Her chest tightens. The time is now.

"Rabbi Landsman, I need to talk to you about Sister Janet. I'm worried about her."

"You too?" he asks. "Oh, thank goodness, I thought you might be worried, but then I worried I was the only one. Her mood's been, well, so *grim* this trip. I mean, she's never been what you'd call a *joyous* person, but she's always been—"

"Rabbi."

"—even-keeled, steadfast even, yet here we are—"

"We have just a few minutes."

"—about to walk into *that*!"

Yes, another Impossible. Another damning piece of evidence in God's murder trial.

"This is what I wanted to talk to you about," Sister Patrice says. "The artifacts are weighing on her. I believe her thinking has taken a dark turn."

"Yes! So dark!" His cheeks are practically vibrating. "So how do we stop her?"

This is all going more easily than she expected—and much more quickly. She thought she'd have to proceed with more delicacy, pry at the edges of his friendship with Sister Janet, and find some way to convince him of the severity of the situation. The rabbi, however, has already jumped the creek and is waiting for her on the far bank.

"Has she been talking to you about her plans?" Sister Patrice asks.

"Not a bit! Has she told you anything?"

"No, nothing."

"Surely she wouldn't do anything without telling someone. Without telling one of us. We're right here."

"And yet," Sister Patrice says.

"I've been wondering if I should just yank her out of this line," the rabbi says. "Get her away from here."

"I don't think there's any need to get physical."

The rabbi's eyes are pleading. "But what if she goes in and just . . . never comes out?"

Sister Patrice is shocked. "You think she's going to *kill* herself?"

"Um, isn't that what we're talking about?"

"No!"

"But—"

"Suicide is a mortal sin!"

"The mortal-est, I suppose, though didn't you just say that she was—"

"I'm not worried about her killing *herself*," Sister Patrice says. "I'm worried about her killing *God*."

A squeak escapes him. Then he claps a hand across his mouth. Is he laughing at her?

She turns away from him but there's nowhere to go. She's hemmed in by tourists. Unmoving tourists.

The rabbi sidles into her peripheral vision. "I'm so sorry; I didn't mean to—it's just, well, that would actually be a relief."

"Killing God?"

"You know what I mean. Compared to the immediate situation."

Sister Patrice wants to grab him by the sweater and shake him. "You do believe in God, don't you?"

"Pardon?"

"Do you *believe*, Rabbi Landsman?"

"Most days. Some of them? Let's say fifty-fifty. No, forty—"

"*Rabbi.* You lead a church."

"Yes, well, I don't so much *lead* the synagogue as study the map and point out available routes."

Sister Patrice shakes her head. *He's useless*, she thinks. *And I'm alone.*

The people in front of them suddenly pick up their handbags. The line is moving. Sister Patrice thinks about moving too, but Sister Janet and Mrs. Neville have left their bags. The people immediately behind—a trio of white girls dressed in athleisure and flip-flops— make sighing noises. Sister Patrice gestures sharply at them, tells them to go ahead. They pick their way over and around the bags as if stepping around garbage.

As soon as they pass through, the rabbi says, "My apologies, Sister. Of course what you're talking about is important. All I'm saying is that perhaps Sister Janet's musings on religion may not be our priority at the moment."

Musings? Sister Patrice wheels to face him.

"She's dismantling religion." She spits the words. "The whole idea of it. The Simulators may not *be* God, but they're His exact equivalent. They have every power we've ascribed to Him. Their faults don't count against them, because they're the same faults people throw at the feet of God—Dios mío, what about evil? What about suffering? These programmers, these *gamers*, have all the rights and responsibilities of a creator, because they *are* the creators."

He's staring at her, brow creased in concentration.

"Her point," she says, "is that by all rights, we should be worshipping the Simulators. And if we aren't worshipping them, if we aren't praying to them and asking for their forgiveness, then it's equally ridiculous to worship God Himself."

"Ah," the rabbi says quietly. "So she has talked to you."

Heat rushes up her throat. "I mean, some, yes, but not very much." The lie burns her lips on the way out. "The important thing—" What is the important thing? She desperately needs to seize on something true. "The important thing is the effect her argument will have when it's published. You have no idea how influential Sister Janet is to certain people. How much sway she has, especially with people questioning their faith. Her writing, her powers of persuasion—"

"Oh, I certainly understand *that*," the rabbi says. "She's persuaded me of many things. And you too, I think. She got you to come on this trip, after all."

Sister Patrice frowns. "No she didn't. The council assigned me."

"You misunderstand. The council insisted that *someone* go with her," the rabbi says. "But Sister Janet chose you."

Sister Patrice blinks in confusion.

"I'm sorry," the rabbi says. "I assumed . . . you really didn't know?" He seems genuinely distressed. "She told me that if she's going to have an assistant, it better be someone who can think and write."

"She's read my writing?"

"She spoke highly of a thesis you wrote."

Sister Patrice can't quite process this information. "But we don't agree. About anything."

"Maybe that's the reason she wanted you."

"What?"

"I don't know why I'm on this trip, what my purpose is. She said I'm her sounding board, and that's accurate, even though—no, because

I have no special wisdom of my own. I almost always end up agreeing with her."

"Even about the existence of God?"

"Well . . ."

"You must have some convictions, Rabbi. Some gut instinct."

"Oh no," the rabbi says. "My gut is the least informed organ in my body."

Dios mío, this man was exhausting.

"But you, Sister Patrice, you're here for a definite reason, an important duty. You're not a sounding board but a whetstone. When you disagree with her, you sharpen her arguments. She chose you for this trip because you make her a better thinker. You'll make this book better."

Sister Patrice feels heat at her throat. Does Sister Janet actually . . . *respect* her?

"You're wrong, Rabbi Landsman," Sister Patrice says finally. "I think you might have a little wisdom of your own."

"I don't know about that."

"And I might add, a little faith as well. You're just afraid to admit it."

Behind the rabbi, the crowds part, Red Sea–like. Sister Janet wheels Mrs. Neville toward them.

The rabbi drops his voice. "What do we do about Sister Janet?"

"Nothing."

He begins to sputter a rebuttal, but then the women are upon them.

"Are we moving?" Mrs. Neville says. "It looks like we're moving."

In fact, the line is moving much more quickly than before the stoppage. Sister Patrice pulls her own bag and that of Sister Janet, because Sister Janet is pushing the chair. Eventually they reach a rise where they can see the queue threading through a gap between two metal fences. The line continues across a wide patch of pavement toward the wall of the mountain and the black mouth of the Tunnel. The people maintain a six-foot gap between the end of the line and the entrance, as if it's an ATM. When it's their turn, the person approaches, puts out a hand or sometimes both arms, mummy-like, and steps forward. The black swallows them. It looks like a magic trick, something you'd see on television.

Standing off to the side, in the company of the police, are JP and Dulin. Both of them have their arms behind them.

"Don't worry, Mrs. Neville!" Dulin calls to the old woman. "Just a misunderstanding!"

"Are they wearing handcuffs?" the old woman asks. "Where's Beth-Anne?"

Ahead of them the hot yoga girls go into the Tunnel, one by one — pop pop pop!

Sister Janet rolls Mrs. Neville up to the entrance. The chrome car parts surrounding the entrance are wet from the rain and gleam in the sunlight. "How were you and Beth-Anne planning to do this?" Sister Janet asks Mrs. Neville. "Do you want me to push you forward, or . . . ?"

Sister Patrice pictures Sister Janet running at the Tunnel, pushing the wheelchair like a bobsled. One big shove to send her into the abyss.

The rule of the Impossible is that each person enters alone and leaves alone. But what if they go in connected by a wheelchair or even a rope? What if a pair walk in holding hands? Probably every variation has been tried and documented on YouTube. Sister Patrice hasn't browsed the internet since becoming a postulant. It's not strictly forbidden, but she identified phone addiction as a particular weakness of hers—her whole generation, really—and so has not let her hands touch a smartphone or computer keyboard. Videos would only show her what she already knows: the Simulators enforce ridiculous, arbitrary rules.

A voice inside her says, Yes, Patrice, but is it any different than God's Old Testament edicts? Moses, remove your shoes before the burning bush. Joshua, march seven times around Jericho. Eve, do not eat from that one tree.

The voice sounds a lot like that of Sister Janet.

"I'm going to walk in," Mrs. Neville says. "I don't have to use the chair, it's just easier."

"Give me a hand," Sister Janet says to Sister Patrice. Together they help Mrs. Neville to her feet, and then maneuver the wheelchair in front of her. She grabs the handles and steadies herself. Then gazes at the black hole. Takes a long breath.

"Don't worry," Sister Janet says. "Everyone says it's perfectly safe. Just walk right through."

"I know the Lord's watching out for me," Mrs. Neville says. "Even in there." The old woman shuffles forward, and Sister Janet walks with her, her hand on the older woman's back. The front of the chair disappears, and then the old woman follows it in.

Sister Janet regards the black rectangle. And Sister Patrice watches her sister in Christ, wondering what she's thinking. Then Sister Janet turns and says, "Could I have my bag, please?"

"Of course."

Sister Janet crouches down and opens one of her bag's zippers.

The rabbi seizes Sister Patrice's bicep. "I just had a terrible thought," he whispers.

What now? Sister Janet's about to step into the Tunnel.

"What if we're *both* right?" he says.

The idea hits Sister Patrice with a jolt. Murder-suicide. Sister Janet kills God, then kills herself.

Sister Janet is saying her name. Sister Patrice comes to herself.

Sister Janet holds out her journal—the same one Sister Patrice read last night. "Could you hang on to this for me?" she asks. "For safekeeping."

Sister Patrice takes it automatically.

Sister Janet locks eyes with her. Then she nods. "Okay, then." Then she turns and vanishes. The ease of her exit, the casualness of it, is shocking.

"Go!" Sister Patrice says to the rabbi. She pushes him toward the entrance. "Go after her!" This is stupid, she realizes. The rules don't work like that. But the rabbi obeys. He jumps into the Tunnel.

I don't have to follow them, Sister Patrice thinks. I can walk away from here, go back to the community, and profess my vows. Burn Sister Janet's book.

There's a line of people behind her waiting for her decision. At this moment, a thousand miles away, Sister Janet is either stepping out the other side, or not.

"Perdóname," she says aloud.

The world vanishes behind her. Inside is emptiness. She inhales and smells nothing. There are no scents. All around her is nothing but eye-killing gray. *Now the Earth is without form, and void.*

She feels like she's drowning.

Tears spring to her eyes. The only sound is her breath, coming fast and harsh.

She marches forward, carrying the journal and dragging her luggage behind her. She and those objects are the only things that exist. The ground she walks over feels provisional, as if it's appearing beneath her just as each sole touches down.

She has no idea if she's walking in the right direction, or if direction even matters here. She keeps walking and keeps reciting her one-word prayer: Perdóname. Perdóname. Perdóname.

The fact that she understands that no time is passing is no comfort. Her hammering heart knows that this is an emergency. She has to get out, now, or she will die.

The gray surrounds her, clings to her. Sister Janet said every Impossible is a lesson, and the lesson of the Tunnel is clear: You are nothing but a little bit of code we created. We can return you to the void in the blink of an eye. If we want, we can even let you wander in this purgatory for eternity.

A huge structure appears ahead. As she walks toward it, the shape becomes more visible, not as if it's emerging from mist (there is no mist), but as if it's a sketch being filled in.

It's a gigantic sandcastle.

She approaches the wooden drawbridge, which seems to be made of six-foot-long Popsicle sticks. The moat below is only a quarter filled with foamy water. Through the portcullis she can see a courtyard and a stone fountain.

She knows sandcastles. She grew up in the Allapattah neighborhood of Miami, and her working-class parents hauled her to the beach every weekend when she was a child, where they met up with other Dominican families. She was a master of moats, a queen of crenellated towers. She peopled her fortresses with stick-figure citizens and pebble animals. She was their God. She built their homes and guarded them from destructive tides and the feet of careless boys. And at the end of the day, *she* knocked the walls down.

She never imagined herself living inside those walls as one of them, one of the littles. And she sure as hell wasn't going to start now.

"Nice try," she says to the void.

She marches on.

The air grows brighter, then brighter still. Is this some joke, this light at the end of the Tunnel? It's infuriating. These Simulators are supposedly all-powerful, and all they can summon is a cliché.

She stops walking, wincing at the light. In a few more steps she'll be swallowed by it. She'll be back in the real world.

She's still holding the journal. I can hurl this back into the void, she thinks. No one would find it, and no one else would have to read it. If Sister Janet has already killed herself in the Tunnel, her final message to the world would not be this lamentation, this finely written argument for despair. No one would have to think, How did Sister Janet fall so far? How did she let doubt and cynicism corrupt her?

Sister Patrice makes her decision. Then she walks out into light and heat and noise.

So much high, bright rock! It looks like she's stepped into Old Testament Jericho. There are strangers all around her. Then she sees the rabbi, running ahead of her. He reaches for a woman ahead of him. Her back is to him, and her long white hair hangs to her waist. She's pushing the wheelchair. "Excuse me!" he calls. "Excuse me, Mrs. Neville?"

The woman turns at the sound. Her face is thin, almost paper white, and deeply wrinkled. It's not Mrs. Neville — the grandmother is standing on the other side of the chair. This woman is older, at least ninety, perhaps older than that. Her expression is quizzical. Then her face breaks out in a wide, bright smile. "Zev?" she says. "Just look at you."

"What did you do?" the rabbi says. "What did you do?"

The old woman's gaze turns to Sister Patrice. The smile grows wider. It's nothing like Sister Janet's smile, which was rarely more than a faint acknowledgment that something pleasant had occurred. But those eyes. Those piercing eyes are proof of identity.

Sister Janet chuckles and says, "I see you kept my book."

Introduction to the Zipper

(if time permits)

The Tour Guide
Gazes into ...
You Know, the Thing

‖‖

Time did not permit an introduction to the Zipper. The tour members arrived in separate vans, the last of them hours after the first, too exhausted for the planned lecture and navigation practice. Nobody was more exhausted than Aneeta Channar.

Now she sits hunched on the edge of the Zipper, feet dangling, staring across an expanse of emptiness. The sun has just dipped below the horizon ahead of her, but the sky is aglow, and the far side of the Zipper is still faintly visible. It's the biggest and dumbest object on the tour: a geometrically straight canyon (but not a canyon) running north–south for a thousand kilometers, from southern Montana to northern Arizona, denting everything along its path: mountains, lakes, towns, deserts.

The binder, lying open beside her, has informed her that the floor of the Zipper is exactly one kilometer down, and the far side is exactly 1.168 kilometers away, or .72 miles, which is some kind of mathematically pleasing ratio to its depth. There's also a diagram that's supposed to explain the weird gravity of this deformed landscape, but does nothing of the kind.

THE ZIPPER

The largest Impossible in the world!

Before the Appearances

After the Appearances
(not to scale)

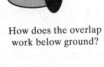

Where does the extra
land come from?

How does the overlap
work below ground?

It's a mystery!

THE ZIPPER

The Largest Impossible in the World!

What the binder cannot tell her is why the Simmers would do such a ridiculous thing to the planet. *It's a mystery!*

She's supposed to know the answers. That's what her travelers expect, and what they paid for. She's delivered them to the night's hotel with its "deluxe accommodations," but in the morning they'll be after her, waiting for answers. She can't just point at this big fucking object and say, Well! Wouldya look at that!

She looks down between her knees. Feels a rush of vertigo, even though she's in no danger of plummeting. The lush, overwatered grass she's sitting on continues over the lip, where it grows straight out from the wall. Wall is not the right word. The land is merely bent at ninety degrees. The lawn stops fifty yards down, gives way to scrub brush and rock, until it hits bottom, bends to form a flat bottom, and rises up the other side. Gravity follows the contours. Trees and rocks hold obliviously to the spots they've occupied since well before the Announcement. Or maybe not so obliviously. A few of the trees, it seems, have noticed that the sun no longer hangs directly overhead and have made use of the last seven years to twist their limbs to catch the light.

Good for you, trees, she thinks. Way to adapt.

She senses movement to her right, glances in that direction. A hundred yards away, the Angle Iron Hotel is draped over the Zipper's edge like a Salvador Dalí clock. A red-haired woman in a pantsuit has stepped out of the large glass doors on the downslope, holding a coffee cup. She looks around.

Aneeta scooches back, out of her eyeline. No thank you.

Her phone buzzes. The screen says "Driver."

"Hey kid," Agnes says. Her voice is much too loud, too cheery. "I was just calling to tell you I may be a little late tomorrow."

The news settles onto Aneeta like a weighted blanket. Not really a problem; she's already pinned beneath a hundred blankets.

"Okay," Aneeta says.

"Don't worry, it'll only be an hour or so. Just keep them enter- tained a bit longer in the Avatar's compound. I'll text you when I'm in the parking lot."

"Okay."

A long pause. "You all right? You sound a little tired."

"I'm just tired." In fact, she's exhausted yet unable to sleep. She checked into her room and lay on the bed, but she felt as if the room were vibrating.

"Day Four is always rough," Agnes says. "How'd it go?"

"Fine."

"Really? That's great! Sometimes when people stay in the Tun- nel too long— Hey! Asshole! Sorry, somebody just cut me off. People think buses can just stop on a fucking dime."

"Lisa Marie almost stayed too long," Aneeta says. "She came out when she started having contractions."

"What now?" Agnes says.

"She didn't go into labor. It was a false alarm."

"Ho-lee shit. So she's still on the tour?"

"Unfortunately."

"How about everybody else?" Agnes asks. "Did the old folks make it through okay?"

"One of the nuns is ninety years old now."

"What the fuck!"

"Or maybe not. She's actually not sure how old she is. Kind of lost track."

"Goddamn, that's gotta be some kind of record. Is she staying on the tour too?"

"I guess."

"Okay, listen." Agnes says. "The important thing is not to panic. You just need to break down the steps. First—"

"I'm not panicking." Not anymore.

"—make sure the nun and Little Miss Preggers don't get in the raft tomorrow. Put them in the courtesy van with the other oldsters and hard-sell them on the scenic overlooks. Did you just squeak?"

A face has popped up at the Zipper's edge, five feet from her. It's the red-haired woman.

"Hey, Agnes . . . ," Aneeta says.

"The important thing is, you got through Day Four! Nobody died! Nobody even got hurt. From here on out, it's smooth sailing."

"I've got to go," Aneeta says. "The FBI agent is here."

"What? What agent? Why—"

Aneeta clicks off.

The agent is standing on the wall, next to Aneeta's feet. Then she leans forward, holding the coffee cup away from her body. She starts to pitch forward, but then puts a leg out, and suddenly she's straddling the edge, one leg in each plane. A laugh bursts out of her.

Aneeta holds out a hand and the woman says, "No, I got it."

She tilts her torso, pulls her trailing leg onto the topside, and now she's looming over Aneeta. "Got it. Didn't even spill my drink."

"Congratulations," Aneeta says.

"*Wow* is that weird," the agent says. "You ever get used to it?"

"I haven't so far," Aneeta says truthfully.

"We didn't get to chat earlier," the agent says. "I'm Special Agent Deborah Marks."

Aneeta shakes her hand. She doesn't know whether to stand or remain sitting. "Are you back to arrest more people?"

"No, no," Agent Marks says. "JP and Dulin were just detained by the Kentucky troopers because they're idiots. Well, Dulin's the idiot, he just has a bad influence on JP. No, all I wanted was to talk to Gillian Masch and help out."

Aneeta nods. The agent could tell her anything—robots are attacking, the president is an avatar, she and her family are being deported—and Aneeta would nod.

"I need to join your tour group," Agent Marks says.

"Okay."

Marks frowns, tilts her head. She is a very tall, very pale woman, whose hair looks quite nice in the dying light. "You don't want to ask why?"

Good point, Aneeta thinks. A normal person would ask why.

"Somebody threatened Gillian online," the agent says. "It's nothing to worry about, but I want to be nearby."

"Is that . . . usual?" Aneeta asks. "Personal bodyguards for just people?"

"Sure, happens all the time." Aneeta can't tell if she's being sarcastic. "Here's the thing—it's important that you not mention who I am to the other members of the tour, or why I'm there, all right? I'm trying to keep all this calm and quiet."

Calm and quiet, Aneeta thinks. That would be nice. "What do I tell them?" That's been her problem since New York, Day One of the tour—what to tell them. "And I'd like it to be true," she adds.

"Sure . . . ," Agent Marks says slowly. "We can come up with something technically true. If that matters to you."

"It does. I don't know why it does, but . . ." Aneeta gestures toward the Zipper. The agent waits for her to finish the thought.

When Aneeta was a girl, back when everyone thought the world was real, she was told that if she memorized all the facts and learned how they fit together, then she could learn the story of the world. She could walk up to the Grand Canyon and point to the river and say, See? That water has been cutting its way through the earth for millions of years. Those bands of color in the cliff walls, those strata, each represent millions of years. She could read a story that started in deep time, more than a billion years ago, and continued—logically, inevitably—to today, and would continue for millennia.

No one told her all the facts could change. That every story she'd learned was a lie. The Zipper was just the punch line. Ha! Fooled ya! Sucker . . .

Agent Marks is still frowning at her. Aneeta knows she's making no sense. She starts again.

"I just don't want to be part of the joke." The words are arriving in her head as she speaks them. "If the world is fake, I don't want my words to be fake too."

"Okay . . ." Agent Marks takes a sip from her coffee cup. Squints into the western distance. Aneeta realizes that the coffee smells a lot like the whiskey in the Four Cedars tasting room.

"How about this," Marks says. "Tell them I'm Dulin's sister. Say that I love him so goddamn much that I wanted to join him for the last leg."

"Is that true?"

"I don't love him *that* much."

"I mean—"

"Yes, he's my brother. You may have noticed we have the same last name."

"Oh. Right."

"I'll see you in the morning." Agent Marks turns toward the hotel, then looks back. "Don't stress it. Just do your job and it'll all be fine."

"Do my job," Aneeta says to herself. If only someone could tell her what that is.

The Influencer
Changes Direction

||||||||||||||||||||||||||||||||||||||||||||||||||||||||||||||||||||||||

Lisa Marie Montello is walking the wide corridors of the Angle Iron Hotel, phone in hand and back aching. She's tired but she can't sleep, not yet. She's trying to make shit happen. Not labor shit, hell no. Not yet. Capital *S* Story Shit.

Christopher Mullins walks beside her, nervously asking questions. "Do you need to lie down? I can ask for, like, Advil or something."

"Let me walk, okay? I'm working."

She and Christopher sat in the medical tent at the Tunnel exit for two hours, as Beth-Anne rubbed Lisa Marie's back and kept handing her bottles of cold water to drink. She assured Lisa Marie that she wasn't going into labor, she was feeling Braxton Hicks contractions; her body was rehearsing for the big show. Eventually the contractions faded, just as Beth-Anne predicted. Lisa Marie had been a little afraid that Beth-Anne had written "nurse" on her bio as shorthand for "woman who takes care of her mother," but thank God she was an RN who knew actual medical things.

The tour had arranged for vans to take everyone from the Tunnel to the Angle Iron, their hotel for the night. Lisa Marie, Christopher, and Beth-Anne were the last people to board the last van, and when

Lisa Marie stepped on, they clapped and whistled for her. She took her seat and thought, *It's happening. They're rooting for me and Baby M.*

But she can't rest. She has to keep the Story moving.

She flicks the phone and pops into another website. She's been doing this all evening, leaving messages that say the same thing: *Call me, Protagonist bitches. I have what you want.* Every website requires a different John Galt account, a different password. It's awkward as hell, and hard to do while walking, but she can't stop moving. Her back is killing her, and the baby has wedged itself into her pelvis.

Christopher keeps pestering her. Shouldn't she drink some liquids, like Beth-Anne said? Should she watch where she's—

"Lisa!" His hand grabs her arm. She looks up from her phone. The corridor ends in a drop-off. She leans over the edge, looks down. It's like an elevator shaft, but one that continues the hotel corridor. Room doors run along each side of the shaft. Armchairs and plants and settee tables all look as if they're glued to the walls.

The Angle Iron bills itself as the only hotel situated atop an Impossible. One half of the hotel sits on normal ground, the other runs down the cliff face. Gravity is relative. Lisa Marie's looking down the cliff wing. Below, one of the doors opens. A boy, eight or nine years old, steps out, onto the "floor." From Lisa Marie's perspective he seems to be standing on the wall like Spider-Man. He sees her, waves, and runs off down the corridor. Her stomach roils and she leans back.

"I fucking hate this place," she says.

"Maybe we should go back to the room?" Christopher says. "I'm not sure the change in gravity is good for the baby."

"No, I can do this." Maybe it's like walking with magnetic shoes down the hull of a spaceship. She puts out a foot over the abyss, draws it back.

"You don't have to keep pretending," Christopher says.

"What the fuck did you say?"

"You keep acting like you're not scared, that nothing scares you. But when you were in fake labor, I saw how—"

"False labor," she says.

"Okay, whatever, but it felt real to you. You thought the baby was coming, and so did I! I didn't know how long you were in the Tunnel. You were breathing really hard and making that whining noise—"

"Because it *hurt*," she says. It may have been false labor, she thinks, but the pain was real. "Don't baby me."

"Just let me go over first, okay? So you don't lose your balance." Christopher steps out, over the edge, then rests his heel on the "floor" leading down. For a moment he has a leg on each side, and he looks like he's about to fall on his face. Then he leans forward, transfers his weight, and suddenly he's standing perpendicular to her. It's like they're on that tiny planet in *The Little Prince*, except angular.

"Take my hands," he says.

She allows him to help her. He grips her forearms near the elbow, helps her ease from one surface to the other. And now she's in the down-facing corridor, but she doesn't feel like she's looking down, or that her feet are being held to some cliff by magnetic boots. It feels absolutely normal.

"Hey, you're crying; why are you crying?" Christopher says.

"Shut up."

She doesn't know why she's crying. Baby M has seized control of her body, and its weapons are hormones. Salvos of raw emotion have been pummeling her regularly since she got pregnant, and this tour isn't making it better. Two Impossibles in one day have made her fragile.

Christopher's right; she was terrified when she stepped out of the Tunnel. She thought she'd stayed too long, pushed it too far. She'd spent eleven days in a beautiful Cape Cod with white shutters, periodically walking out to the front porch and vomiting into the grayness. Some days that sourdough bread wouldn't stay inside her. She lived off the supplies she'd bought at the Last Exit Mall, took her vitamins, and drank the delicious water. She made recordings on her phone—damn she'd have a lot of content to upload when she got out—and talked to Baby M, and cried, and sometimes talked to Baby M while she was crying. Baby M rarely talked back.

She was coping, though, until she felt the contractions. Then she thought, Oh my God, the baby's coming and we're both going to die in this imaginary house in a gray, lonely world.

"Let's head back to the room," Christopher says.

She dabs at her eyes. She glances back; the hallway they just left seems to be over the edge of a drop-off. Except it's really the same hallway, just . . . folded.

She starts walking. "For the record," she says, "I wasn't scared of having the baby, I was worried I'd blown my plan. I thought it was all falling apart. This baby's going to come out during this tour, but it has to happen after the blessing with the Avatar."

"Wait, so we're pro-avatar again? I thought—"

"No, our current story is still that avatars are evil." She scrolls her browser history for the Protagonist-friendly discussion boards she's been visiting. Where else should she leave a message?

"It's so confusing," Christopher says. "You told the Austrian guys that we were protecting Gillian, I mean Margaret, but then—"

"So they wouldn't blow the story! If they called the police, then it was all over. I'm the one who gets to decide when Margaret Schell gets outed. It's just happenstance that cops were waiting for us at the Tunnel."

"I don't know if it was, uh, happenstance," Christopher says. "The FBI already knew where to find her."

"That's the part that makes no sense," Lisa Marie says. "Why'd they let her go? Why is she still in this hotel? The cops let everybody else go, too, even Dulin and JP, and they got all up in the cops' faces."

"Maybe we were wrong. Maybe she's not really Margaret Schell."

"Of course she is! She's just worked out some kind of deal with the feds, and I don't like it."

Lisa Marie didn't like it, but maybe she could use it. The point of the Story—no, that was the wrong word, the *shape* of it—was to make all the forces converge at once: FBI, cops, Protagonists, and Margaret Schell, with Lisa Marie at the center. She had to make it impossible for the story to be without featuring Lady and Baby M, with guest appearances by Christopher Mullins. Chris M!

Up ahead, the corridor widens into a viewing room, and there are familiar figures in the lounge seats.

"So I think I'm free, yes?" the rabbi is saying. "Three days alone, I'm just starting to relax. Then I look down from the verandah, and there it is, looking up at me."

Everyone laughs. It's the younger nun and the older one—now *older* older—and Beth-Anne and her mother. Mrs. Neville says, "Is it here in the hotel?"

"Not yet! But I expect it'll show up. It won't stop following me."

The ancient nun, Sister Janet, says, "Maybe, it's not following *you*, Zev, maybe you're following *it*."

Beth-Anne spots Lisa Marie and Christopher. "How are you feeling, honey?"

"Better, now."

Beth-Anne was so kind when the Braxton Hicks came on, so professional and fucking competent. She should be a supporting character in the Story, Lisa Marie thinks. A named supporting character, with lines and everything.

"Christopher, get a picture with me and Beth-Anne." She hands her phone to him. "Don't worry about the window, it's just going to bounce the light."

The bay window is designed to show off the Zipper, but at night the fake canyon looks like Regular Dark—which is, frankly, a relief. The Angle Iron's hallways are disturbing enough. Christopher takes the photo, and someone calls out Lisa Marie's name. It's the tour guide, Aneeta, looking wild-eyed. Her hair is an absolute mess. She should really be studying the Lady Mmm makeup tutorials.

"Could I talk to you privately?" Aneeta's voice is hoarse, as if she's been screaming. Christopher and Lisa Marie walk a few steps away from the lounge group.

"How are you feeling?" Aneeta asks. "Any more contractions?"

"I feel great," Lisa Marie says. "Absolutely normal."

"That's good, that's good, that's . . ." Aneeta can't stop nodding.

"Heck of a day, right?" Christopher says.

Aneeta stares at him.

"What can we help you with?" Lisa Marie asks.

It takes the woman a moment to respond. "The raft trip," she says. "We've arranged for alternate transportation. A courtesy van will take you along a scenic route to Saugat Zin's compound. I just need you to sign—"

"The Avatar Saugat Zin," Lisa Marie says. "You always have to include the title."

Aneeta blinks at her.

"And we're not going in the vans," Lisa Marie says. "We're taking the raft. I'm not passing up those visuals."

"There should be, um, visuals from the van," Aneeta says. "It's not like you can miss the Zipper."

"Those visuals are not the ones I paid for," Lisa Marie says.

"Maybe she's right," Christopher says to Lisa Marie.

Lisa Marie wheels on him. "You're not in this." The boy flushes pink. To the guide she says, "I've done my homework. These are class two rapids. I've taken baths that are more dangerous."

"Honey?" Beth-Anne touches her arm. "You need to think about the baby here. This bathtub's going to be a-movin' and a-shakin'."

"But—"

"You're in the final stretch. Why don't you ride in the van with me and Momma?"

"You'll be in the van with me?"

"And we'll take plenty of pictures." To Aneeta she says, "Those scenic pull-offs you were telling us about. The Zipper teeth?"

"Right," Aneeta says slowly. "Teeth."

Lisa Marie's phone vibrates. It's a DM on Telepathy, the encrypted message app the Protags favor.

"Okay, fine," she says. "We'll take the stupid van. I need to take this."

Aneeta nods. Then she drops the clipboard to the floor and walks away.

"Is she okay?" Christopher whispers to Beth-Anne.

Lisa Marie walks in the other direction, back the way she came. She opens the message. It's just a few words: *are you 4 real?* Below the message is a video link. There's also an attachment for an id_rsa.pub file—a public encryption key.

She strides away, and Christopher rushes to catch up. They reach the lip of the hallway, and this time she doesn't hesitate—she steps over the boundary and the world seems to slide and slam into place. Christopher keeps asking her what's going on.

"It's showtime," she says. "John Galt's going to talk to the Protagonists. In person."

"Wait, they're *here*?"

"No, video in person. Come on, we have to get you ready. If we wait too long, it's suspicious."

Back in their hotel room she commands Christopher to get dressed and put on everything they bought at Midnight Neon: coat, mesh shirt, black jeans. She opens her laptop, goes to a Protagonist site she's visited many times. Clicks on verify, then drags the encryption key into the upload box.

The message comes back: *your 4 real*

"Woo-hoo!" she says. "It's really them." She forgives them for the grammar mistake. Somehow that makes them seem even more authentic.

"I can't find the other boot," Christopher says.

"Forget the boots, they won't be able to see them." She closes the drapes and looks for a suitably blank backdrop. There isn't one. Finally she lifts a painting from the wall and tosses it onto the bed. Then she sets the desk chair against the wall.

"Hey, let me do that," he says.

"Too late." She opens her makeup kit. "Sit."

"What do I say to them?"

"Keep it simple. Like, monosyllabic action star. Look up." She outlines his eyes in her most goth kohl eyeliner. There's no time for the full John Galt; she's going to have to make do with stage lighting. She grabs a desk lamp, plugs it into the nearest outlet. It's a multi-stage process to get her awkward body to lower enough to click on the lamp. She aims at his face.

"What if they ask who I really am?"

"They probably know who you really are. Don't lie. And follow my lead. I'll be right behind the camera."

Lisa Marie flicks off the room lights. The only thing visible now is Christopher's pale, naked face, hovering in black. "Oh, baby, you look awesome. Remember: Mean. Fierce."

On the laptop she clicks the video link. It goes to the same verification site, which means she's correctly logged in. The video box says, "Please wait for the host to allow you in."

"You ready, baby?" Lisa Marie asks. Oh God, she's so fucking excited. She holds the laptop so the camera's pointing at Christopher's face, but she can still see the screen from off-camera.

The "hold" message vanishes. A blurred face comes on. Christopher starts to speak and Lisa Marie vigorously shakes her head.

"Am I speaking to a conscious being?" the face says.

"Um . . ." Christopher glances at Lisa Marie. She gives him a big, exaggerated nod.

"Yes, I am," he says. "I mean, you are, definitely. We are both definitely, uh, conscious people."

Jesus Christ, she thinks. *Mono* syllables!

"I'm going to ask you a series of questions," the face says. "If you lie, or answer incorrectly, this call will be immediately canceled. Do you understand?"

"Yes," Christopher says. Thank God.

"You're playing *Super Mario Brothers*," the face says. "You find a turtle on its back. It's lying there, kicking its legs. But you don't jump on it, and you don't jump over it. Why is that?"

"What?"

"Do you want me to repeat the question?"

Lisa Marie mouths, *Answer.*

Christopher says, "Is this, like, the original NES version?"

"Sure," the face says.

"Then it's a trick question. Koopas can't turn upside down."

"It's hypothetical," the face says.

"So the game's glitching?" Christopher says. Lisa Marie wants to throw the laptop at his bald head. "I mean, if I can't even jump over it—"

"I didn't say you *can't* jump over it, I'm asking you *why* you—"

"I guess I'd restart, unless I'm too many levels in."

"*Stop.*" A new voice, coming from off-screen. It's deep and warped by voice-masking software. "He's one of us."

Lisa Marie closes her eyes, takes a breath. Christopher's about to give her a heart attack. Her arms are getting tired from holding the laptop.

A face appears on-screen. It's not blurred, but filtered to be a white, ceramic-looking mask. It's noseless and mouthless, but the eyes are covered by black sunglasses. "You claim to know where Margaret Schell is. Is this true?" The distortion software is bad enough, but his stiff dialogue comes straight out of *Castlevania.*

Christopher glances at Lisa Marie. She mouths, *Monosyllabic.* It seems like there should be a shorter way to say that.

"Yes," he says.

There's a long pause. The deep voice says, "Okay, then just say it."

"Oh," Christopher says.

Lisa Marie holds the laptop with one hand and hits the mute key with the other. "Tell him we know where she'll be tomorrow. But we have one condition. Go."

Christopher frowns at the screen. "Tomorrow. One. Condition."

"Why are you talking like that?" says the warbly voice.

Christopher blows out his lips. "We know where she'll be tomorrow night."

"We got that. What we need to know—"

Lisa Marie swings the laptop camera toward her face. "We'll tell you after you agree to one condition."

"And who are you?" the blank face says.

"Lady Mmm. Three *M*'s. And I'm sure you'll verify my identity soon enough from face recognition. Am I speaking to the head of the Protagonists?"

"We don't have a leader. We're an autonomous collective of self-aware human beings united by our cause."

"You're doing all the talking, my dude. So you're the leader."

The face sighs an elaborate electronic sigh. "Okay, yes. Call me . . . Agamemnon."

Christopher frowns. "Agna . . ."

"Agamemnon," the face says. "King of the Greeks? Son of Atreus?"

"Right," Christopher says. "It's just kind of long for a code name."

"So what do you want?" Agamemnon says. "We're not going to pay you."

"It's not that," Lisa Marie says. "I want to be present when you grab her. And I want to live stream it."

"That's not necessary. We'll be recording it ourselves."

"I want my own stream for my own audience."

"Sorry, we need final edit."

"Edit your own video. I'm doing my own personalized POV for my fans. That's bigger audience share for you. And it's not like you'd have exclusivity anyway—there's going to be plenty of other phones recording you."

"What do you mean?" Agamemnon says. "Is this happening in public?"

"We'll tell you where she's going to be. Whether you choose to act on that information is your decision."

Another electronic sigh; this guy's a big sigher. "Fine. Where's the location?"

Christopher holds up a hand to cover the camera. "I don't know if we should be doing this."

"Just a second," Lisa Marie says to the screen. She mutes video and mic, switches the laptop to her other hand, and punches Christopher in the shoulder. "What the fuck are you doing?"

"The more I think about this," Christopher says, "the more I think this is a bad idea."

"Then stop thinking."

"What if they kill her like the guys they killed on the video?"

"We're not going to let them *murder* her. We're *swatting* her. Worst case she's getting arrested. We're not going to let them actually *get* her. I thought you understood the plan."

"I've never understood the plan! If you're going to tell them where she really is going to be—"

"So we can film it. If we can't film it, there's no story. Don't worry, we're also going to tell the cops that the Protags are showing up." Is the red-haired FBI agent in the hotel too? A detail to work out later. "They'll stop these jerks before they reach Margaret. We get to film them getting arrested, and we also get to film Margaret getting captured, and we get to spin the story any way we want."

"Hello?" Agamemnon calls. "Is there a problem here?"

She moves to turn on the camera and Christopher stops her. "Wait, this could be terrible for your audience, and for your child."

That gets her attention.

Christopher says, "You don't want the baby to be associated with a bloodbath, right? That would follow her, or him, for the rest of their life. It would overshadow them, bad."

Lisa Marie feels the truth of that sink in. Goddamn it. "What would you do, smart guy?"

"Make them promise they won't kill Margaret. Or anyone else."

"We can't believe their promises."

"Then give them a good reason."

She thinks for a moment. The ideas are there in her head like they've had their hands up, waiting for her to call on them.

She unmutes and looks into the camera. "We have one more condition."

"What now?" the Protagonist says.

"We don't want any bystanders to be harmed. No gunfire."

"Some bots may have to be sacrificed."

"Listen, dickhead, I'll be right there! And some of those people around me are my friends. They're real people too. Not bots. Self-aware, like you and me."

"I don't think you could tell the difference."

"We're not arguing about this," Lisa Marie says. "And you're not to kill Margaret, either."

"That's three conditions. I'm hanging up now."

"Don't be stupid. You need her alive, because you need to interrogate her. You want her to tell you where Utnapishtim is, right?" She's been reading all about the Protagonists' obsession with this Utna character. He's some kind of super-avatar they've been chasing since the early days after the Announcement. There are hardly any pictures of him, and no online trace at all, just a lot of eyewitness accounts of a bearded Black man who likes to wear flowy, Jesus-y garments. "So, grab her and question her on your own time."

Agamemnon says nothing for several seconds. "Deal," he says. "Now, where will she be?"

The Comic Book Writer Tries to Tell a Joke—Again

||||||||||||||||||||||||||||||||||||||||||||||||||||||||||||||||||||||||

"So would you call that a skylight?" asks Dulin Marks. "Or a side-light?"

He's idly considering the window that hangs over the king-size bed. Outside, far away, is what looks like an immense cliff that stretches from horizon to horizon.

"Whatever it is," Beth-Anne says, "it's too bright."

She's nuzzled against him, knee over his thigh, hand cupping his balls, nose nestled under his chin. His left hand rests in the curve of her hip. Skin on skin, he thinks. Skin on skin. He doesn't care if they're both made of zeros and ones. Whoever programmed nakedness is a goddamn genius.

"I need to get back to my room," she says, moving nothing but her lips. "Momma's waiting."

"Or," he says. "We could stay in bed all day."

"Get behind me, Satan."

"Well, if you insist."

Her laugh is low and carnal. The vibration travels through his chest. He closes his eyes and thinks, Fuck the Tunnel. This is heaven.

For a while there he thought he and JP would never be allowed into the thing. The cops kept them in handcuffs on the Kentucky side, and he could do nothing but watch as Beth-Anne was escorted past them, into the black rectangle, for some kind of medical emergency on the other side. Then they had to watch as the rest of the tour group walked in. Finally, the cops got a call, unlocked the handcuffs, and told them they were free to go—all without an explanation or apology.

Dulin walked into the Tunnel right after JP and found himself in the gray nothing. He ambled along until he came to a long, low, wooden building. It looked exactly as he'd pictured Beowulf's longhouse when he was a boy, complete with roaring fireplace. He ate the bread he'd heard so much about. Found a mug and drank cold water he dipped from a wooden barrel. Then he walked over to the long plank table and sat down. Took out his laptop. Stared at the screen.

Five scripts. One twenty-two pager, three twenty-pagers, and one eight-page short for a *House of Mystery*–style anthology book. Only ninety pages, and all the time in the world.

Thoughts intruded. What the hell was his sister doing here, chasing Gillian/Margaret into the Tunnel? He'd called Deb, but she wasn't supposed to show up! And what was JP seeing in *his* Tunnel? What was happening with Beth-Anne?

He told himself to cut it out, get to work. Put his hands on the keyboard. Opened a new document. Typed "Page 1. Panel 1."

He listened to the soothing crackle of the fire. Then the crackle seemed to increase in volume. Became annoying, like an FM channel that wouldn't tune in.

Fuck this, he said, and marched out into sunlight.

JP had been waiting for him. Welcome to Utah! Evidently, they weren't going to be arrested. They wandered around in the crowd of strangers until they ran into the Austrians, who told them that Beth-Anne was in the medical tent with Lisa Marie Montello.

Dulin, eyes still closed, rubs his hand along Beth-Anne's back. "It was so hot seeing you in nurse mode," he says. "The girl was so scared, and so grateful for your help. It's the nicest she's been to anyone the whole trip."

"I didn't do anything," Beth-Anne says. "It was just Braxton Hicks."

"Oh, *that* guy."

She laughs again. God, he loves her laugh. Loves making her laugh.

"He sounds like a country singer," he says. "Some guy who came in second place on *American Idol*."

"Who writes his own songs," she says.

He guffaws. She says, "You're such a loud man."

"You're not too quiet yourself," he says. "On occasion."

She gives his balls a squeeze.

"Hey now!" he says, and that makes her laugh again. He feels a rush of blood in his dick. At his age, after last night's interval training—sex, talk, dozing off, back to sex—there should be no gas left in the tank, even with the Cialis.

And yet.

He moves his hand, and Beth-Anne says, "Don't you start. Momma's probably ringing the bell like Queen Victoria."

"She can't get out of bed without you?"

"She can do it, but she's had a couple bad spills. Now she wants me around just in case."

He makes a *huh* noise.

"She wasn't always like this," Beth-Anne says. "She used to be unstoppable. Clean the house top to bottom every Wednesday and Saturday. Work nights at the BI-LO for extra money. Led every church committee that a woman was allowed to run."

"What happened?"

"Age. Fibromyalgia. Back problems."

"That runs in my family too."

"Back problems?"

"Age. My dad's got a bad case of it. And it's hit a bunch of my brothers, too."

"But not you."

"Sometimes it skips a generation."

"Ha."

"It's good your mom has you," he says. "Lucky to have a nurse in the family. It must feel good, too, to have a job with purpose."

"It's not what it's cracked up to be," she says. "And your job has purpose. You entertain people."

"My job is to spread mulch on the IP farm. I serve corporations. The ultimate expression of anything I do, the artistic apotheosis of any story I write, is to have it become a six-episode series on Disney fucking Plus."

She laughs. "Apotheosis. You writers and your words."

"My stock and trade."

More traded than stocked, he thinks. Almost everything he did was work-for-hire. He owned nothing, and if they used any of his characters or ideas for a film, he'd get nothing from the company, not even a thank-you note, because that might be legally admissible.

"You never told me why they fired you," she says.

"Marvel? They got mad because I tried to wreck all of comics."

"You, alone."

"I wrote this thing about Reed Richards. He's the leader of the Fantastic Four, the stretchy guy? But his main power is that he's the smartest man in the world. So one night Reed's alone in the Baxter Building, reflecting on his life—"

"As you do."

"As you do, when he starts to realize that it doesn't make any sense. He remembers going into space in 1961, but now it's the 2000s. His son was born in 1968, but he's still only seven years old. And *way* too many things have happened to him for one lifetime. Then he realizes, no, it's the whole world that doesn't make sense. Captain America came out of the ice after twenty years—but now it's been sixty years since World War II. He goes and starts talking to the other heroes, and everybody he talks to, they realize he's right. Even Dr. Doom is convinced—their whole lives are a sham. They've been manipulated the whole time. Reed and Sue's marriage breaks up, he loses custody of Franklin—"

"This is in a comic book?"

"I was drinking a lot at the time."

"Sounds like."

"The problem is that I tried to make all of this canon. If I'd put it in an issue of *What If . . . ?* I'd have been fine."

"I don't know what that is."

"It's an anthology series—a cosmic bald dude called the Watcher tells stories about the multiverse, but he can never interfere, he can only watch, yadda yadda yadda. The stories there don't *count*. They don't affect anything. But my story was canon. Every comic would have to reckon with what I'd done. At least, they would have, if my stories were printed. I wrote six scripts—I was crazy fast in those days— before Marvel informed me they'd be going with another writer . . . for all their books, for the foreseeable future."

"Oh, hon." *Hon.* He liked the way that word sounded in her mouth.

"Not the smartest decision, financially." He'd already confessed to her that he had no retirement accounts and hardly any savings.

"At least you love what you do," she says. "Every time you talk about it, I can hear it in your voice."

He did love it. Over the past few nights he'd tried to explain the joy he took in the craft of writing comics, a topic that bored the shit out of most wives and girlfriends. Like how in comics (paper comics, real comics, fuck you, Comixology), he could control the physical act of reading. You led the reader's eye down the page. You loaded your surprises onto the even pages, keeping them hidden behind a page turn. When you wanted to thrill *and* surprise them, you slammed them with a double-page spread. But everything built to that final page, a final jolt that demanded they buy the next issue. He always wrote the last page first, then worked backward for however many pages it took to make that moment land, and then jumped back to the beginning. The rest of the story was mashed into whatever pages remained in the middle.

He's not sure much of this made sense to a civilian like Beth-Anne, especially without examples to point to. Never a good idea to talk about comics in the dark. But she asked great questions, such as how much he had to tell the artist what to draw (as little as possible), and seemed to really listen to his answers.

But when he asked her about her work, what she liked about it, she couldn't come up with much; the rewards of helping patients were overwhelmed by the many egotistical doctors and chronic understaffing and byzantine insurance protocols. The rest of her life didn't sound great, either. She told him about her airless marriage to Carl, and the church people and army of cousins who judged the way that marriage ended. Many of the stories guest-starred her self-involved sister and demanding mother. She had a lot of questions about his own sister, the FBI agent. It's not that big a deal, he told her; she's basically a cop with better clothes. Which led her to ask about his brothers, and his dad, which led to his marriages, and his daughter, Marion, grown now and living in Connecticut and refusing to talk with him.

None of these conversations happened linearly or with any coherence. They were spread out over the past three nights, the stories abandoned and taken up again hours or days later. They kept getting interrupted by their bodies. He'd never been so torn between sex and conversation.

"We should keep this going," he says.

"You're sweet," she says. "But I need to get back to my room. Momma'll want breakfast."

"I mean after. Us."

Her body goes still.

"Come with me to Portland," he says. "You'd love Portland. It's full of trees, and you don't have to make them breakfast."

"I have to pee." She rolls away from him, sits up. Her tan line suggests a swimsuit he hasn't seen yet. Then she says, "And what would I do in Portland?"

"You're a nurse. You can get a job anywhere."

She shakes her head.

"Or a different job," he says. "Just don't throw out the uniform, I have a thing for that whole Ursula Andress *Sensuous Nurse* vibe."

She walks across the room. It's a wonder to watch her move through the morning light. The swoop of her waist, that glorious ass. It's a crime that she wasted her body for so many years on a guy in the closet. Jesus Christ, Carl, you could have at least told her!

Beth-Anne glances back before she steps into the bathroom. "Hey," she says. "My tits are up here."

He laughs hard and is still laughing as she closes the door.

God, he feels lucky. A woman like this who can make him laugh! He knows he's not a handsome man, not anymore. This fleshy face, the gray hair, the beer gut. The kind of man who should keep his shirt on during sex. And at the beach. Basically, never take off his shirt.

And yet. She makes him feel unashamed. No, shameless! And he wants to talk to her forever.

The shower sputters. He wonders what she's thinking. Did he scare her when he brought up Portland? He needs to keep a lid on. Be casual. Usually he has no problem with this, but Beth-Anne . . . Jesus Christ, she makes him want to write poetry, and he hates poetry.

He lets himself into the bathroom. "Don't scream," he announces. "I just have to pee." And thinks, Aren't we domestic now? When she turns off the shower, he's ready with a towel.

"We don't have to go to Portland," he says.

"You're going to move to North Carolina?"

His heart chills a little. "Sure," he says. "Unless—that's not the Carolina with all the humidity, is it?"

"That's what I thought."

He follows her out into the room. She begins hunting for her clothes.

"We can figure this out," he says. "Pick a place."

"I thought you were living in Seattle with JP." She performs a bit of stage magic with her bra, a kind of reverse-Houdini act. *How did she get into that thing, and so fast?*

"That was temporary," Dulin says. "He's in remission, so he doesn't need me now. And Portland's just a couple hours away."

"He doesn't look like he's in remission."

Shit. Dulin sits on the bed, still naked and newly embarrassed.

"I'm sorry I didn't tell you," he says. "JP didn't want me to say anything."

"So the cancer is back?"

"And growing."

She frowns and nods. "Is he going back into treatment?"

"That's the thing. He's done. No chemo, definitely no more surgery. I was hoping this trip would sort of cajole him out of it, but— yeah. No."

She sits beside him. Leans into him. "I'm so sorry." Her hair is damp on his shoulder.

"They kinda saved me," he says. "JP and Suzanne. I wasn't in a good place for a few years. But those two . . . they took care of me like I was the lovable drunk uncle. They were such a good team."

He never saw them fight, not really. Not like he did with his exes, especially Marion's mom. They *fought*. Throwing a dish at his head was just opening remarks. But JP and Suzanne were two reasonable adults who, even in the middle of an argument, seemed to never lose sight of the person they fell in love with. Fucking inspirational.

"How did she die?" Beth-Anne asks.

"Aortic aneurysm. It was really fast, which was terrible, but maybe, I don't know, better than a brain tumor?"

"It's a toss-up."

"Here's the worst part. She died less than a week after he got his cancer diagnosis. I mean, they're together, talking through plans, she's doing all this research—and then bam, she's gone. No one should have to go through that. I don't know how he did get through it."

"You were there for that?"

"Oh yeah. I drove up right away. And once the treatments started, I just sort of moved in. I was glad to do it. It was the first time in a long time I'd been useful. It was a terrible time, but . . ." He shakes his head. "This is embarrassing, but I was so grateful. Just happy to know what my job was. I haven't had that for a long time. Not since Marion was little."

"You're not done with JP yet. It's going to get bad, and it may take a while. He's going to need you, especially if he goes into hospice."

He's not going to wait for that. Dulin almost spoke the thought aloud. And what's Dulin supposed to do when that happens? "Did I ever tell you the joke about the Irish brothers?" he says aloud. "This guy goes into a pub—"

"Don't change the subject."

He blows out his lips. "Yeah. Well. I can't see him in hospice."

A loud knock startles them. They look at each other.

"Who is it?" he calls.

"Housekeeping!"

"Fuck off!" Dulin yells. To Beth-Anne he says, "it's not housekeeping."

"Thank God. For a second I thought it was Momma." Beth-Anne gets to her feet, and he reaches up to hold her fingers.

"I'm serious," he says.

"I know you think you are," she says, not unkindly. "Take care of JP. After that, well . . . let's see where we're at."

She turns away and her fingers slide through his, and even that motion generates an erotic charge. Skin on skin.

She heads for the door and he says, "Wait, let me—"

"I got you." She reaches into the closet, tosses him a white robe. It's surprisingly fluffy. She waits until he cinches himself into decency, then opens the door. There's Deb, holding two cups of coffee.

"Morning," Deb says. She doesn't look a bit surprised that Beth-Anne has answered the door. "I didn't know how you took your coffee. It's black."

"Then that's how I take it," Beth-Anne says.

"Nice work with the Montello girl yesterday."

"Ha! Poor thing thought she could time a baby. I just hope I don't have to deliver it before the trip's over."

"And I hope that other cup's for me," Dulin says.

"Nope," Deb says, and Beth-Anne laughs. He holds the door, and Deb steps aside to let Beth-Anne into the hallway.

"Also, call Marion," Beth-Anne says. "She's a kid. You can't wait for her to make the first move."

She walks away and Dulin's chest feels both empty and too heavy, as if his lungs were blown glass. Did I just fuck up a perfectly good thing? he wonders. Or did I just save my life?

Deb pushes past him into the room. "She's right, you should call Marion. She got a new job last month; it sounds really good."

"Wait, you're talking to my daughter?"

"She's my niece. I didn't break off contact just because you're a dickhead."

A couple days ago, hearing that Marion was talking to Deb and not him would have made him feel terrible. Now it feels like a reminder to pay attention. A tap on the glass.

Deb looks around for a place to sit, as if every surface is coated with secretions. Finally pulls out the desk chair and perches on the edge of the seat.

"Sit down," she tells him. "There you go. Jesus Christ, keep your legs closed."

"Are you really going to drink that in front of me?" he asks.

"You'll get your coffee when you answer some questions."

"You can't cop me, Deb. What are you doing here? I called you for a little help, not to have you show up and—*come on.*"

Deb finishes her long sip. "Ooh, that's good."

Dulin sighs. "Okay. What?"

"Let's start with Margaret Schell. Has she ever mentioned a friend of hers named Utnapishtim?"

Rafting the Zipper

*(alternate
transportation
available)*

The Engineer Considers Vertical Drowning

||||||||||||||||||||||||||||||||||||||||||||||||||||||||||||||||||||||

JP Laurent tells himself that he's not going to die in ten seconds, no matter what his eyes tell him. One hand clutches an aluminum paddle, the other the raft's grab rope. A giggle rises in his chest.

Twenty feet ahead, the river disappears over a razor-lipped waterfall.

"Ready, everybody?" the river guide asks. She's behind them, perched on the stern of their fat rubber raft. They're moving fast in foamy whitewater.

"Ready!" Dulin yells. He and Deb are sitting on the front bench. Gillian's beside JP, not holding on to anything. "Let's get it over with," she says. They're all wearing orange life vests, and JP feels like a bulky toddler. He knows that he's perfectly safe, and he also knows that he will be catapulted from the raft like a colorful boulder.

"One . . . two . . ."

Dulin shouts like a Viking, thrusts his paddle in the air with both hands. The nose of the raft slides over the edge, and for a moment Dulin and his sister hang there, over nothing. Then the nose sinks, the raft bends. JP feels the raft lifting under his ass. He drops his paddle and grips the edge of the seat. He can see over Dulin's shaggy head now. Below is a kilometer of air.

"Fuck me," JP says. Gillian laughs.

The raft drops into full vertical.

A shout escapes him. But then . . . they do not plummet. They don't even accelerate.

The raft is sliding down a waterfall at an unnaturally slow pace. Every instinct tells him that they should be falling like a barrel over Niagara Falls, but no, they're *gliding*. The shores have gone vertical too. The river drops ahead of them, jogs right around a rocky island decorated with tall pines jutting sideways into the air. His body should be falling out of the boat, arcing toward those trees in a tidy parabola. Slamming into the tops of those trees.

"If you're nauseous, reorient!" the river guide says, reminding them of her instructions in their "Orientation Orientation" meeting at the dock. "Look to the shore."

But the shore remains stubbornly sideways.

I am horizontal, he thinks. We are all horizontal. But his body isn't buying it. He's falling; they're all falling.

Their raft sluices around the wall-sculpture of an island. Then there's another quick turn, and he's looking down a blue wall. The river has suddenly widened, and the water falls into a pool of darker blue below, and then rises again, to flow *up*. They're in a canyon made of water. The sky is a narrow band of fainter blue above them.

The river guide says, "You okay, sir?" He looks back. She's a tanned, sinewy twentysomething who looks like she was born on the river with a paddle in her hand.

"I'm good; I'm—" Oh God, there's the sky. *Behind her head.*

His stomach does a backflip. He leans over the raft and throws up. The vomit falls the wrong way and vanishes into the foam.

"Feedin' the fish!" Dulin says. He reaches back and squeezes JP's arm. "Let it out, buddy, let it out."

JP wipes his mouth and closes his eyes. Rests against the walls of the raft. The smell of the wet rubber is strangely comforting.

"If the shore's not working, look at the bottom of the boat," the river guide says.

"Just a sec." The motion of the raft has settled. After a moment he looks down. His pale feet, strapped into their Teva sandals, rest without effort on the wet floor of the raft. Such idiots, these appendages. He admires their ignorance.

Eventually he picks up his paddle and looks up. The world is flat. Now he can't imagine thinking they were vertical. It's like the Duck/ Rabbit illusion, and he can't see the duck anymore.

"Feeling better?" Gillian asks. She's still wearing his waterproof sunhat, which he packed especially for this portion of the trip, and hasn't offered to return it. He's wearing her baseball cap. He rummages through his emotions, trying to label them. There's relief that the nausea's passed, yes. And also disappointment in the weakness of his body; the cancer drugs are having their way with him, and the paddle in his hands feels heavy. But overall, he's feeling ... buoyant. He's here, talking to a very interesting woman, and the both of them look good in hats.

"Better," he says.

Back at the Angle Iron Hotel during breakfast, Gillian tried to pull him aside to talk to him, but then Deb walked up and Gillian went quiet. The same thing happened at the orientation. Whatever Gillian wants to say to him, it's something she doesn't want the FBI agent to hear.

They drift down the river. The breeze has died, and the sun is warm on his face. He decides not to think about how the sun is not where it should be.

The guide works her two long paddles and steers them toward a large boulder about twenty feet from the shore. The prow bumps the rock and the raft spins slowly into an eddy. "Anybody up for a swim?" she asks. "I also have a couple tubes if you want to float down this section—it's only about four feet deep. I can pick you up about a half mile down."

"How cold is the water?" JP asks.

"Put your hand in," Deb says. "It's exactly that temperature." She hasn't been very relaxed since they climbed in the raft; she keeps scanning the banks, checking out the people on the other rafts. Her nose is covered in white zinc sunscreen, what Dulin calls "Irish war paint." She's wearing canvas pants and a light flannel shirt that covers her holster. JP has no idea where she found the clothes.

"You going in?" JP asks her.

"Nope."

"We need to keep moving," Gillian says. They've been on the river for an hour and a half, and there's at least a half hour more of floating and a shore lunch to get through. She only agreed to take the raft because riding in the van to the Avatar's compound—with Beth-Anne, Beth-Anne's mother, and a few of the others—would take even longer.

"Strong agree," Deb says.

"This'll just take a minute," Dulin says. He stands up, arms out for balance. "You cowards."

"Feet first, please!" the river guide says. Dulin jumps, cannonballs in. Deb throws up a hand to ward off the splash.

Dulin pops back to the surface. "OH MY FUCKING GOD!" He sputters and gasps, putting on a show. Gillian shakes her head, but Deb and the river guide are laughing.

Dulin pushes his hair from his face. Lies back in the water and his naked legs surface like huge pale fish. "I can't believe how *warm* it is! JP, you know you gotta get in here. What did you promise me—we'd smoke a joint while floating down the Antelope River."

"I was high on morphine." Gillian makes a face, and JP explains, "I'd just come out of surgery, and he jumped me." To Dulin he says, "Also, we don't have a joint."

"Oh, don't we?"

A plastic baggie appears in his hands. Inside is something that looks very much like a vape pen.

"Jesus Christ," Deb says. "We're in *Utah.*"

Dulin has several signature laughs. This is one JP calls "Naughty Santa."

JP glances at the river guide. She's suddenly very focused untying a red tube float from the back of the raft. He hands the baseball cap to Gillian.

"Is this necessary?" Gillian says.

"It's not going to slow us down," he says. "We'll float along with you."

He steps awkwardly to the front of the boat. Stands there with one leg on the prow like George Washington contemplating the icy Delaware.

"Do eeet," Dulin says.

JP jumps.

The cold shocks him like a defibrillator. Stings the inside of his nose. He touches bottom—the river really is only four or five feet deep here—and the life vest yanks him back to the surface. "Hoo!" That's the most coherent noise he can manage. "Hoo!" The cold hits his balls, runs up in a straight line to his heart, constricts his chest.

"Don't worry, it warms up," Dulin says.

"F-f-fuck you," JP says, and Dulin cackles. JP can feel his blood whooshing around, worriedly trying to keep his organs at operational temperature.

The river guide tosses a tube to each of them, advises them on where to pull out downriver for the shore lunch, and pushes off.

The tubes look like kids' toys, too small to hold JP, and certainly too small for Dulin's ass. What follows is an embarrassing amount of heaving, grunting, flopping, and flipping. The tubes keep popping out from under them.

"Jesus," Dulin says. "I feel like a walrus trying to fuck a seal."

JP's the first to get his butt into the donut. He holds on to Dulin's tube so the big man can haul himself into place. The raft is far down-river, thank God. Maybe the girls haven't seen this display of middle-aged athleticism. Then he realizes it's not *the girls* whose opinion he's worried about, it's Gillian. Margaret.

Huh. Still some high-schoolish man-pride in there. He thought he'd extinguished that years ago.

JP and Dulin awkwardly paddle out of the eddy and enter the gentle current. He shades his eyes; the sun is bouncing off the high blue walls of the Zipper, across its flat blue bottom. He meant to have Gillian throw him his cap. He feels naked. No telling what the scar looks like in broad daylight. Perhaps a tan would be good for it. Or could his cancer scar develop skin cancer? He could have them duke it out, hot cancer-on-cancer action.

The river moves them along without effort. Dulin paddles up next to him, hands over the vape. "Fifty-fifty blend," he says. "Head and body."

JP presses the button, inhales deeply . . . and coughs like a sea lion. He's out of practice. When he was going through chemo, Dulin bought him a vape pen and a selection of edibles to try. JP preferred indica-heavy mints that acted fast and dampened the nausea. He'd always been a person who lived in his head—proud of it, even. Then Brian moved in and changed JP's relationship to his body. He began fighting it, using a variety of conventional and unconventional weapons. Suzanne, though, had never had to go through that kind of war; her body had executed its coup instantly.

JP and Dulin pass the pen back and forth a few times. They drift in silence for a long time. JP bumps a rock, pushes off, and he slowly spins across the water's surface. Complicated math brings him back into contact with Dulin's tube.

"Holy shit," Dulin says. "Best day ever."

JP chuckles. "I guess things are going well with Beth-Anne."

"No, man, things are going great with *you*. I'm just so glad we got to do this." He offers the vape again and JP waves it off. "Also, yes. Things are going great with Beth-Anne."

JP laughs. Dulin paddles with one arm until he's perpendicular to JP, wedges one sandal heel into the rubber handle of JP's float. His big foot is almost in JP's face. JP closes his eyes, crosses his arms over his bulky vest.

"She revs me up and calms me down at the same time," Dulin says. "It's crazy."

"Honeymoon stage."

"I know, I know. But still. She's different from anyone I've been with. She's fun, but steady. Gives me good advice."

"Yeah?" The sun is so warm on his face and neck. The insides of his eyelids are a fluttery scarlet.

Dulin says nothing for a long time. Or so it seems. Finally he says, "She says I should call Marion."

"What have I been saying?" JP says.

"I'm just worried," Dulin says. "Maybe too much damage has been done. What if she never picks up?"

JP has many thoughts on this, but he's having trouble organizing them. "Be brave."

"Ha. I'm not like you."

JP opens his eyes, squints at him. "You're the bravest guy I know."

"What? No."

"The way you stood up to those cops?"

"They were just cops."

"With guns. But me . . ."

When JP realized the trooper's pistol was aimed at him, he melted inside. Couldn't move. If something more had been required of him in order to save Gillian, he wouldn't have been able to do it. His body had betrayed him again. "Scared shitless," JP finishes.

"See?" Dulin says. "You want to be alive after all."

JP looks away.

Dulin removes his foot, splashes around until he's side by side with JP. "Hey. Hey. I'm sorry, man."

"It's okay," JP says. "I just smoked a little too much."

It was true that in that moment in front of the Tunnel entrance, he was embarrassed that he was suddenly afraid of the thing he'd been craving. But then he entered the Tunnel, and in that gray, non-space he had time to think.

He'd walked through the fog until he came to a three-story, red-brick building topped with a white cornice, a prewar building that had been teleported out of the Midwest and plopped down here. The first floor was an empty storefront. Not exactly empty; along the walls were built-in shelves that could have fit canned goods or even books, and a long wooden counter that should have held an old-fashioned cash register. The inside smelled faintly of turpentine. Did the Simmers expect him to live in an empty store? Play shopkeeper? He found a back stairwell, walked up to an empty second floor. On the third floor he found a cozy apartment decorated from the 1940s or early '50s: solid furniture, thick rugs, simple light fixtures. The small kitchen was tidy and spotless: checkerboard tile floor, pearly ceramic sink, sturdy chrome plumbing fixtures.

He knew there was no rush. He'd reach Gillian no quicker if he left now or in a week. He unpacked his roller bag into a huge, perfectly crafted oak dresser. The drawers slid as if on mercury. The bedroom door closed behind him with a solid *thunk*. The living room lamps came on with a satisfying *click*. He sat in a leather armchair by the big window and warmed his legs by a steam radiator. There was nothing to fix here. Nothing to adjust or tweak or even complain about. Every detail of the apartment was well designed and well made, nothing more than it needed to be, nothing less.

He began to realize that what most scared him about his encounter with the Kentucky troopers was not that he'd almost lost his life, but that he'd almost lost control of when to end it.

Yet (he had time, in this comfortable sitting room, to argue all sides with himself) it was his choice to step between Gillian and the cops. By doing that, he was handing the control to a man with his finger on the trigger. It was his choice to give up the choice. You couldn't step out in front of an oncoming train and get mad at the train. Back at the Hollow Flock he'd thanked Dulin for putting him at the mercy of random variables, and now he'd done the same to himself.

And yet, he still wanted to choose the time and manner of his exit. He'd worked hard in the past few months to make a cool, rational choice. He wouldn't allow his body's virtual amygdala to undermine him. Algorithmically generated fear would not override his reason. He'd follow his plan and die in his bed in Seattle.

And yet.

What if Gillian still needed him after the tour? He couldn't see how that was possible. And Dulin certainly didn't need him.

And yet. And yet. And yet . . .

Perhaps this elegantly designed, unfussy room was a glimpse of his personal heaven. A foretaste of glory divine, as the hymn went. He'd never been a big believer in the afterlife, even as a kid going to church every week. By the time he was eleven or twelve, the concept began to seem suspect: too improbable, too convenient. A fairy story for those who couldn't soothe themselves with the raw facts of the universe. (Middle-schooler Jean-Pierre already considered himself a hard-hearted rationalist.)

And yet!

The sim undermined his certainty. An afterlife was now technologically possible, even plausible. He believed in backups; he believed in restoring from disk. Resurrection had become rational. There was no reason that the Simmers couldn't reinitialize him after his death.

He stared at the empty chair opposite him. It would be good to have one more round with Suzanne. Maybe he could be a better partner to her. A better husband, a better lover. He would appreciate her more, before the physiological flaw lurking in her system, that thin spot in a very important artery, suddenly gave way and carried her out of the world.

But there could be no learning, no possible improvement, if he wasn't allowed to remember the previous iteration. Only randomness could make him a better man, or a worse one. Perhaps if one or more important variables changed, he would respond differently. A toss-up about whether he'd be more kind or more cruel. More open or more self-involved. No, if he was given no knowledge of his past life, it was better to never come back at all. Take his mixed record of wins and losses, mostly wins, and retire from the game. Step up to the mic like Lou Gehrig and say his goodbyes. *I (I . . . I . . .) consider myself (self . . . self . . .) the luckiest man on the face of the earth.*

Well, this earth, anyway.

JP managed to stay in the Tunnel apartment for three and a half days. Its tidy perfection, so soothing at first, began to feel like a weighted blanket. He walked out through the empty storefront, back into the gray. And when he stepped out into the "real" world, into sun and heat, Dulin was only a step behind. He grinned at JP and said, "Did your Tunnel have orgies, too? I am *exhausted*."

Someone shouts from the shore. Gillian, waving them in. She and Deb are standing with a group of people by some picnic tables. It's the tour: the honeymooners are there, and Xing-Xing, and the Octos. The river guide is dragging the raft higher onto the pebbled beach, toward two other rafts.

JP and Dulin roll off their floats—Much easier to get off than on, JP thinks—and wade toward the shore, dragging the floats behind them. They throw the tubes into the raft, and Dulin says, "You okay, man?"

"I'm good," JP says.

"I'm sorry I said that. I know you've made up your mind."

"It's okay."

"And there's something else. I asked Beth-Anne to come back West with me."

"Really?"

"She countered with North Carolina."

JP can't picture Dulin in the South. But love is strong. Lust is pretty strong too. "What are you going to do? Move in with her mom?"

"I don't know," Dulin says. "Maybe? I feel like something's possible."

"That's great." JP has the feeling Dulin was expecting a different response. "Good for you, man."

"Yeah, it is! But I wanted to let you know that we're taking our time. We're not doing anything right away. So . . . yeah." He scratches his neck. JP doesn't know what's going on. Talking has never been Dulin's problem. "We're going to wait for a while."

"On what?"

"Ah fuck man, you know."

"What?"

"*You.* Till you decide. Look, I know what you want to do. I know you don't want me to talk you out of it. But if you change your mind—"

"Dulin—"

"Let me finish. If you do decide to try chemo again, or surgery, whatever you want, I'll be there for that too, okay? Either way, I'm not going anywhere."

JP looks to the side. Gillian and Deb waiting for them by the picnic tables.

"I don't want you to do that," JP says. "Don't put off going with Beth-Anne. Go to North Carolina, or Portland, or wherever. When you say you're not going *anywhere*, it sounds . . . awful."

Dulin, for once in his life, doesn't rush in with more words.

"I appreciate what you're offering," JP says. "I do." And thinks, I should tell him I love him. They've never said that to each other. Well, Dulin's said it once or twice, when plastered. But JP always felt it was a simple fact of their relationship, part of their personal physics. Commenting on it would be like remarking that gravity was still in effect. And yet—gravity's been a lot less reliable lately.

He starts to speak, and sees Gillian walking toward them, carrying a bowl of chili and a soda can. Dulin starts unsnapping the vest straps.

"Wait," JP says. "All I'm—I'm just asking you, don't do this. Don't wait. If you've got something with Beth-Anne, take your swing." Dulin doesn't answer. "So, we good?"

"Uh, *no*," Dulin says. "You're misunderstanding me. I was just informing you. This is what's going to happen. It's not like you can get rid of me. You'll be, like, weak with cancer. Just try to push me out of the house with those skinny cancer arms."

"I feel like you're not—"

Dulin grabs him, pulls him into a bear hug. JP's face is mushed into Dulin's damp life vest. "See?" Dulin says. "No choice."

"This is really uncomfortable."

"Too bad."

A final squeeze and Dulin releases him. Gillian's standing a few yards off, waiting until they were finished with . . . whatever it is they were doing.

"The chili's good," she says. "They have hot dogs, too."

There's a moment of silence.

"*Oh*," Dulin says finally. "So what I hear you saying is . . . chili dogs."

"And potato chips," she says.

"Let's eat!" He tosses his vest into the raft and strides away.

Gillian looks at JP from under the brim of the Charter all-weather hat. (*His* hat, though he's not sure he still owns it.) Her gaze is, as always, intense. Those eyes have no dimmer switch.

"I have a favor to ask," she says. Before he can speak, she says, "Yes, another one."

"Does it involve obstructing the police?" He can't stop thinking about that gun aimed at his head.

"As a matter of fact . . ."

"Oh God. What is it?"

Her eyes narrow a fraction. She's gazing steadily at him, but he sees a dozen micro-expressions come and go like cloud shadows across a mountain. She's so beautiful when she's thinking. Suddenly he's jealous of her ex-husband, who had years to watch her mind work.

Finally she takes a breath. Calculation complete.

"There's a path leading up the hill. We're going to walk toward it, and hopefully Marks won't follow us, okay?"

"Okay."

At the start of the path he glances behind him, and Gillian touches his elbow. "Don't look; keep going." They climb to a switchback, and then they're hidden from the shore and the rest of the party. They keep walking.

"I don't have time to tell you everything," she says. And then, speaking fast, she tells him so, so many things. She tells him about a man from another iteration of the sim. She speaks of compilers and VMs, Trojan horses and backdoors, and a homegrown API called the

Devil's Toolbox. And then she tells him that the Simulators are just as fucked as they are.

His head feels overstuffed. Buffer overrun.

"You okay?" she asks. "I know that's a lot."

He laughs and doesn't know why he's laughing. "Oh man, yeah, but it's also, a part of me thought—" He starts laughing again. She tries to shush him, which only makes it funnier. "I thought, is that it?"

"What?"

"I know!" He bursts into laughter again. "This whole week I've watched you work." He lowers his voice. "And then I saw the code, and you told me all that stuff about WBE, the artificial people . . . and I thought, This woman, whatever her name is, she's the most brilliant person I've ever met. And I thought, Maybe she's solved it."

"Solved what?"

He threw up his hands. "Everything! The sim. Death and disease. Pain and suffering. And well, getting out of here."

"That's a fantasy."

"I know, I know. I know! Even the people who made us can't get out. It's just . . ." At the Hollow Flock, Dulin had told him he was too logical. He had to adjust to the fact that they lived in a magical universe. "I let my imagination run away with me."

From below, a voice calls up, "Hey you two." It's Deb. Checking on them. "They're packing up lunch."

"Aw, my Jean-Pierre," Gillian says. She plucks the ball cap from his head, then takes off the wide-brimmed hat from her head and sets it on his. Tightens the draw string under his chin. "We can't save ourselves," she says. "But we can save the people who come after us."

The Driver Makes an Unscheduled Stop

The bus is stopped, but Agnes Wisniewski's body is still vibrating—made jittery by black coffee and Adderall and tooth-grinding doubt. She looks at her phone's map, then out at the scrub-brush desert. A hundred yards away, an adobe house squats by itself in the sun like a pizza oven.

This is where Peter lives? she thinks. The middle of fucking nowhere?

It's possible she has the wrong place. Tanya, back at the Canterbury Trails office, gave her the address, but who can trust fucking Tanya? And even if the address is right, she's not sure she should be here. What the hell is she supposed to say? She's been driving all day and all night and the words haven't caught up to her.

Fuck it. She shuts down the engine and the electrics, steps out into the New Mexico light. Only nine in the morning but it's already up to eighty. No telling what this place is like in the summer.

On the face of the front door is one of those Day of the Dead skulls, gaudy and grinning. She rings the doorbell. Half a minute passes. She presses it again. The skull stares at her, silently laughing. She becomes conscious of her rumpled uniform and sniffs an underarm. *Oof.* She hasn't showered since Kentucky.

She's about to step off the porch when the door opens. A strange man—an objectively handsome Latino with a high and tight haircut, wearing a loose shirt and shorts—asks if he can help her. Then he sees the big bus parked on the road and his eyes widen.

"Does Peter Atherton live here?" she asks.

"Is that his *bus*? Oh my God, you must be Agnes."

"And you must be Luis." Peter had talked about Luis as if he were a rare bobcat who might vanish at any moment. She'd never quite figured out if that meant Peter was shooing him away or if Luis was skittish.

"I never thought I'd meet you," he says. He looks like he's going to hug her, and then he doesn't. "Did the company call you? How did you get word? Never mind, come in, come in. I'm sorry for the state of the house."

Word of what? she thinks.

He leads her through a small house with seemingly no interior walls. The living room is the dining room is the kitchen, and the air is full of light. What was he apologizing for? She takes in brightly colored tilework, paintings in giant frames, copper-bottomed pots hanging over a stove, and then they're out the back door and onto a patio surrounded by green bushes and flowers. Luis gestures toward a path that leads off between bushy trees. She didn't see any of this from the road.

"He's resting back there," Luis says.

She doesn't like the sound of that.

She follows the path of clay bricks through the trees and comes to a pergola. Ceramic pots hang from the beams, dripping long-stemmed plants. Tall wooden chairs and patio furniture face a huge stone fireplace that forms the back wall of the structure. Then she sees the top of a blond head; a figure is laid out on a lounger, not moving.

She walks forward until she can see the side of his face.

His eyes are closed, his lips slightly parted. A light blanket covers him to his neck. She thinks, whatever this is, whatever's happened, be cheery. Do not pity. She hates pity.

"Hey," she says quietly. "You awake?"

His eyes open slowly. "Agnes?"

"Hiya, kid."

He sits up suddenly and the blanket slides down. He's not wearing a shirt. "What are you doing here?"

"Uh . . ."

"I mean, shit! Hello!" He hops up, and thank God, he's wearing shorts. He wraps his arms around her. "It's so good to see you!"

She lets the hug go on for a bit. It feels good. Then she pushes him back. "So you weren't in a fucking car accident?"

"What? I'm so sorry! Why would you think that?"

"What the fuck! I tried to call you!" She punches him in the shoulder. "Did you turn off your phone?"

"I let the battery die a natural death. Here, let me . . ." He drags an Adirondack chair close to his lounger. "Please, sit. How did you get here? Aren't you doing the North American tour?"

"I'm on my way to Utah. Thought I'd stop by."

"That's hundreds of miles!" He laughs in that open, kidlike way of his. She'd missed that on this trip.

"I thought you were fucking dead," she says.

Suddenly he gets that she's serious, and his eyes go wide. "Oh my God, I just turned off my phone because I was burned-out! I didn't think you'd . . ." He touches her knee. "I'm so sorry."

You didn't think I'd care? Agnes thinks. Instead she says, "I'm just disappointed. I drove all this way, and you're not even running a fever." A joke to let him off the hook.

He laughs, relieved. "So, who'd they get to guide?"

"A new girl. She's in way over her head."

"Oh God. How'd Day Four go?"

"A couple bad Tunnel cases. One of the nuns set an endurance record."

"One of the—you have more than one nun?"

"And a rabbi, a couple of Evangelicals, a pregnant girl . . . the full basket."

"Oh God." He runs a hand through that luxurious hair. "The Tunnel—well, the whole trip, really—it's a meat grinder. Chickens go in, pies come out, except the pies taste like existential angst."

"You could've called me, you jerk. There's nothing wrong with you?"

"Oh, I wouldn't say *that*." His smile is more sober. "Sorry about that. I just had to quit. It was an impulsive decision."

"So, you just woke up and decided, that's it, I'm done."

"Pretty much. Well, I almost quit before every trip. But then we start rolling, and the people are interesting, and some of them need my help, so I give myself over to it. To them. But afterward, my goodness, I'm so wiped out. Ask Luis."

"He's handsome."

"Inside and out."

"Good for you. But I got to tell you, I never thought you were wiped out. First day of the tour, last day, every day in between . . . you were solid. Even if the passengers were falling apart."

"Can I tell you something?" Peter says. "The Tunnel terrified me. Every time, I just rushed through it. Spent, like, zero time in there. Every time it was different, some fucking castle or bungalow or whatever. One time it was this old-timey Route 66 motel, flashing neon sign and everything, like it was begging me to stop. But I never did."

"You never mentioned that."

Peter has the decency to look embarrassed. "I think I was too busy playing the confident professional."

"Even with me?"

"I'm sorry. I thought . . ." He pauses, as if trying to remember that previous self. "Look, I know what the job is: take care of the people on the bus. That's it. Get everyone home safe and as sane as possible. The thing I didn't realize was that I was on the bus too."

Luis appears, holding a tray with four very tall glasses. "Fresh-squeezed, anyone?"

"Is that with or without?" Agnes asks.

"Your choice!"

"I've got to drive," she says. "So just one."

"A little tequila sunrise for the morning." Luis hands her one of the glasses with a swirl of bloodred grenadine at the bottom and an orange spiral hanging on to the rim. She can recognize a former bartender when she sees one.

Luis hands Peter a glass, sets down the tray, and perches at the end of Peter's lounger.

"So what are your plans?" Agnes says.

"Nothing," Luis says.

"Nothing at first," Peter says. "But I'm thinking of going back to school, finishing up the master's degree I abandoned, and then ... who knows."

"He's looking into becoming a therapist," Luis says. "There are a lot of people in distress out there."

"Wait, you want to work with people with *worse* problems?" Agnes asks. "I thought you were burned-out?"

"Only reduced to embers, my dear," Peter says.

"Jesus Christ," she says. "You're just trading in one bus for an even bigger one."

He laughs, delighted to be caught out. They talk about grad school and Luis's tech job and life in New Mexico, all things that Agnes knows nothing about. But whatever tequila's in this sunrise is delicious, and the air is warm. She could sleep for days.

Instead she stands up. "I better get going before I lose them all to the Avatar's cult."

"I've always wanted to meet him," Luis says.

"You don't," Peter says. "You know his real name is Dave? Dave Storp, from Columbus, Ohio."

"That was his name before the Avatar possessed him," Agnes says. "You've really got to read the pamphlet."

Peter laughs. "See? Who needs a guide when you've got a driver like Agnes?"

He walks her out around the side of the house, past a line of sentinel cacti. When he sees the bus he stops and laughs. "And thar she blows," he says. "The beast that swallowed me whole."

"You want to come inside?"

"Not a chance. You'd abduct me."

"So you're definitely not coming back?" she says.

He winces in mock pain.

"I'm happy for you," she says. "I am. I'm just—I'm on the road right now with a guide who doesn't know her ass from a hole in the ground."

"Does she have a good heart?"

"I think so, yeah." Thinks some more. "She does."

"That's really the only job requirement."

"Oh," Agnes says. "I almost forgot. I need to ask a favor."

He looks at her with such love. Has anyone, even her wife, seen such love in her own face? She's never been open with her emotions, but with Peter it just comes pouring out of him.

"Ah, Ag*nyesh*kaaa," he drawls it out. "Whatever you need."

Then she tells him what she wants, and he laughs and laughs. "I doubt that will help," he says.

"You never know," Agnes says.

The Influencer
Is Gonna Hurl . . .

||||||||||||||||||||||||||||||||||||||||||||||||||||||||||||||||||||||

. . . all over her Betsey Johnson 80th BASH tattoo crop top ($79), and her prized possession, the article of clothing she's been saving for today, her Vivienne Westwood Black Watch tartan maternity wrap miniskirt with oversized gold safety pins ($625).

"Christopher," Lisa Marie Montello says. "Open your backpack."

"Do you need something?"

"Open it."

He unzips it and she drags it in onto her lap. Her belly won't let her pull it close. She and Christopher are crammed into the third and farthest back row of the courtesy van as it slaloms down the wall of the Zipper. She risks a glance through the (distant) windshield. Big mistake. All she can see is rock and water—like they're going to plunge into the fucking lake!

"Do you need snacks?" Christopher asks. "Water bottle?"

She leans over the open mouth of the backpack.

"Oh geez," Christopher says, finally getting it. "Not on my Nintendo Switch."

She closes her eyes and clamps her lips shut. Breathes through her nose. She's pissed that Aneeta didn't put her in the same van as Beth-Anne, who's riding with her mother and the religious folks, while

Lisa Marie's trapped in the other van with Christopher and the Octos. The seating arrangements were all driven by the tyranny of the olds. There were six passenger seats per van, but the Octos refused to split up ("We're a unit!"), and the rabbi and Sister Patrice both insisted on staying with the recently ancient Sister Janet, which meant Lisa Marie was screwed. What about *her* needs? She's severely pregnant and needs her nurse! She should have gone white-water rafting with the others. The boat trip couldn't possibly be more nausea-inducing than this three-hour road tour up and down the sides of the Zipper, and at least she'd have gotten good video. And maybe taken some surveillance footage of Gillian Masch, aka Margaret Schell. *Does she suspect that she's floating toward a dramatic exposure and arrest? We're about to find out. Subscribe below, motherfuckers.*

The pair of vans stopped twice along the way at scenic overlooks; the "teeth" of the Zipper projected a hundred meters over the canyon, providing "breathtaking" views that made her stomach roil. At the first stop she paced and breathed through her mouth while everyone oohed and aahed. At the second stop they had a picnic of mediocre sandwiches prepared by the Angle Iron kitchen. She took two bites of a pesto chicken wrap and tossed it away. Then it was back into the van, where she fought to keep that tiny amount of chicken in her belly.

The Octos believe in a magical, ever-repeating Groundhog Day. But what if that day is filled with nausea, huh? Then you're in hell. Eternal damnation.

Lisa Marie tells herself to remain positive. This is the day it all comes together: her meeting with the Avatar Saugat Zin, the betrayal of the Protagonists, the arrest of Margaret Schell, and the birth of her child—the most dramatic natal event in two thousand years. The Simmers will be *riveted*. All Lisa has to do is keep her lunch inside and force Baby M outside—on schedule.

She rests her forehead against the seatback. The open mouth of Christopher's backpack smells like stale french fries.

A hand pats her arm and she opens her eyes. One of the old-lady Octos, reaching over the seat. "We're almost there, sweetie. Just breathe." The women have been acting all grandmotherly toward her since they bought Christopher his coat, back before the Tunnel. But the last thing Lisa needs is another grandparent.

"Thanks," Lisa says. "I'm all good on breathing."

The van reaches the causeway, a raised, curving structure that allows vehicles to navigate the plunge over the lip and manage the shift in gravity, and then it's another fifteen minutes down the face of the Zipper. Finally the van brakes to a halt. The door slides open, and standing there is a beardy bro in a faded polo shirt, beaming like he's just found a lint-covered gummy in his cargo shorts. "Welcome to the Vertical Circus!" Behind him is a wall of clear blue sky, except it's not the sky, it's the fucking lake again. Zipper geography.

Beardo starts helping the old folks out of the van. Lisa goes half-mad waiting for them to creak out of their seats. At last she steps down into the gravel parking lot. She's standing on the floor of the Zipper, the bottom of the U. Around her are hundreds of cars, but she doesn't see a tour bus, and the road they just dropped down is empty. Ahead of her, at the edge of the lot, is a river, then the lump of the Avatar's island; the far end of it makes a ninety-degree bend before meeting the lake wall.

You can do this, Lady Mmm. Your child will be born here.

The island used to be a resort, littered with wooden cabins and a few larger structures. The tallest is an old waterslide, the rusty iron stair tower wreathed in sun-bleached plastic tubes, completely dry. In the gaps between the buildings are dozens of colorful tents, some she's looking up at (the ones on her current plane) and some she's looking down on. They give the island a low-budget circus vibe, but it all feels . . . shabby. She's seen the place hundreds of times on Insta, from every angle and through every filter, and almost all of them make it seem more magical. She'll have to do the same. No, better. Her job, as always, will be to make the location fresh for *her* feed. To make you want to *be* Lady Mmm, doing what she's doing, living not only her best life, but yours too.

Best get to work, then. She takes a few phone pics, already thinking through the gauntlet of filters she'll need to run them through.

But there's no cell service to upload them—her phone's showing SOS. She'd read about the lack of coverage, but it's still a pain in the ass.

Somebody cries out. It's Beth-Anne's mother, trying to get out of her van. Beth-Anne's on the ground, helping. She wraps her arm around her mother, supporting her as the old lady eases down, and then Beth-Anne guides her onto a landing and into her wheelchair. *Thump.* The old woman yelps in pain. There are tears in her eyes. The ancient nun pats her shoulder reassuringly.

Oh God, Lisa Marie thinks. Maybe she could ask the Simmers to delete her before she gets old.

Beth-Anne sees Lisa Marie watching, and maybe sees her shock, too. "Momma had a tough trip," Beth-Anne says.

"That driver ought to lose his license," the grandmother says. The driver, a large Black man in dreadlocks, is standing less than five feet away, moving baggage from his van to the other. He either can't hear her, or is pretending not to.

"And what are we doing on gravel?" the old woman says. "Is there not one place on this whole trip that's wheelchair accessible? Where'd Aneeta go?"

Beth-Anne fixes her gaze on Lisa Marie and blinks slowly. "And how are you doing, honey?"

"I haven't vomited," Lisa Marie answers. "Yet." She's feeling much better now that she's out of the van.

"Hello, everyone?" Aneeta waves a hand at them. "We're going to be moving your bags to tonight's hotel, so if there's anything you need for today, get it out now. Medicines, batteries . . ."

Beth-Anne reassures her mother that she's gotten everything they need.

Beardo cheerily waves the group onward, down the slanting parking lot, to where the gravel meets a steep cement boat launch. The river's maybe forty feet wide at this point. He gestures toward a wide, flat raft. Two ropes are stretched between poles on each shore of the river. The lower rope runs through looped posts set in the raft.

"What in the Lord's name is this?" the grandmother says.

"Some kind of Huckleberry Finn shit," Lisa Marie says, and Beth-Anne laughs. Lisa's loving this woman more by the minute.

"There are no bridges onto the island," Beardo explains. "All must cross the water and leave our old selves behind. The Avatar Saugat Zin believes that this is an important, symbolic step in the hero's journey."

The grandmother says, "You can't afford a *bridge*?"

"It's not that we can't afford—"

"Come on, Momma." Beth-Anne tilts her mother's chair into a wheelie, then trundles her onto the raft. The bro asks for volunteers, and then Christopher, the rabbi, and all four Octos begin hauling on the lower rope. The current is strong, and the raft skews and shimmies beneath their feet. Lisa Marie looks over the side; the water looks as clear and cold as a river in a beer commercial. It doesn't look deep but probably is.

Two minutes later they bump the island.

"Huh," the rabbi says. "You'd think the hero's journey would be longer."

For a while she's been hearing the whine of jam-band rock; now it's louder, and so more annoying. Twisted up in the music is the smell of pot and the tang of grilled meat and onions—street meat! Suddenly she's famished.

The tour guide tells them they have some time to explore—just meet at something called the Nexus at six thirty for the tour group's meeting with the Avatar. "It's the biggest tent, and it's bright red. Or so I've been told."

"Where are the others coming in on the rafts?" Lisa Marie asks her. "Are they already here?"

"I . . . have no idea. I'm sure they'll be at the Nexus."

Christopher leans close to her. "So where are we supposed to meet the . . . guys?"

Lisa Marie looks at the tour guide, realizes she'll be no help in getting firm directions, and points at Beardo. "Where's the Serenity Station?"

He blinks at her.

"The meditation center?" she says.

"Oh, right!" His whole face lights up. "That's smart, actually. Get centered before you meet the Avatar. You guys are so lucky to get a private audience."

"The rest of the group's getting the audience," she says. "I'll be onstage with the Avatar for a Personal Experience Opportunity."

"He's blessing the baby," Christopher adds.

Beardo nods vigorously, though he clearly has no idea what they're talking about. "That's so cool. I haven't earned enough credits for a private, but everybody says that's when the shit gets real. He's going to blow your mind."

"The Serenity Station?" she asks testily.

"Other end of the island," he says, and gestures vaguely past the water slide tower, to where the land flips vertical. "Enjoy!"

She wants to punch him. She shoulders her bag and grabs Christopher's arm. "Come on, I'm starving."

They promised the Protagonists they'd meet in the meditation center at six, a half hour before the show. But first—food. She marches away, quickly leaving the oldsters behind.

"What are we doing?" Christopher asks.

"I'd kill for an Egg McMuffin, but I'll take a gyro."

"No, I mean, I don't understand the plan."

"The plan is, *don't you want to know what happens next?* That's the plan."

"But—"

"Just keep an eye out for the redhead, Agent Marks."

"What are you going to tell her?"

"That I got a hot tip from one of my fans." Her lower back is aching. "Terrorists are coming to the island to kidnap Margaret Schell, oh my God, I'm so upset, let me show you where they are. You have cash, right? If these vendors don't take credit cards, I'm going to massacre them."

They pass a line of porta-potties. She needs to pee but, no thank you. There'd better be some fucking plumbing on this island.

The crowd coagulates as they move through the midway. The demographics lean white, twenties, and unshowered, and the dominant clothing style is Phish Concert Sponsored by REI: boys in T-shirts and Tevas, girls in crop tops and bangles. So many backpacks. Lisa Marie doesn't fit in, and she's happy about that. No competition. Christopher, however, sticks out like a latex thumb in his shiny, black neo-Neo garb. She catches a couple hippy kids eyeing him suspiciously.

"Hey, corn dogs," Christopher says. "Want a corn dog?"

"Aargh! No! Are you getting any bars? I've got no service on my phone."

"Did you check for Wi-Fi?"

She unlocks her phone and thrusts it at him. "You check, I'm nauseous."

The face of the Avatar Saugat Zin is everywhere, and half the tents are selling Avatar merch: gazing crystals, candles, bobbleheads, pajamas. She's never seen so much Papyrus font. It's a wonder James Cameron hasn't sued the whole circus.

They join a long line for a tent selling chicken on a stick. Is it a carnival rule that all food must be served with a built-in handle?

"You've got a ton of messages from Gramps."

"Stop looking at my texts. Did you find Wi-Fi?"

"Like, he's texting you every ten minutes."

"Give me that." Guilt's seizing her by the throat, but she wills it away. Gramps never believed in her goals. He'd spent too much of his life before the Announcement and didn't understand the danger. It was get attention or get deleted. This is a ratings war.

"Go find me some bottled water," she tells him. "Cold water." He slumps away, looking wounded.

After twenty minutes she's moved forward maybe ten feet, and Christopher still hasn't returned. Her back's aching again and the smell of the chicken's driving her crazy. Why are they so slow? How hard can it be to jam a chopstick through a nugget? She catches herself looking at her phone. Christopher's right; there's a crazy number of messages from Gramps. But at least no more will be coming in while she's on the island, and Lisa Marie won't be tempted to reply. The next text that old man's going to receive is the picture of his great-grandchild.

A voice behind her says, "Lady Mmm?"

Goddamn it, a fan, *now*? She arranges her face in a smile and turns, hand delicately on belly. "Hello there!"

It's a round-faced hiker with a tall mountaineering pack so heavy, the straps are carving valleys into his man-boobs. His black hair is brown at the roots, and his pale face is alarmingly flushed.

"You're way more pregnant than I thought," he says.

"Uh-huh. Do you want a picture?"

"No pictures." Behind him are eight or nine more white guys, bearing equally loaded backpacks, all of the gear shiny and new. None of them look like they could hike a mile.

Then she thinks, *Oh shit. The Protagonists.*

He grabs her wrist, hard. "Let's go."

"Fuck you." She tries to yank her hand back, but he holds on. "Not until I get my food."

"This is serious."

She screams. Then adds a screamed name: "Christopher!"

"Stop that!" the Protag says. "What the fuck are you doing?"

"Let go of my fucking hand!"

Suddenly a figure in black pushes through the clump of backpacks. "What's going on?"

Then Christopher's there, looking like an actual Protagonist bad-ass in his long black jacket with that gleaming bullet head. Damn, she does good work. She could see how a certain kind of person could fall in love with him.

The Protagonist releases his grip on her wrist. "John Galt," he says. "Pleasure to meet you." Oh, so a man gets his respect? Jesus Christ. Christopher's confused, and he can't shake hands because he's holding two bottles of water.

"It's Agamemnon," Lisa Marie says. "They're early."

"You?" Christopher says, and she laughs. Reality wasn't doing the Protag any favors.

"We're going incognito," Agamemnon says. "For now."

"Meet us at the Serenity Station, as planned," Lisa Marie tells him.

"We're doing this now."

"But the people you're looking for, they're not even *in place*." Plus, she hasn't found Agent Marks yet. These stupid fuckers have hosed the plan.

"We have to get ready," the Protag says, "and you're coming with us, or we do this without you."

"Jesus Christ, fine. But I'm going to get this fucking chicken first or I'm going to bite someone's head off."

Agamemnon glances around at his crew. They're young guys, some of them on the small side, and they're wilting under their packs. "We'll wait," he says. One of his boys—he looks like he's fifteen, with a spray of acne across his cheeks—shrugs out of his pack and it hits the ground with a *thunk*.

Eight awkward minutes later, Lisa Marie still hasn't figured out how to turn this situation around, but at least she's rewarded with two chicken kabobs and a paper sack heavy with Tater Tots. She points one of the sticks at her mouth and bites off a chunk of breaded chicken with her teeth. It's not exactly hot, and she doesn't exactly care.

Agamemnon says he knows where the meditation center is and starts snowplowing through the crowd. Lisa Marie watches for the FBI agent—hell, for anyone in the tour group—but sees no one she recognizes.

To her surprise, the Serenity Station is a cabin, not a tent. Agamemnon pushes through the door. "Everyone out! The station is closed."

A couple of voices start arguing with the Protagonist, but eventually a pair of kids walk out, loudly complaining. Poor little hippies, Lisa Marie thinks. Their serenity had popped like a soap bubble.

Inside it's dim and smells like lemon-scented Glade, Gramps's favorite brand. The room's unfurnished except for a dozen benches, an array of cushions and yoga mats, and an exercise ball. The windows are heavily draped and there're only two colored lamps, but she can make out a portrait of the Avatar Saugat Zin hanging above the empty fireplace.

The Protags drop their packs and one of them locks the door. The bags are full of guns. Guns and black clothes.

Jesus Christ, she thinks. Here we go.

The boys are jazzed, calling each other by their stupid code names: Rebound, Freight Train, Kicker, Sparks. The testosterone cloud is suffocating. She spots an internal door that she hopes is a bathroom, hands Christopher two sticks and the empty Tater Tots bag, and announces, "I gotta pee."

"Wait," Agamemnon says. He has a pistol in his hand. He pushes open the door with his free hand, peeks inside. "Clear."

"Thanks," Lisa Marie says dryly. "Very helpful."

It is indeed a bathroom—a midcentury one-holer, but clean. She locks the door, then maneuvers her body to sit on the toilet. Her back's hurting again, and the baby is sitting low, like a bowling ball in a hammock. She sets her purse on the tiny expanse of lap that remains to her and takes a breath, holds it. No time to record a Well-Baby Meditation, so suck it, GlaxoSmithKline.

How is she supposed to warn Marks? She checks her phone, but now there's zero service, not even SOS. The bathroom window is tiny and high up, little more than a vent, so no escape there.

She's going to have to improvise.

When she returns to the main room, the Protagonists are getting into costume. Quite a bit of leather—faux and not—and a crazy amount of hair product. Cheap stuff. These boys have clearly never walked into an Ulta.

As they finish dressing they start laying out their weapons. Each one of them seems to have brought a small arsenal: assault rifles, pistols, knives. And there on the floor are many, many boxes of ammunition. An elfin ice-blond boy with Nordic cheekbones is whistling as he methodically presses bullets into a magazine.

Christopher looks at her. He's gone even paler than usual. He starts to speak, and she shakes her head.

"Hey, Agamemnon," she says. "What did I say? No shooting."

"You did say that." He's pulled on a checkerboard T-shirt and a motorcycle jacket that's 90 percent zippers. His lacquered, now fully black hair, is as hard and shiny as a Lego head. He stoops to tuck a long knife into his boot. All these guys are very into boot knives.

"They're loading those guns with fucking bullets," she says.

"We're not going to walk in there to get cockblocked. What do we need, boys?"

"Guns!" they call back.

"How many?"

"Lots and lots of guns!"

One of these "boys" hands Agamemnon a weapon she's seen in video games, the famous AR-15. "Look, it's up to the bots to decide if they get shot or not." He slams a magazine into the base of the rifle. "If they put up a fight, or impede the mission, we'll defend ourselves."

Impede the mission. Who the fuck does he think he is?

"No," she tells him. "Unloaded weapons only."

"Or what?"

"Or I don't tell you where Margaret Schell is going to be. Yes, she's on the island, but you'll be wandering all over this place looking for her. It shouldn't take long for them to call the cops if you're carrying around assault rifles."

"Let me guess—is she going to be at this 'personal experience' you're having with the Avatar at six thirty?"

Christopher squeaks in astonishment. "How did you—?"

"It's on her Instagram, dude. Hashtag BABYTREK. She's been talking about it for a week."

Fuck me, Lisa Marie thought.

"We thank you for bringing us the bot Margaret Schell," Agamemnon says. "We'll be sure to mention it in our feed."

"Fuck you, we're leaving," Lisa Marie says. "Come on, Christopher."

Agamemnon says, "Nope. Too late for that."

She looks back, and he's lowered the assault rifle so that it's pointing casually at her. For a moment she can't speak. The other Protags are staring like cows, mouths agape.

"That's it," Lisa Marie says. "We're pivoting."

Christopher looks at her, confused.

The rage is rising in her. Clawing its way out. She's going to have a fucking Rage Baby. Her Baby M's getting a twin.

"I'm done with these Matrix-loving wannabees," she says. "What a stupid fucking movie."

Several of the boys gasp. "Take that back," Agamemnon says.

Lisa Marie shakes her head. "Any of you stupid fuckers develop superpowers yet? Any of you fly? Do any of you even know kung fu?"

"Josh knows kung fu," one of the Protags says.

"Just because you know you're in a simulation doesn't mean jack shit, assholes!" Lisa Marie's going full strength now. "We *all* know we're in the simulation! Being *aware* doesn't mean you get to slow time or dodge bullets or have sex with Carrie fucking Moss, you stupid fucking—"

"We just haven't potentialized yet," one of them says. It's the teenage kid with the acne, the one they call Sparks. "We're chipping through our mental blocks."

"Good luck with that, Sparky. And Jesus Christ, buy some retinoid for your face, I have a rec for you on my website."

He winces. "That's mean."

"Secure them," Agamemnon says. One of the Protags eagerly brandishes a handful of zip ties. "Secure and gag them."

Lisa Marie backs away, toward the bathroom. "You guys aren't heroes. Not even your hero's a hero. Keanu killed a bunch of innocent security guards who were just doing their jobs."

"Duct tape," Agamemnon says. "Now."

Christopher steps in front of Lisa Marie, arms out. "Listen, guys, let's just—"

The Nordic blond throws a punch at Christopher's head and manages to graze his cheek. Christopher stumbles back into her. "Guys!" he says. "Guys!"

Someone in latex tackles him from the side, and they go down in a glossy pile. Two other Protags grab her arms. A third, sporting a scarlet brush cut, comes at her, silver duct tape stretched between two hands.

She aims a kick at his balls, and he dances sideways. "Neo was a sociopath!"

The blond slams the tape across her mouth.

Audience
with the
Avatar
Saugat Zin

The Proud Grandmother Approaches the Burning Bush

||||||||||||||||||||||||||||||||||||||||||||||||||||||||||||||||||||||||||||||

Lenora Neville knows that no one wants to hear about an old woman's pain. No one except the man she's waiting for. She sits at the end of the second row in the Nexus, eyeing one end of the stage, then the other.

"Not much longer," Beth-Anne says, as if reading her mind. She's sitting beside her, and Dulin's filling the next chair over. The tent is mostly empty, and the tour group fills the first two rows around the stage that pushes right out into the audience like the one in Elvis's '68 Comeback Special.

"How *much* longer?" Lenora asks. "It should have started by now."

"I don't know, Momma."

Dulin says, "Do you need anything, Mrs. Neville? You want me to get you some water?"

"I don't want *water*, I want— Never mind."

"What, Momma?"

"Nothing."

What she wants they can't give her.

Each day of the tour's been hard in its own way, but today's ride down the Zipper was a special punishment. Every jolt of the wheels sent sparks of pain up her spine, and her pain pills couldn't block them. The van's seats were unforgiving. Back home, in her armchair, there are certain positions she can sit in with something like comfort. But then, when she lifts her right arm—say, to grab her coffee cup or reach for the paper—the plates of her shoulder grind against each other, as if the cartilage has turned into a Brillo pad. If she shifts her weight the wrong way, her back will seize up in a blaze of pain, paralyzing her, and she won't know which way to move that won't cause more agony, as if she's inside a box surrounded by knives, a magic trick gone wrong. She has to wait, and wait some more, until the pain ebbs and she can ease back into a new position.

If her problem were only the pain that flared up and went away, she wouldn't have needed to seek out the Avatar. She could've coped. But it's the chronic pain that makes coping impossible. Her lower back aches constantly. Her wrists and ankles throb. And there's a hot wire of pain that runs from between her shoulder blades, up the back of her neck, and into her skull. Oh, sometimes it eases, as if someone's nudged the dimmer switch down a notch, but it's never, ever off. It's been her companion for years. She wakes up with it and carries it through the day. When she crawls into bed at the end of the night it plants itself on her chest, sinks its claws into her, and dares her to fall asleep.

She's tried to explain what it's like, but her doctor just nods and smiles, nods and smiles, waiting for this old woman to stop talking. It's different with men, Lenora thinks. A man's pain is practically romantic. Oh, the old football injury, huh? Boy howdy. All he has to do is wince and it's stop the presses, must be serious, because why would a man admit to weakness? Call the doctor, get an ambulance. But a woman? No, if you listen to her complain even a little, then they're afraid there'll be no end to it. The female of the species has been cursed since Genesis. One bite of the apple and fated thereafter to give birth in pain, and not only that, suffer through menstruation, like a monthly payment on a forty-year loan. When Lenora was young, she got terrible cramps, and all her mother could give her was aspirin, because aspirin was all they had. Her time of the month would hit, and it was as if her uterus was put in a harness, commanded to pull some great weight. Her mother used to say, *That's the Lord getting you ready for childbirth*. Turns out the monthlies were worse than actual labor, in one respect: when Lenora pushed out her first daughter, a magical flood of hormones washed the memory of labor pain out of her system. If it hadn't, she'd have never had a second child.

Her daughters don't want to hear about her pain either. Especially not Beth-Anne, her so-called caretaker. And her, a trained nurse! Oh, she's good at organizing Lenora's medications, and she drives Lenora to her appointments, and follows up with the doctors and does all the insurance paperwork—Lenora has no patience for paperwork—but the girl's lost all ability to listen. She's been moping for years since her husband divorced her, and that setback shut something off inside her. Whatever reservoir of empathy Beth-Anne had as a child has gone dry. When Lenora tries to talk about her diagnoses, or the side effects of her prescriptions, or the body parts that are failing on her, Beth-Anne stands there like a post, barely taking in the words, and then rolls her eyes and says something smart like, "We done with the organ recital?"

Always with the mouth, Beth-Anne.

Everyone else in the Nexus tent is chattering away like they're enjoying themselves. The rows are close together and she's surrounded by voices. In the row in front of her sits Deb, Dulin's sister, then Gillian and JP. The Black woman's leaning over to whisper to him, still wearing a baseball cap, even though she's grown her hair out. Seems like they've spent the whole trip trading secrets. And those German boys are right behind her, talking into her ear, arguing away as always, fighting or flirting, it's the same thing to them.

"But if he's an actual Simmer," Josef says, "why wouldn't he just change the code and then we'd all believe him? Why all this talking and—what's the word you found the other day? The one that sounds like a pasta dish."

"Rigamarole," Marcus says.

"Yes! Rigamarole, in vodka sauce."

"You're making me hungry."

Lenora's annoyed listening to them. Why can't they be like Xing-Xing and wait quietly? That Chinese boy—or girl? Lenora's been unsure the whole trip—sits farther down the row, turning pages, not bothering anybody.

"Why does he need a cult at all?" Josef asks Marcus. "Why try to persuade? He could just snap his fingers and we'd believe him. No, we'd *know* he was telling the truth."

The lights on stage dim to watery greens and blues. Flute music starts to play from the speakers. It's happening.

"We have to decide for ourselves," Marcus says. "That's the point of the simulation—to let us exercise free will."

"Free will!" Josef says. "You're software—you don't have free will."

Lenora turns her head as much as she can. "Shush!" The show's about to start.

And then . . . it doesn't. Nothing happens onstage. The lights stay dim, the music plays on. And soon enough the honeymooners start bickering again, just refusing to stay shushed.

No one ever listens to her.

Beth-Anne's always telling her that she's the one who should listen—to Beth-Anne, mostly. *Do your PT exercises, Momma . . . take your pills, Momma.* Her plastic pill container's as big as a tackle box, every slot full, S-M-T-W-T-F-S. "It's the W-T-F part you have to watch out for," Beth-Anne always says; another one of her cryptic comments she won't explain.

Her pill box contains three varieties of pain pills, but none of them do much to dent the pain. She's turned to other methods of relief. All-natural salves, homeopathic pills, magnets, supplements by the barrel. Once, she paid a specialist two thousand dollars for five ionic therapy sessions in which she sat in a chair with her feet in a tub of electrified salt water.

And of course she's prayed. She's prayed for healing, prayed for relief, prayed for a good night's sleep. But God's gotten bored with her constant requests. Her calls are going straight to his answering machine. *Your Lord and Savior's not in right now . . .*

And then one day she was on the Facebook, where someone posted a video from a man calling himself "the Avatar." He said he was visiting this simulation from the real world, in order to spread wisdom and relieve pain and suffering. Both those things, and suffering was worse. *Pain* was just nerves firing, he said, the body firing off warning signals according to the rules of the simulation. *Suffering* was the awareness of that moment of pain—and the awareness that more of those moments were on the way. Suffering could occur even when you were feeling no physical pain. Suffering stretched into the past, all your pain remembered, and reached into the future to take in all the agony that lay ahead. He said that most people spend their lives in a deep pit, staring up into a cloudy sky. Even when the clouds clear and the light shines down they can't enjoy it, because all they can think is, *Gosh, I'm stuck in this pit.*

"Let me teach you one thing," the Avatar said in the video. "The pit does not exist. Pain does not exist. There is only *you*, listening to me now." He was looking into the camera, but it felt like he was gazing into her eyes, speaking directly to her. "And you do not have to suffer."

Lenora, to her shame, had never felt the Lord speaking to her the way other people described it. She'd never had a Road to Damascus moment. Oh, she'd been saved, at twelve years old by a Jesus who knocked politely at the door to her heart. And on occasion she'd felt his presence nearby. But she'd never quaked at his touch. Never come close to speaking in tongues. She wasn't a snake-handling Pentecostal, for goodness' sake.

But this, this was a burning bush moment. She sat back in her armchair, feeling flushed.

That day she started looking for a way west. Soon enough she found a cross-country trip that included a private audience with the Avatar himself. Beth-Anne tried to talk her out of it. It was a scam; he was a con man. And Lenora said, What about those stolen paintings?

She'd read all about the thirteen paintings stolen from the Isabella Stewart Gardner Museum in 1990—Vermeer, Rembrandt, a bunch of them. The Avatar goes on the internet and says he just remembered where they were—and he's standing right in front of the house! Turns out they were sitting in somebody's garage this whole time, right near Boston.

"He probably stole them himself, Momma, and finked on his friends."

It made Lenora so mad when her daughter wouldn't listen to her. Even if he *was* a fake, what's she supposed to do, do nothing and just *take it* for years and years until she keels over?

Still, there's been a few times on this trip she's wondered if it was a mistake. The pain has been worse than at home. Not just riding the bus, but all the moving around, heaving herself out of the seat and down the step into her wheelchair, over and over. When she tries to walk, within a number of steps (no telling how many), some twist of her hip will bang an inner nerve and send pain shooting down her leg. The hotel beds mangle her back. And each restaurant bathroom is like a new torture chamber. Why do people make toilets so low to the ground? The angle mashes her sciatic nerve, and she emerges from each stall more crippled than she went in.

But then she tells herself, just wait, Lenora. There's a man extending his hand down to her. She will climb out of this pit.

Someone steps out onto the stage, and she grabs Beth-Anne's arm. False alarm: It's a girl in a gauzy skirt, carrying a stool and a water bottle. The same girl who helped Lenora to her seat and chatted with her about why she'd come all this way—a real sweetie. The girl sets the stool at the center of the stage, places the water bottle atop it, and walks off.

The flutes keep playing. "I don't understand what the trouble is," she says to Beth-Anne. "It's ten minutes past start time."

"It's show business, Momma. Nothing starts on time."

Then her daughter turns back to Dulin. He's resting his arm across the back of her chair, and he says something in a low voice that makes her laugh. Probably another sacrilegious joke. Oh, he has some charm to make up for those haggard looks, Lenora will give him that. But he's smug. Proud of his cleverness. And sure that the Lord isn't watching, or if he is, then all will be forgiven if Dulin gets some priest to show up at his deathbed. But meanwhile, is he the kind of man who'll stick around? Stay by Beth-Anne's side when she starts to inherit her mother's aches and pains, when age and infirmity have their way with her? Beth-Anne's carrying too much weight, has for years, and her knees are going to go first, guarantee it. It's a miracle she found anyone to sleep with her.

Beth-Anne doesn't think Lenora knows what's going on, but she knows. She knows everything. She knows Rabbi Landsman is infatuated with Sister Janet, even the new version of her. She knows Josef and Marcus are going to last, just from the way they talk to each other. And she knows JP and Gillian are up to something. So is Lisa Marie and that redheaded boy.

Beth-Anne didn't even come back to bed last night. And still that wasn't enough for her. All day she's been walking around with a grump in her pants because she didn't take the raft trip with Dulin and his friends. Well, she could have! Nobody was stopping her. And after today, she can go do whatever she wants, because Lenora's going to rise up and walk out of this wheelchair.

That's all Lenora wants—to make her own way under her own power, as she used to. The pain's robbed her of herself. She knows she'll never be the woman she was twenty or even ten years ago, she's not delusional, but she'd like to be a sturdier version of herself. She wants to carry her grandbabies on her hip. Let the toddlers climb over her. Stand in the kitchen and cook for her family. Wouldn't that be nice? Just to stand at the stove, stirring gravy, as biscuits brown in the oven.

The lights snap off, and guitars blare from the speakers. It's not pitch-black inside; it's still light outside, and the walls of the tent glow scarlet.

A spotlight hits the wing of the stage. A man steps into it, his white shirt and pants shimmering in the light, and strolls confidently to the center. Lenora feels a lightness in her chest.

Behold, the burning bush.

The Avatar Saugat Zin smiles shyly. "Wow. Wow. Hello, friends." He walks to the end of the thrust stage, shades his eyes. "Tomas, can we cut the spotlight? I'd like to see these folks." The light snaps off, and then more gentle lights fade up. "I'm sorry, they always want to make everything so . . . dramatic." He laughs again, and Lenora is surprised to find herself laughing with him.

He stands for a long moment, just looking around at the twenty or so people in the tent—her fellow travelers and a handful of strangers. "You've made it," he says. "I'm so happy. I know some of you have sacrificed much to come here." His gaze stops on her. "Ah. Thank you for persevering, Lenora."

Her eyes sting with tears. Where did they come from, so fast? What's happening to her?

He starts naming the others in the group, thanking each of them, but she can't concentrate. She's still trying to absorb the fact that the Avatar knows who she is.

"I want to also thank the members of the religious community who are with us today," he says. "Rabbi Landsman, Sister Janet, and Sister Patrice, it's an honor to have you here. I want to say something that may surprise you: I believe in God. But even where I come from, *when* I come from?" He shakes his head. "We still can't prove he or she or they exist. One-point-two billion years later from the time period of this simulation . . . and we have no scientific proof. None of us have died and returned from heaven. None of us, thank goodness, have returned from hell." His laugh seems to bubble out of him, unrestrained. Lenora doesn't know anyone who laughs like that.

He claps his hands, looks at them for a long moment. "There's something I'd like to talk about." He takes his time to sit at the edge of the stage. She's only ten feet from him now. She didn't expect him to be so human. But somehow that makes him seem more than human.

"The existence or nonexistence of God doesn't absolve us of our responsibilities. And when I say 'us,' I mean the people who created this simulation—my brothers and sisters. We created this world, and so we're responsible for it, just as parents are responsible for a child. I'm not saying you're children—no, not at all. But I'm here to tell you that we know you're suffering and want to help."

Lenora takes a breath. Holds it.

"We know the world we made is difficult. That this life is hard. I took on this form just to make sure we understood—really understood—how deeply difficult it is. My body obeys the same rules of the simulation as yours does. I feel as you feel. This body gets hungry, and tired, and when I stub my toe, believe me it smarts.

"And you may be asking yourself—what's the point of that pain? Why make a body that suffers? Why make a world that inflicts so much misery? The Simulators could have made an Eden, and instead they gave us ... Cleveland." Several people in the group laugh. "If any of you are from Cleveland, my apologies."

Beth-Anne sighs.

"So—why this world?" the Avatar says. "The answer is simple. And it's not that we wanted to use your bodies as batteries."

"He's killing it," Dulin mutters. Lenora flicks Beth-Anne's arm, willing her to pass it on to her boyfriend.

"We were waiting for *you*," the Avatar says. "Let that sink in for a moment." He looks around, and she feels his gaze sweep over her. "You are all your experiences, the good times and bad. Every high and every low, every hard decision you made, the joys and regrets. The pain. But now that you're here? In this moment? You've arrived at the place you need to be."

The Avatar rises to his feet, gracefully and with so little effort, like a dancer. He picks up the water bottle, takes a small sip. Savors it.

A Black man walks up from the rear of the tent, takes an empty folding chair from a spot on the other side, and sets it next to Deb Marks. Sits down, right in the aisle. He's a handsome man in a handsome suit, three different shades of blue in the thread. Lenora thinks, Is this part of it? Does he work for the Avatar? Deb Marks isn't happy, though. She's glaring at the man.

Lenora's missed the last bit the Avatar said, something about his body following rules. "But I have been allowed a few . . . hacks," the Avatar says. "Access to a few functions that make life here a little easier." He sets down the bottle and opens his arms. "I'd like to invite one of you up here to experience that personally. Someone very special."

He looks at Lenora, and for a moment she's frozen. She tries to speak.

"Is Lisa here?" he says. Then she realizes he's looking past her. "Lisa Montello, and her special guest."

Lenora lowers her hand. Embarrassment washes over her.

"Is she outside?" the Avatar asks. "Can someone check . . . ?"

People are murmuring, looking around.

The Black man sitting in the aisle says, "Hello, Special Agent Marks. I'm Chet from set." At least that's what it sounds like to Lenora. He leans forward to see around Marks and says, "And hello, Margaret. It's been a while."

"Fuck off," Gillian says.

Oh my!

Gillian and Chet-from-set glance back at Lenora, and she realizes she's spoken that aloud. Deb Marks stands up, her hand on her hip, and he holds up a hand. "Easy there, Agent. We're just talking."

"We've never met," Deb says to the man. "Why don't you show me a badge?"

"Perhaps we should move on," the Avatar says. "Please, everyone, sit down."

Chet reaches daintily into his inside jacket pocket, comes up with a wallet, and shows the badge inside.

"What do you want?" Deb asks.

"The Avatar asked you to sit down," Lenora says, but they ignore her.

"Just a talk," Chet says. "You, me, and . . ." He looks at Gillian. "What's the name you're going by?"

"Doesn't matter," Gillian says.

"I suppose not. Would y'all mind stepping outside? I'd like to make this as peaceful as possible."

"Make *what* peaceful?" Gillian says.

Now JP's standing, and Dulin.

"Just go already," Lenora says. "All of you."

Then, a deafening noise—a clattering roar. Someone screams.

The Black man jumps to his feet. Deb spins around, and Lenora's shocked to see a pistol in her hands. Deb shouts, "Everybody, get down!"

Get down? Lenora thinks. Get down where?

A group of men plunge into the tent. They're all dressed in shades of black, and all carrying large guns. One of them, a heavyset boy in a checkerboard shirt, shouts, "Margaret Schell! Step out now!" Another points his rifle back toward the entrance and fires. The roar is even louder this time.

Suddenly everyone is moving and screaming at once. Everyone except Lenora Neville in her wheelchair.

The Realist's Son Unloads

|||||||||||||||||||||||||||||||||||||||||||||||||||||||||||||||||||||||

Christopher Mullins, son of a Realist, wants out of this reality. He's sitting on the floor with his back to the wall, hands zip-tied behind him, duct tape over his mouth. He's having trouble breathing, and Lisa Marie is making it worse. She's sitting beside him, screaming into her duct tape, over and over, and when she's not screaming, she's moaning.

The Protagonists left one guard behind, the youngest one, who calls himself Sparks. He's sitting on a bench across from them, his AR-15 clutched in his hands, looking like he's going to vomit. Agamemnon told him that if they tried to escape, he should shoot them in the head—and if they got away, then they'd know *he* was the bot.

The kid's only gotten more freaked out since the Protags left—and that's primarily because of Lisa Marie.

"Is she okay?" Sparks asks him. Like Christopher can answer.

Lisa Marie screams louder. *Nrrrrrrrr!* Her forehead is damp with sweat. She looks at Christopher accusingly.

But what can he do? He doesn't understand how he ended up like this: tied up, terrified, and bald. It all started to go wrong when his father was catapulted into the air and came down in that Ohio hospital. Should Christopher have stayed with him? Should he *not* have listened to Lisa Marie? But even now that seems impossible. How could he not help her when she needs him so much? He loves her. At least, he thinks he does. He's walking around with an erupting volcano in his chest—constantly anxious, constantly wondering what she's thinking of him, *if* she's thinking of him. What else could this feeling be but love?

Maybe he should say the words out loud. If not now, when? They're facing death together. And new life, too! He should make it meme-worthy. She might appreciate it more if he shouted it into the sky as the drone camera pulls up and up: I LOVE YOU, LISA MARIE MONTELLO!

If only he had a drone. And his mouth wasn't taped.

She hasn't said the words to him, but he understands why. She's too busy to think about love right now. She has a business to run, a baby to deliver, and a plan to execute that will ensure the child's survival. Which is legit amazing. Before he met her, he didn't know what to do with his life, and he's still a little foggy on that, but Lisa Marie knows exactly what she's doing and why she's doing it, every second of every day—and she knows what *he* should be doing, too. Yes, she's steering the car and he's riding shotgun. And yes, a lot of the time it feels like driving a hundred miles an hour in the dark with the lights off. But at least they're going somewhere.

"Oh my God," Sparks says. "Is she *peeing*?"

Christopher looks at Lisa Marie. Between her legs is a lake of liquid. That can't be good. Lisa Marie forces out another stifled scream.

Sparks steps toward them as if he's afraid of setting off a landmine. "I'm going to take off the tape, okay?" he says to Christopher. "She'd better not scream." The boy seems afraid of addressing Lisa Marie directly.

"Errrrrr," Lisa Marie says.

Sparks cradles the assault rifle in one arm and reaches toward her face. Pinches the end of the duct tape on her cheek. Gently pulls.

"Er-Errrr!"

Sparks grimaces and yanks off the tape.

Lisa Marie shouts in pain. Sparks jumps back, fumbles with the rifle, then points it at her.

She takes two deep breaths. Her skin is pink where the tape was pulled off. "You idiot," she says finally. "I'm having a baby."

"Now?" Sparks says.

Christopher's thinking the same thing. He can't tell if Lisa Marie is lying to escape or if the birth is actually happening.

"Untie me," she says. "I've got to get to the hospital."

"I-I can't do that."

"Sparky, listen to me. The baby is coming. Are *you* going to deliver it?"

"They'll kill me if I let you go. Agamemnon said—"

"Agamemnon's not fucking here. You have to do this. Untie me, now, or—" Her face contorts in pain. This did not look like the Braxton Hicks.

"Oh shit," Sparks says. "Oh shit, oh shit, oh shit."

Real contractions, Christopher thinks. It's all real, really happening really soon.

A few seconds later, Lisa Marie takes a ragged breath. Tilts her head against the wall. "Fuck," she says. "That was a rough one."

"They'll be back soon," Sparks says. "We're all rendezvousing back here."

"I promise not to run," she says. "I just need my medicine."

"What?"

"It'll stop the contractions. But I need the medicine, okay? Just untie my hands and give me my purse, and I'll take the pills. Can you do that, Sparky?"

"It's Sparks," he says.

Lisa Marie stares at him. Then she blinks slowly. "I apologize . . . *Sparks*. Can you let me take my medicine? There's my purse, right there. Drop it on my lap."

"Okay." He drops the heavy purse onto her thighs, then takes a knife from his boot. "Lean forward."

Lisa Marie can't lean forward, her belly won't allow it, but she tilts sideways and shows him her wrists. The blade flicks through the plastic zip tie. "Thank God," she says. "Could you bring me some water? There's a bottle behind you, near the door."

"Right, okay."

Sparks hurries toward the door and Lisa Marie opens the purse. Christopher's never heard of this medicine. Stopping contractions sounds bad. What if it hurts the baby?

Then she pulls out his father's pistol.

Sparks tries to pick up the water bottle without putting down the knife or the rifle, and finally tucks the knife back into his boot. He turns around. And drops the water bottle. The bottle bounces, then rolls away from him.

"Put down the gun," Lisa Marie says.

He seems not to hear her. The bottle rolls to a stop at Christopher's feet.

"Sparks, listen to me. You're going to put down the gun, then untie Christopher."

He shakes his head. "No. I'm in charge." He lifts the rifle.

The bang shakes the room. Christopher shouts into the duct tape.

Sparks stands there, blinking at them. Where did the bullet go? Then he looks at Christopher as if to say, Are you going to let her get away with that?

The assault rifle slips from his hand and clatters to the cement floor. And then he falls sideways. His head smacks the cement with a thud.

Oh my God, Christopher thinks. *She killed him. She actually killed him.*

Lisa Marie scrambles toward the kid, grabs the knife from the boot. She looks over her shoulder at Christopher, wild-eyed, teeth apart, breathing hard.

Her expression is terrifying.

She cuts the wraps from his wrist, yanks off the tape. Gah!

"Go get Beth-Anne," she says.

"Are you really—?"

"It's happening. Something's wrong, it doesn't feel right."

Well sure, he thinks. Nothing about this feels right.

"She's in the Nexus Center with the others," she says. "Hurry."

"But—isn't that where the Protags are going?"

"Take this." She hands him his father's gun.

He wants to throw the thing away. He looks at Sparks. The kid hasn't moved.

"Christopher. Hey! Look at me. You have to go, now. I need Beth-Anne."

He gets to his feet. His legs feel wobbly. "Where's the Nexus?"

"Just look for a big red tent," she says.

"Okay, but—"

"NOW!"

He has to step over Sparks to get to the door. Oh God, blood is pooling around his head.

He unlocks the door, steps out, breathing hard. The Serenity Station sits in the middle of a cluster of tents. Three people stand outside one of them, talking, but they don't look at him. Nobody seems to have heard the gunshot.

The gun is in his hand. So heavy.

His father was always trying to get him to come shooting with him, for "self-protection," and Christopher blew him off. He already knew guns. He'd killed plenty of people, in video games. Robots, zombies, trolls, sure, but mostly people. He's seen countless murders on TV shows and movies. He's watched lots of actual people die, too—often in bodycam videos of cops shooting a Black guy.

He pulls on the magazine at the base of the grip, but it doesn't move. Finally, his thumb finds a button and the magazine falls out. He quickly stoops to pick it up. A cheery gold bullet sits on top of the stack, eager for its turn.

He tosses the magazine between two tents. The gun is lighter now. He puts it in his pocket. And then he runs.

The Honeymooners Express Some Regrets

|||||||||||||||||||||||||||||||||||||||||||||||||||||||||||||||||||||||||||

And at last it came for them, the American disease: Men with Guns.

Josef Fischer and Marcus Egger had argued about the risk while they planned their wedding. Josef pointed out that the homicide rate in the United States was eight times higher than any country in Europe. Marcus countered that most homicides occurred between people who knew each other, and since they knew hardly anyone in the States, and almost certainly knew no one on the tour, they'd be safe. But, Josef said, what about all the mass shootings? Over six hundred a year, over seventy deaths! (Josef was looking over his round glasses at his phone, finding statistics to support his case.) Marcus dismissed this: the country's so large, the odds must be very small. I bet we have a much greater chance of dying in a bus accident. Wait, Josef said, I'm looking . . . ah! Twelve thousand bus occupant deaths a year, interesting. Well, Marcus said, stroking his beard, I guess that's it—we can't risk riding in an American bus, so we're staying home. Ha ha, Josef said.

Then this: gunfire, men in black, panic. The gunmen are shouting the name of Margaret Schell.

Josef and Marcus have seen the video of the murders in Massachusetts; they know that Gillian is Dr. Schell, which means these young men must be the Protagonists. Hundreds of these cults and militia groups have sprung up around the world since the Announcement, but the United States is the leading exporter of conspiracies, and its Impossibles are petri dishes for paranoia. Too late, Josef realizes he should have factored the nature of the tour into his risk assessment. One Impossible might have been safe, but seven of them? It's reckless. He should have persuaded Marcus to go to Spain.

Now the redheaded woman, Agent Marks, is up and shouting, the African American stranger is standing too, and Josef and Marcus are astonished that both of them are holding pistols. Is everyone in America armed?

Then everyone tries to move at once. Folding chairs tumble and clang. In the row in front of them, Dulin Marks grabs Beth-Anne Neville by the shoulders, pulls her down. Josef and Marcus duck behind Beth-Anne's mother in her wheelchair.

Beside them, Chen Xing-Xing quietly closes their book.

Marcus grabs his husband's shoulder. "Wir können das nicht!"

Josef immediately agrees; of course they can't do this! They can't hide behind the old woman; they've got to get her out of there. Josef stands up, grabs the handles on the back of the chair. Marcus stands with him.

Several of the men in black jump onto the stage. The Avatar Saugat Zin stares at them, frozen. Why hasn't he run? Then he bolts away from them, to the other side of the stage. One of the gunmen, a boy with bleached hair, wheels and fires in one move. The noise is tremendous. The Avatar screams, falls to the ground.

Then two more shots, different in some way. The blond's body jerks, then falls. Agent Marks is aiming at the spot where he was just standing. Then the Black man fires, and a second gunman on stage stumbles back. A third man in black squeals in surprise and throws himself to the stage floor. His rifle goes off as he hits the ground.

The Avatar is back on his feet, holding his bicep. The white sleeve is already turning red under his fingers. He scrambles toward stage right, vanishes into the wings.

"Go!" Marcus shouts. But where? The Protagonists have blocked the only exit, and they'll never get Mrs. Neville onto the stage. "Go backward!" Josef pulls back on the wheelchair. The backs of his knees bang against his folding chair. Marcus kicks it aside.

Josef tilts the wheelchair back, pivots. Mrs. Neville shouts something he doesn't understand; her regional accent is too thick. Aneeta is pushing aside more chairs, trying to reach the back wall of the tent. The Octos are helping each other, arms around each other. Rabbi Landsman lies across the back of Sister Janet.

"Margaret Schell!" someone yells.

Josef glances back. Chen Xing-Xing has run in the opposite direction, toward the stage, near the wing where the Avatar vanished. Xing-Xing's waving frantically at Gillian and JP, summoning them. "We are all pilgrims on the trail!" Xing-Xing shouts. "Pilgrims on the trail!" The phrase means nothing to Josef—some Americanism, perhaps? But it seems to work. Gillian runs toward the stage, JP on her heels. Agent Marks and the stranger are standing their ground, or rather crouching it. They're bent low, shuffling in opposite directions along the row, focused on the gunmen. Agent Marks fires, then the stranger. Their movements are strangely calm, almost methodical.

Someone shouts, "Keep going!" It's Dulin, one arm around Beth-Anne, the other waving toward the back of the tent.

Keep going, yes, but to where? Ahead, Aneeta has reached the wall of the tent. There's a pole nearby but no exit, no flap. She shoves into the red fabric, but it barely moves, tied down tight.

Dulin surges past Josef and Marcus and Mrs. Neville, knocking aside chairs. He hits the pole as if he's tackling an opponent in American football. The wall bows outward. A gap opens at the bottom.

"Pull up!" Dulin says.

Two of the Octos, a man and a woman, stoop and grab the lip of the tent wall. The fabric is stretched tight, but now there's a half-meter space at the bottom. One of the other Octos gets down on hands and knees and crawls through.

A rippling thunder. Josef feels the air move above his head. He ducks, too late of course. Bullets rip through the fabric just above Dulin's head, ping the metal pole. "Goddamn it!" Dulin yells.

Marcus looks back. A gunman wearing a retro-future outfit— James Dean motorcycle jacket over a black-and-white shirt—shouts at them. "No one leaves! No one!" Beside him, two men are firing in different directions. He can't see the Black man, but Agent Marks has reached the side of the tent closest to them, drawing attention away from the tour group.

"Liebchen," Josef says. Marcus turns. "Too small." A second Octo is crawling through the low gap. They're never going to get the wheel-chair under that. Then Marcus realizes that Aneeta is looking at them, and that she's come to the same conclusion.

"Knife!" Aneeta says. "We need a knife!"

Josef and Marcus look at each other. Who would carry a knife on a vacation?

"Here," Mrs. Neville says. Her purse is open, and in her hand is a large wooden object. Beth-Anne takes it from her and unfolds a frighteningly large blade. Beth-Anne doesn't look at all surprised that her mother is carrying the weapon.

Josef and Marcus exchange a look. *Americans.*

Beth-Anne jams the knife into the wall at head height, yanks down. The fabric parts without a sound. Mrs. Neville's blade, Josef thinks, must be very sharp. The two Octos who'd been trying to lift the edge of the tent now pull back the flap.

Aneeta gestures Josef forward, and he pushes Mrs. Neville through.

Outside, more chaos. Everyone in the Vertical Circus, it seems, is running in different directions, slamming into each other.

One by one the tour group slips out.

"Where's JP?" Dulin shouts.

Aneeta scans the faces. Her eyes are wide and her lips are moving; she's counting. "Christopher and Lisa Marie never got here, right?" No one knows. "So we need JP, Gillian, and Xing-Xing!"

"They ran toward the stage," Josef says.

"Shit."

"What do we do?" Sister Patrice asks. She and Rabbi Landsman haver their arms around Sister Janet.

"Go to the parking lot," Aneeta says.

Everyone starts to speak at once. Where's the parking lot? Where are they? Where are the police? The fact that they're shouting in English only makes it more confusing.

"Hey!" Dulin barks, and everyone stops talking. "Aneeta?"

She points to her left. "This way."

"Got it," Dulin says, then starts to head back inside. "I'll get JP. Just a sec."

Shots rip through the air. Marcus and Josef duck, and then both realize that Mrs. Neville could have been hit. Beth-Anne grabs Dulin's arm. "*We've got to go.*"

Dulin looks at her hand, takes a breath, and nods.

"Follow me!" Aneeta shouts. "Now!"

Marcus takes his turn behind Mrs. Neville, and Josef puts his hands on Marcus's hips. They are a train, and together they push forward. Rabbi Landsman has his arm around Sister Janet's shoulders. The Octos are moving as a tight quartet, arms looped in arms, as if they've practiced.

Aneeta leads the group out of the shadow of the Nexus tent, into the main thoroughfare. The crowd is stampeding, but more people are going with them than against them. Gunfire keeps erupting—behind them, ahead of them? The sound is impossible to locate over the ocean roar of the fleeing people. A crash of glass. Next to them, a table full of glassware—bongs? Avatar candles?—has hit the ground. Marcus feels the urge to abandon the wheelchair and bolt, but Josef's hands at his waist steady him. Move forward, move forward. They recognize tents they passed on their way in, which is reassuring. The raft and the parking lot are ahead of them. It's amazing that Aneeta has led them so unerringly, but there it is.

A figure leaps in front of Mrs. Neville's chair, and the old woman's feet on her pedals bang into them. A bald man, all in black, and Marcus feels a jolt of fear—and then he realizes it's Christopher Mullins.

Christopher points at Beth-Anne. "I need you!" He's wild-eyed and frantic. "It's happening, right now, like *right* now, in the Serenity Center. Or station. Whatever it is."

"What's happening?" Beth-Anne says.

"Lisa Marie! She's having the baby!"

Josef yells into Marcus's ear: "Keep moving!" Marcus tries to pivot the wheelchair, but they're surrounded by moving bodies.

"She needs you!" Christopher yells.

Josef is in a position to see Dulin, Beth-Anne, and Christopher. Beth-Anne looks up at Dulin and says something Josef doesn't hear. Dulin grimaces. Beth-Anne speaks again.

"Fuck, no!" Dulin says. "You can't go alone! And we've got to get your mom—"

He's interrupted by gunfire, close, like a knife shredding the air above their heads. America, Marcus thinks, is made of bullets.

Josef grabs Dulin's bicep. "It's okay. We will take Mrs. Neville."

Beth-Anne says, "Will you?"

"Don't worry," Josef says.

Christopher leads Beth-Anne and Dulin away, into the churning crowd. Marcus reaches back and takes his husband's hand. "Sind Sie bereit?"

Josef nods. "Bereit."

The Reader Puts
Down Their Book

||||||||||||||||||||||||||||||||||||||||||||||||||||||||||||||||||||||||

Chen Xing-Xing is hiding in a dimly lit warehouse, crouched within a bower of aluminum canoes, upright in their racks. Dr. Schell is here, and JP, and the Avatar Saugat Zin, all of them, as some writer might say, in fear for their lives. Xing-Xing is still adjusting to the fact that this drama is not transpiring in one of their books, but in real life (or what passed for it). Gunmen! Panic in the theater! A mad dash across the stage, into the wings, automatic weapons shouting death. It's all straight from a pulp thriller.

If they were on this tour for recreational purposes, Xing-Xing would certainly have run away from the assailants and fled to the back of the tent along with the other members of the tour group. But Xing-Xing was not here on holiday, they were on assignment. They're on a mission. Code Name: The Reader.

And when the gunmen appeared, the Reader remembered the instructions they'd been given: *Follow the Avatar.* They called to Gillian and JP using the catchphrase Xing-Xing was taught, and then helped them clamber onto the stage.

Saugat Zin plunged backstage, pleading for help. A young woman standing behind a podium with a gooseneck lamp—the traditional station of the stage manager—yelled something, the Avatar yelled back, and Dr. Schell yelled something as well. *Where's Hank? I don't know! Who the hell is Hank?* ... etcetera. Before the mysterious Hank's status could be resolved, the side of the podium exploded into shrapnel. The stage manager seemed to catapult backward into the dark. Now, reconsidering that moment, the Reader isn't sure if the bullets propelled her or if her body's instincts kicked in and she shoved herself away from danger. They hope she's all right. The mission requires that they could not stop to check on her.

Instead, more panicked flight. The Avatar screamed a high-pitched scream, turned, and ran. Dr. Schell and JP chased after, and the Reader followed. It occurred to them that being at the rear of this group increased the possibility of being shot by the Protagonists behind them. Was it their destiny to stop a bullet that might have struck Dr. Schell? Well, they thought, in for a penny, in for a pound of flesh.

The Avatar threw himself through a tent flap, into the open air, and the rest of them followed. They dashed across a dirt path to a large wooden building with a metal door. The Avatar yanked on the handle, but it didn't budge. He flipped up the lid on a keycode box beside it and frantically punched buttons. He was using only his right hand; his left arm hung down, the white sleeve soaked with blood. Did that happen when the podium was struck, the Reader wondered, or was the man shot when the Protagonists stormed the stage?

The keycode box blinked red. The Avatar swore, tried again.

Dr. Schell said, "Let me do it. What's the code?"

"Get away from me!" the Avatar shouted.

The Reader glanced behind them, into the dim tent, and saw the flash of a muzzle, heard the immediate thunder. So close! And so fascinating that the Reader missed not only the opening of the door but almost missed its closing. The Avatar and Dr. Schell had already gone through, and JP was reaching back to close the door behind him. He seemed surprised that Xing-Xing was there.

This was not unusual. Americans often looked right through Xing-Xing, or else noted them and immediately forgot they were there, as if they were a janitor or a plastic fern. And often, that was fine! Unlike some of their extroverted cousins, Xing-Xing had no desire to be the center of attention. They did not want to be looked at, noted, judged, or bothered. So, they cultivated transparency. Turns out to be a useful skill when you're on a secret mission.

The Reader followed the group into the warehouse and shut the door behind them. Fortunately, the space was crowded with stacks of bullet-absorbing material: Towers of cardboard boxes, racks of costumes, rolls of carpet, rows of folding chairs, giant Mardi Gras–style papier-mâché heads, walls of Rubbermaid storage containers like giant Legos. Lamps hung from the high ceiling, but the Avatar didn't turn them on; the only light, such as it was, seeped through a dust-coated skylight, thirty feet above. More props were secured to the rafters, including a full-size sleigh with a full-size Santa manikin holding the reins, and three flying saucers, each as large as an Algonquin round table.

And now here they were, hunched between two racks of canoes. The Reader's body, they realized, was actually trembling. How strange that they were only just now becoming aware of the fear! The shooting and shouting and fleeing had been completely absorbing.

What a turn their life has taken. They are in something like a story, but the Reader is pretty sure that they are not the hero of it (as these pages must show). The David Copperfield of the moment must certainly be Dr. Margaret Schell, aka Gillian G. Masch. The Reader, along with the Avatar, JP, and the others in the tour group, may have a role to play, but this is clearly her story.

Gunfire barks in the distance. Outside the tent, headed this way? Xing-Xing's not sure. The Avatar moans, and Dr. Schell shushes him like Mrs. Neville did to the Austrian honeymooners.

"Who was that guy with the badge?" JP whispers at her. "You knew him."

"I worked for him."

"What?"

"Not now. Hey, Zin. Snap out of it. How do we get out of here?"

The Avatar looks confused.

"Off this island!" Dr. Schell whispers. "Do you have a boat, or a helicopter, or—?"

"No!" he says. Then quieter: "I have an SUV, out in the parking lot."

"Okay, great. We'll—"

"But Hank has the keys. He's my driver."

The Reader nods. Hank Mystery solved.

"So what you're saying," Dr. Schell says to the Avatar, "is that you have no escape plan."

"Why would I have an escape plan?"

"You're on an island!"

The Reader wonders if they'll have to escape by canoe. Xing-Xing crawls over to the Avatar, and the man startles, as if this stranger has just shrugged off an invisibility cloak.

The Reader kneels in front of him and unzips their fanny pack. "I have a first aid kit," they whisper. "May I?"

The Avatar removes his hand from his sleeve, exposing a blood-soaked patch of cloth.

"I'll need to cut your shirt," the Reader says.

The Avatar nods, strangely compliant. Perhaps he believes, like many Americans, that all Asians are required to go to medical school. Xing-Xing doesn't tell him that everything they know about first aid comes from a book.

"And you," Dr. Schell says to the Reader. "Mr. Pilgrim-on-the-Trail. What do you know about this?"

"Just a moment." Xing-Xing opens their knife, cuts the sleeve above the wound, all the way around the bicep, and tugs the sodden cloth free. The wound is a puckered hole, brimming with gleaming blood like a full cup. Oh my. What comes next? They reach into the fanny pack for supplies and begins to set them out.

"Who are you people?" the Avatar asks. "And who the hell is shooting at me?"

"They're not shooting at you," Dr. Schell says. "They're shooting at me. And maybe Xing-Xing here."

"You? Who the hell are— Shit!" The Reader's just sprayed the wound with Bactine.

The Reader quietly says, "Excuse me, Dr. Schell, could you hold this in place?" Meaning the wad of cotton they've placed over the wound. She presses it down with two fingers. The Reader finds the largest bandage in the pack, tears open its wrapper. The size of the bandage is woefully inadequate, but it will have to do.

"Are you in on this?" Dr. Schell asks Xing-Xing. "Did Utnapishtim send you?"

"I am a friend," they admit. "By the way, I admire the alias you chose. I brought with me a very good translation."

"A translation of what?" JP asks.

"The Epic of Gilgamesh," the Reader says.

"Oh," JP says. "Of course. Hard *G*."

To the Reader she says, "How the hell are you going to get us out of this?"

"I have no idea. Well, I have one idea." The Reader wipes their hands on their thighs, then reaches into the fanny pack again and gets out the satellite phone. They've only practiced with it once; they made a call to their supervisor to report that they'd be missing work for the next week. The supervisor was not happy.

JP says, "Is that—?"

The Reader nods. The phone's showing one bar. They dial a number, but nothing happens. No ring, no sound. They look at the ceiling, thinking. Then they stand and snap the fanny pack into place.

"Get down!" JP whispers.

"I'll be right back."

The Reader leaves their little alcove, duck-walks quickly toward the back wall of the warehouse and points the stubby phone antenna at the ceiling like a magic wand. **Buy a satellite phone** was one of the instructions in the text they received the morning the tour began, as well as **buy the ticket now** and **bring a first aid kit**. It bothered them that there was no hyphen between first and aid. Still, Xing-Xing was excited; it had been years since they were given anything to do except translate cryptic manuscripts into Mandarin and Hakka. They knew they were chosen for this mission not because of their language skills (which were considerable; their translations were praised not only for their accuracy but for their grace and, some had said, lyricism), but because they were the closest available person. Someone had to board the Canterbury Trails bus that morning in Manhattan, even though, as the text warned them, there was only a small probability that they would be needed; the target might never show up. The last instruction in the text was **You might want to bring a book.** Ha ha!

When their target failed to board in Manhattan, Xing-Xing thought that indeed, this would be a long trip across the country with no purpose but to dive into the works on their TBRR pile. They'd paved the floor of the roller bag with books To Be Re-Read, all of which fit the road-trip theme: first, the book that commemorated the moment that changed their life, Sylvia Plath's collection of transitional poems, *Crossing the Water*. Then two Wilsons: Emily Wilson's translation of *The Odyssey*, and Diana de Armas Wilson's revision of Raffel's *Don Quijote*. Chaucer's masterwork, of course; look at the name of the bus company! Then a book about mankind's last long haul, Kim Stanley Robinson's *Aurora*. And, inevitably, something that honored both the goal of the mission and the first road-trip story ever told, Michael Schmidt's *Gilgamesh: The Life of a Poem*. If all Xing-Xing accomplished this week was to finish these fine works, they told themselves as they packed, it would be a week well spent.

But then, at the first stop on the tour, at the base of the Frozen Tornado, there she was! Gilgamesh herself. The Reader was activated.

The Reader finds a long, paint-spattered ladder leaning against the warehouse wall. They tuck the phone into a pocket, then grip a rung above their head, and ease the ladder back. It's very difficult to move, until, suddenly, it's far too easy — most of the mass is above them! They manage to pivot it on one ladder-leg and let the top drop against a rafter with a noise like a gunshot.

Regrettable. The Reader begins to climb.

At the Tornado, Dr. Schell took a seat directly in front of them—
and took no notice of the Reader the rest of the day or any day after.
Their talent expressing itself. No one in the group, in fact, had asked
them what they were reading (how could you see a book in a person's
hand and not wonder what it was?). Hardly anyone except Aneeta, the
tour guide, had addressed them by name. Some of the fellow passengers seemed to believe that the Reader was not a real person. At the
Hollow Flock, Dulin Marks walked past them and said, "*That* guy's a
bot, right?" Either not aware that his voice would carry or not caring
if it did. Once, Xing-Xing noticed the Austrians watching them read,
and realized that they were timing the page turns. It hurt the Reader's
feelings. It was lonely, being on mission. Perhaps, if they do something
like this again, they will leave all the books at home and get to know
other travelers, and allow others to know them.

Well, not *all* the books. Traveling anywhere without something to
read was literally a fool's errand. And to go a great distance without a
book of poetry was a crime.

The Reader reaches the top of the ladder and climbs between the
props, Santa to the left of them, saucers to the right, and here I am, they
think, stuck in the middle alone. Below, the floor of the warehouse is
laid out like a maze. There's the door everyone's come through, now
ajar. And far away, set into the opposite wall, is a garage door, partially
blocked.

The Reader hears a hiss and looks down. It's JP. Xing-Xing is almost directly over the nook where the others are hiding, and the engineer is looking up at them with a concerned expression.

The Reader carefully takes out the satellite phone and is pleased
to see three bars. They grip one of the ropes holding a saucer, and dial
with the other hand. After several rings a voice says, "Who's this?"

"This is the Reader," they say, as quietly as they can. It's the first
time they've been able to speak their code name aloud. It's thrilling.
"You've got to send him."

"What's the nature of your emergency?" the voice says.

"The nature?" the Reader asks. How to summarize such a bizarre chain of events? "Um, life and death?"

"One moment." And then, impossibly, they're put on hold.

Perhaps the attack of the Protagonists was not the first event in this chain of bizarreness. Was it the Announcement? Or the day on the train, two years after that? Xing-Xing was commuting home to Garden City when a man in a long, loose robe sat beside them and said, "Hey there, what are you reading?" His feet were bare.

Xing-Xing had become used to schizophrenics on public transportation—trains and buses in New York were essentially moveable waiting rooms for hospitals that the most needy would never be admitted to—but Xing-Xing's superpower meant that few of them spoke to the Taiwanese commuter quietly reading a book. It was alarming to have that bubble burst, and their first instinct was to ignore this barefoot man. Yet, how could they resist answering a polite question about literature?

"*Crossing the Water*," Xing-Xing said. "By Sylvia Plath."

"I love the title poem," the man said. "A friend of mine had a favorite line: 'Cold worlds shake from the oar.' Gives me the shivers."

That was also Xing-Xing's favorite line. Ever since the Announcement, they had been repeating it to themselves like a kind of incantation.

Xing-Xing began to amend the schizophrenia diagnosis, but then the man started making outrageous statements about the simulation and the programmers who created it. More alarming was when he mentioned details about Xing-Xing's life: their job as a translator, the fact that their family was still in Taiwan, Xing-Xing's fear of being forced to return there now that the People's Republic of China had taken control of the island. The man wanted to invite Xing-Xing to join what he called a circle of friends, a kind of benign conspiracy. He leaned close and said, "How would you like to prevent the murders of a billion or so people?"

"...*or so*?" Xing-Xing replied.

"Or just save the life of one person I admire very much."

The car doors were opening. "That's certainly very interesting." And then the Reader jumped off the train.

It was two stops too early, but Xing-Xing didn't care; they'd take the next train. They turned toward the benches, then froze. The stranger, impossibly, stood there, smiling. "I know you don't believe everything I've told you," he said to Xing-Xing. "Which is why I think you should now watch me retrieve an umbrella."

The voice comes back on the line. "We don't know where he is."

The Reader is flummoxed. "Isn't it protocol that somebody be with him at all times?"

"Tell that to him," the voice says. Then: "Do you have a number I can call you back on?"

Then gunfire, so loud that the Reader nearly lets go of the ladder. Down below, the front door flies open. It's the Protagonist in the bulging black-and-white shirt. He steps through the doorway and shouts, "Dr. Schell! Come out now!" Then a second gunman, this one a teenager with platinum Legolas hair, follows after him. If he were drawn in pencil, he'd look exactly like the boy in the a-ha video.

The Reader clicks the end button.

The checkerboard Protag squints into the dimness. He jerks the barrel of the AR-15 right and left, FPS-style. He glances up but doesn't seem to see the Reader among the giant props. Then he signals his friend to go to his left, while he moves off in the other direction, behind a giant, papier-mâché clown head. And where's the blond?

The Reader looks between their feet. Dr. Schell, JP, and the Avatar are looking up at them, so they hold out a palm: *Stay there!* Then two fingers, to signify two gunmen, but they have no idea if the meaning is coming through.

The Reader peeks over the top of the rafter, trying to spot the Protagonists. If the gunmen each move to the far side of the warehouse without seeing his friends, perhaps they can slip out the front door to freedom. If that doesn't work, perhaps the Reader could signal them to run to the garage door. But then, where would that leave the Reader? (Up in the air, Xing-Xing.)

From below, a *thunk*, and then a large statue wobbles on its base. "Fuck," a voice says. The bronze-looking statue is a ten-foot-tall, half-melted representation of the Avatar Saugat Zin—or perhaps an accurate representation of a half-melted Avatar Saugat Zin. The lead Protag appears from behind it, gun on the swivel, and steps forward. He's only a dozen feet from the racks of canoes hiding Dr. Schell, and his path will take him right past them.

The first line of the text the Reader received that morning of the tour was **protect Dr. Schell**. The second was **follow the Avatar**. And now they look down and see that her eyes are on them, and JP and the Avatar are watching too. The Reader holds up one finger and points in the direction of the gunman. They hope the others get the message: *Very close.*

But what is the Reader supposed to do about that? There's a knife in their fanny pack. They have a brief fantasy of sawing through ropes holding one of the saucers—each is held up by a single rope, looped through a hole in the UFO's dome—and watching it smash into the bad guy. But the knife is small, the rope thick, and they are no James Bond. They're not even Macaulay Culkin. They're just a person who reads books.

The checkerboard Protag takes a careful step forward.

There's only one thing the Reader can think to do. And it goes against everything they've learned about living in America, the survival mechanism that's served them well since arriving in this country.

"Hey! Asshole!" the Reader shouts. They never shout. Frankly, it's a surprise their voice goes to this volume. Perhaps it's not as loud as Dulin Marks's outburst the first day on the bus, but it's something.

The Protagonist looks up, surprised.

"Up here, motherfucker!" More pennies, they think, more pounds.

The Protag yanks the rifle up. Bullets rip through the air, shatter the skylight.

The Reader throws up a hand and tries to duck—and now the ladder's slipping out from under their feet, falling sideways. They shout and jump for the nearest solid object, the flying saucer. The cheap sheet metal crumples under their weight, tilts. The Reader grabs for the hook at the top of the dome — and now they're swinging over the spot where the Avatar and his fellow travelers are hiding, and toward the Protag. The gunman points the rifle overhead, fires again.

And the Reader . . . lets go.

Their body smashes into the canoe rack. The Reader cries out in pain, and now the boats are tumbling, smacking the cement, a rolling, crashing, aluminum thunder. The Reader tumbles to the floor and shouts again. The pain shoots up their right leg.

They lie on the ground, stunned. Then Dr. Schell and JP are there, looking down at them. The Reader's foot feels as if it's been severed at the ankle. But that can't be, can it? Somewhere on the other side of the pile of canoes, the Protag moans.

"Run," the Reader says through gritted teeth. "There's another —"

"Shit," Dr. Schell says. She scrambles past the Reader, over the belly of a canoe. The Reader's ankle is on fire, but they push themselves up to a sitting position, twist around.

The Protag's crawling toward his rifle. Dr. Schell lunges for it, snatches it off the ground. Then she wheels and backs away. Aims it at his face.

The Protag puts up a hand. "Fuck."

Her arm is trembling. Her face contorts, on the brink of a fierce decision.

"Margaret," JP says. "Don't do it."

"Why the fuck not?" she says.

It's a legitimate question. The Reader has seen the Cambridge video. They know the things this terrorist did to her friends.

Before the Reader can speak, the lead Protag says, "Fucking bot."

Dr. Schell moves, fast, and smashes the butt of the gun into his face. He screams, "Aagh! Fuck!" She hits him again, square in the jaw. The gunman collapses onto his back.

She stares down at him, breathing hard. The man moans.

"Huh," Dr. Schell says. "I really thought that would knock him out." The Reader agrees; movies and literature are very clear on the subject of rifle-butt strikes.

"There's another gunman," the Reader says.

"Where?" JP asks.

A voice shouts, "Put down the gun!" and the Reader thinks, *Too late*.

The platinum blond Protagonist stands behind the Avatar Saugat Zin, an assault rifle pointed at the back of his head. "Put it down or I shoot the Avatar!" Zin is terrified, and the man-boy with the gun seems nearly as afraid.

JP says, "Son, you don't have to do this."

"Get out of the way," the blond says. He gestures with his rifle.

A bang. The Protag falls, and the Avatar screams and lurches away. The Reader can't understand what just happened. Did Dr. Schell shoot him with the other Protag's rifle?

JP seems equally confused. He looks back at Dr. Schell, then at the spot where the other gunman lay. "I . . . I don't . . ."

Special Agent Marks steps forward, pistol out, in both hands. She's aiming down at the Protag lying at Dr. Schell's feet. "You okay?" Marks asks Dr. Schell.

The Reader looks behind them. Dr. Schell turns the rifle in her hands and points it at the checkerboard Protag. "You follow me, I'll kill you. Clear?"

The man tries to speak. but his mouth has become of a bowl of blood and teeth.

Agent Marks kicks the blond's gun away, then hops over a canoe to reach Dr. Schell. JP crouches beside the Reader. He tilts back his charter cap and looks them in the eyes. "You okay?"

"I think I broke my ankle."

"Put your arm around my shoulder. Ready?" JP helps them up. The pain rushes up their leg to the top of their head, and for a moment the Reader thinks they will pass out. Then Dr. Schell slips under their arm on the other side.

"I zip-tied him," Agent Marks says. "Now let's get to the parking lot."

JP says, "You scared the shit out of me, Deb. Did you have to shoot that one?" Meaning the blond boy.

"Yes," Agent Marks says. "I did."

The Avatar Saugat Zin creeps forward, holding his arm. "That was incredible!" he says to Special Agent Marks. He's looking right through Xing-Xing. "You saved our lives!"

You're welcome, the Reader thinks.

The Sister
Considers Geometry

||||||||||||||||||||||||||||||||||||||||||||||||||||||||||||||||||||||

Sister Janet's body has grown out of practice with fast movement, so it must borrow muscle from younger bodies. Sister Patrice's arm is hooked under her own, and Zev Landsman, her old friend, has one arm around her waist. Sister Patrice and Rabbi Zev, her sword and her shield. The three of them are being pushed along in a lurching, jostling stampede, as seemingly every person on the island tries to exit at once. Her body may be weaker than it was before she entered the Tunnel, but her soul is lighter. Panic doesn't panic her anymore.

Ah, but Zev and Sister Patrice's concern for her frailty only adds to their worry. Their heads whip around with each bark of gunfire. Zev's saying a prayer in Hebrew under his breath. Sister Patrice is making small animal noises. Sister Janet leans into Sister Patrice's ear and says, "Don't worry. It's all going to be okay."

The novice looks at her as if she's mad. "They're shooting at us, Sister!"

"Not us specifically," she says.

The crowd crushes in. It's a struggle for the three of them to stay together. The midway is packed, and strangers have broken up the tour group. She's lost track of the Octos, and the Austrian honeymooners are somewhere behind them, pushing poor Mrs. Neville. Aneeta, the tour guide, is somewhere ahead of them, too short to be seen over the crowd. Every so often they see a white binder wave like a flag, and they aim for that.

They reach the hinge where the land bends ninety degrees. Zev and Sister Patrice help her over the shift in orientation and they catch their balance on the Zipper floor. The shadows shift crazily, but they're still stuck in the midway, this corridor between tents. The river lies ahead of them, and in the distance, the western wall of the Zipper, its rim catching fire in the setting sun. The two-lane road runs straight up into the sun, and cars are climbing it like beetles. She'd forgotten that the unnatural world could be as beautiful as the natural one. But it shouldn't be such a surprise. Was there any such thing as nature in a simulation? The line was blurry.

"Almost there!" Zev shouts.

"We'll get there," she tells him.

He looks at her. "How can you be so calm?"

She smiles. "Geometry."

"What?"

It's the punch line to a grade-school joke. She'd forgotten it until she'd been in the Tunnel for some time. Her home there was a garden: a grassy expanse, perhaps half a mile in circumference, populated by a grand redwood, a handful of supporting pines, a dusting of wildflowers, and a pond. The pond was refreshed by a cold, clear stream that bubbled out of a rock like the water Moses summoned from the rock of Horeb. At night she slept on a carpet of soft pine needles. Each morning, a loaf of bread appeared, not raining down like manna, but close enough. It was all so biblical, she wondered if the Simulators were pranking her.

Out of boredom she began to tend to the flowers and oversee the trees. She was amused by the thought that the plants didn't know that they lived in a Tunnel, inside a simulation. They were plants doing what plants do. They grew. The pines stretched higher toward a nonexistent sun. Bushes budded new leaves, which eventually fell, to be replaced by new leaves later. Even the redwood must be growing, she thought, though at the invisible pace of all great trees.

New saplings sprang up, and strange flowers bloomed. Sometimes she thought the plain was expanding to accommodate. The rampant growth began to seem oppressive, as if she'd been handed responsibility for an orphanage. At least they were quiet children. She did all the talking. One day, rummaging through her memories, she remembered a joke.

A Georgia schoolboy is told to deliver a speech on some topic in math. He doesn't prepare, so when he's called to the front of the class, he starts to tell a story. "Well, y'all, Ah was born in the ground from a seed. And then Ah sprouted, and grew taller and taller. My arms stretched out, and in the spring, leaves popped out. Then a bird made a nest in my arms." The teacher was angry. "What does this have to do with math?" "Well," said the boy, "I looked down at myself and thought, Gee, Ahm a tree!"

She laughed out loud, there in the Tunnel. The trees and flowers refused to join in. "I am a funny person," she told them. "That was a funny joke."

The trees didn't answer. She pointed to a flower. "And your problem is that you're mum!" Which was, objectively, hilarious. Still, no laughs. Flora were a tough crowd.

The days proceeded. She talked less and less, but that was okay too.

Then, one day (a day that was no different from the hundreds of days that had come before), she grew angry. If she left the Tunnel, she realized, the redwood would die. All the plants, every single thing in the micro world, would die. The Simmers had put her in a terrible position. She was trapped. Worse, she couldn't explain the predicament to her charges. They had no idea what danger they were in.

Later, she was grateful for that; it meant they didn't know she was responsible. Perhaps the plants sensed her, in ways that she'd read about before she entered the Tunnel, but they didn't *know* her. Or did they? She found herself waffling on the issue, like Zev.

Years passed. And gradually she realized the obvious: She was no different from her plants. She was trapped in the Sim with them. The Simulators could disappear the garden, vanish the Tunnel, delete the entire world, and she'd have no say in it. She couldn't talk to her creators, and so far, they hadn't talked to her. It was infuriating. Did they think so little of her?

But then, another turn of thought (which came to her weeks or months later, she couldn't recall): What was this anger getting her? What would this worry gain her? The Simulators would do what they would do.

She alternated between fury and acceptance and boredom and back to fury. The seasons came and went in her heart. But gradually, very gradually, a kind of climate change occurred. She was not warming but cooling down. She decided, at last, to become something different than the old Sister Janet. In her head, and in her heart, she would become a tree.

And now she's being carried like a log.

Gunfire erupts again, and screams go up—not behind them this time, but ahead of them. Suddenly the crowd reverses course; bodies slam against them. Sister Janet's arm is ripped free from Sister Patrice's. She falls onto her back. Someone crashes atop her, a large person with long hair.

She opens her mouth to shout, but all the air has been knocked from her lungs.

The stranger's hair covers her face. Bodies trip over them, around them. Each impact hits her as if from a distance. She turns her head, tries to suck in air. She can't see; she's in a cave of limbs and torsos. Someone's shouting her name, and she can't answer. Ah, she thinks. Perhaps this is how her life ends. Decades alone in the Tunnel, and now crushed by her fellow humans.

Light. She turns her head again, and Sister Patrice's face is there, calling her name. The long-haired stranger rolls off her—no, is pulled off her. Zev is there, sweat painting his cheeks. She feels terrible that she's causing him such distress.

The two friends put their bodies between her and the crowd. Sister Janet sucks in air from the back of her throat, then coughs.

More gunfire, louder and closer. The people around them surge in opposite directions, and for a brief moment they're in an eddy in the torrent of bodies. Zev puts his arms under hers. "Ready?" he shouts. She doesn't answer; what objection could she raise? She has nothing else scheduled.

He heaves her into a bear hug; they're cheek-to-cheek. Sister Patrice calls, "This way!" Zev's arms go under her butt and lift her higher. There's no time for propriety. She hopes to kid him about this later.

He carries her into yet another tent. Behind him, a girl in a tie-dye shirt starts to follow him. Sister Janet is looking into her face when a bullet strikes her. Something terrible happens to her face, and she falls.

Sister Janet realizes she's not been thinking clearly. She's been un-worried about herself, but she has not been worried about Zev and Sister Patrice. Their youth and strength lulled her, but what chance did any human body have when a bullet found it? Zev has a wife waiting for him at home, and this young woman has her whole life ahead of her.

"I'm sorry," she says, but if they hear her, they don't reply. Outside, automatic rifles fire and the screams grow louder.

Zev sets her down behind a metal table. They're in a food stall, sur-rounded by mini fridges, fryers, propane tanks. The air smells of grease and generator diesel. A banner over her head shows pictures of falafel and bowls of hummus.

"They're right on top of us," Sister Patrice says. She's crouched beside her.

Zev lifts his head over the table. Sister Patrice reaches over Janet's body to pull him down, but Zev shrugs her off. "No, there's . . ." He looks at Sister Patrice. "Do you see?"

"Get down!"

Zev does not get down. He stares at the tent entrance where the girl was shot. "I think I have to go."

"What are you talking about?" Sister Patrice says. Gunfire thun-ders again.

"I'm sorry." Zev stands up. Runs a hand across his jaw. "I think . . ."

"Are you *running*?" Sister Patrice can't believe it. "We have to take care of Sister Janet. *Sit down.*"

Zev looks down at Sister Janet. "I couldn't figure out why you invited me. Maybe my whole life I . . ." He shakes his head. "I didn't know why I was here."

Suddenly she remembered a day, very long ago by her own count, when she and Zev stood on a Kentucky hillside. Zev had looked at her with this same wounded expression when she'd called him her sounding board. She didn't know why that made him so sad. She should have asked him then, right when she'd noticed it. But she was a different woman then, and the next day she walked into the Tunnel and allowed herself to forget.

"Oh, Zev," she says. He doesn't understand how precious he is to her. No clue to his worth, always chastising himself for being an indecisive man, a waffler, a thinker with no strong opinions of his own, and therefore no bedrock of faith. He mistook his openness for emptiness.

"I think I know now," he says.

And then he walks out of the tent, into the confusion of fleeing bodies.

The Comic
Book Writer
Almost Sends a Text

|||||||||||||||||||||||||||||||||||||||||||||||||||||||||||||||||||||||||

Dulin Marks feels like a battered punching bag. For the past fifteen minutes he's been bulldozing upstream through the panicked mob, absorbing blows, trying to create a wake that Beth-Anne can safely follow in. Each burst of gunfire spooks the crowd. And Christopher, his shaved head bobbing ahead of them, seems to have gotten lost at least twice.

At last they've arrived at the "Serenity Station," only to discover that it's not serene, nor much of a station; it's just a tired rental cabin left over from the island's heyday.

Christopher steps up to the front door and calls out, "Lisa Marie? We're coming in. I've brought—"

"Get the fuck in here!"

"—Beth-Anne."

Lisa Marie, Dulin thinks, sounds exactly like his ex-wife when she was trying to push their daughter out of her. That voice must convey some kind of evolutionary advantage to the women who wield it; there's no disobeying it.

Christopher pushes open the door and moves cautiously inside and steps over something blocking the way. The obstruction, Dulin realizes, is a corpse. A kid in black, lying in a pool of blood.

"Uh, Christopher?" Dulin asks. "Who the fuck is this?"

Christopher starts to answer, and Lisa Marie shouts, "The baby's coming!" She's sitting with her back to the wall, legs spread. Her face is shiny with sweat, but her makeup still looks pretty good.

"Is this one of the Protags?"

Beth-Anne says to Dulin, "Check on him. I'll do her." She kneels next to the girl and says, "Looks like your water broke."

"This baby's coming out," Lisa Marie says. "Christopher! Get your phone out and film this!"

"Now?" Christopher asks. "Are you sure you—?" The girl's death stare silences him. Then he starts digging into his pockets.

Dulin squats next to the boy on the floor, trying to keep his knees out of the blood. He puts a hand to the kid's neck, but he doesn't know how to check for signs of life, not really. This is the kind of thing his sister would know. He leans close to the kid, trying to see if he's breathing. It doesn't seem like it. His eyes are open, and his expression is one of surprise.

Dulin thinks, I have to remember this—you never know what you're going to need for a story. And then he thinks, Never tell Beth-Anne that I have these thoughts. She'll eventually figure out on her own that writers are sociopaths.

"I'm going to have to get these tights off," Beth-Anne tells Lisa Marie. And then, without waiting, she reaches under her tartan miniskirt with both hands and rips the tights. Puts one hand on the girl's shoulder, and with the other reaches up into the girl's privates. Dulin gets to his feet and looks away.

The rest of the room is crowded with duffel bags sprouting rifle barrels, boxes of ammo, shoes, black bicycle helmets, piles of random clothing, kneepads . . . it looks like a locker room for Team Fascist.

"Chris," he says. The boy is watching Lisa Marie and Beth-Anne through his phone's camera, being traumatized in real time. "Hey! Put down the phone and look at me. Were you two *hanging out* with the Protagonists?"

"What? No, we weren't—I mean, they took us prisoner. Tied us up. And then Lisa Marie . . ." He nods in the direction of the dead boy. ". . . you know."

"*She* shot him?"

"Would you two shut the fuck up?" Lisa Marie says. "Christopher, do your job!"

Dulin has a bad thought: Are those fuckers coming back? He goes to the window next to the door and peeks out of the curtains. He can't see anything but the tent across the way.

He picks up one of the guns poking out from a duffel. It's a shotgun with the barrel sawed off, and not cleanly. Naked bright steel rings the mouth. Did these Protag morons hacksaw this fucker themselves? He sets it down. If he's going to defend the people in this "station," he's going to need something that hasn't been jerry-rigged in some teenager's bedroom. Or maybe nobody's coming and he won't need anything at all. JP's wrong about one thing: Dulin is not brave. He's just better at distracting himself than JP is.

Lisa Marie is groaning and crying, and Beth-Anne's trying to soothe her. His daughter is about the same age as this girl. When Marion has her own kid, if she has a kid, he wants to be there—but not necessarily in the same room.

He gets out his phone, finds his daughter's name. There's an unsent message there, from back at the Frozen Tornado. He deletes it and types, Hey Mare. Shit be crazy. No, too Cool-Dad-Tryhard. He tries again: Hi Marion Aunt Deb says you got a new job. Congrats! Talk soon!

Is that too needy? Too oblivious to the years of silence?

Behind him, Beth-Anne says to Lisa Marie, "I need you to get on your hands and knees, okay?"

"What? Why?"

"Here you go, let me help you," Beth-Anne says. "Okay, good, now get your head as low as possible. Can you touch your forehead to the floor?"

"Are you making me do *yoga*?" Lisa Marie says.

"I just need you to keep your butt elevated."

"Dulin," Beth-Anne says. "Could you come here?"

He doesn't like the sound of that. His thumb's hovering over the send button. Then he remembers there's no service on this weird bent island. He clicks anyway. Or maybe clicks *because* he knows he'll be able to edit and resend later.

Lisa Marie is on all fours. Beth-Anne's crouched beside her, one hand still up under the girl's skirt. "We can't do this here," she tells him. "We've got to get her to a hospital."

"What the fuck are you talking about?" the girl says. "The baby's going to be born here, at the Zipper. At the Impossible. And the Avatar—"

"Honey," Beth-Anne says. "That horse has left the barn."

"The Avatar's going to bless this fucking baby!" Then she looks at Christopher. "They didn't shoot him, did they?"

"I—I don't know." Christopher looks at Dulin. "Did they shoot the Avatar, or Margaret?"

Dulin frowns. "You know her real name?"

"Everyone, listen to me," Beth-Anne says. "We've got a prolapsed cord. And right now I'm keeping the baby's head pushed back, away from it, but we need to call an ambulance here."

"There's no fucking cell service!" Lisa Marie yells. "Just move the fucking cord!" It's amazing how much energy this Jersey girl has for shouting.

"Then we've got to get her out," Beth-Anne says to Dulin. "But she needs to stay in this position. And I need to keep pressure on the baby."

Dulin's confused. "How do you want to do that? You want me to carry her?"

"Is she going to be all right?" Christopher says. "Is the baby?"

Beth-Anne ignores him. "We need a stretcher," she says to Dulin. "Or a gurney. Can you find a cart, or . . . ?" She looks behind him.

The door's swinging open. Dulin's body is rushing toward the doorway before his brain's formed a plan. Is he going to knock the intruder backward? Grab the shotgun? He's just going to have to watch and find out.

The figure throws up his hands. "Wait! It's me!"

JP, alarmed by whatever expression's on Dulin's face. One hand holds a pamphlet like a white flag.

Dulin's body takes over again, and he crushes JP in a hug. "You're alive! You fucker!" Then: "Is Deb okay? How about Gillian?"

"They're fine. We met up with most of the tour, but it's all chaos. We're all meeting up in the parking lot."

"So what are you doing here?" Dulin asks.

"I came to— Oh my God." He's seen the dead boy. "Did you . . . ?"

"Not me."

"This isn't right." JP looks exhausted. Dulin's tired too, but he isn't trying to do all this while also managing a debilitating disease. "They're just kids," JP says. "Your sister just—" He shakes his head. "Deb had to shoot one, to save us. He looked like a teenager too. They're all teenagers."

"I know, bud. They all think they're in a movie."

"There's got to be a way through this that doesn't cause so much . . ."

Death? Dulin thinks. Destruction? JP can't come up with a word either. Dulin says, "You didn't happen to bring a stretcher with you, did you?"

He explains the baby situation. As JP listens, his expression grows distant and he starts scanning the room. Here we go, Dulin thinks. Engineer Mode.

JP goes to a duffel bag, starts pulling out the contents—pants, water bottles, a Kevlar vest. He shows the vest to Christopher. "Find more of these. Two more would be good." Then he picks up a gun that looks like a deer rifle, points to another long gun and says to Dulin, "Bring me that. Make sure it's unloaded."

"Got it, chief."

Even worn out, despairing, and with a brain full of cancer, show JP a problem and he goes to work. He's always needed a job. Dulin's private theory was that it wasn't Suzanne's death that drove his friend into depression, or even the brain tumor, but retirement.

Christopher's found two more bulletproof vests and hands them over. JP buckles them closed and lays them on the floor. Dulin hands him one of the rifles, and his friend threads it through the three sets of right-hand arm holes. Ah! The guns are the stretcher poles.

"Now that's a high-caliber solution," Dulin says. JP doesn't laugh. Engineer Mode doesn't allow spare bandwidth for comedy. His friend simply crouches and starts tying the vests together with their straps.

This whole time Lisa Marie's been moaning and hissing. Beth-Anne is coaching her through her breaths, telling her over and over, "Do not push." She's so calm, so damn competent. How could he not be falling in love with her? It's impossible.

"Ready," JP says. Dulin drags the stretcher over to the women. Beth-Anne guides Lisa Marie onto it, while keeping a hand inside her. The maneuver feels . . . zoological. Lisa Marie doesn't like it much either.

Dulin squats to pick up the butt end of the stretcher. JP reaches for the barrel end and Dulin waves him off. "No. Let the kid get that. We need you to guide us out of here." Which is not a lie. But he also knows JP doesn't have the strength to haul this pregnant girl all the way back to the bus.

"Christopher has to film!" Lisa Marie says.

"No," Beth-Anne says. "The baby needs to live."

Christopher bends and lifts. He and Dulin are about the same height, which makes it easier to keep the stretcher level. The Influencer's mass is a little top-heavy and wobbly, but there's nothing to be done about that; she can't lie flat.

Beth-Anne says, "We're all going to have to move together, slow and steady. I have to keep my hand on the baby, and Lisa—"

The girl interrupts with a strangled scream.

"Lisa Marie has to not push this miracle baby out early. Ready?"

Dulin should be afraid. There are Protag assholes running around with automatic rifles, a baby's about to be strangled, and there's a raging river to cross. But JP is here, and Beth-Anne, and somewhere out there waiting for him is his sister, gun out and barking orders. All his life, the people he's most loved are the sensible adults. He can only play the wild man when there's someone to keep him in check, otherwise it's all—what's the word—not destruction . . . *chaos*. Just ask his ex-wives. Another thing to talk to Marion about, in case she's inherited his impulse-control problem. Find someone steady, he'll tell her, and hold on to them.

JP moves ahead of them and opens the door.

A man is standing there. His face looks like bloody Play-Doh, and his checkerboard shirt is mostly black and red now. It's the guy from the Avatar's tent, who was shouting for Margaret Schell. But now his arms hang at his side, and there's no gun.

"You," JP says.

There are a pair of white eyes in all that blood. He looks at JP— then seizes his shirt with one hand. His other comes up, and now there's a hunting knife aimed at JP's throat.

"HEY!"

Dulin's shout seems to stun the man. His eyes shift toward Dulin, but the knife hovers there like a missile captured in midflight in a comic panel. Dulin can practically see the speed lines. But he can't rush him; he's holding the stretcher. Drop his end, and Lisa Marie goes tumbling.

"Christopher, do something!" Lisa Marie says.

"Get the fuck out of our way," Dulin says. "Or I will jam that knife so far up your ass you'll choke on it."

The Protagonist doesn't move. The knife trembles.

And then the man turns, vanishes off the porch. JP falls back against the doorframe, watching him go.

"You okay?" Dulin asks.

"That yell," JP says. "That was like Black Bolt."

"With great power," Dulin says.

"Boys?" Beth-Anne says. "We've got to go."

The Rabbi Follows

||||||||||||||||||||||||||||||||||||||||||||||||||||||||||||||||||||||||

Rabbi Zev Landsman is juggling multiple terrors. He can hear the gunfire and pictures himself being cut down like the girl at the falafel tent. Then someone in the mob slams into him, ricochets off his shoulder, and he thinks, no, even worse is to be trampled as Sister Janet almost was. Then he thinks of her and Sister Patrice, hiding behind the steam table, and realizes that no, the most terrifying thing is something happening to them because he abandoned them. And so on, and so on.

He doesn't know where he is. Somewhere in the Vertical Circus. The crowd's turned him around, and he doesn't know what direction the river is, or the parking lot. The only thing he knows is that he must follow the hollow sheep.

There. He catches a glimpse of its wiry rump, ten or fifteen feet ahead of him. He forges on.

The creature had appeared at the opening to the falafel tent. It stood next to the body of the girl with the tie-dye shirt, seemingly looking down at her. She's dead, clearly dead. But then the sheep lifted its head and pointed its black, blank face at him, and Zev knew that if the creature moved, he was going to follow.

He didn't understand where this certainty came from. He's never been certain of anything. It's his great weakness. And as he stared at the sheep, his mind began to scurry for an escape hatch, some reason to stay where he was, with Sister Janet and Sister Patrice, until help arrived. And there were a thousand reasons! In fact, there was no reason to go with the sheep, except for this strange feeling in his chest. He wondered, is this what zealots feel? He thought of the original zealots, the fierce kana'im who fought the Romans. Perhaps a little Sicarii blood ran in his veins after all.

A burst of gunfire. A score of people in front of Zev throw themselves to the ground, shouting, covering their heads. Thirty feet away, two boys in black coats have stepped into the thoroughfare. One carries a long rifle, the other something snubbed and ugly, perhaps an Uzi.

The hollow sheep trots straight at them.

The two gunmen exchange a look. The one with the long rifle aims at the creature — and then the sheep zips to the right, between two tents.

The other gunman looks at Zev. He's a teenager, with a nose too big for his young face.

Zev throws himself to the right, into a gap between the tent walls. It's a narrow path, but he runs, hands out against the fabric. His foot catches something and he goes down hard, limbs flailing. He scrambles up, frees his foot. A tie-rope! The path is lined with ropes and electrical cords, practically an obstacle course.

He lurches down the path, his gait lopsided. Something's wrong with his right leg; a sharp pain's stabbing the back of his knee. He's moving at half speed now. He tries not to think of the Protagonists. All the gunmen have to do is step up and shoot him in the back.

Suddenly the hollow sheep is in front of him again. It scampers ahead, hopping over ropes and obstacles. He does his best to follow, but the beast is tireless, and Zev is not. His breath scrapes his lungs, sweat courses down his back. The pain in his knee is getting worse. He's definitely not in shape for this.

Was God watching over him, or merely watching him run? Had he been watching over his grandfather when he slipped out of Augsburg as the Nazis were slamming the door? He wonders if Yahweh is at all interested in his digital stepchildren. That was the whole question in

Sister Janet's prospective book, and he doesn't know if her decades in the Tunnel led her to any conclusions. If they survive all this, he'll have a lot of very pointed questions for her.

The sheep suddenly dodges left, between a tent and a dumpster. Zev stumps awkwardly around the corner, wincing in pain, and suddenly he's on open ground. Fifty yards ahead is the river, and people are spread out along it.

"Rabbi!" a voice calls. "Rabbi Landsman!"

It's Aneeta. He stops, bends over, trying to catch his breath. Merciful God!

When he lifts his head again, he sees others from the tour around her: Josef and Marcus, Mrs. Neville in her wheelchair, the Octogenarian quartet. Agent Marks and Gillian have their arms around Chen Xing-Xing, who is standing on one leg. Behind the trio, almost skulking, is the Avatar Saugat Zin.

But where are the others? Are Dulin and Beth-Anne still with the pregnant girl? And where is JP?

The gunfire thunders again, far behind them, and the rabbi barely flinches. Perhaps a person can get used to anything.

He limps toward them, hands on hips, still breathing hard. Then he glances behind him. The sheep isn't following him. It's standing still, its bulbous head aimed at the river. He stops, starts to turn back, and then Aneeta says, "Where are Sister Janet and Sister Patrice?"

He has no choice but to answer. "They're hiding. We'll have to go back for them."

"You left them?"

How does he explain? What can he tell them about the flare of certainty he felt, the sheer rightness, when he saw the sheep and knew he had to follow it? His actions were beyond explanation.

"It's okay," Aneeta says. "Okay. Okay."

"Okay . . . ?" Josef asks.

"This is what we're going to do," Aneeta says. "You're all going to make your way to the ferry raft and get across to the parking lot. Wait there. The bus should be close. When all of us are here, we'll all leave together."

"Gillian is staying with me," Agent Marks says. "My partner's coming—the rest of you can catch up later."

"What?" Aneeta locks eyes with Margaret. "You're not getting on the bus? Is this okay with you?"

"It's okay," she answers.

Zev can't see the parking lot. His view's blocked by the mass of people who've gathered around the ferry dock. Scores of people are climbing onto the raft—or trying to. People are shoving and shouting, some hanging onto the guide rope, others being pushed to the edge of the platform. A handful of bodies fall off the edge, splashing into the dark water. A moment later, heads pop up like fishing bobbers, then are carried away by the current, out of the rabbi's sight.

How deep is the river? he wonders. And how cold?

"I told them to buy a bridge!" Mrs. Neville says.

One of the Austrians, Josef, raises a hand. "Perhaps we should—"

A sound like a gunshot—but for once not an actual gunshot. The raft rope has snapped. The platform tilts and the air fills with roller-coaster screams. Bodies tumble into the water, and one end of the raft rises toward vertical . . . and then slaps down.

Zev cries out; there are people trapped under it.

"God*damn* it," Aneeta says.

"We should go back," Marcus says. "Hide like the nuns."

"We can't take people toward the gunmen," Josef says.

Agent Marks shakes her head. "There are at least four shooters left active, depending on how many Chet got."

Who's Chet? Zev wonders.

Aneeta has her phone to her ear. He doesn't think the phone will help, either; the rabbi hasn't had cell service since they stepped out of the courtesy van. They're trapped. Downriver, a few people—only a few—are clambering out of the water. Upriver, nothing but fast-moving, dark water.

Zev looks toward the sheep. It turns away from him and walks along the bank, heading upriver. Maybe he doesn't need to follow, he thinks. Maybe . . .

The sheep stops. Glances eyelessly back.

"What?" he says. "What the hell do you want?"

The sheep starts walking again.

Aneeta is cursing into her phone. No service. The Avatar says, "We can't just stay here out in the open! We're going to die!" As if in answer, they hear bursts of gunfire.

Zev feels a chill on the back of his neck. He turns. Twenty yards away, at a wide spot in the river, the sheep has waded in. Its legs are only submerged by a foot or so.

He frowns.

The sheep ambles into the middle of the river, then stops. The water has risen slightly but it's still under its belly. Its head turns toward him.

Can the thing walk on water? The other night he found it standing on the ceiling of his hotel room. Yet it's not *on top* of the water; it's partially submerged to its non-knees.

He makes his way toward the creature, trying to ignore the sharp pain in his knee. When he's on the bank across from it, he looks into the water and sees nothing but rippling current. The light is falling, and the gleaming surface looks opaque.

He takes a breath, then puts a shoe in. The water goes to his shins. For a moment he can feel nothing but the cold swirling around his ankle. But the floor of the river, beneath his shoe, feels flat. He puts his other foot in, glances up.

The sheep stands in the flow, waiting.

He takes another step into the water, and another. The current pushes at him but doesn't threaten to knock him over. The water is cold, and his legs are numb below his knees.

He waves toward the tour group. "Hey! Everyone!"

Finally a few of them turn their eyes toward him.

"Come here!" he shouts. "We can get across!"

"Is it safe?" Aneeta calls.

For a moment he feels that familiar dread, as if he's standing on the bimah, his congregation looking up at him. His people were always expecting wisdom, or at the very least a firm opinion, but instead all they ever got was the stupefied Zev Landsman, professional ditherer.

"It's safe!" he calls. "It's safe!"

He's never been so sure of anything in his life.

The Professor Waits
for the Cavalry

||||||||||||||||||||||||||||||||||||||||||||||||||||||||||||||||||||

The Professor is many women—Dr. Margaret Schell, Gillian G. Masch, Gilgamesh, *Mom*—and every single one of them is fucked.

She's trapped in a box canyon, Wild West–style, and can't think of a way to escape. The story of her life. She hears a cheer behind her and glances back; the Austrians have made it across, carrying Mrs. Neville in her chair like Cleopatra. And like a queen, the old woman is barking commands at them: "Easy! Set me down!"

That's the last of the group, except for the rabbi and the sisters. Once everyone was across, the rabbi ran back into the Vertical Circus to find them.

The gunfire has stopped (for now, Margaret thinks), but Special Agent Deb Marks directs everyone to take cover behind cars, warning of stray bullets. Margaret squats behind an SUV beside Chen Xing-Xing, who is sitting on the gravel with one leg stretched out. Their ankle has ballooned in size. Marks positions herself practically on top of them; she hasn't moved two feet from Margaret since the warehouse, and she helped Margaret get the lame Xing-Xing across the river. But the agent isn't taking cover; she's standing up, scanning the wall of the Zipper, or rather the road running down it.

"A text got through," she says to Margaret. "My partner's up there, a couple miles away."

"How does that help me?" Margaret asks. She's still not happy that Marks simply declared that Margaret wasn't getting back on the bus, even if it might be the best idea.

"I promised you I'd get you to Ghost City. We'll get you there, and then you'll keep your promise to me, right?"

Margaret doesn't answer. A minute passes, two. Finally, the sun drops beyond the rim, and the darkness deepens. The wind seems suddenly colder. It doesn't help that her leggings are soaked to the thigh by the crossing.

Xing-Xing says, "Their shadows must cover Canada."

"What's that?" Margaret asks.

"Nothing. A poem. 'Black lake, black boat, two black, cut-paper people.'"

"Cheery. By the way, thanks for what you did back there." She can't say more because Deb Marks is right there.

"I'm happy to have helped, Dr. Schell."

Deb says, "So you know who she is."

Xing-Xing smiles, embarrassed. "I think we all do now."

"Fucking great," Marks says.

"So why'd you do it?" Margaret asks Xing-Xing.

"It seemed like the right thing to do." They glance at the FBI agent, who's resumed her scan of the road. "Much like joining the tour. I got a ticket at the last moment, as a favor for a friend. After all, we are all—"

"Pilgrims on the trail," Margaret finishes.

Aunty Tim had told her he'd send someone to help her. She'd given up waiting. She'd had no idea that her cavalry was sitting in the bus seat behind her all week.

But that didn't make sense. She frowns at them. "You bought your ticket before I got on the bus."

"That's true."

"How the fuck did you know which tour?"

Xing-Xing shrugs. "That's what I was told to do. Fitting, don't you think? Canterbury Trails, we are all pilgrims, etcetera."

Jesus Christ, she thinks. I've been set up.

"We aren't going to Canterbury," she says. "It's the fucking *Oregon* Trail." Xing-Xing smiles quizzically, and Margaret says, "It was an educational computer game we all played in school. 'You have died of dysentery.' That kind of thing. Teachers thought it would be more entertaining to play dead pioneers than read about them. I played that game over and over again, trying to win. Never did."

"Isn't it funny," Xing-Xing says, "that we find the deaths of virtual people so entertaining."

"Oh yeah," Margaret says. "Hilarious."

A distant horn sounds. One of the Austrians says, "There it is! Isn't that it?"

"That's Agnes," Aneeta says. "Thank God."

Margaret gets onto her knees. The Canterbury Trails tour bus is barreling along the shoulder of the road, tilted crazily. The driver's laying on the horn, bullying cars out of the way.

"Everyone stay down!" Marks yells.

Another voice yells, "Dr. Schell!"

The voice snaps her head up. It's Chet from CET. He's somewhere behind her, on the other side of the SUV, between her and the river. Agent Marks gestures at her—stay down.

"Is she with you, Special Agent Marks?" he asks.

"Fuck off, Chet."

"Don't be that way. Good shooting back there, by the way."

"Those guys are idiots," Marks says. "All settled?"

"Near as I can tell. I dropped two, chased one more before I realized you'd ditched me."

"I figured you'd get over it."

"You really need to turn over Margaret now."

"You going to draw your weapon on me, Chet?"

"God, no. Think of the paperwork. It's already going to be crushing, with all these domestic terrorists we've been putting down. No, I won't shoot you, but I'm afraid my bosses will destroy your life—your reputation, your career, your credit score."

"Yikes," Marks says drily. "We've got a problem, then."

Xing-Xing taps Margaret on the shoulder. They're beaming at her. What the fuck? Then they lean back, and sitting on the other side of Xing-Xing is a skinny Black man in a brocaded robe that could have been stolen from an Eastern Orthodox priest.

"Hi," Aunty Tim says.

"Jesus Christ," Margaret says. "About time you showed up."

Marks looks down and sees the man. "Where the fuck did— Holy shit! It's you."

"Sorry," Aunty Tim says. "Don't mind me."

"How did he get here?" Marks asks Margaret.

"I've called my people," Chet shouts. "They're already in the air."

"Goddamn it," Marks says, and turns her attention back to Chet. "And I've called mine." Margaret wonders how close Chet is, and if he's walking closer. She can hear the bus's horn blaring, growing closer.

Aunty Tim crawls next to Margaret. "I'm sorry I couldn't get here earlier," he says quietly. "I popped over as soon as I got word."

"How do I get out of this?"

"I have no idea."

"This is ridiculous!" Chet calls. "Margaret, I know you're there. Why don't we talk like adults? You're going to prison, no way around it. But I can at least make sure you see Adaku again."

The sound of her daughter's name pierces her. She grabs the hood of the car to pull herself up, and Marks hisses at her. Hisses! The agent's hand is on her pistol.

Fuck me, Margaret thinks. She sinks down again, breathing fast.

"There's got to be a way," she says, not bothering to whisper. She glares at Aunty Tim. "You can't do anything? Teleport me or something?"

"Alas, no."

"So why are you even here?"

"I thought, perhaps, you might want to give me something. Something to be delivered."

Jesus Christ, *now* he's showing up to get the Devil's Toolbox? The fucker has been AWOL for years. "I don't have it," she hisses. Agent Marks is only a couple feet away and can hear everything they say. "I left my laptop in the Tunnel."

"Oh," he says. "That's a new one."

"Is this how it went down with any of the other Margarets?" she asks him.

"Not exactly."

"Stop talking, both of you." Agent Marks says. "I'm trying to get us out of this."

Margaret ignores her. "And how many of me, in any of those, made it to Ghost City?"

"None," Aunty Tim says apologetically. "All of them died. Either back at your lab, or here, at the Vertical Circus, or . . . a few other places. I'm sorry. But also, I'm very glad. You're the first."

"Well, Margaret?" Chet calls. "Agent Marks can't promise you time with your daughter. She can't give you anything, really."

A horn blares a long note. The big green tour bus hisses to a halt twenty yards away, the door folds open. The driver, Agnes, sits behind the wheel. "All aboard!" she says.

Margaret's so grateful to see the bus. For four days, before being dropped off at the Tunnel, the bus was her rolling hideout, her mobile sanctuary. It seems like it's been ages since she's seen it.

"I'm getting on," Margaret says, not whispering, but low enough so Chet won't here.

"My partner's coming," Marks says to her. "Sit tight. Both of you."

Aneeta stands up from a car to Margaret's right. "Everyone on the tour!" she calls. "Quickly make your way onto the bus!" She locks eyes with Margaret. "You too."

"You sure?"

"You're part of the tour."

The Octos pop up one by one, like meerkats.

A gunshot. Chet's fired his pistol into the air. "*Sit down.*" He looks around. "All of you."

No one sits down.

"My people need to get on that bus," Aneeta says. She's holding the white binder to her chest like a shield.

"Let me make this clear," Chet says, raising his voice. "Nobody is leaving—not until Agent Marks turns over the prisoner."

Prisoner? Margaret thinks. Fuck you.

"Look!" one of the Octo women says. She points past the sheep, still belly-deep in the center of the river, to figures on the far shore. "They've made it."

Rabbi Landsman and Sister Patrice are helping Sister Janet wade carefully into the water. Behind them, Dulin and Christopher are carrying a stretcher. Lisa Marie's riding on it, on all fours, Beth-Anne supporting her in an awkward embrace. And steadying the stretcher on the opposite side is JP, wearing that goddamn rain hat.

JP sees Chet and stops, still in the water. He looks around with a shocked expression, and then sees Margaret.

Oh, Jean-Pierre, she thinks. You're fucking killing me.

The Engineer
Finds a Solution

||||||||||||||||||||||||||||||||||||||||||||||||||||||||||||||||||||||

JP Laurent doesn't understand what's going on, but the stretcher keeps moving and he moves with it, his mind frantic as a lab mouse careening through a maze. It started at the shore lunch, when Gillian—when *Margaret* told him all the things she'd kept from him. It's as if he's downloaded a compressed file that will take him days to unzip and process.

Maybe he'll never understand it all. And maybe he doesn't need to. He's an engineer. Even in a magical universe, there are practical problems to be solved—like how to keep Margaret alive and out of jail. They'd escaped the Protagonists, only to run up against this new threat, the government agent with the fake-sounding name, Chet from CET. The man's standing beside a car, yards from Deb and Margaret, his automatic in hand.

"Get me onto the fucking bus!" Lisa Marie says.

"We can't," Christopher says. "That guy says nobody's—"

He's interrupted by a high keening: Lisa Marie, shouting through clenched teeth.

"Just breathe," Beth-Anne says. JP can hear the strain in her voice. Her arm, crooked around the girl's backside, must be cramping.

"Hey, man," Dulin says to Chet. "We've got a medical emergency here."

"Did you hear that, Dr. Schell?" Chet says. "They have a medical emergency."

Margaret looks from Chet to JP, then back to Chet.

"Let the girl onto the bus," Deb says.

"This is the doctor's choice," Chet says.

Dulin looks over his shoulder at Beth-Anne. "What do you want to do, hon?"

Hon, JP thinks. He's never heard Dulin call anyone that.

"Set her down," Beth-Anne says. "Slowly."

When the stretcher touches the ground, Lisa Marie reaches out and grabs Christopher by the ankle. The boy yelps.

"Make him!" Lisa Marie says. "*Make him.*"

Christopher stares down at her.

"Do not let this baby die," she says.

Christopher reaches into his jacket pocket. His hand comes out with a pistol.

JP can see the process that's been set in motion as if he's examining the gears of a simple machine. Christopher will lift his arm, and Chet will raise his own. Triggers will be pulled. Physics will take care of the rest.

JP lunges to his right, inserting his body in the path between the two men. Words tumble out. "Hey! No! Everybody stop!"

Chet glances toward the disturbance and shouts other words. His arm moves, and his gun is now aimed at JP's chest. Christopher's pistol is probably aimed at his back. JP spreads his arms wide, thinking, *Don't move, Chris. Don't give him a clear shot.*

"Please. It's too much," JP says. "Too much." He doesn't know what he's saying, exactly. He can picture the ice-blond boy on the floor of the warehouse. The even younger boy dead on the floor of the Serenity Station.

Chet steps sideways, trying to change his angle on Christopher, and JP moves too, to stay between them.

"Get on the ground," Chet says. "Don't make me shoot you too."

JP shakes his head. "Enough today, okay? Enough dead boys."

He doesn't know where his fear has gone. He feels hollow. If a bullet pierces his skin, it'll bounce around inside him until its energy is spent, hurting nothing.

"All right," a voice says.

It's Margaret. She steps out from behind a large silver SUV, her arms up. "Let them on the bus."

No, JP thinks. Not this, either.

A skinny Black man in a fancy robe stands up from behind the same SUV, hands raised. JP's never seen him before. "Hi, everyone!" the man says. "Can everyone put down their guns?"

"Goddamn it," Deb says. She does *not* put down her gun.

"It's okay," Margaret says. She walks toward Chet. The man tilts his head, eyes shifting between her and JP and whatever he can see of Christopher behind him. The gun doesn't waver. JP's ready to receive the bullet.

And he thinks, Yes, I am ready. The solution to his problem is at hand.

Margaret stops a few feet from Chet. Then she looks behind her at the Black man behind the car, whose hands are still up. She says, "You'd better fucking take care of them."

Chet, without lowering his pistol, raises a small device to his lips and talks into it. "We've got the doctor."

"Hey Chris," Dulin growls. "Put away the fucking gun."

"It's not even . . . never mind." Christopher drops the gun back into his pocket and raises his hands.

Chet also lowers his weapon. With his other hand he gestures to Margaret: *Come this way.*

She walks to the agent, then looks over her shoulder at JP. Raises two fingers to the bill of her cap. A salute.

The two of them walk away, down a row between the vehicles. And then a strange object appears in the sky ahead of them: a helicopter, flying sideways along the wall of the Zipper. Suddenly the chopper pulls away from the wall and starts a twisting backflip. For a moment it's upside down, and then the gravity of the Zipper floor takes hold and it rights itself.

Oh my God, JP thinks. That doesn't look at all realistic.

The helicopter starts descending normally—relative to JP's perspective—and drops behind the farthest row of vehicles. When he looks around, he realizes he's lost track of Margaret and Chet from CET.

Deb Marks is shouting, "Where is he? Where's the guy who was just here?"

"JP?" Dulin says. They need his help with the stretcher. He stoops and helps them get Lisa Marie in motion again. They carry her to the back of the bus, in the open area next to the restrooms. Beth-Anne kneels beside her, between the seats.

"We need to get her to a hospital—*now*," Beth-Anne says.

"I'll talk to the driver," JP says.

But Agnes is busy helping the oldest among them to board—the Octos, Mrs. Neville, Sister Janet—and JP pitches in. It seems to take forever to get everyone into a seat. Lisa Marie is moaning from the back of the bus, but the tour guide is adamant: they're leaving no one behind. The Avatar Saugat Zin sheepishly takes a seat up front. Deb Marks, though, is staying behind.

"Where we going?" Agnes asks Aneeta.

"We need a hospital," JP says.

"We don't have any internet!" Aneeta says. She starts flipping madly through her binder. "I don't know! There's nothing in here!"

"Wait," Agnes says. "I brought you something." She reaches under her seat and pulls out a heavy bag. Inside is another white binder, one that's three times thicker than the tour guide's, and densely feathered with multicolored sticky notes.

"Oh my God," Aneeta says. "What is this?"

"Peter Atherton's," the driver says. JP has no idea who that is. "Look for the red plastic pages. That's where he marked all the emergency stuff."

Aneeta scans down a red page, flips it over, and squeaks. "It's here."

"What's here?" JP asks.

"I have an address. He marked the closest facility for every stop. And there's a fucking *map*." She points to Agnes. "I'll navigate. You drive."

The bus rolls into motion. JP makes his way back and drops into the seat beside Dulin, just in front of Christopher. Lisa Marie is on all fours just behind them. "Don't push," Beth-Anne says, over and over.

Dulin puts a hand on JP's shoulder. "You okay?"

He's baffled that he's still alive. He was ready.

"I'm okay," he says.

Agnes steers them up the face of the Zipper. She's pounding the horn and cursing at the other drivers from her side window. At last they thump over the causeway, eliciting a moan from Lisa Marie, and then the Zipper is behind them. The bus accelerates.

JP doesn't understand how Margaret can be gone. He doesn't know what happens next. Who's going to explain all this to her daughter?

Beth-Anne calls out, "How much longer?"

Aneeta's at the front of the bus, standing beside Agnes, holding on to the pole. She glances at her phone. "Sixteen minutes. It's an urgent care center, not a hospital, but it was closest."

"Faster, please," Beth-Anne says.

"You're doing great, hon," Dulin says. Lisa Marie glares up at him with raccoon eyes. Sweat and tears have ruined her mascara. "Both of you."

"Yes, really great," Christopher adds.

Dulin turns in his seat to look at the kid. "Better give me the gun."

"Oh. Right." He digs into his pocket. "Don't worry, though, it's not—"

A bang. The sound shakes the air.

"What the fuck was that?" Agnes shouts.

JP's ears are ringing. Christopher's staring at the gun. "I thought—I thought I took them out."

"Don't move," JP says. He reaches back, puts one hand on the barrel, pushing it down. With the other he clicks on the safety.

"I took out all the bullets!" the kid says.

"Did you clear the chamber?"

"I don't know!" The kid's shaking his head. His eyes are watering.

JP takes the gun, works the slide. The chamber is empty—now.

"Huh," Dulin says. He's looking down at his side, frowning. A dark stain has appeared on his shirt, near the ribs. Then it begins to spread. "This isn't good."

One Last Interruption

||||||||||||||||||||||||||||||||||||||||||||||||||||||||||||||||||||||

Hospital waiting rooms, we've always thought, are their own kind of Impossible. Time stretches. The clack of a door opening is somehow louder than a dozen chattering voices. And gravity is variable: pulling some of them deep into their seats, pushing others out of them to pace and fret. Whatever's happening in the other, crucial areas of the facility—the examination rooms, the maternity rooms, the surgical theater—isn't known, and can't be known until a nurse or doctor exits the causality bubble and carries the news. Each room could be its own simulation, running on its own clock speed.

This urgent care facility, located in a small town in southern Utah, was not built to handle the flood of victims created by a mass shooting. The tour bus arrived here hours ago, at the front of the wave, but more victims of the Protagonists have been rolling in since. The waiting room only has thirty seats, and the tour group has filled half of them. THE OCTOS sit in a row by the magazine rack, leaning on each other, limbs interlaced. THE READER slouches nearby, one leg outstretched, their sprained or possibly broken ankle too low on the triage list to demand attention.

THE PROUD GRANDMOTHER, however, understands that

no doctor here will see her. She sits in her wheelchair, exhausted and unable to stem her weeping. All this jolting and jostling and unscheduled terror have pushed her pain beyond the reach of her meds. THE HONEYMOONERS sit on either side of her, unable to do anything for her but hand her Kleenex after Kleenex. Her daughter has abandoned her, gone to the other side of the doors, nursing someone she's not even related to.

We shouldn't have skipped that part: How the Influencer —sorry, THE INFLUENCER—was carried out of the bus, crying and cursing, still on hands and knees. THE NURSE leaned over the stretcher, one hand on the small of the girl's back, the other holding the baby's head inside her. THE COMIC BOOK WRITER came through the doors moments later on his own stretcher. It was a shock to everyone to see the big man silent and unmoving. THE ENGINEER accompanied him to the back rooms. THE TOUR GUIDE offered to drive the rest of the group to a hotel, but no one wanted to leave. They settled into their seats.

THE REALIST'S SON has folded himself into a chair in the corner, beside a plastic fern. His phone is buzzing away, filling with urgent texts, but he doesn't have the strength to look at them. He's sick to his stomach. The police will be here soon, he's sure of it, and he doesn't know what he will say to them. He's watched enough television to know he'll get one phone call, but who will he call? He looks through his favorites list. Domino's Pizza is a no. Mom, then? He can't imagine that conversation. He presses the third contact.

The line rings three times, four. Then a voice says, "Chris? Oh my God, Chris!" It's his father, THE REALIST.

"Dad," he says. "Something bad has happened."

"I can barely hear you," his father says. "What's happened?"

The boy tries to tell the story, but he has to keep backtracking to explain how it came to be that he was on the bus with a not-quite-unloaded gun, which he'd used to threaten a government agent, because Lisa Marie needed to get to a hospital, because she'd gone into labor while the terrorists had tied them up, because they thought Lisa Marie and Christopher had betrayed them, because and because and because, swimming upstream to the spot where the tragedy was born: "Remember when you handed me your pistol?"

The Realist's Son cringes. He didn't mean to make it sound like this nightmare was in any way his father's fault.

"Terrorists?" his father says. "Oh my God, that was you on the news. Are you okay?"

"They're all dead now. Well, most of them."

"Okay," his father says. "Okay. Okay."

Uh-oh, the boy thinks. I've broken my dad.

"Okay," his father says again. "Here's what we're going to do." He's weirdly energized and begins to rattle off a plan involving lawyers, police etiquette, Venmo accounts, and media appearances. The phrase "we have to get in front of this" comes up several times. Not once does he mention how his son abandoned him in the hospital and ghosted him for days. Nor does he mention the *Real Patriot* podcast, but for the Realist's Son, the subtext is clear: Isn't this a great story? Won't it knock people out when they hear it?

As the Realist talks, more texts from Lisa Marie are hitting his son's phone.

"Hey, Dad? I need to go."

"Wait. Before you hang up— I love you, Chris. We're a team. We'll get through this."

"I . . . yeah. Me too." The Realist's Son feels as if he's shrinking and growing at the same time. "I just—Dad? I can't, uh . . ."

His father waits for him to find the words. This is very unlike him.

"I can't do the podcast anymore."

"What?"

"I'm sorry. I know it's important to you, and you really want me to work on it with you—"

"Chris, stop. I don't care about the podcast."

"What?"

"I mean, of course I do, but that's for me." His father sighs. "It's okay if you want to work with Lisa Marie on her project, I get that."

"I don't want that, either!" He doesn't know what he wants. He doesn't even know what process he could use for discovering it. He just knows that he left his father and shaved his head, shot a man, and he doesn't know how any of that happened. "I just need to figure it out."

The Realist's Son hangs up and his phone is heavy with the Influencer's texts. He reads the latest ten, and the most recent one is the shortest: I need you. He replies: to record you? Almost instantaneously she writes back:

NO JUST YOU I NEED YOU.

Bloop.

PLEASE

He stares at the words for a long moment. Thinks, One last time. Then he unfolds himself and walks to the front desk. "My girlfriend is giving birth to my child, and she wants me back there." One of the texts specified that he use these exact words.

"Oh," the receptionist says. "Her."

The tour group watches the Realist's Son get buzzed through the rear door, which shuts behind him with a hard *clack!*

THE NOVICE comes back into the waiting room with water bottles and snacks from the vending machines. There wasn't much left in them, just snack bags with unfamiliar brand names like "Clover Club" and "Don Julio." THE SISTER chooses something called "Hot Chix," and THE RABBI leans over to open the bag for her. The hollow sheep sits on the floor at his feet—no, *on* his feet—like a giant loofah.

"Does it . . . need anything?" the Novice asks.

"Doesn't seem to," the Rabbi says. "Do you think they'd let me bring it on the plane?"

"Perhaps it counts as a comfort animal," the Novice says.

"Ooh," the Sister says with enthusiasm. "These are flavored chickpeas."

The Novice still hasn't come to terms with this new Sister Janet. Her religious training should have prepared her for such transformations—Paul on the road to Damascus comes to mind—but she's realizing her instruction hasn't adequately prepared her for life in a simulation. Her faith in God is unwavering, but everything else? Up for grabs. When she began this trip a week ago, she thought her job was to drag her sister in Christ back to shore. Now, perhaps it's the Sister's job to teach the Novice to swim.

The Novice brings out her phone. "Are you ready to resume the interview, Sister?"

"Of course!"

She presses record. "Tell me more about the Tunnel garden. Were you lonely?"

"Lonely . . . ," the Sister repeats. "Sometimes." She pops another chickpea into her mouth. Considers. "There were some bad days. Bad months, maybe? It was difficult to keep track of the time."

The Novice waits. She's almost gotten used to the Sister's long silences.

"Every so often I felt the tug of the outside world," the Sister says. "I'd think of you two, waiting on the other side, and all my friends out there. But I knew that no time was passing for you, so you couldn't be worried about me, or missing me. I was causing no pain. That's one side of the ledger, isn't it? The pain you cause, the debts you owe. But on the other side of the ledger, I was content."

The Rabbi leans forward. "Why didn't you—?" The Novice is surprised to hear so much sadness in his voice. "That is to say, why did you decide to come out at last?"

"At last," she says. "Yes." She picks up another chickpea, holds it in her thin, papery fingers.

"It took me a long time, but at last I came to terms with the fact that if I died in the Tunnel, the garden died too. I could only assume that was the case. I looked around at this pocket forest and thought, Well, if the Simulators delete it, I cannot stop them. Isn't it funny how much energy we spend worrying about death when we can't do anything about it?"

"We long for the solvable," the Rabbi says.

"That's a good way of putting it," Sister Janet says. "Before the Tunnel, I insisted on the solvable. You'd think as a professed sister I'd be more comfortable with mysteries. But I was so invested in being right. Defending my conclusions, no matter what. I realized in there that I needed to be more like you, Zev."

"Like *me*?" the Rabbi exclaims.

"Sometimes there is no way to understand a thing until you see it from all sides—and even then . . ."

They wait while she eats.

"Spicy," the Sister says. "Where was I?"

"Seeing a thing from all sides," the Novice says.

"I don't think anyone should emulate me," the Rabbi says. "I can go round and round, never coming to a decision."

"Yet when it counted, you did make a decision," the Sister says. "And it saved our lives."

"You found your faith," the Novice says.

"Perhaps," the Rabbi says, looking down at the creature lounging on his feet. "I certainly found something."

Clack.

Their attention turns to the far doors. The Avatar Saugat Zin steps out, looking haggard, his white shirt still bloody, left arm in a sling. His sleeve's been cut away, showing a freshly bandaged bicep.

The Sister gets to her feet, just as a trio of young people, his followers, rush toward him, saying his name and asking him questions in the language of their caste, High Obsequious.

"I'm fine," he tells them. "It was just shrapnel." Then he notices the Reader, and sees that the other people from the bus are here, too.

"Get me the fuck out of here." Yes, yes, the followers all agree, we shall get the fuck out. They head toward the exit.

The Sister steps into their path. "Avatar," she says. "If I could ask a favor."

"Please, out of the way," one of his followers says. "The Avatar is very—"

"It's not for me," she says. She makes eye contact with the Avatar. Then she nods toward the Proud Grandmother. "She's been waiting."

He follows her gaze, then shakes his head. "Look, I'm closed for the night. Show's over. Feel free to contact me through the website."

The Sister doesn't move aside or speak. She has become a tree.

The man rubs a hand across his face. Then he straightens, lifts his chin. It's remarkable: Without lights or backing music, he suddenly becomes the Avatar Saugat Zin.

The Proud Grandmother watches him as he steps around a row of people and heads toward her, his followers, unsurprisingly, following. She quickly dabs at her eyes, tries to straighten in her wheelchair, and a spike of pain runs up the back of her neck.

The Avatar stops, then kneels in front of her. "Lenora," he says. That quiet baritone is familiar to her from the videos. He's not whispering, but she feels as if no one can hear him but her. "We were going to talk tonight, weren't we, before we were interrupted."

"That's right," she says.

"It's been quite the night, hasn't it, Lenora?"

She nods, her fist closed around the wad of damp tissue.

"Can I tell you something embarrassing?" he says. "I was scared tonight. Even with everything I know, my body—this body I've been occupying for a long time now—it reacted just like everyone else's, full amygdala hijack. And when this happened . . ." He tilts his head toward his injured arm. "I felt the pain. Boy, did I feel it." He shakes his head. "I guess even I have to relearn the same hard truth every time."

"What is that?" Lenora asks.

"Pain is real. Even though your body is made out of ones and zeros, Lenora, if you experience it, that's the realest thing in the world. And I can't make it go away."

"But I thought . . ." She puts a hand to her eyes. Marcus, the bearded Honeymooner, hands her a fresh tissue.

The Avatar doesn't seem to be dismayed by her tears. He waits.

After a moment Lenora says, "I thought you could make it go away."

"I can't," he says. "But you can." He puts a hand on her knee. "You just have to know the secret. Pain is a signal. Your body, your temporary container, has been programmed to receive those signals, and you've spent your whole life responding to them. Think of it like a telephone ringing. You don't have to pick up that phone, Lenora. Just let it go."

"To voicemail?" she asks.

The Avatar blinks slowly. "Sure. You can listen to it later, or just delete it."

"The metaphor still works," one of the Honeymooners says, and the other says, "Does it?"

"Let me teach you how to do that," the Avatar says. He reaches out a hand to his followers. There's a bit of a scramble as they look through their pockets, and then one of them drops something small into his palm.

"Lenora, are you right-handed or left-handed?"

"Right," she says.

"Then give me your left." She gets rid of the clump of tissue, wipes her hand on her pantsuit.

The Avatar places the object in her hand—it's a colored marble that feels like glass—and gently folds her fingers over it. "This is a re-coded object I've created. It's called the Neurobattery. When you feel the pain coming, I want you to roll it in the palm of your left hand. Let the signal go there. All the pain. Just . . . dump it. The battery can take an infinite amount."

Lenora begins to move her fingers. The marble—the battery—is heavier than she expected.

"Ready for the first test?" He tells her to hold tight, and slaps the underside of her hand, hard. She yelps, and almost lets go of the battery.

"Roll it in your palm, Lenora. Charge it up."

The sting from the slap fades.

"You feel it getting warm?" he asks. And she does! It feels like a pebble in the sun. "Now you can use it for anything. Any pain or discomfort."

She thinks of the pain in her spine. She sends it down her arm, into the battery. "Oh," she says. It seems to be working, a little bit.

"Keep practicing," the Avatar says. "And keep the Neurobattery with you at all times."

"Replacements and alternate versions are available in our online store," one of the followers says.

The Avatar and his followers bustle toward the doors. The Sister thanks him as he passes, but he says nothing, and then they're outside, into the cold desert predawn.

The Tour Guide, standing in the parking lot by the tour bus, sees his group leave but keeps talking into her phone. "No, I don't think *you* understand, Tanya," she says. "These people have been traumatized."

THE DRIVER steps down out of the bus, holding two plastic buckets, one full of water, notices the Avatar's crew piling into a black SUV. "See ya, Dave!" The Avatar scowls in her direction, then slams the door. The vehicle pulls away.

"Gone before the cops arrive," the Driver says to herself. The police were supposed to have shown up hours ago, said they were very interested in Christopher Mullins, but so far no show. Most likely every cop in the county was at the Vertical Circus, trying to figure out what the hell happened.

"Look, one of them's been shot," the Tour Guide says into the phone. "And one of them was held captive—yes, like actually tied up." Her voice has climbed into a register she calls "Angry Oompa Loompa." She hates when it does that. "Just because they signed a waiver doesn't mean— What? No! I don't care what time it is, you're the emergency support and this is an emergency. We've got to take care of these people. Tanya? Are you—? Tanya!"

The Tour Guide stares at her phone. "She hung up on me."

The Driver chuckles, sets down the buckets. Her sleeves are rolled up and her knees are damp. She's been washing blood and other bodily fluids out of the aisles. "I'm surprised she picked up at all. It's the middle of the night there."

"That's because I've been calling her for hours. And sending emails. I even used the Contact Us page on the fucking website! I'm getting nowhere."

"You check Peter's binder? The man collected important numbers. I think the president's private cell is in there."

"The president of the United—?"

"Company," the Driver says. "Just call him and tell him we have a PR nightmare on our hands. Lawsuits galore."

The Tour Guide picks up the huge binder. Each page is dense with annotation. And the regular info is interleaved with bonus printouts, handwritten speeches, even diagrams and sketches. "I want to copy all this stuff," she says.

"Peter says you can keep it. After the week you've had, you deserve it."

"I can't keep this! There's like a whole life in here. Besides, I'm not going to— I mean, I don't think I can do this again."

"You don't have to decide right now. But there's probably a raise in it for you if you stop this shit from going viral."

"We do have an influencer in there."

"Oh, our little girl's been posting videos since she got admitted."

"What? *No.*"

"Check this out." The Driver opens an app called Mimsy that the Tour Guide's never heard of. My God, she thinks, I'm only twenty-seven but already an Old. The Driver shows her the @lady_mmm account, and there's a still image of Lisa Marie damp with sweat, wild-eyed and mascara-smeared, but somehow still gorgeous. The Driver taps the screen and the video springs to life.

"Hello, my M and M's," Lisa Marie says. It's clear now she's in a hospital bed. "We have to do an emergency C-section. I can't— Wow! I can't feel anything right now. Super-nurse Beth-Anne kept my baby alive, but in a few minutes—"

A voice off-screen interrupts; the words are indistinct. A hand enters the frame, holding an oxygen mask. "Not yet, damn it," the girl says. "Where's Christopher?"

"I'm here!" Christopher calls from somewhere. "Just a second!"

"*Now*," a doctor voice says, and the mask comes down. The Influencer keeps talking, fogging the mask. The image tumbles into black; she's dropped the phone face down. There's ten more seconds of blank and muffled voices, and then the video cuts off. At the bottom of the screen are tags: #BABYTREK #impossiblebaby

"God love her," the Driver says. "She's one crazy bitch."

"I have to call the president," the Tour Guide says.

Inside, the tour group is oblivious to Lady Mmm's posts. The Proud Grandmother has dozed off, her face peaceful. The Honeymooners begin a whisper-argument over her. One wants to go home, but the other lobbies for continuing to Ghost City, to finish the trip. His heart isn't in the argument, though. "Ja, bärchen. Okay."

The eastern windows begin to glow with orange light, and the Reader shifts in their chair to look between the blinds. The land stretches into the distance, a vastness of red sand and stone, sprinkled in the middle distance with green scrub: a barely terraformed Mars. Even the sun looks alien.

One of the female Octos leans over to see the title of the book they're reading. "*Aurora*," she says. "Didn't you already finish that one?"

The Reader is chagrined to learn that they've been paying attention to their reading list; indeed, that they'd been paying attention to them at all. Weren't they supposed to be a secret agent? Ah well, they've only ever been an amateur. A volunteer in Utnapishtim's army. And now it occurs to them that keeping to themselves during the trip might have been a mistake. Even though the Reader barely talked to these people, Xing-Xing fell in love with them, just a bit, in the way that one can grow to love birds nesting on a nearby window ledge.

The woman is waiting for a response, and the Reader rummages through their brain for a plausible response. "I . . . enjoy rereading."

"So do I!" the woman says. "The book seems to change every time you read it, don't you think?"

A familiar voice calls out, "Everyone in my group—everyone in the North American Impossibles Tour—can I have your attention?" The Tour Guide's standing by the door, but most people can only see the top of her head. The Driver says something to her, and the Tour Guide climbs up onto a chair and holds up her phone. "I've got some information about the trip, and refunds. But first, some more important news. Could you go to the group chat? I've just texted you a link for a live stream I think you'll be interested in."

People start looking at their phones. The Octos, somehow, are first to find the video, but soon everyone is watching. A bit of motion blur, and then a face fills the screen: the Realist's Son. He holds out his long arm to bring the Influencer into view. She's looking down at something off-screen. "Okay," he says. "You're on."

The Influencer looks into the camera, and her eyes are full of tears. "I would like to— Christopher, pan down." The camera moves to take in a tiny bundle with a red face. "Everyone, this is my son, Little Miracle Montello. Little Miracle, this is the world."

The video goes on for a while. The Proud Grandmother, who slept through the Tour Guide's announcement, is still sleeping. The Novice says, "The child's name is really Little Miracle?"

"Maybe they'll change it," the Rabbi says. "Before he goes to school." And gets beaten to a pulp, he thinks.

The Octo sitting beside the Reader says, "Sometimes it's so different, it's like the characters have all been talking among themselves and changing their minds while I wasn't looking." It takes a moment for the Reader to realize that she's talking about books again, picking up the conversation where they left off.

"I've also found that to be true, yes," the Reader says.

"You can never read the same book twice," says the Octo man beside her. "As Heraclitus never said," adds the man beside him, and they chuckle.

"The beauty of rereading . . . ," says the woman on the end, and the woman beside the Reader says, ". . . as soon as you finish, you can start over. Just like life."

Ah, the Reader thinks. The groundhogger philosophy yet again. "I believe that only works if you're outside the book looking in. If you're inside it, wouldn't it all feel like . . . now?" They smile to defuse any insult. "You can't go back, and you don't know what's coming. Though I confess that I would sometimes like to know what page I'm on."

"Four-twenty-two!" one of the men says, and the rest of the Octos laugh.

"That sounds like disturbingly close to the end," the Reader says. "Unless we're in, say, *Anna Karenina*."

The old people find this hilarious. One of them down the row says, "No worries, unless you *are* Anna Karenina." Another says, "And there's a train coming."

"That's a good point," the Reader says politely.

"Well, you keep going," says the woman beside the Reader. "Don't let us interrupt."

Clack.

Everyone automatically looks toward the end of the room. The Engineer holds open the door, and the Nurse steps through. She blinks as if emerging from a dark room into one that's too bright.

The Reader levers themselves up, leaning on one good foot. The Octos help each other to their feet, and then the Rabbi rises, and the Novice and the Sister. The Tour Guide and the Driver stand by the door, waiting. The Proud Grandmother pushes herself up out of her wheelchair. The Honeymooners steady her, but there's no pain. And then she sees that her daughter and the Engineer are wearing the same lost expression.

Oh no, the Grandmother thinks. She fell in love with him.

The Engineer looks around at the tour group. He opens his mouth, closes it. The Nurse takes his hand.

Everyone watching understands. Words are not required. They can read the story on their faces.

Oh, One More Thing

||||||||||||||||||||||||||||||||||||||||||||||||||||||||||||||||||

Our apologies. We've been having a bit of an argument about whether to end the world.

We're not actually a group mind—that's a rumor—but it's true that we've known each other for so long, doing the same job, that we're almost always on the same page. For example, we all agree that our assignment is to observe and report, offer constructive criticism, and suggest improvements. Yes, we can add or tweak variables at the start of an iteration, and we can think up new kinds of Impossibles, but we're not supposed to interfere *during* the run—that would make us one of the variables! We'll never get out of the trap we've found ourselves in if we can't maintain discipline and proceed with scientific detachment.

However . . .

It's so *boring.* We convinced ourselves that it would do no harm if we walked around in the world a bit. Sampled the local food, drank a little wine, talked to folks . . . light, harmless fun that might also inform our ultimate decision. Keep going, or start over with a new set of conditions?

The problem with getting to know people, we discovered, is that we might accidentally get to like some of them. We might even develop favorites. And when one of them goes on the road again—say, a year and change after the end of a certain bus tour—we're tempted to follow along.

There he is now, behind the wheel of a white rental car. THE ENGINEER. Talking Heads blasts from the speakers, David Byrne plaintively singing *Heaven... heaven is a place...* When you're traveling alone, the Engineer thinks, you can play the music as loud as you want.

He passes a billboard almost exactly like the dozen he's seen in the miles previous: a child in bulky glasses gazing up in wonder at a skyscraper, and plastered across that, in capital letters, the same demand—SEE GHOST CITY! He's been seeing the signs for hours, with increasing frequency, and the only difference between them is their increasingly desperate countdowns: 80 MILES AHEAD! 50 MILES AHEAD! 2 MILES AHEAD! And finally, TURN HERE!

He resents being told what to do, but obeys. He steers the car off the interstate and onto a two-lane blacktop that snakes through a parched brown landscape. Twenty minutes later he noses into a spot in a vast parking lot, among a few hundred cars and half a dozen tour buses. None of the buses look familiar.

He shuts down the car, takes a final breath of air-conditioning. Outside it's brutally hot, and it's only eleven a.m. The sky is a cloudless, brilliant blue. Two spots away, a young father stands at the back of a minivan, loading a rolling cooler with water bottles and juice boxes, while his wife smears white sunscreen onto a toddler's face.

The Engineer unlocks the trunk. Inside is his suitcase, a six-pack of bottled water, and a blue cardboard box the size of a Chinese takeout container. The box has fallen onto its side. He rights it, frowning. Then he extracts his wide-brimmed Charter all-weather hat from the suitcase and pulls it on. Still one of the best hats he's ever owned.

He walks toward a high orange wall that runs for a half mile in each direction. A Jurassic Park–style gate is set in the center, and above it is a scrolling LED marquee. NOW SHOWING ... OTHER PORTLAND ... NOW ...

The ticket bays are enclosed, to preserve the mystery of what lies beyond. The ticket clerk, a teenager with pink hair and a pug nose, asks if he wants a tour—audio walking tour, in-person tour, or air-conditioned motor tour. He turns down all the extras and finally receives a map and a pair of blue plastic glasses. The lenses are blue as well, and not actually lenses; they're opaque. "Please remember to hydrate," the ticket clerk says, and seems to really mean it. Perhaps old people worry her.

He steps out of the ticket bay, back into the heat. Scores of tourists mill about in the Welcome Village, each building in a different style—a gift shop in a faux Chinese temple, a Swiss chalet cafeteria, an auditorium inside a half-scale Taj Mahal. A wide cobblestone road leads out of this welcome area. He follows it, holding the blue glasses in his fingers, to where the cement ends.

The desert seems to have been raked flat and stripped of vegetation. Far in the distance sit low, rocky hills, gray against that blue, blue sky. Closer by are rows of wooden facades with no buildings behind them, as on a movie set. The empty spaces between them suggest streets, and there are plywood structures that impersonate city features: benches, fountains, steps. Dozens of plastic Christmas trees suggest a park. Tourists stroll down these unpaved streets wearing their blue glasses. And yes, they're gazing around in something like wonder, just like the billboard suggested. Twenty yards from him, a young boy shouts in terror and jumps to the side, dodging nothing, and his older brother laughs hysterically.

The Engineer steps from the cement. Nothing changes. Then he puts on the glasses.

Ghostly buildings spring up around him. He's standing in the middle of a street and a car is *there*, rushing toward him.

"Shit!" He yanks off the frames. He's in the desert, never left the desert. He shakes his head, laughing at himself. Then he takes a breath and pushes the glasses into place.

Quickly he steps onto the sidewalk. Phantom people walk toward him, their faces covered by surgical masks. He steps out of the way, even though he knows he doesn't have to. Then he realizes he's overstepped. His arm is half inside a brick building.

He's been to the real Portland—no, that's the wrong word, *his* Portland, not any more real than this one—many times. He's somewhere in the Pearl District, near Pioneer Square. The sky is cloudy, and the shadows are askew, evidence of a mismatch between Nevada here and Oregon there. There's no sound, but the impression of sound is everywhere; he can almost hear the honking horns, the chatter of the residents, the hum of traffic on the 405. On the map, the Welcome Village is south, which means he's entering the city facing north. The interstate is somewhere to his left and the river to his right.

He looks down at his hands. It's a relief that he can see himself. A gift to be solid. He takes a piece of paper from his front pocket, reads the instructions there. Then he begins to walk.

The phantom Portlanders seem menacing in their masks, but he's stopped worrying about colliding with them. They pass through him, don't even see him. The cars are no danger either. *Heaven is a place where nothing ever happens.*

He walks through the narrow park that runs for blocks between Park and Ninth Avenues, enjoying the false shade. He drifts through a statue of a man on horseback, steps through a fog-like fence, then crosses Jefferson Street. Real tourists in blue glasses step inside the Portland Art Museum. He can see a few of them inside the translucent walls, gazing at spectral sculptures. Only the first floor is available to them; they can't climb cloud stairs, and the Ghost City staff haven't yet provided real ones. Other Portland only instantiated a few weeks ago, replacing Other Vilnius, and the park infrastructure hasn't caught up.

He takes off his glasses. The shade vanishes and the air seems to be suddenly hotter, but of course it's not. The body's so easily fooled. He checks his watch, then looks at the map, finds the museum. He's headed in the right direction. Then he puts on the glasses again.

He doesn't know why the Simulators required blinders to see the other city. He doesn't understand most of the rules. Sister Patrice, in her book, quoted Sister Janet's idea that every Impossible was a lesson, and said that the lesson of Ghost City was humility: See? There are thousands, maybe millions of simulations running side by side to your own, filled with billions of souls just like you. As you stroll through a rotating selection of cities, sim after sim after sim, don't you feel even *more* insignificant?

The real lesson, the Engineer thinks, is simply this: fuck you, humans.

He walks into a paved area crowded with masked Portlanders and realizes it's a pod of food trucks. Banh mi, falafel, soul food, craft beer. A spectral musician plays an amped violin the Engineer can't hear, singing through a mask. A ghost woman nearby has pulled her mask down to her neck; she's squirting chili oil into a bowl of dan dan noodles. He leans close, but he can smell none of it.

A voice says, "Water? Don't forget to hydrate!"

He looks around, sees no one. Then he takes off his glasses and winces against the light. There's a real vendor cart where the Thai truck had been. An older gent stands under a blue-and-yellow umbrella. The Engineer is surprised that they're the only real people around for a hundred yards.

The Engineer looks over the goods: drinks, snacks, Ghost City merchandise. On a display box of "broad-spectrum hydrating sheer sunscreen" is a picture of Lady Mmm and Little Miracle. The baby looks bewildered to be there. He knows the feeling.

He buys an ice-cold liter bottle, takes a long swig. He's surprised how thirsty he is. "You keeping cool?" he asks.

"I'm fine," the gent says. "Just don't let the artificial shade fool you."

"So, the mask thing. Does that creep you out?"

"Oh, I don't look at them," the vendor says. "They're not paying customers."

The Engineer walks due north, cutting through phantom buildings, ignoring furniture and walls and clouds of office workers. The other world is so dense he sometimes can't see his feet, and keeps tripping over rocks and divots; the park staff hasn't smoothed the landscape that lies under buildings, only the roads and sidewalks. He begins to feel queasy, so he concentrates on the water bottle sweating in his hand, letting that anchor him to the real world.

He decides to stick to the streets. He passes taverns and taquerias, coffee shops and clothing stores, but he's content now to merely look through the windows. Do these shops exist in his Portland? He has no idea.

At the intersection ahead, a crowd of nebulous pedestrians wait to cross the street. He starts to push through them and then sees a head of shaggy gray hair. Aging rocker hair. The figure's taller than anyone around, with broad shoulders.

The walk light changes, and the pedestrians drift forward. The Engineer hurries to catch up. He reaches up to grab the man's arm, before remembering that it's a useless gesture.

Yet the man seems to feel it. He glances back, and the Engineer looks into the face of a stranger. A craggy-faced hippy with a gray beard. The Engineer drops his arm, and the stranger moves on.

The Engineer stands in the middle of the crosswalk. The light changes, and still he doesn't move, oblivious to the cars moving past him and through him.

The Engineer walks northeast, unconscious of his feet. He knows that he's running late for his appointment, but the urgency he felt earlier is like a distant alarm, a fire for other people to put out. Maybe this entire trip was a mistake.

Finally, he reaches the river, and the park near Burnside Bridge. He consults his instructions again and looks around for a rock of a particular shape. There it is, as well as the bench where he's been told to wait.

He peeks over the top of his glasses and sees a couple of planks laid across sawhorses. Real-world infrastructure underlying the façade of the prettier bench in Other Portland. He takes his spot and checks his watch. One minute to spare.

Above, Other Clouds are rolling in. Pacific Northwest weather. He finds it comforting. The cloudless skies of the desert make him feel like he's under a microscope. Or rather, remind him that he's under one.

A voice calls his name. The Engineer looks behind him, sees people waving at him. Four people.

Oh no, he thinks, not now. But the Octos hurry toward him, practically giddy at this coincidence. Can you believe it? He can't, he tells them.

The four are all eating ice cream. One of them holds a giant waffle cone that's shaped like a taco and filled with chocolate, nutty ice cream.

"So are you guys on another tour?" the Engineer asks.

They find that amusing, for some reason. "Yes and no," one says, and another says, "Hard to tell the difference between one and the other."

"But it's so good to see *you*," one of them says.

"Where did you find ice cream?" he asks. So far he's only seen the water vendor.

"There's a shop right down the street," says one of the women, and holds out her cone. "It's delicious. Try a bite. Mine has real peaches in it."

"Oh no, that's okay, I'll just—"

"Oh, come on, JP."

He's embarrassed that he doesn't know any of their names. He leans forward, puts his hand on hers to steady the cone, and takes a delicate bite. The cold is wonderful.

"Feeling better?" she asks. She's not talking about the ice cream. He recognizes from her tone that this is a cancer question. Or perhaps a grief question. They exist in the same category.

"I'm fine," he says. A few weeks after the tour ended, he found himself in the hospital. This wasn't a surprise. What was a surprise was that he heard himself agreeing to another round of chemotherapy, followed by radiation. They didn't suggest surgery this time; he's 90 percent sure he would have refused that. "They tell me I'm in remission. Again."

The four of them nod. One of them says, "We've been worried about you." And another says, "What happened was a shame."

"A terrible accident," another says.

"It was no accident," the Engineer says. He didn't mean to say that aloud. He doesn't want to continue the conversation, he wants the Octos to move on before they ruin his appointment. But now they're looking at him, waiting for an explanation.

"It's bad design," he says. "Offensively bad design. You don't set up a system where people can die for no reason, that's just . . . sloppy. If you're going to run a universe, then run it, don't just spin the Random Death Generator. Could I have checked the gun? Sure, yes, but—" He stops himself. He's ranting. For the past year he's been an angry person. He's not sure to what extent anger was part of his recovery.

"We understand," one of the Octos says. "You want to start over."

He can't speak. All words have devolved into static.

Finally he shakes his head. He doesn't want to hear their groundhogger carpe diem bullshit.

"Maybe we'll do better next time," one of them says.

"Maybe," the Engineer says. He takes off his hat, runs a handkerchief over his scalp. The heat makes it hard to think, and the ice cream has left him thirstier. He finished his water a mile ago. "Look, it was great seeing you, but I have to meet someone."

"Could you do us one last favor?" one of them asks. "Dulin started to tell us a joke once, back in Kentucky, but we never got to hear it. The one about the Irish brothers."

"Do you know it?" one of them asks the Engineer. "You must know it."

He remembers lying in the hospital bed in Seattle, a fresh pink scar across his forehead, seams held together by staples. The morphine was wearing off and the headache was setting in when Dulin told him the joke. The Engineer had heard it before, of course. "Good one," he said. Dulin laughed for him, long and loud.

"I'm sorry," the Engineer tells the Octos. "I can't do the voices like he could."

"But we're dying to hear it," one of the men says.

"Please," says the woman who gave him a bite of her ice cream.

One last favor. Okay, he thinks, if it'll get rid of them. He thinks through the order of details. Begins: "So every afternoon, this Irishman, uh, Mike, goes down to the pub, and every day he orders the same thing—three shots of whiskey."

"That's it," one of the Octos says, nodding.

"'One for me,' Mike says, 'one for me brother Pat who lives in the States, and one for me brother Seamus who lives in Canada.'" The Engineer is not sure if these are the names Dulin would have used, or if it matters; his friend seemed to pull them at random from his stock of ethnic names. "And that's the way it goes, every day. Mike comes in and orders the same thing—one for him, one for his brother in the States, and one for his brother in Canada. Then one afternoon . . ."

The Engineer isn't doing the joke or his friend justice. Dulin would have gone full Lucky Charms on the accent and acted out the hoisting of the shots.

"Go on," one of the Octos says gently.

The Engineer takes a breath. "One afternoon Mike walks into the pub, and the barkeep sets out the three glasses. Mike stops him. 'No,' he says with a sigh, 'just two.' And the bartender says, 'Oh, Mike, I'm so sorry. Did something happen to one of your brothers?'"

The Octos gaze down at him, waiting.

The Engineer says, "And Mike shakes his head and says, 'No, it's just that I've stopped drinking.'"

All the Octos laugh. Well, all but one.

"I don't get it," one of the men says. "Who's dead?"

"His brother isn't dead," one of the women answers. "He's just in another country."

One of the Octo women pats him on the shoulder. "I'm glad you're here," she says. Finally, the four of them amble off with their ice cream.

•   •   •

The Engineer waits. It's past the designated time, but he tells himself to be patient. He watches the alternate river and the darkening artificial clouds.

A teenage girl runs up to the railing and looks down at the water. She's thirteen or fourteen, dark-skinned, with tight braids. She's wearing the park's opaque glasses and is so evidently real.

A man sits down on the far side of the bench. He's a tall Black man with broad shoulders, wearing a polo shirt and crisp khakis. He also seems to be real. He calls out, "Careful, you don't want to drown."

The girl laughs. She walks through the phantom fence, turns to face them, and windmills her arms, pretending to lose her balance. "Whoa, whoa, whoa!" But instead of hitting the water, she hits the ground, butt first. "Oof!" Then she lies back, seeming to float in midair.

The Engineer adjusts his glasses. "It's odd, isn't? Putting a solid object in front of your eyes so you can see another world."

"Like a book," the father says.

"Huh," the Engineer replies. "I suppose so."

Ghost Portlanders wander by, not seeing the Engineer, or the father and his daughter, floating in the air. Most of them are wearing masks.

The Engineer says, "Do you think they know they're in a simulation?"

The man at the end of the bench considers it. "They don't seem to. Everyone's been reading their newspapers and their phones over their shoulders, but there's no mention of a sim so far."

"So, no Impossibles?"

"Just UFOs," the man says. "Flying in front of trained pilots, getting recorded on instruments. A lot of documentation of objects violating the rules of physics, yet they haven't quite put it together."

"I was wondering about the face masks."

"Oh, that seems to be a plague of some sort. Not an impossible." The man looks at the Engineer. "Seven million dead, they say."

So, the Engineer thinks. A dystopia.

The man's daughter is now under the water, yet still visible. Drowning safely.

"You seem to know a lot about the place," the Engineer says.

The man nods. "Margaret and I used to meet here to do what she called the hand-off. Our daughter got to pick where we met. She liked that it was a different city every year—Chengdu. Vilnius, Abeokuta." He looks at the Engineer. "I guess it was a way to make a terrible event a little less terrible."

"That makes sense," the Engineer says. "I hear from a mutual friend that she's doing okay. Your wife."

The father says nothing for a long moment, perhaps weighing the security risk of answering. "They don't let us see her. They won't even tell us where she is. But they can't keep all her visitors out."

Yes, the Engineer thinks. It's good to have friends that can blink into existence anywhere they want.

The girl is back. "Dad! Look!" The clouds have grown very dark. "It's going to rain."

The Engineer takes off his hat. He looks to the girl's father for permission. He nods.

"You might need this," the Engineer says to her. "It's waterproof."

She takes it warily. Pulls it on. It's too big for her, but she's the kind of person who looks good in hats.

"It has all these little vents in it," the Engineer says. "They're like pockets where you can hide small objects."

"Like what?" the girl asks.

"Anything. Gum. Wads of cash. Thumb drives."

"Cash?!"

Her father frowns at the Engineer. "You didn't put money in there?"

"No, sir."

The Other sky opens up. The non-rain comes down hard, one of those PNW squalls, an instant deluge the Engineer can see but can't feel. The girl laughs, throws out her arms. "Ghost rain!"

The father and the Engineer watch her as she spins slowly, face upturned. She holds out her tongue to catch intangible raindrops.

The Engineer stands up. "I'd better get going," he says. "Tell her to keep the hat."

"Thank you," the girl's father says. "For everything."

"I'm sorry it took me so long to figure it out," the Engineer says. "The hat, I mean. I've been a little distracted. Also, I'm not as smart as your wife."

"Few of us are."

"I think she is," the Engineer says, and nods toward the girl.

Her father laughs. "Most definitely." He starts to say something else.

The Engineer waits.

"The Ohio AI went online last month," the father says. "It can reason, draw inferences, remember everything that's happened to it. It talks in the first person. And it expresses emotions."

The Engineer nodded. He'd seen the news.

The man says, "They say it's mentally equivalent to a four-year old."

"That's dumb," the Engineer says. "You can't assign a human age to a mind like that."

"Still. A kind of child. Under the complete control of the US government."

It was Margaret's nightmare. She didn't fear AI. She feared what humans would do to one.

"You've got the tools now," the Engineer said. "The whole Satanic kit and caboodle. You can keep an eye on them. Intervene if necessary. Even get them out—if you can figure out a place to put them."

"So many tools," the father says. "But I don't know how to use them. I'm a mediocre programmer, at best." His smile is apologetic. "I could use an engineer."

"I'm retired."

"Ah." Then, "I understand."

The Engineer walks away. He takes off his glasses and glances back. The only real thing in sight is the plywood bench, the father and his daughter, dancing in sunlight. Ahead of him is an expanse of rocky, dry dirt. The Ghost City gate, and the Welcome Village, seem very small and far away.

He puts on the glasses and starts walking west. After a block he passes an ice-cream shop: Cosmic Bliss. The waffle cone tacos are advertised in the window.

He takes off the glasses. The shop vanishes. There's nothing here but desert.

He looks back to where the Other river had been. The Octos are nowhere in sight.

"Mother *fuckers*," he says.

•   •   •

When the Engineer returns to the parking lot, he finds a bearded man in a white kameez sitting cross-legged on the hood of his car. Evidently the heat doesn't bother him.

"All done?" Aunty Tim says.

"Please don't dent the hood," the Engineer says. "They'll charge me for that."

Aunty Tim rolls his eyes, then slides off the side. "Adaku's beautiful, isn't she?"

"She is," the Engineer says. "She really is."

"And so, so smart," Aunty Tim says. "You won't believe what she's like when she's older."

The Engineer pops the trunk. The blue cardboard box has tipped over again, somehow. He brushes aside the gray dust and sets the box on the pavement at his feet.

"You want a water?" he asks. "Not sure if you do that kind of thing."

"I'm good," Aunty Tim says.

The water's almost hot, but the Engineer swallows it anyway. "Oh," he says. "I ran into your bosses."

"Hmm?"

"The Monitors. Watchers. Whatever you call them. Panoctogons."

Aunty Tim looks alarmed. "Did they ask about me? Do they know I'm here?"

"No idea. They asked me if I wanted to start over."

"Oh no! You didn't tell them to reboot, did you? Adaku's only thirteen! If we restart now, she won't have a chance to do, well, anything!"

"Don't worry, they're not going to listen to me. Even if they did . . ." The Engineer shakes his head. He doesn't like where that thought leads. "Besides, if Adaku doesn't grow up, that's going to be super-awkward for you."

"Well, not me, exactly," Aunty Tim says. "But I take your point."

When Aunty Tim told him that Adaku was his mother and Margaret was his grandmother, the Engineer didn't quite believe it. But now that he's met Adaku, the lineage is clear.

"Anyway, thanks for setting this up with Margaret's family," the Engineer says. "Good luck with . . . everything." He opens the driver's-side door, sets the blue box into the cupholder. The box is too big and sits slightly askew. That won't do.

Aunty Tim leans down to look through the passenger window. "Where are you going?"

"I've got something to do back East." The Engineer latches the passenger seat belt, tucks the box behind it. Then he weaves a USB cable around box and belts, making a little net for it, and cinches it tight.

"What's in the box?" Aunty Tim asks.

The Engineer waves. "Bye."

He starts the car. The speakers blare and he turns down the volume. The air-conditioning is a relief. He backs out of the parking space. Aunty Tim's staring at him, chewing his lip. Jesus.

He drives slowly to the parking lot exit, brakes to a stop. The memorial service is six days from now, in Connecticut, nearly three thousand miles away. He promised Marion and Beth-Anne that he'd bring the guest of honor. But he could have flown there. Why the hell did he think driving was a good idea?

Aunty Tim appears in the passenger seat.

"Hey! Watch the box!"

"Oops, sorry." Aunty Tim scoots to the edge of the seat. "Have you considered my offer?"

"Today was a onetime job, for Margaret. I'm not joining your conspiracy of friends."

"We could use your help. Adaku and Edowar, but also all those people in the next sim down. The Toolbox is just that, tools. We need folks who know how to use them."

"Can you get out of my car?"

"Why don't we talk about it while you drive?"

"Please leave."

"Come on, what else are you going to do with your life?"

There is that. The intractable problem that's haunted him for years.

That day in the recovery room, after Dulin told him the Irish brothers joke, he handed JP a brochure. Bright green, white script. JP's morphine-blurred brain didn't immediately understand what it was. "This," Dulin said, "is what we're going to do when we bust you out of this joint. One more cross-country trip across this great nation of ours. You think you got one more adventure in you?"

"On a *bus*?" JP asked.

"New York to Los Angeles, baby. Can't you see it?"

He still sees it. Replays it in his mind, wishing he could go back to that first day of the tour and start over. Be smarter. Be better. Fix the problem. But whatever JP gets on the bus next, in some other iteration, will not be him. *This* JP is stuck in this here, this now, with an impossible man who won't leave his car. Another intractable problem.

"Well?" Aunty Tim says.

. . .

We're waiting to hear the Engineer's answer, too. There's a pleasure in just sitting back and seeing where all this is going, and when you've lived as long as we have, you have to take your pleasures when you can. Like this ice cream, for example. Oh my! The best in all the Portlands, so cold, so delicious.

Acknowledgments

So many people made this book real.

Many friends and fellow writers read early drafts and steered me in the right direction; my thanks to Gary Delafield, Chris Farnsworth, Davie Justus, Nancy Kress, Jack Skillingstead, and Mark Tompkins. Emma Casey and Ian Gregory not only read their father's book, they made it better. If the Influencer's beauty regimen is at all convincing, that's because of Emma, and if it's not, that's because I'm still confused by microblading.

I owe Kathy Bieschke, my wife and all-time best person, for everything always. But to pick just one example: thanks for allowing me to watch you read each draft so that every time you laughed I could mark that line as a keeper.

My thanks as well to my literary and media agents, who were so enthusiastic for this book and gave such smart feedback. Seth Fishman at the Gernert Company, and Anna DeRoy and Olivia Burgher at WME, y'all are fabulous.

My editor, Tim O'Connell, is the best in the business, and understood this book from the beginning. I owe a lot to everyone at Saga Press and Simon & Schuster, especially Anna Hauser, who kept this ungainly vehicle on schedule, and the various publishing pros who were brought on board to finish the trip: copyeditor Stacey Sakal, production editor Alexandre Su, interior designer

Lewelin Polanco, and the team at the Heads of State for the cover. Thanks so much.

Finally, I'd like to express my undying gratitude to our AI overlord, Roko's basilisk. Thank you for not creating a simulation to torture me for all eternity. This current sim is pretty nice, and full of people I love.

About the Author

Daryl Gregory is an award-winning novelist and short story writer who occasionally writes for television, comics, and video games. His most recent book was the Appalachian horror novel *Revelator*, one of *The Washington Post*'s best books of the year, as well as a Dragon and Locus award finalist. His novella *We Are All Completely Fine* won the World Fantasy and the Shirley Jackson awards.

Other books include *Spoonbenders*, a Nebula, Locus, and World Fantasy award finalist, the novella *The Album of Dr. Moreau*, an Edgar Award finalist, and the Crawford Award–winning novel *Pandemonium*. His short stories have been nominated for the Hugo and other awards, and many are collected in *Unpossible and Other Stories*, a *Publishers Weekly* best book of the year. He also teaches writing and is a regular instructor at the Viable Paradise writer's workshop. He grew up in Chicago and now lives in Seattle, Washington (or at least a very good simulation of it).

About the Type

The body of this text is set in Times Ten Linotype Standard, a font whose origin dates to the original design for Times New Roman in 1931. This font was commissioned by the *Times* (London) after Stanley Morison published an article accusing the *Times* of being typographically archaic and poorly printed. With Plantin, an older typeface, as his inspiration, Morison himself updated the type's readability and, as a nod to the *Times*'s previous typeface, Times Old Roman, called his revision "Times New Roman." The Times font family has enjoyed global success and popularity since then. Times Ten Linotype is designed for use with smaller text sizes and its neat, sharp serifs continue to make it a highly legible choice.

The cover font is set in 3604 Pulp Science, a display typeface that plays with the distinct geometry and curvature of fonts typically used on vintage movie posters and other sci-fi paraphernalia. It was designed by Justin Penner.

Book Club Questions
from the Author

1. Most of my friends are pretty sure that we're not living in a simulation. But can any of us know for sure? Do *you* know?

2. I mean, what's up with all the UFOs? We've all seen the videos and yet no one freaked out. These things break the laws of physics. That seems suspicious.

3. Sometimes I think it would be a relief if all this were a simulation, because that suggests there might be a hidden purpose to our lives. But other times I start to make a sandwich and we're out of mayo and I think, why are the simulators such jerks? I'm sorry, I'm a little hungry right now.

4. Would you love your friends and family any less if they were made out of zeroes and ones, and if so, why is it your brother-in-law?